I0688453

PROLOGUE

'Drop the mask and revel in the beauty of being bare.' The only directive Phoebe has to adhere to.

. . . Getting off the bed and slowly approaching me, "Well, at least, unlike you — who's barely covered with this short towel — I'm wearing my pants."

Like water over rocks, his comment went over my head. All I could think of as I openly ogled at Federick was how **God damn** tempting and inviting he was. He was a freaky Greek God. With his sexy bed hair, broad-shoulders and sturdily built physique, he left little to the imagination. Regardless of his pants covering his long legs, I had already gotten a glimpse of how toned and firm it was, just like his eight packs.

I was well aware Federick was an eye-catcher and every girls' dream, but **this much.** I had no idea. With how sexy, hot, handsome, and dashing he seemed in that moment, I didn't blame all these girls for throwing themselves at his feet. For worshipping the ground he walks on. They had seen in Federick Archer something I was now seeing — the guarantee of delicious sex that had the power of erasing the world around.

However, I knew better than to fall in his alluring web. I knew behind all these sexiness, and the promise of a taste of heaven was an arrogant son of a bitch.

"Stop gawking and drink this. It will help with the hangover and the bright light that's causing your head to pound." Federick uttered a bit too politely for my liking.

Snapping me out of it and confused as to why Federick was suddenly being helpful, kind and considerate towards me, when he is supposed to hate me, I was even more worried about what might have conspired last night. Pointedly and suspiciously scrutinising Federick, I snatched the glass of water and aspirin from his hand.

Washing down the pill and relishing in the cooling effect of the water, "Thanks."

UNMASKING REVIEW

"Another great turn of events. I've been going through a hard time in my life, and this book has really helped me get through it. There are plot twists at every corner, and the ending — I love how you did it. This 2nd book in the Tame Series had a lot of high expectation to live up to, and it met each one of them. This book is truly amazing and won't disappoint."

— Rachel M. Cordero

"You are a talented writer. Unmasking was a great read."

— Juliano Agertt (Jusky), Singer & Songwriter

"I really enjoy your books... It is nice and interesting... Nice work."

— Wattpad Reader

OTHER BOOKS BY AUTHOR

THE SPY WITHIN

AFFAIR OF THE HEART

UNMASKING

BOOK 2

TAME SERIES

Ж DROP THE MASK AND REVEL IN
THE BEAUTY OF BEING BARE Ж

LAVINIA DASANI

L.D PLUMITIF

An Imprint of Plumitif Press, LLC

1309 Coffeen Avenue STE 1200

Sheridan, Wyoming, 82801

This is a work of fiction. Names, characters, places, and incidents are either the product of the author's imagination or are used fictitiously, and any resemblance to actual persons, living or dead, business establishments, events, or locales is entirely coincidental.

Cover by GetCovers.

Visit Plumitif Press, LLC at www.laviniadasani.com.

This is the 2nd edition of the novel. The 1st edition was previously published on Wattpad, year 2016.

ISBN (pbk): 978-1-7339857-5-8

ISBN (ebook): 978-1-7339857-6-5

ISBN (Hardcover): 978-1-7339857-7-2

Printed in United States of America

WARNING

The following material contains S-ensuous contents. These are described as containing graphic romantic details that are not as explicit as an erotica novel would. Then again, like any romance novel; be it action or not, expect love scenes. However, I will give a fair warning that there might be some gruesome details within the literature.

This ROMANCE book is entirely entertainment literature, and you've been warned of its potential 'Dangerous' contents in advance. Keep out of reach of children.

Proceed with cautious – Not for the faint of heart.

DEDICATION

To Michaël Aaron Akash Dasani, my brother

I dedicate this book to you

Thanks for your help with building my website

And being my other creative eyes when it comes to designing & arts

With love and affection

Your 22nd Birthday gift

From me to you.

ACKNOWLEDGEMENT

To all my readers, especially those from Wattpad, I would like to thank you once again. Your support and comments have meant a lot to me. Thanks to your critics, I have been able to edit better and reconstruct the final draft of this novel. Your love and presence despite the rollercoaster I often throw you in will forever be appreciated.

To Jonathan Ventura, the Chief of Arlington Police Department, thanks for letting me pick your brain so I could have more accurate information within my writing. Your insight in weaponry and the justice system has been more than valuable. You've been a friend that one would forever cherish.

To my family, like always, you've stood by my side no matter what. And for that, I would be forever grateful.

Thank you so much for following the Tame Series and waiting a whole year for this novel.

CHAPTER 1
PARTY CRASHER

PHOEBE

Breezing through some last-minute paperwork, the natural chemical in my body, acting like amphetamine, I tied up all the loose work I left behind the day before. I was so immensely ecstatic by the sudden appearance of my childhood best friend; I made the mistake of overlooking my daily security routine.

But not today. Making sure everything was clean and adequately locked, I bolted out of Archer & Associate before anyone could stop me. Tonight was going to be a special night — a landmark even.

Rushing home, I began all the preparations for tonight's grand dinner. I have been waiting for this specific day ever since Damien left us — left me.

Preparing Damien's favourite dish, I couldn't help but ponder how shocked he would be to see Wyatt and Teo so grown up — as almost young adults. They were no longer those jumping high-energetic toddlers running around. Now, they were just high-energetic teenagers running around. Teenagers full of love and compassion.

UNMASKING

But most importantly, teenagers who still needed a father figure in their lives. I'm sure once Damien meets them and gets to know the boys on a more personal level, he will regret all those beautiful years he missed. Years when they most needed a father figure. However, I'm convinced if given a chance, Damien would make a wonderful father. I just have to prove to him that there is more of Mia in Wyatt and Teo than there is of Cole.

Aware Damien will eventually have to leave, and I won't have much time to show him this reality, I was determined to make the most of Damien's time here with us — as a family. He was going to see there was nothing but pure love inside the boys.

By 16:30, some of my dishes were set aside, marinating, and awaiting to be cooked at a later interval. With half of the preparation already completed, I had time to kill until my sons returned home from their soccer practice.

Relaxing on my couch and aimlessly browsing through the channels, I envisioned how I would break the news of Damien's return to the boys when they don't even remember him. They had no idea how their lives were going to drastically change in a blink of one night.

Nervous and worried I might freak my kids out, I prayed I don't mess things up.

'Oh! Get a grip, Phoebe! You are Angel! Fearless. Confident. The best assassin. And the Angel of Death!' My inner voice confidently chimed to encourage me. And it was right.

I was feared by many, and yet, here I was, nervous like a clam at the thought of divulging a little secret to my sons. That on its own got to be a whole new level of pathetic.

But I couldn't escape the inevitable. The question about their origin and bloodline was there. I knew there would come a time when I would have to answer to my boys. And the time for them to learn the truth about Damien was here.

By 17:30, Wyatt and Teo trudged into the house with dirt and mud stains all over their body and cloth. Scrutinising their poor state and furrowing at the mess they must have made on their way in, "You boys look like shit."

My white furniture was so going to suffer. But thank God, the maids usually clean up after the boys before I'm home; otherwise, I would have had a heart attack by now.

"Hello to you too, your highness." Wyatt sarcastically greeted.

"Hi, Mom, you're home early." Teo innocently added.

One could definitely see who was the sweet one and who was the sarcastic troublemaker.

"Hi, my sarcastic and sweet angels . . ." Using an overly fruity tone to hide my nervousness, "We have a special guest coming over for dinner tonight. So, would you please tidy up, wear something nice and clean your rooms while you are at it." Without skipping a beat, I showed all my cards.

"Do we know this special guest?"

"Yes, Teo. But I don't know if you remember him. So please, I want you and your **brother** to behave the whole night." I purposely emphasised on the brother part, because Wyatt was well, just Wyatt.

"Hey, I can behave when it's needed."

"Sure, you can."

"Who is this guy, anyway? I would have guessed your boss, but since we don't remember this special guest, it can't be him. Is that *'guest'* your boyfriend or something? — Because if he is, we will have to take a good look at him. Right, Teo?"

I was surprised and perplexed as to why Wyatt would think of Federick of all people. Teo, on the other hand, just nodded his head like the young, innocent brother he was. I swear this attitude of his sometimes worries me. I would prefer for Teo to be as vocal and annoying as his brother, rather than being so shy. He needed help, that's all I knew.

"No need to go all protective on me, dear father." Fluttering my eyelids, I teased in a childlike tone.

"Puff . . . I am not."

"You so are . . ." Switching conversation before we start bickering like children, "I'm curious, why did you think Federick was the one invited? He is a supreme asshole, remember."

"Sure, whatever helps you sleep better at night."

"Getting mouthy, aren't you, young man?"

"Just saying."

"Whatever. The guy who is coming is not my boyfriend, but an old friend of mine. He has been my best friend since kindergarten, and I haven't seen him for years; so, both of you better behave your asses tonight. Your post-derrière depends on it." I sternly added.

Quietly nodding their heads like the well-mannered children, I raised them to be, they headed to their respective rooms. Aware I wouldn't have enough time to run to the store, finish my special dish and get ready for tonight by 19:00, I called for my protégé.

An avid lover of cooking, Luke, my sons' best friend and brother figure, was everything I needed. Talented and loving, he was also secretly my sons' bodyguard and my protected prodigy at the agency. With his help, everything, including me, was ready before 19:00. Lost in a Tv show all three boys obsessively followed, the doorbell recaptured my attention, announcing Damien's arrival five minutes before 19:00.

'Well, I guess he was anxious and came a tad bit earlier.' Leaving the kids in the living room, I mentally added.

"Damien, you are a bit early . . ." Stopping mid-sentence, my whole being was struck dumb.

In front of me wasn't Damien who rang the bell, but **Federick** freaking **Archer**.

'What the heck was Federick Archer doing standing on my front porch?' My brain internally screeched like a skidding tire. No matter the reason for his presence here, I was sure of one thing; he was here to spoil my perfectly planned evening. It was just like the jerk he was.

"What in the greatest world are you doing here?" I whispered-yelled. Trying to be patient, and not wanting the boys to hear us, I couldn't be blamed for my exaggeration.

"There's an important matter that needed to be discussed." The inconsiderate asshole that Federick had proven to be, purposely drew attention to him.

"Lower your voice!" I lowly hissed; my displeasure as bright as the moonlight.

"What could you possibly want to talk about in the middle of the freaking night?" Pointing at the clear starry sky above his head, I made my point.

"Mom, who is it? — Is your guest here yet? We are hungry."

Turning around to face Wyatt, who was suspiciously regarding Federick, I plastered a fake smile on my visage. I didn't have to acknowledge Federick's presence. I could simply dismiss him like he was a mirage.

"It's nobody, Wyatt. Go back to your show. As soon as the guest arrives, we are going to serve dinner, don't worry."

"Mom, remember what the little birdie once said; lying is bad for health. If you are trying to hide your boss and the guy behind him with the door and your back, let me tell you, it's not working." Wyatt stated, slightly jokingly and slightly seriously.

"What are you talking about?" Confused, I asked Wyatt's departing back before turning to face the entrance of my home. It was then I noticed Damien standing a few feet away from Federick.

Figuring Damien had just shown up, "Oh sorry, Damien, I didn't see you coming. Clearly, someone's gigantic head is doing a great job at blocking my view. But come on in, Damien." Sending a glare at Federick, I was trying my best to order him to piss off. But like the stubborn brat he was, Federick stayed still.

"Hi, Mr Archer, what a pleasant surprise. What brought you here at this hour if you don't mind me asking?" Damien politely and professionally asked.

Glancing between Federick and myself with a frown and questioning look, it was clear Damien was curious and confused. Heck, even I was confused as to why Federick was at my doorstep at this hour.

"My boss was just about to leave, right, Mr Archer." I pressed, dropping another clue for Federick's stupid and stubborn head.

"Hi, Mr Ambrosh, I was having a little chat with Miss Smith."

Given Federick was standing closer to me than he was to Damien, I could hear his low, "Wish I could say the same about you", together with something along the lines of, "Yes, I mind everything about you."

"Okay. I'm sorry to bug in like this again, but playing soccer for hours then being forced to clean my room really made me hungry. So. . . if the three of you would, please come in, I would love to start eating." Breaking the awkward silence floating above — Federick, Damien and myself —Wyatt made his renewed arrival known again.

Pausing for a breath, "You are not thinking of staying out here for hours, are you?" Wyatt added with a hint of anxiousness.

Truthfully speaking, I wasn't shocked by Wyatt's behaviour. I knew how impatient and relentless he could get when he was hungry. And it's better not to kid with him if you value your life. Hungry Wyatt was no good.

"Okay, Wyatt. Tell Luke to wait for me in the kitchen. You and Teo go sit at the table; we will join you shortly."

"Come on, Dam, you don't want Wyatt too hungry if you want to survive this night." Completely ignoring Federick, I teased with a sweet smile. But just as I was about to close the door, Federick walked right behind Damien.

"What do you think you are doing, Mr Archer? You are leaving this house."

With Damien a step ahead of me, I mumbled to Federick; annoyed he wasn't taking no for an answer. Then again, I shouldn't be expecting much from **'The Federick Archer'** — he never knew how to take no for an answer — not even when he was a toddler and annoying the life out of me.

"You are wrong, Miss Smith. Didn't you hear your son? He just invited me inside for whatever you are doing tonight." Federick smugly mumbled beside me, as if he had just won the lottery.

"This is a private dinner between my family, Mr Archer! So, if you could, please leave. We can talk about whatever you want tomorrow or better yet, at work on Monday." Trying my best to keep my temper in check for the sake of Damien and my kids, I tightly stated.

"MOM! I am super-duper hungry; even Teo is starving. He is whining like a girl who is *'means-trating'*. He might just faint, you know." Getting his tendency to exaggerate and be a drama queen from me, Wyatt called out.

"You heard your son, Miss Smith. You don't want them to start *'means-trating'* or faint on us now, do you?"

"UGH!. . . . You are so annoying! Let's just go."

I guess my perfect dinner was not going to happen anytime soon. If not someone else, it is Federick Archer who ruins everything. I sure as heck cannot tell the boys about Damien with Federick around; this would have to wait another day.

CHAPTER 2
POSTPONED

PHOEBE

"Go ahead, Mr Archer. Walk straight from here, pass the living room, then take your left. You will find the dining room. Damien and I will be right behind you. I hope you can handle this much by yourself."

Merely raising his perfectly arched eyebrows as a response, Federick followed my direction but not before grazing his fingers against my arms as he passed by me. Intentionally ignoring Federick and his stupid touch, I gave Damien my full attention.

"I am sorry, Dam, we can't tell the boys who you really are to them, tonight. I wasn't expecting Federick to show up and ruin tonight for us. We will have to wait for the next most appropriate time. However, you could always spend some alone time with them to try to get to know them, to — you know, bond." My mind going through different scenarios where my problems would be resolved, and my anxiousness would dissipate, I blurb out in one breath.

"It's fine Phebes, do what you seem fit. But truthfully speaking,

I am kind of relieved Federick Archer crashed in. I apologise, but I don't think now is the best time to tell them anything. You are trying to move things too fast, and that will only create problems. Let us slowly get to know each other first — you get what I mean, right." Damien explained with patience and caution.

"Yes, I do. I just thought it would be great for them to finally know some truth about their life. I guess I am trying to push things too fast, and I apologise. But I promise I will try my best not to repeat this." Realising I was indeed at fault here, I uttered with a smile and understanding. If the boys were to find out any truth about themselves, they will in due time.

"Hey, Miss Smith, you're coming or what? I'm famished too. What do you say, Wyatt?"

"Definitely. Drag yourself in here."

Since when did Federick and Wyatt become buddies? A few days ago Wyatt hated Federick guts, and now they were agreeing with each other and being best buds.

"Yes, I'm coming," I shouted back.

"Dam, we will continue this conversation later on. Go and have a seat at the table. I will be bringing the food in." Pointing at the dining table, Damien and I gave each other an encouraging smile.

Marching around my kitchen like my bum was on fire, still baffled and annoyed at Federick's intrusion, Luke and I hurriedly garnished the entrée. With Damien left all alone in the dining room with my boys and Federick without a proper introduction, my nerves were all twisted up. There was no doubt in my mind that the air in that room was filled with awkwardness.

Hurrying back to the dining table with Luke following behind, all proper etiquette was out of the window. Hit with the awkwardness shrouding the dining room like a hammer hitting a nail onto a brick wall, my gut feeling was yet again proven right.

Teo and Wyatt were whispering amidst themselves while stealing glances at both men in front of them. Federick and Damien, on the other hand, were glaring and scrutinising each other with suspicion and wariness.

Sensing my arrival before everyone else, Federick snapped his head in my direction. In the spotlight, there was no escaping it.

"Okay . . ." Stretching my words, as if it would magically extinguish the awkwardness in the room, "Luke, here, is going to do us the honour of serving dinner tonight."

"The honour is all mine, Phoe — Miss Smith, I mean." Profesuly blushing, Luke corrected his near slip.

"As cute as you are, sweetheart, I think Wyatt is way too hungry for good manners. Serve him first, then Teo, the guests and lastly me." Winking at Luke, he instantly turned beetroot. I still couldn't believe how a fantastic fighter as Luke could blush so much on the simplest thing.

Having groomed and trained Luke over the year, he had become like a third son to me, and the knowledge of him hungry in his corner, while I was eating, didn't sit well with me. Particularly, when I knew he too played soccer with Wyatt and Teo after school hours. Allowing my motherly instinct to kick in, I couldn't stop myself from reaching out to Luke before he could leave.

"Hey, Luke, you can dine with us if you want too." Smiling and holding onto his wrist, "Especially now that this dinner is not as private as I had originally planned." Glaring at Federick, I let him know the last sentence was meant for him and I was still pissed at him.

"It's okay, Miss Smith, I'm good. I might be extremely close to this family, but right now, I'm on duty. Besides, I don't want to intrude on your dinner."

What did I say — Luke was one of the sweetest boys ever, despite not having someone to call his own. And surprise, surprise, he had more common sense than Federick Archer.

But unlike the intruder sitting at my table, Luke was family. "No such thing, sweetheart. Just have a seat beside me and enjoy this fresh homemade food."

"If you say so. Thanks, Miss . . ." I lightly shook my head, cutting him off.

"I mean, Phoebe." Smiling at Luke, I was proud of him. Months ago, he could hardly understand my body language or silent instructions and regard, but today, he made this skill look as easy as 1, 2, 3 would to a 6-year-old.

Federick's consistent glare capturing my attention, I recollected my racing thoughts. Perplexed, I met his questioning glare, but that didn't seem to deter his sleeted gaze. Oblivious as to why Federick was suddenly angry when it was me who should be furious, I let his abnormal behaviour slide once more and turned my attention to the only important person in this room.

Taking a bite off my plate, I observed Damien take a mouthful of the dish I prepared specially for him. Swallowing the first few morsels, Damien's eyes nearly popped out of its socket. Gradually lifting his astonish gaze at me for confirmation, I slightly nodded, anticipating his response. I have, after all, not made this particular dish in ten years, and I wasn't sure if I was still any good at concocting this specific variety of assortment.

"Umm . . . This is delicious, Phebes. Don't tell me you of all people have started cooking again." Taking another spoonful, Damien jested with fake surprise.

"No, Dam, I've been starving my kids all these years, while awaiting your grand return." Sarcastically responding, I wanted to give Damien a hard time. Then again, it proved hard to keep a straight face and not smile at his missed-face.

"Ha-Ha, you think you are so funny. You know that's not what I meant, dumbass. It's just been so long since I've had such delicious real home-made food, especially one made by the great Phoebe Smith."

"Why, your many girlfriends didn't cook for you?" I jested with a raised brow. "Besides, it might as well have been my chef who cooked this for us."

"Well, dummy, your chef wouldn't leave your famous trademark." Arching his fine eyebrow, Damien smugly smirked.

"Oh well, thank you. I did my best to make you feel at home." Throwing a dirty look at Federick, "I tried, anyway."

Taking notice of Federick and the others' weird and confused stares, I remembered I yet again forgot to introduce Damien adequately.

Not giving me time to clear their confusion, the boys quickly took matters into their own hands; probably concluding their sweet mother was in danger of humiliation. Little did they know Damien and I were simply messing around.

"Sorry to interrupt you, Mister *I-don't-know-who*, but I'll have you know, my mother has always been the greatest chef and perfect mom. Yeah, she might be over-protective and secretive, but it's part of her. So, if you would, please be more respectful when speaking to her, because trust me, if you misbehave towards her, all good manners will be thrown out the window — no matter who you are." Wyatt dramatically finished with a huff.

And this is why Wyatt was not allowed to learn extensive fighting skills. He had the temper of a bull.

Despite being proud of Wyatt for always being so protective and sticking out for me, I couldn't let him speak to his father in such a manner. I could understand him, but Damien wouldn't. He barely knew Wyatt.

"Wyatt, I'm touched by your words, but son, this is no way to speak to Damien. I suggest you apologise to him right away." Turning towards my other son, "And Teo, if you don't want to end up in trouble with your brother, I suggest you stop agreeing and nodding your head to whatever your brother says, like the good little follower you've become."

Narrowing his eyes at me then at Damien with a hint of glower, Wyatt was palpably pissed and disapproved of my request. While Teo yet again nodded. I swear this boy had a problem.

"But MOM . . ." Fire dancing in the depth of his eyes, Wyatt tried to argue.

"Do it now, Wyatt Smith! I'm not kidding. It's no way to speak with your —"

"It's okay, Phoebe, don't worry about it. Wyatt did nothing. In fact, I apologise for the misunderstanding between your sons. I forgot they were still kids and don't understand the way adults joke around." Placing his hand on top of mind, Damien rapidly cut in, like a sharp knife chopping meat, stopping me from making yet another stupid mistake.

Taking in a deep breath, "You are right, Damien. I'm sorry, Wyatt, for being so hard on you. I forgot you don't remember him. This is Damien, my childhood best friend. I call him Dam, but you can all just call him Damien." Pointing at Damien, I introduced with a small smile.

"As you may have already realised Dam, the one without any filter and is super protective of me as if he is my father is Wyatt. While the one who keeps nodding his head and has become shy for some unknown reason to me, yet, is Teo. But when it comes down to it, he too is super protective of me."

"Nice to meet the two of you," Damien politely added.

Ever polite, Teo was about to respond but stopped midway. Noticing Wyatt's slight body movement, I knew he had kicked Teo under the table to stop him. Left with no other choice, I threw a harsh warning look at Wyatt so he would stop being so stubborn and rude.

"Nice to meet you too." Wyatt forced out a fake smile, followed by Teo's less forceful one.

'Oh my God . . . It was like I saw another Federick in Wyatt, and they haven't even hung out for a week.'

"I'm sure all of you know my boss, Mr Archer, who in my opinion is hugely annoying. Last but not least, this sweet guy beside me, who seems very uncomfortable right now is Luke. My splendid young chef on special occasions, but most importantly, my sons' best friend. They go to the same high school. Though Luke is a senior this year." Concluding the introduction, I threw a reassuring smile towards Luke. The unfortunate thing really wasn't used to normal family life.

"Now that all of you have made acquaintances let's get over the awkward part of this dinner and finish our meal. Luke and I worked hard to prepare all of these." Pointing at the table full of food, I was done with the awkwardness around me.

The rest of dinner went by quietly — except, of course for me. Federick's stare ceaselessly boring on me, I couldn't help myself but squirm in my seat every now and then. Glancing at each other while eating, everyone was trying to make this evening less awkward. Luke, on the other hand, couldn't stop blushing whenever I would look his way — immediately bringing a smile to my face. This boy was genuinely intimidated by me despite knowing I viewed him as my son.

After dinner, all of us moved to the living room, to make small talk and use the Tv as background noise to lessen the discomfort of our situation. Seeking to ease the atmosphere, I offered Damien and Federick a glass of wine while Wyatt, Teo and Luke were handed sodas.

Every now and then staring at the Tv screen, I was almost out of ideas of how to lessen the tension floating above our heads. A tension mainly caused by Federick freaking Archer.

"Okay, I've had enough. The atmosphere in here is going to strangle me to death. What do you say if I have some wine with you, Mom? It would really help make the night bearable." Winking at me for more effect, Wyatt tried one more time to convince me to let me consume alcohol. However, it was not going to work, especially not when Damien was here for the first time.

"Ha, nice try baby, but it's not gonna happen. The answer is still *NO*. Be happy with your drink. Or do you want me to take this one from you as well?" My face supporting a smile, I winked at Wyatt.

"Okay fine, heard you loud and clear." Pouting, Wyatt gave up.

"But Phoebe, I'm older than them, so why not me." Luke tried his turn.

Teo better not even try if he doesn't want to be grounded for all of eternity. He was way too young for this shit.

"Not big enough for me, Luke. Remember, you are still a senior. I think you are hanging around Wyatt way too much. He's having a bad influence on you." I jocularly added.

"Hey, I'm right here if you haven't noticed. So please, do insult me more when I'm gone. Besides, I thought I was your real son, not that asshole." Wyatt playfully whined.

"Language, young man — unless you want to be grounded or spanked. In case you have forgotten, I am still your mother, and I have every right." I faked a motherly tone when all I wanted to do was laugh.

I was moments away from cracking up when the ever-stony frigid ice-statue that was Federick Archer beat me to it. Hearing his big fat genuine melodious laugh for the first time in my life, I was awestruck.

All my smiles and laughter flying away, I turned my head towards Federick with such swiftness, I heard a 'Click' inside my neck. Lost for words, all I could do was gawp at Federick with bulging eyes and agape mouth, like a cute little goldfish. I couldn't believe my ears and eyes.

Gaping like a wonderstruck statue, I loved his silvery open laugh. It was music to my ears. So much so, I was starting to consider inviting Federick over more often just to hear him laugh for hours. At the same time, a surge of jealousy coursed through my veins at the thought of him laughing this magically with his other women.

Gosh, what was I thinking! Where the heck did this stupid idea came from? Why would **I** want Federick in my house more often? This was crazy! I was going crazy.

Federick might possess the most beautiful and angelic laugh I have ever heard, but this doesn't mean I will start crushing all over him.

No, I won't! No way to that arrogant presumptuous asshole despite his alluring laugh. I needed to regain full control over myself.

CHAPTER 3
ODD NIGHT

PHOEBE

Matching my captivated stare with utmost intensity, Federick and I held each other's gaze without an ounce of hatred, annoyance or ickiness for the very first time in our lives. Forgetting about everyone else in the room, I couldn't deny there was something invisible in the air. Something I couldn't quite put my finger on.

Beholding Federick's enticing grey orbs, I was flabbergasted and somewhat bewitched by how our relationship was stealthy changing and becoming increasingly confusing. I still didn't like the man and his arrogance, but for some unknown reason, I didn't feel like choking him to death anymore.

In fact, I was fascinated by him. Particularly after he came back into my life after graduating business school — after he had disappeared from the face of the earth years ago.

Unbeknown to me, mine and Federick's little moment became the night's special show. The next thing I knew Damien was beside me, loudly clearing his throat to grasp my attention. Internally struggling with the idea of whether I wanted to know more about this invisible cloth lingering over Federick and me, I was upset Damien managed to grasp my attention and broke mine and Federick's unique moment.

Hearing another insistent clearing of a throat, "UH . . . yes . . . What do you want Damien?" Secretly stealing glances at Federick, I inattentively inquired.

"What do you think I want?" Folding his arms in front of his chest as he stood tall in front of me, Damien sarcastically exclaimed.

"Umm . . ."

Letting my words hang, I couldn't give two shits about Damien's rhetorical question. I was too distracted and desperate to take another look at the smiling man who had taken Federick's place. I will do anything to avoid Mr Federick Arrogant Stony-face Archer. But Mr Federick Smiling Charming-face Archer, I would gladly like to know more about.

"My God, Phebes! I'm trying to get your attention here. Will you please stop gawking at your boss in front of me?" Damien reprimanded in an annoyed voice.

Jerked me back to reality, "Huh . . . What are you talking about? Did you hit your head? Why would I of all people be ogling at someone as arrogant and annoying as Federick Archer."

'Is he now?' A voice inside my head quipped with sass. Instead of ignoring it as I've been so far, I began considering that stupid voice's comment, propelling me to blush for being so obvious with my staring.

"Yes, Miss Smith, stop ogling at your irresistible boss . . . Or, at least be less obvious. Until we make it official, anyways." Federick alluded.

But hey, at least he was still smiling.

'Infatuated, much. . .' That persistent voice again.

'So what!' I mentally scolded.

If this continues, I am going to need a doctor to operate on my brain. And what was this shit about hearing voices in my head all of a sudden . . . I must be unwell and dying, or ghosts really do exist.

"What do you have to make official, Phoebe? Is there something going on between you two that I should be aware of?" Damien asked both sternly and confused.

Shoving my absurd thoughts under a pile of rocks, "No! Of course not, Damien. I promise. Federick is joking and being his usual jerk."

My earlier mesmerised gaze turning into a glower as I look back at Federick, "Keep your nasty dreams and stupid jokes to yourself, Federick. You might just start worrying my family." In the most unpleasant tone I could muster, I bit back at the asshole.

"Okay . . . Okay . . . I'm sorry, it was a low joke. I apologise for worrying you, Damien." Lifting his hands halfway up in defence, Federick quipped.

Briefly glancing between Damien and me with mischievousness, "But Damien — even if there was something between Phoebe and me, it shouldn't bother you, given you two are **only** childhood best friends . . . right?" Purposely stretching on specific words, Federick blatantly questioned mine and Damien's friendship.

"Don't fret it, Federick. Everyone has their own sense of humour. I don't mind your jokes, and I'm sure Phoebe doesn't mind either. Do you Phebes?" Damien contended with defying confidence, evincing Federick his commentary left him unaffected.

"But I do mind —"

"Phoebe Smith." With a hard look indicating I shouldn't defy his words, Damien firmly cut in. I swear Damien has intentionally learned to cultivate my dad's hard look and tone so he could use it against me.

"Whatever. Sure, I don't mind. I'm going to bring the dessert."

Enjoying our dessert, it occurred to me that my kids were awfully quiet, to the point where they were almost invisible. Their peculiar silence — when they had plenty of opportunities to bug or make fun of me quickly gained my attention. It was unusual for them, especially from Wyatt, my chatterbox of a son.

Turning my attention away from Damien and Federick, I carefully observed Wyatt, Teo and Luke sitting in their little corner beside Federick. They were so engrossed into their phones and hushedly talking to each other, they didn't even notice my scrutiny on them.

Surveying them with narrowed eyes, my curiosity grew with each passing second — or was it with each mouthful of ice-cream I was gulping.

Letting my inquisitiveness get the best of me, I discreetly kept my ice-cream cup on top of the small glass round table and stealthily moved towards them. With ninja stealthiness, I stood a few feet behind their couch and attempted to peek at their phone screens.

Other than Luke who seemed to have noticed my presence but didn't act on it, my two sons were as oblivious as an empty clam.

'If these two didn't have so many bodyguards around them at all times and were naturally this oblivious when someone was a few feet away from them, they will already be six feet under.' My brain vocalised.

And heck was it right. The amount of time Cole had sent an assassin to track these two down to eliminate or kidnap them was unbelievable. But thanks to mommy dearest, they are still breathing, and those assassins have forgotten the meaning of oxygen.

Perceiving the confused look on Federick and Damien's face through my peripheral vision, I stopped dead on my tracks. Placing my forefinger on top of my lips, I instructed them to zip it and not move a muscle. I didn't have time for their questions.

With a smile plastered on his face, Federick seemed to have gotten an idea about what I was planning. Damien, on the other hand, was just plain confused, and if this were a cartoon world, there would have been a huge question mark in place of his head.

Shifting my attention from the two grown men to the three teenagers, as their whispering increased, I was further sure they were hiding something from me. Edging closer, I crept up to them to the point where I could literally touch Wyatt's head with my forehead, and they still didn't feel my presence behind them. I guess I am pretty good at being a ninja then.

Pushing that thought at the back of my head before my mind begins to wander in all different directions, I return my attention to my sons. Brows furrowed and eyes narrowed, I tried to listen in on their private conversation.

Resembling the diet coke that burst from its container when combined with mentos, my mouth popped open at the words; **Girls, Party** and **Tonight**. Getting out of my buzz state, I picked my jaw off the floor and snatched their phones from their hands at warp speed. My original plan of solely listening in ruined, I took a few steps back and waited for all three teenagers to get out of their stunned state.

"What the hell, mom!"

"MOM!"

"What the heck was that for!"

Letting their foul language slide, I grinned at their dumbstruck figures. "Three words. Girls, Party and Tonight." Observing their priceless facial expression, I simply had to continue teasing them to death.

"Okay . . . Let's make it four words, **sex**." With a playful grin, I relentlessly jibed. At this their faces turned so pricelessly red I couldn't handle it and cracked up.

"Mom, are you done yet! It's not funny. And I would really like my phone back, please." Beetroot, Wyatt complained after about five minutes of my unceasing laughter.

"My goodness . . . You guys . . . are so cute. Especially you, Luke." I mumbled between laughter.

Seeing Luke so profoundly immersed into my family, in addition to already knowing my most important secret, really arose my desire to divulge my final decision about bringing him in as an official member of my family. Not only was Luke one of my best spies, but he could eventually carry out my legacy in our spy world.

Realising where my train of thought was leading me, I let it slide from my crazy-mother and Angel head and concentrated on annoying the boys. Besides, I sort of told Joseph I would wait for him to be present when announcing my decision to Luke.

"Okay, I apologise." Taking in a deep breath to control my laughter, "But your faces were so priceless. All three of you looked like I caught you about to do something wrong."

Their guilty regard upon hearing my statement, however, clogged my laughter as a rusty, debris-filled pipe would to a sink. "You boys weren't planning on going to that party tonight, were you? Because it's written on all three of your faces that you've been caught red-handed in your attempts to make plans to sneak out tonight."

"Well, mom . . . We wouldn't exactly call it sneak out. Let's just say; we would have gone without letting you know about it until tomorrow morning." Wyatt enumerated with a guilty grin.

"Is this what you kids call it these days?"

"Sorry, but we didn't want to ruin your reunion with your child-hood best friend. And I promise we would have been back before he left for his place."

Louring at all three teenagers, even though it was Wyatt who was doing all the talking, I was piqued at their behaviour. First, it was Federick who was head bent on ruining my supposedly perfect night to welcome Damien back into my life — now it was my kids. It was vexing how I've waited ten years for Damien's arrival and the world; or better yet, the people in my life were doing everything to refrain me from open-heartedly welcome the one guy who knew me the longest and even more than myself.

Slowly exhaling to calm my rising temper, "So, if I get this straight; you were going to ditch your mother to go to some stupid late-night party to have sex with some bimbos without having the decency to inform me ahead of time. And might have been ready to lie to me if you had too. WOW . . . This is just awesome. It seems I have the best kids ever."

Usually, I'm cool with them partying at night, but right now I was a little pissed off. Sneaking out at night with Vanderwill sneaking around town again, looking for them — what were they thinking!

"Well, if you put it this way, it sure sounds bad."

"No shit, Sherlock!"

"But believe me, we were going to tell you . . . Tomorrow."

Crossing my arms over my chest, stern like a General, ready to deliver the deadliest punishment, I glared at them in burning silence. Maintaining my sharp posture as time ticked away, the intensity of my glower sent chills down their backs. Gulping, the boys dropped their gaze to the floor, fixing it with new admiration.

Forgetting about the other adults in the room, my attention fixated on my boys; I was taken by surprise when a wide body closed behind me, its heat intermingling with mine. Its firm muscles unashamedly pressing against mine. The self of this person itself was exuding control and something else — something more significant that was relaxing me rather than annoying me.

The warmth of this person's body was welcoming, despite its sly attempt to wash away my anger and guard. However, I wasn't going to let the comfort of this man's body divert my initial plan. Slowly turning my head around, I was praying it was Damien because if this was Federick, shit was going to get further complicated for us.

Unfortunately, as luck would have it, the person who was causing my body to react in such a bizarre manner was none other than Federick freaking Archer.

Attempting to resist the pull my body felt towards his was, however, fruitless once Federick gave me his rare sweet yet innocent smile. My lips stretching into a smile without my accord, I was an outsider in my own body.

Reckoning my smile as an encouragement, Federick wrapped his arms around my waist with utmost carefulness and pulled me into him. Confused as to what Federick was doing so close to me, or why my foul temperament was insisting on disappearing, the urge to fall in his comfort was intoxicating.

Despite our history, I yearned to let Federick's smell and the warmth of his body melt my cold heart. It was as if his body — his self, was commanding me to let go into his arms, but I knew I couldn't. It would be complicated, unreasonable, weird and awkward later on.

With this in mind, I returned my attention to my boys, who were standing in a disciplined line in front of me, prepared to be grounded. Contenting the absurd urges within me by pressing my back against Federick's chest, I was amazed by how our bodies — even though differently structured — moulded perfectly into each other. Like two perfect pieces of puzzles have finally been paired, which on its own, was crazy.

Realising I was hesitating to relax completely, Federick slowly brushed his lips against my ear. His breath hitting my earlobe, a shiver ran down my body. "I'm here for you. Let go." Federick lowly whispered for only the two of us to hear.

The whole situation was so bizarre. His whisper carried an authority I never encountered before — one that had the power of an alpha — just like the tone I use when commanding my army of spies.

I couldn't pinpoint why I was unable to fight Federick's order when I, myself, am not fond of being ordered. Perhaps, it was our close proximity — his hot breath fanning over my ear and neck, or the overpowering manly smell of him wounding around me. All I know is, I for once, did as asked without putting up a fight.

My whole body fully relaxing against Federick, the stiffness encompassing my hard posture was long forgotten. I knew I had to get a grip over myself and concentrate on the matter at hand, but before I could do anything, Federick motherfreaking Archer beat me to it.

CHAPTER 4
AN ADDITION TO THE FAMILY

PHOEBE

Tightening his grip around the small of my waist, "So care to explain, boys?" Federick sternly admonished.

'WOW . . . I've never heard Federick speak in such a tone.'

Federick is usually stern, hard, cold and heartless, but the tone he had just used was utterly different. It was identical to the one my father would use whenever he would catch me sneaking out to party at the rave, or when I would be in deep shit. Yep, I did it all — the main reason why the boys' sneakiness intrigued me so much.

In comparison to how I felt when my dad would use this tone, Federick's tone had an entirely different effect on me. His voice carried an authority that propelled me to involuntarily snuggle deeper into him. A wave of prurient chill coursing down my core, I was somehow turned on — which put more weight on my theory of me losing my sanity.

Like a bat out of hell, Wyatt, Teo and Luke looked up at Federick and me, shocked at how we were holding each other. Heck, even

I would be stunned to see Federick and myself in such an intimate position. Conscious Wyatt would unashamedly talk back to Federick and say something along the lines of *'You are not my father'*, I took the first step and warned him with my fiery motherly glare.

"I am sorry, mom . . . I promise this will never happen again. I don't know what overcame me. It was stupid — I guess we will be going to our room now. We are grounded, right?" In a low voice, his puppy dog eyes full-on, Wyatt apologised with a heartwarming innocence.

Yes, Wyatt was cute when he wanted to. This was precisely how he got himself and his brother out of trouble. I was weak when it came to them, but I couldn't help it. Swayed by Wyatt's apology and adorableness, I was about to smile at him, but then my eyes landed on Luke.

This was the perfect opportunity to give Luke a taste of what was awaiting him when I do pop the question, and he accepts my proposition of officially becoming my son. After all, the last thing I wanted was for Luke to complain he didn't have a clue of how overly motherly and protective I am.

It was time to give Luke his ***'Welcome to the family as my son'*** wrath.

Pulling my best pissed off face, I focused my attention on Luke, "As far as you are concerned, Luke, I am upset with you. I would have never expected such reckless behaviour from you. You are supposed to be the most responsible one between those two imbeciles."

Luke's demeanour changing like he was near to tears, I was ready to crack up. How a brave and strong boy, like himself, could become so emotional when it comes to tasting my raft was still beyond me.

"I am extremely sorry for upsetting you and being such a disappointment. And before you punish us, I want you to know; it was all my idea, not Wyatt or Teo's."

Albeit, I was intentionally pulling Luke's leg, I couldn't let him continue his illogical rambling about being a disappointment to me. Not when his words hit closer to home than I would have expected.

His words evoked the deep and sad memories of me uttering the same phrase to Mia and my dad before they got killed. And, no matter how much I tried to suppress those memories, I couldn't stop the images of their last moments on this planet from flashing in front of my eyes.

"That's not true, mom. It was all my idea. Luke is being nice and doesn't want us to get into trouble."

Bringing my attention back on the boys right when Luke cast Wyatt one of his *'What the fuck are you doing!'* look, "I already know this, Wyatt. No need to point out the obvious." Feigning a glare at a nodding Wyatt, I was glad they were finally starting to take responsibility for their actions, especially *Mr Wyatt I'm-never-wrong Smith.*

Since Federick didn't seem ready to let go of me, I pointed for Luke to step towards me. "Look at me, Luke." Gently raising his chin with my index finger, I captured his apologetic gaze. A gaze which told me, he was bashing onto himself.

Maintaining a soft tone, "Sweetheart, I want you to understand something tremendously important. There will be times, like today, where I will be upset with either you, Wyatt or Teo, but hear me loud and clear. No matter what happens, you will never be a disappointment to me. Whoever dares to tell you otherwise is wrong and one of the biggest imbeciles known to humankind. Heck, if someone ever dares utter such nonsense to you, I want you to come to me. I will personally deal with them." I passionately vocalised.

Widely grinning, the sad glimmer in the depth of Luke's eyes disappeared.

"But, if you can't handle the insult, just hit the bastard where you know it will hurt the most — well, not too hard. The last thing you need is me picking you up from a jail cell." Ruffling Luke's hair with motherly affection, I added with a wink to terminate the tension. Nodding his head, Luke was picture-perfect of a satisfied innocent child.

Breaking free from Federick's hold, it was like a piece of myself was ripped from my core. The warmth and relaxation my body had become accustomed to, vanished into thin air. Unfamiliar with these feelings, I stuffed all those irrational thoughts at the back of my mind, wishing for it never to resurface.

Enveloping Luke into my embrace, forgetting about the men behind him, I whispered the good news I had meant to keep a secret until later this week when Joseph would be present.

To say Luke was euphoric would be an understatement. He was on top of the world — radiating brighter than the sun on the warmest summer days. The ray of his jovialness shone with such intensity, it lightened my mood to the point where I forgot about them trying to sneak out, about my failed welcome-back dinner for Damien, or Federick stuck to my ass like my tightest leather skirt.

"Really, Phoebe, do you honestly mean it? — I am not questioning you, but I know you were waiting for the perfect time, and this seems so sudden. I don't want to force myself into this family . . . I mean, are you saying this out of sympathy, sadness or something else? Because I will hate to put you in such a position. I am rambling, aren't I? I am so sorry, but I am just —"

Having had enough of his illogical rambling, I hugged Luke again, effectively cutting him off.

"Don't you want me to legally be your mother, Luke? Because I would be my honoured to call you, my son." Raising one of my fine eyebrows, I lightly mused with a smile.

"No, it's not what I meant. Of course, I want you to. You are one of the best mothers known to humanity . . . The only mother I have known so far, anyway." Thankfully getting a grip over the grim thought that had popped into his mind, Luke plastered another radiant smile on his face.

"Confirm with Wyatt and Teo first, though. I value our friendship more than anything, and I wouldn't want them to feel uncomfortable around me or jealous of the attention I might get at first. Or worse, start hating me."

Acknowledging Luke's worried tone, I glanced behind him for confirmation from my two sons. Grinning like maniacs and nodding their head like a bod-head doll in response to my questioning eyes, "I will take a wild guess and say they want you in this family as much as

I do." Still eyeing these two boys of mine like they were a pair of crazy people who could pounce on me if I averted my eyes from them, "I just hope they don't creep you out to the point of running away".

"Mother, stop trying to push Luke away. He finally accepted to become our new bro after weeks of discussion— the most boring part, might I add. I can't even start to comprehend how you survive all these hours of meetings every day."

"Well, you boys are really creepy, shaking your head as such. I can't help but state the facts."

See what I said about not being able to stay angry at them for long.

'You forgot to add that the reason behind why you don't get bored during those long hours of meetings is because Federick Ashton Archer constantly keeps your mind running.' Ms Inner voice decided to pinch in her unwelcome and obviously false statement.

"Um . . . Phoebe, does this mean I can finally call you mom, instead of using your name." With a blush, Luke shyly questioned.

"Of course, sweetheart. I want you to accept me as your mother from the very core of your soul because I will be treating you like I treat Wyatt and Teo. How about I call my lawyer first thing tomorrow morning to formalise your adoption as a Smith."

Crushing me into a hug. "Thank you so much, Phoe — I mean, mom." Turning tomato red again, Luke exclaimed with heightened emotion.

To sum up, I now have one son who is way too timid and quiet. One who is blunt and talks without any filter whatsoever. Another who blushes all the time and is in between Wyatt and Teo when it comes to attitude. Just great — I got all the characters in my home.

"I will caution you, though, if you feel I'm being too strict or controlling within the first few months, let me know. I will try to go easier. Afterwards, however, you will have to handle everything that comes with this relationship. But don't worry too much, I don't see Wyatt and Teo complaining.".

"I expect no less." Luke happily added.

Focusing on welcoming Luke into the family, I forced my body to stop imagining Federick's heat and comfort. However, the more I was refuting this persistent desire, the more my body was craving for him. Motherly on the outside, I was a woman desiring the warmth of a man on the inside — a woman who until tonight had no desire to get close to any man, much less Federick Archer.

'*You should just ask him to hold you again.*' The damn voice in my head suggested. But there was no way I was going to fall this low. I was going to suck it up — I didn't need anyone.

As if reading my internal struggle, Federick closed the distance between us and wrapped his arms around my torso again. Embarrassed Federick could notice what I internally needed, and slightly shocked at how in-tune someone who is continuously standoffish was, I felt compelled to mutter my appreciation.

"Anything for you, sweetheart," Federick whispered with his infamous smirk.

In lieu of fiercely reacting to Federick's arrogance as I usually do, I leaned further into his strong embrace and relinquished every second of whatever was happening between us tonight. Because God knows my body hasn't been able to relax to this extent in a very long time. Tomorrow I will deal with the problem that tonight will definitely bring.

Bringing my attention back to the three teenagers who were eyeing Federick and me suspiciously, "So, let's get back to your guys' sneaking out to party and have sex, shall we?" Returning to the other main topic of the night, I seriously stated.

"Okay, mom, we get it . . . We are going into our respective rooms to await your punishment." Wyatt voiced out with his puppy dog eyes in full effect, followed by Teo and Luke.

"When does the party start?" I cut in.

"At nine, why?" Sharing a questioning regard with his brothers, Wyatt inquired.

"Good, it's like eight something now." Still confused but with hope written on their faces, they nodded.

"Well, does this still give you guys time to get ready for the party?" Doing my best to hide my smile, I posed without excitement.

"Really, mom! Of course, we have time. We love you . . ." All three of them excitedly professed, as if I had just offered them the world.

"Tsk, Tsk . . . not so fast. I'm not done yet. You will still be punished. But I realised I hadn't been the best mother or friend in the past few months, so to make it up, I will allow you three to attend this party." Stopping them on their way to Federick and me, "There is a condition.".

"Which is?" Luke and Wyatt asked at the same time, while Teo patiently waited for me to continue.

"Damien is coming with you."

From my peripheral vision, I noticed Damien's astonished face, clearly thunderstruck by my condition. It was as if I had just brought him back to a harsh reality, plucking the invisibility coat he has been wearing all this while.

"But why?" Wyatt and Teo simultaneously whined.

"Because I said so. And in the event of any trouble — I mean any trouble at all, as insignificant as it might seem at the moment, give Damien a call. I will text you his number." Picking up on my indirect hint that Damien was one of us and could help protect Wyatt and Teo if needed, Luke stepped down from protesting like Wyatt and Teo.

"However, if it's one of your girl problems, please leave Damien out of having to bail you out of their claws. Also, I can't emphasise enough — but **do not** under any circumstances leave Teo alone. As for you, Luke, please don't let these two leave your field of vision for a prolonged amount of time. Did I make myself clear enough for you boys?"

As easy-going as I was as a mother, their security was something I never mess with. Especially with Vanderwill lurking closer than ever, like the devil he was.

"Do we have any other choice?" Wyatt pleaded.

"Nope. It's either accept my conditions or no party; which also means no sex for both you and Luke tonight."

"Okay, as you wish. But why do we have to take Damien, why not Federick? I don't mean to be rude or offensive, but I think I speak for all three of us when I say we prefer Federick over Damien. Federick is so much cooler and fun."

Shocked at Wyatt's statement and the other two boys' nods, I honestly didn't understand what was happening. It was supposed to be the other way around. Even though the boys didn't know it yet, Damien is to be the father figure in their life. He should be the one winning over their hearts, not Federick freaking Archer.

Not knowing what to do with their response or of Federick's victorious smirk, I focused my hard warning glare on the three teenagers standing in front of me.

"Fine, got it, Ma'am. We feel and get you straight to the point. We are going to get ready."

"Do that," I added in a deadpan tone.

With the kids out of the picture, the buffer they were subconsciously representing in lessening the awkwardness and weirdness of the night was gone. Federick still wrapped around me like the meat around rice sushi, while Damien was quietly sitting on the couch beside us, I was in a real pickle.

Nonetheless, I didn't want Federick to let go of me just yet. Refusing to face and acknowledge the awkwardness of my situation, I slowly turned my attention to Damien's shocked self.

"I am so sorry for everything, Dam. I know this is not how you wanted tonight to go. But you were right. We should give the boys more time to know you before we tell them the truth."

Instantaneously Federick's whole body stiffed up behind me, his uneasiness clear as a sharp stainless steel knife poking at me.

"I guess it's all right . . . But Phebes, you should have at least considered asking me if I wanted to babysit them while they were out partying. Don't take it the wrong way, but sweetheart, remember what we talked about before dinner? Because you are doing the exact opposite of what we agreed on. Besides, they don't seem to appreciate my company. So why not do all of us a favour and let Federick babysit them while we do some catching up?"

"As promising and nice as this idea seems, the answer is still a no. I get it, I am going a little too fast for your liking, but try to see all of this from my perspective. I only mean well for you guys. Why don't you want to see this?"

"Hey, if none of you has realised, I am standing right here. So, would anyone mind asking for my opinion about the whole matter?" Federick cut in before Damien could utter another word.

"How can we forget you're here when you are clinging onto Phoebe so hard you could practically knock her out."

"Damien, please behave!" I uttered with seriousness, my patience wearing thin with his renewed amount of rudeness.

"Oh come on Phebes, stop being so easy."

"Excuse me!" One could say I was astonished by Damien's crude words.

"Let's be real, Phebes . . . Federick utters a few sweet words, holds onto you longer than necessary and you are already taking his side. Next thing you know, you are sleeping with him — if you haven't already done so, that is."

Irked by the accusation and prudeness in Damien's tone, "If this is your new way of trying to protect me, let me inform you right now, it's not working. You know damn well it's nothing like that. So please, stop behaving like a kid, because I swear, even my sons don't act as such."

"Of course they wouldn't. They are not me, nor resemble anything like me."

Standing frozen like an icicle, shocked as his words replayed in my mind, the double meaning in Damien's statement was painfully obvious. Till this day, Damien was still refusing to acknowledge Wyatt and Teo as his own.

Noticing my flabbergasted state, Federick rubbed the side of my arms in a circular motion in an attempt to relax my tense self. Doing my best to ignore the chill that ran through my bones as Federick blankly and stonily glared at Damien, "I hope for your sake, you did not mean what I think you meant." I uttered in a low voice.

"Let's forget about it, Phebes . . . It's just . . . your comment about me not being like your sons touched pretty close to home, and I snapped. Notwithstanding, I think you and I should discuss your idea of taking in this Luke boy — in private. We need to have a dire talk about your behaviours and emotional state."

"What the heck are you babbling about?" Damien's words making no sense whatsoever, I demanded in confusion.

"Let's face it, Phoebe. When I came back, I had high hopes of seeing a completely different and more mature Phoebe Smith. I expected the evolving time and our difficult conditions to have transformed you. Alas, it's not what I see here — no worries though, it's not too late for a change."

"Whatever you say; but, this doesn't change the fact that you are bringing the kids to the party tonight. I am in no mood to drive, and you are our best bet, so please, do me this one favour."

"Okey-dokey," With a sweet reassuring smile, Damien affirmed, propelling me to smile back at him.

Nonetheless, I couldn't shake the feeling that something was wrong with Damien. He was acting bizarrely, saying illogical things along with switching from mood to mood — almost, like a girl on her menstruation.

I was starting to worry about Damien. About what all those years away had done to him. And as much as I wanted to speak with his commanding offer in Rio to get a clear picture of what was exactly happening, I promised Damien ten years ago that I wouldn't interfere in his life unless it were life-threatening.

CHAPTER 5
EVENTFUL

FEDERICK

Dismissing half of what came out of my father's most prominent client's mouth, and speedily wrapping this unexpected meeting my dad dropped on my lap, I risked the chance of a speed ticket on my way to Phoebe's place. The staggered and anxious expression on Phoebe's face when she opened her door, however, was well worth all the trouble. Not to mention her sweet and innocent demeanour while she was addressing her children. It made up for any inconvenience and brought an honest smile on my face.

This motherly and loving version of Phoebe Smith was so new to me; I couldn't help but be internally google-eyed.

A sentiment I never once experienced in my life.

However, once Damien Ambrose showed his face, the spell this version of Phoebe had on me saw a depletion. My frustration, on the other hand, saw an increase. But I couldn't possibly show it. I had to be polite and pretend to like Damien. Not because of the business he was bringing to me; I could care less about it with the way things were developing. But because he was polite towards me.

Dang him!

Although I am usually capable of keeping a tight grip over my emotions and mouth, I couldn't for the life of me stop myself from muttering how much I disdained everything about Damien when he kept getting into the picture. What caught me by surprise, however, was my nonchalant reaction at being interrupted by Wyatt.

Being one of the most ruthless tycoons in New York, I despised being interrupted — especially when a situation was awkward. I thrived in crushing people's emotions and walking all over them to get what I want. Yet here I was, being interrupted on more than one occasion by a teenager.

Listening to Phoebe apologise to Damien on several occasions for something she had no control over further infuriated me. To top it off, Damien had the audacity to bluntly admit he was glad I crashed this dinner where he was supposed to introduce himself as the kids' father. That jerk even went as far as making Phoebe feel guilty when it should have been the other way around. All these, plus his poor excuses stirred the anger within me with flaming intensity.

Swallowing my anger like a snake swallowing a whole egg, I silently scanned for any similarities between Damien, Teo and Wyatt. Alas, I was left further baffled. The two teenagers resembled nothing like Damien, much less anything like Phoebe. What was clear though, was Wyatt and Teo's pull on Phoebe. They had her wrapped around their fingers.

As time went by, with me quietly studying each member at the table, it dawned on me that something was terribly wrong with me. I was irked for Phoebe when all she was doing was enduring Damien's stupid comments. It shouldn't have concerned me that Damien was jokingly insulting Phoebe, yet I found myself wanting to punch his arrogant face.

Comparatively, when Phoebe reprimanded Wyatt for coming to her rescue, I practically had to retain myself from giving Phoebe a piece of my mind. She was being impractical, which, it seems made no sense to her kids. However, I had no right whatsoever to lecture Phoebe on how to educate her kids — especially when she has way more experience than me at being a parent.

Taking in my surroundings and Phoebe's weird, almost beta-like behaviour, I realised it was going to be a long, insufferable and nerve-wracking night. What gave me little consolation throughout the dinner, however, was that both Damien and I were still on point one. And if he continues with the way he was in front of Teo and Wyatt, Damien was sure going to lose a lot of points, and I will be here to pick up the slack. Not to mention, witnessing Phoebe slightly squirm under my ferocious gaze was a significant plus.

Subtly observing Phoebe's carefree relationship with her kids, I had to admit she had an amazing and amusing family. One so out of the ordinary, I couldn't help myself but genuinely and freely laugh at their sweet innocent bickering. A laugh, I don't show to anyone other than those extremely close to me.

Catching Phoebe's bulging mesmerising eyes, I lost myself into its unique depths. The cherry on top of the icing, however, was Phoebe's irritation when Damien yanked her out of our once-in-a-lifetime trance. At that moment, I realised if I play my cards right, I could push Damien away and have Phoebe all to myself. Obviously, Damien would be allowed to visit his kids, but Phoebe was mine and mine only to hold and love.

Then again, I should have known with Damien in the picture; my happiness would be short-lived. The gigantic asshole that he was, dared to force Phoebe to say she didn't mind my low comments when I knew damn well she did. Fuming with rage at Damien's audacity, I didn't even care that I would have minded Phoebe's sarcastic response to my question about her relationship with Damien. All I cared about was punching Damien's stern voice out of him.

He had no right to speak to Phoebe so sternly!

Only I had the right to speak to Phoebe as such.

Languidly breathing out the darkness within me, it dawned on me that I've been addressing Phoebe as mine and using the word love for a while now. On top of that, my possessiveness was spilling out like the fizz from an overtly-shaken soda. To make matters worse, I was enjoying the company of her family and felt a need to be part of me.

I was in so much trouble — especially when I knew practically nothing about the woman I supposedly love.

God, I needed help.

I could easily deal with liking Phoebe more than I usually like other women. But actually falling in love was something far more dangerous, and I wasn't sure if I could come to terms with the latter.

Paying heed to Phoebe's every movement for the remainder of the night, I discerned a tint of my mom's habit within her. Squinting her eyes and stealthily zeroing her attention on the inert teenagers, Phoebe resembled my mom. Even the way her mood swiftly changed from easygoing to pissed off, and motherly was parallel to my mom.

As I was holding onto Phoebe in an attempt to relax and comfort her while she was chastising her kids, I was perplexed at Damien's indifference to the situation. He was sombrely sitting on the couch, watching us as if we were an unfascinating drama Tv show.

Notwithstanding, what captivated me was Phoebe's willingness to permit me to hold her so close, that too in front of her family. The fact that she succumbed to my authoritative tone instead of fighting me or hitting me was a major surprise to my already confused mind. All I knew was that I was starting to affect her — I could feel it through her body as she pressed herself against me.

Weirdly enough, Phoebe and her kids felt like mine despite their birth father being in the same room. But I knew this feeling was only temporary. From the very day I found out about them, it was crystal clear that Phoebe was both the father and mother to Wyatt and Teo. And given the respect both boys treat Phoebe with; there was no doubt they acknowledged the latter.

Granted, I was delighted to discover that deep down Phoebe was caring, generous and compassionate; I was still amazed and flabbergasted when she openly announced adopting a nearly grown man like Luke. I was not one to judge, because, from the looks of it, her decision seemed to have been well pondered over. But at this rate, it would be difficult for her and me to have our own children when we do marry.

'WHOA!... SLOW DOWN THERE, COWBOY!'

My brain screeched at an alarming speed, spawning me to mentally bang my head against an invisible wall for even thinking about such a thing when Phoebe and I were not even a couple.

'Let the couple thing go, you dumb ass. Think . . . You don't even know her! And what about her relationship with the people around you? Think you dumb ass. Think.' The little annoying voice of reason vocalised. Probably making more sense than my possessive rants.

'You think!' It pointed with a high note of sarcasm.

'See, without me, you are nothing.' The not-so-little voice bugged me again.

'Don't be so proud of yourself.' I mentally retorted.

Any person going through my head right then would definitely think I was crazy. Heck, even I thought I was losing it. However, the instant I caught sight of Phoebe's eyes — at the desires she was battling — my mental argument was a distant memory.

At first, I was head-bent on ignoring Phoebe's ache for me until she swallowed her pride and asked me to hold her again. However, when I noticed her unconsciously rubbing and caressing her arms, my ego ate itself out, and the battle was lost. My need to be close to Phoebe was somehow more significant than my pride — which was a complete first for me.

Comparatively, I also recognised Phoebe wouldn't do anything rash in front of her sons. She valued their opinion way too much.

Although it was nice and unexpected of Phoebe to allow all three teenagers to attend their wild party, I was vexed that she once again blamed herself for something she had no control over. And from the expression on her kids' faces, they held the same sentiment as me. Then again, after hearing Phoebe's condition for the party, my earlier exasperation seemed insignificant.

Contemplating Phoebe's condition, I had to agree with her. Going to a party filled with booze and girls with someone who could be their dad was indeed a punishment. Discerning the teens' displeasure at their mom's condition, it was clear they didn't like Damien one bit.

Sure enough, Wyatt vocalised my suspicion and blankly stated his preference — which if you ask me was a significant point for me. But, Phoebe didn't particularly see his comment in the same light as me. Nevertheless, I was already winning by 3 points, and the sucker that was Damien was still on point one.

'Stop being so childish, will you?' The voice inside my head reprimanded.

How dare my own voice inside my own head scold me when I was winning . . . This was a good thing.

'Well, if you stop acting like a teenager who has fallen in love for the very first time and instead, act like the tyrant you are supposed to be, maybe I would reprimand your ass less often.' That little annoying voice, I would beat the crap out of it if I could.

'But you can't.' I could mentally envision it, sticking its tongue at me.

'Oh, just shut it, will you! I'm holding a special woman in my arms if you haven't noticed.' I inwardly exclaimed like a crazy person.

'Oh, I know, believe me.'

Blocking whatever else this little shit was going to say, I concentrated on the matter at hand — on Phoebe trying to persuade and pressure Damien to spend time with his kids when all he wanted to do was run away from his responsibilities. He was one of those men who were way too willing to carelessly drop their pants at every opportunity, then disappear at the sight of anything that resembles a problem.

Studying Damien with a new disdain, it was clear he had a way with words around the ladies and Phoebe was no exception to his deceptive spell. For one split second, however, when Phoebe defended me in front of Damien, I fooled myself into thinking she had made a breakthrough and recognised Damien's inappropriate manners. But I was left facing an explosion of my oversight.

Then again, given how Phoebe has been acting, I would bet she has been taking shit from Damien for way too long to even recognise the game he was playing. Let alone realising when actually to say enough is enough. I, on the other hand, was way too choleric from his accusation about Phoebe being easy, to not see right through him.

Slowly breathing out my anger, and maintaining a tight grip over my emotions, I did my best to remain in control. Deep inside, though, I felt Damien's insult to Phoebe directed right at me, and whoever knows me knows I don't take insult — like **ever**.

Relentlessly throwing another punch at my cracking composed self, Damien audaciously stated Phoebe was emotionally unstable and needed to undergo a few changes that would be more pleasing to his royal assholeness. This guy was clearly the one emotionally unstable and sick out of his mind.

Why on earth would he want to deprive this earth of someone like Phoebe? She was an angel. It was he who needed to have his head checked.

Oh, how I wished her sons were here to hear Damien's latest comments. I bet they would have eaten him alive.

I really couldn't comprehend how Phoebe could maintain a smile after that bastard said such rude and insensitive things to her. Stormy, I was itching to bang Damien's head against something hard, so he would understand how to speak to a lady — better yet, how to talk to my woman.

Phoebe was **mine** only. And she deserved to be treasured, nothing less.

Albeit, I still had to figure out the whole being in love with Phoebe — I wasn't sure where this was going. All I knew was that I liked her with extreme passion. But the idea of loving a girl, let alone Phoebe Smith, who I barely knew anything about, scared me to death.

And I, Federick Ashton Archer, cannot afford to be scared. I am impeccable, cold, standoffish and bring fear on others.

CHAPTER 6
THE SMITH PLAYBOYS

PHOEBE

"Look who has finally decided to grant us their presence." Terminating our discussion, Damien and Federick followed my gaze towards the staircase.

"What's taking you girls so long? Come on, hurry up . . . It's not like you are going on a date or anything."

In comparison to my sons, who were used with these types of playful behaviour from me, Damien and Federick looked at me like I was crazy or even eccentric. And the bizarre thing was, I completely agreed with them. I seem to behave oddly when I'm around my loving and annoying kids.

"Take your sweet time, girls. We have all night in front of us." Grinning, I sarcastically taunted.

"God, let the teasing of the month start. We are never going to hear the end of this." Luke sarcastically added.

Softly asking Federick to fully let go of me as the boys leisurely approached me, he reluctantly complied instead of throwing a fit. And despite my better judgement, some stupid part of me felt the need to get rid of the chagrined look on Federick's face.

"Don't worry, Fede, you can hold me as much as you want after I'm done teasing my sons," I whispered for only the two of us to hear and winked at him.

'MY GOD!' I mentally screeched.

This was embarrassing and crazy . . . Who in their right mind would behave so inappropriately towards the person they are supposedly working for?

First, I gave Federick a nickname, flirted with him and lastly, I winked at him. I must have drunk way too much wine way too quickly, or I was losing my mind.

Sensing Federick's smirk and picturing it, I couldn't possibly turn back towards him. Instead, I paid attention to a beaming Wyatt, Teo and Luke, who were waiting for their fair share of teasing. A responsibility I was more than happy to take on.

"Look at what the cat dragged out . . . Three breathtakingly gorgeous young men."

"Why, thank you, milady," Taking a bow, Wyatt exclaimed in a British accent.

"You are more than welcome, my excellency." Curtseying and being just as dramatic as Wyatt, I exclaimed in the same British accent.

"There's going to be a lot of girls tonight literally throwing themselves at my three Lordships, isn't it?" I further stated.

Not giving the boys time to respond to my teasing, I circled them like a predator looking for its prey. Scrutinising their attire, I quickly found my kill of the night.

Stopping short in front of Luke, "You may be brilliant, cute and all, but your sense of fashion is an ultimate disaster."

Messing with Luke's neat, sleek comb-over hairstyle, I arranged it in a high and tight messy hairstyle. "It's high time you learn to be more presentable and dress accordingly to compliment all your features. Especially if you want someone absolutely beautiful and sexy in your bed more often."

Stepping back after successfully giving Luke a bed-head look, I admire my handiwork. This new look completely transformed his appearance, giving him an air of bad boy. The combination of his voluminous messy hair with his dark leather jeans and a black t-shirt that wonderfully fitted his muscular body was perfection.

"Oh come on Mom, you are not making this any easy on me."

"What?" Looking at Wyatt as if he was stupid, I was confused.

"Because of you, Luke is now more likely to win our bet." Wyatt all but huffed at me.

Laughing and smiling at him and his reasoning. "A bet, hmm . . . Do tell." Cocking a brow, I inquired with curiosity.

"You know, bets between guys."

"No, Wyatt, I don't. If you haven't noticed yet, I am very much a girl."

"You are! I surely didn't notice." Wyatt jokingly taunted.

"Should I strip for you to prove how much of a girl I am or what?" Utterly forgetting about Damien and Federick's presence, I playfully goated.

"As if you would have the courage to strip." Wyatt defiantly chafed.

"Oh, you think I can't."

"I know you can't." He provoked.

"You don't want to dare me, young man." I challenged.

"You don't have the guts, but go on, do it. We wanna see." Sharing a playful glance with Wyatt, Luke tested me.

"Not me," Teo exclaimed, earning himself a flick over the head by both Luke and Wyatt.

"Ouch!" Massaging the back of his head, Teo bleats.

"Hey, don't abuse my sweet boy, now."

"Changing topics." Wyatt and Luke vocalised in unison.

Quirking an eyebrow at their open challenge, I unbuttoned my blouse at a snail's pace. Completely taking off the blouse, I glided my hand to the straps of my top and playfully drooped it off my shoulder.

"Phoebe!" Federick vociferated — the growl in his tone, capturing my attention.

Perplexed, I halted and turned towards Federick to only be astonished by his stupefied expression. My dear Damien, on the other hand, wasn't a party pooper like Mr Federick Archer. With a faint smile on his face, his brows lifted in anticipation.

Returning my regard onto Federick, I remained still for a beat and blankly stared at him. But there was only so much I could do to maintain my laughter. The confusion laced on his face at my explosion did nothing to calm my hysteria. In fact, all it did was make me laugh to the point of clutching onto my stomach so I could remain standing and not roll onto the floor like some crazy person. I had no desire to visit a mental institution, believe me, it is terrible. Certain unfortunate missions do, in fact, force one to infiltrate places no one would want to go.

"My God . . . You . . . Really believed . . . You believed . . . I . . . was actually . . . going to do . . . it . . . REALLY . . . I . . ."

"Would you stop laughing like a madwoman?"

"Not sure she can. I think she has long lost her mind." Damien added with a tone of amusement.

"Anyway, of course, I believe." Completely ignoring Damien, Federick declared. "How could I not when you were about to remove your top after already removing your blouse — which you are going to put back on by the way." Picking the blouse by my side, about ready to hand it to me, Federick stated with utter seriousness.

Restraining my laughter with much difficulty, I was ready to drown Federick in my well of sarcasm and ask what crawled up his ass, but his befuddled face threw me into another fit of laughter. Laughing hard, I wholly dismissed the fact that Federick had just tried to order me around.

"She wasn't going to strip fully. We would have stopped her before it went too far. It's always like this between us," Luke and Wyatt cared to explain on my behalf.

"Mom, if you are done teasing us, do you mind if we take your leave now?" Teo asked, surprising me and putting a stop to my wave of laughter.

"Okay, gosh . . . I get it, no need to fuss."

Taking advantage of the timing, Federick shoved my blouse into my hand and given I was busy talking with Teo; I ignored the fact that I unconsciously complied to Federick's 'Request' and buttoned up my blouse.

What was Federick's sudden obsession with my blouse, anyway? I still had a top and a bra on.

"So, does this mean we can leave?"

"Oh no, not so quick, dear Wyatt. Not before you tell me a bit more about your bet." I asserted in my motherly tone — aware they couldn't defy this tonality.

"Well, actually . . . Umm . . . Luke and I made a bet on who will pick up the most girls by the end of tonight." Wyatt hesitantly professed.

"As in just making out, or phone number?" I asked for confirmation.

Blushing and scratching the nape of his neck in embarrassment, "Umm . . . As in sleeping with." Luke divulged.

"Ewe! I should have never asked, and you should have never told me. This is DIS-GUST-ING," I emphasised. "But I guess all of your specimens are like this from a young age. A perfect example would be the one behind me." I pointed at Federick, who was holding his laughter.

Crossing his arms in front of his chest after my comment, his muscles flexing under his dress shirt, Federick raised one of his eyebrows as if to say *'Oh really.'*

Tell me how Federick could manage to look so sarcastic, domineering and so hot at the same time. Umm . . . I mean . . .

"You asked for it, Mom. We simply had to comply." Wyatt conveyed, thankfully interrupting my crazy train of thoughts.

"Yes, mom, there's no way we can defy you when you are in **mother mode**, using the *'Just try to disobey me, and you are dead'* tone." Following his brother's footstep, Teo elaborated.

Turning my attention to Teo, "For your own sake, young boy, I certainly hope you are not a part of their bet. You are far too young to be sexually active. Wait at least until your next birthday before doing such foolish stuff." At this, I heard a cough on my right and behind me.

"Now. Now. Damien. Federick. Better not strangle yourself on your own spit."

Noticing Teo fidgeting, I turned to his brothers to only find them trying to hide a knowing smile. Dreading the answer behind their not-so-sleek behaviours, "Please tell me I'm wrong for once, and you didn't already fuck someone without speaking to me beforehand. Because if this is true, I'm either going to get drunk or faint."

Immediately lowering his gaze and turning red like an overripe tomato, my suspicion was sadly confirmed.

"My God! At 15, Teo! What went through your thick head? Do you even know the risks involved in sexual intercourse? The type of girls you need to be extremely careful with and how to be prepared to prevent any misadventure in the future? Heck, do you even know how to use protection? — Dear Lord, please tell me you used protection . . . Gosh, why didn't you come to me to expound that you are not my little boy anymore and are sleeping around? Where's the trust —"

"Please no, not THE TALK!" Teo, Wyatt, and Luke sharply begged, putting an end to my rambling.

"Go ahead and breathe," Wyatt instructed, unaware they had just given me a devious idea.

"What's with the smirk?" Luke cautiously mouthed.

"Well, you guys just gave me a mind-blowing idea, but you didn't have to shout so loud if you wanted the **'Sex talk'** so badly. I would have gladly given it to you even if you had asked gently."

"NO! No, please, Mom. You have guests over, and we are already late."

Looking at the clock over the dining room entrance wall, I found out that I, unfortunately, had to let them be, *for now*.

"Okay, you win this time. But know it's only because I love you boys so much."

"Thank you so much." All three verbalised in relief.

"Damien, could you please drop them off? You don't have to wait until their party is over. They will be returning with one of the new bodyguards I assigned this week. Make sure you inform them before you leave, though."

"Another one!" Wyatt and Teo exclaimed, quite irritated not knowing why they had bodyguards following them around.

"Well, the more, the merrier." I jested as a way to prevent further questions.

"You mean, you hired more than one." Shrugging, I pleaded the 5th and remained silent to Wyatt's questioning.

"What number will this one be, Teo?" Wyatt turned to his little brother, aware I wasn't going to answer anytime soon.

"I think it would be number five."

At this, I couldn't escape the thought of what they would do if they found out there were at the very least seven of my agents following them around.

"Come on, Teo, Wyatt. We don't want to keep Damien waiting." Luke came to the rescue.

"But aren't you a bit curious as to why we keep having so many bodyguards around us these past few months?"

"Okay boys, if you want to go to this party, we should get going." As if reading my thoughts, Damien came to my rescue.

"Sure." All three responded, dropping the subject for the time being.

"Don't forget to use condoms, boys. I have no intention of becoming a grandma at such a young age." I shouted at their retreating back to break the tension.

"Mom!" Three different loud pitches screeched at me.

Given the boys were way ahead, Damien halted on his track when he reached the front door and decided it would be nice to give me a piece of his mind about the whole partying and sex situation.

"Not to sound rude or too old fashioned, Phebes . . . But as funny as this whole scene was, I strongly disapprove of the idea of **your sons** partying all night to have a series of sex. I don't understand how you can allow such a situation to take place or even accept such behaviours from someone you call your **own**."

Glowering at Damien, I was now royally pissed off. He might be the '*Father*' and my best friend, but he sure as hell didn't have the fucking rights to judge my parenting styles. And as far as talking about my sons like they were trash goes, he was way out of line. I knew they slept around — except for Teo of course — but they were boys. They were teenagers with their hormones at their peak. And well, the girls know what they are getting into when they decide to sleep with renowned playboys as themselves.

Suppressing the urge to snap at Damien and kick some sense into him, I plastered a fake smile on my visage, " Look, Dam, I know you are trying to be a sweetheart and only mean well, and I love you for it. But, **do not ever**, I mean **EVER** judge or question my upbringing style again. You are in **NO** place to do so anymore. So you better leave **my sons** be and let them enjoy life as much as they can."

Catching sight of my sons turning towards us with a perplexed look, engulfed in their layer of overprotectiveness for me, I smiled, pretending like everything was alright and blew a flying kiss to them. Catching the invisible kiss in their closed fists, they kissed their fists and laid it on top of their chest — releasing my love for them in their heart.

"Okay, boys, leave before you are too late to be fashionably late. And Teo, keep it in your pants tonight. We are going to have a little chat about your *'adventures'* sometimes this week — oh, and just so you know, you are going to be under surveillance." Smirking at Teo's flushed face, I was loving the idea of having his every movement reported to me.

"Okay." Gulping, Teo meekly muttered.

"Oh, man, you are so screwed." Wyatt and Luke taunted as they left with Damien.

God knows why Damien is suddenly so rude. I mean, I'm aware I'm responsible for everyone's misfortune, mine included. But this doesn't mean he should make it so plainly apparent with his words and actions. It wasn't like I wanted everyone I loved to be killed in front of me by the same person. So maybe, Damien should cut me some slack.

Turning around, I watched Federick approach me with his trademark smirk. Gulping the sudden lump lodged in my throat, I realised we were now completely alone in the same room — with nobody to interrupt us and nowhere to escape.

Why did I want to escape, anyway?

Nothing was going to happen. I was going to send Federick away and enjoy some me-time — everything was going to be perfectly fine.

But then, the promise I made to Federick earlier replayed in my mind — creating a sense of anxiousness within me.

CHAPTER 7
WASTED

PHOEBE

Swallowing the nervousness coursing through my body and trying to ignore my sweaty hands or thumping heart, "I need a drink. If you want one, follow me to the bar."

Secretly hoping Federick would deny the offer, I marched to my open bar. Unfortunately for me and my state of mind, Federick followed behind.

"Are you always like this around your sons? Speaking so freely about their personal lives without any boundaries whatsoever." Federick inquired as I was choosing which bottle of wine would help me better digest his presence and my nervousness.

His question, however, immediately brought up what I was dreading from the beginning. Federick was judging and disapproving of the way I raise my kids — same as Damien and almost every other person out there.

Telling myself bashing Federick's stupid head against my wall once he starts criticising my parenting methods would be a crime I shouldn't commit, I sucked in a deep breath. Forgetting about the bottle of wine I had my eyes on, I picked a bottle of Spirytus — the strongest and most intoxicating drink known to humankind — and quickly fixed myself a couple of shots.

Taking a shot of my drink and turning towards Federick, "Why do you ask?" Narrowing my eyes at Federick, I was ready to defend the ways I raise my kids.

"Will you, for once, just respond to my question with a real answer instead of topping it with another question? I believe it's a simple question."

Quaffing a second, almost bitter shot, "No Federick, I'm not kidding this time. What exactly do you mean by *'Am I always like this around my children or if I always talk so freely with them?"* With a sleeted glare, I quoted his question, waiting for him to show his disapproval; just like Damien did minutes ago.

Drawing in a deep breath, "I didn't mean it in a bad way, Phoebe. In fact, I think you've raised your boys quite impressively."

My distrust as bright as the stars in the dark sky of the country-side, "But? There's always a but, so go on."

"But, one of my real questions is; do you always talk and joke about their sex life with so much ease? I mean, don't you or them feel uncomfortable? Then, there's also the fact that you seem so different around them; you are more easy-going and relaxed."

"And your point is?" I exclaimed without any emotion.

"My God, Phoebe . . . Do I need to spell out every single detail for you to understand? No wonder my mom still threatens you with the *'I'm going to ground you'* warning."

"Look, if you are going to start insulting me, now is not the best time. I'm too tired. So can we please do this another day?" Chugging my third shot, I blinked away the slight haziness behind my eyelids.

"And, by the way, I'm not a child who's going to be intimidated by mommy dearest. The main reason I listen to Alicia is that I respect her. Not because I'm scared of being grounded."

"Main reason? There's another reason then."

"Have you met your mother? Of course, there is another reason. The woman really does what she says she will, and believe me, being grounded for a month or a lifetime is not part of my plan. I had my fair share of it during my transition into your family, and these days, I'll prefer to take a pass."

Smirking in the cutest way possible, instead of his usual arrogant and prick-ish smirk, Federick knew precisely what I was talking about.

"I agree; my mom can be controlling and motherly." Doing my best not to make any wild movement, I took the last shot with me to the couch.

"Anyways, I was not insulting you. I was actually praising you on how well you handled the situation, especially after Teo gave you such a shock. Then again, I must admit, I would have never imagined this side of you. You were cute, charming and funny — not your usual sassy and arrogant self."

"Thank you — I guess. But I'm not arrogant. It's you who is ." Not taking the crap I was throwing his way, Federick raised his left eyebrow as if to say *'Oh really'*.

"Okay . . . I guess I am. But I'm only this bad with you. I can't help it if you bring my worst attitude."

"Oh, why thank you. At least I now know I can get some reaction out of you — even if it is the worst." And he could joke too.

"You are more than welcome, Mister Archer."

Flirting with Federick, the flicker of logic that was slowly dying recognised I should stop drinking and kick Federick out.

"So kind of you, Miss Smith."

Not helping my case with his alluring voice and the way he pronounced my last name, it was high time to change the topic — at least, until I got a hold of my mind.

"I'll let you in on a small secret."

"Is this our bonding time?" With a tone of amusement, Federick quipped.

"Shush . . . It's about your previous question. Yes, I'm extremely at ease talking about my sons' sex life with them. As the only parent, I have to be informed of those things, especially when they are known playboys. I may have come to love being a mother at a young age, but I have absolutely no desire and interest in becoming a grandmother at the young age of 26."

Reaching for Federick's wrist, I pulled him towards me, compelling him to sit next to me, instead of standing at the far end of the couch. Peering up at him and placing my hand over his clothed chest, I lightly trailed my delicate fingers upward to his neck, the warmth of his skin prickling the tip of my fingers and coursing through my veins like a surge of electricity. Slowly making my way down, his clothing a barrier, I lost the intoxicating physical contact with his skin.

Sadden I couldn't touch more of his hot skin, I stopped by his waistline, "Plus, you know what? There are 'wa-aay' too many bitches nowadays, especially at their private school. I don't want those posh opportunists coming over my house claiming they are carrying my sons' baby when it could be from another man, or simply a lie for child support. And let's not forget, those girls would kill for the chance to be called their girlfriends, fiances or worst, their wives. You surely can relate. Both you and my sons have the same habit of fucking every single girl you can get your hands on. I bet that's why you guys became such good friends, so quickly."

"Phoebe, are you doing fine? You seem tipsy." Turning a deaf ear to whatever I said, Federick asked with uncertainty.

"Shush! Stop interrupting me." Pressing my forefinger on top of his lips, I stopped Federick from uttering another word.

"You know," Fisting Federick's dress shirt and tugging him towards me, his face only a hair away from mine, "In the normal world it's considered rude to interrupt someone while they are talking."

Dismissing the shadowy cloud encompassing my senses, I paused. Releasing his stupid dress shirt, and shoving him back, I gave Federick a false sense of security before edging towards him again. Seeing his dress shirt as an unnecessary apparel, I leisurely popped open each button, my slender fingers grazing against his soft yet firm chest with each advance. The same rush of electricity coursing through me with each touch, this moment was torture for both of us.

With a darkened piercing gaze and heightened breathing, Federick watched me droop his dress shirt and throw it on the other end of the couch. Eyeballing his bare muscular chest, his biceps, his eight-pack abs and the v-shape muscle running diagonally from his hip bones to his pelvic region, a swirl of desire danced within me, making me tingly and warm inside-out.

"And you should be punished for it." Brushing my hand on his now exposed chest, I seductively coaxed.

Hissing in an almost inaudible growl at the back of his throat, Federick caused butterflies to dance and make pirouette inside my stomach.

"As I was saying before you so rudely interrupted me, you and my sons seemed to have grown a connection when you have just met them. Tonight should have been about them getting to know Damien. About them getting used to him being in their life again. But no . . . things are never this easy for me! Is it now? — You had to pop in and ruin everything I had planned. And now, all of my kids like you more than they like Damien. But no worries, I will make sure Damien, Wyatt and Teo eventually accept and like each other."

"Phoebe, I think you should stop. You can't be touching me like this and talking about another man at the same time. This just doesn't do it." Taking hold of my wrists in an attempt to stop me, Federick cut me off. Alas, for him, I didn't want to be stopped.

"What did I say about interrupting me, Mr Archer?" Lightly shaking my head at him for once again, not listening to me, I sultrily inquired and swiftly got my wrists out of his grip.

"Not to interrupt you." Attempting to resist the temptation that I had become for him, Federick softly quavered.

Seeming to draw in a dose of self-restraint, "But I cannot help it when you are here with me and still talking about another man."

Federick firmly contended.

"Fine, no Damien for tonight." Straddling Federick, I surprised both him and myself with my bold action.

Placing my hands on top of Federick's shoulder blades, I locked eyes with him and drowned myself in its intoxicating depth.

"But, you know, Damien had no right to judge the way I raise Wyatt and Teo . . . No right at all . . . I've done the best goddamn job I could to raise those kids all by myself — actually, how dare he come in here after disappearing for ten years and criticise me? **Me!** Who took the responsibility he refused to!"

"Phoebe, I agree with you, but you are talking about him again while fondling me, and that's unfair to me." Keeping his hands on my outer thighs and increasing the distance between our face, Federick broke the intimate contact we were experiencing.

Letting go of his shoulders, I dragged my sultry touches down his chest, and along his sides. "I'm sorry, does it annoy you." Fluttering my eyes at Federick, I peered at him through my eyelids before returning my attention to my dancing fingers.

"I'm the jealous type, Phoebe. I don't share. So yes, it annoys me."

Lingering my caresses by his waistline and listening to Federick wheeze with desire, jealousy and need, somewhat greatly satisfied me. But I wanted to do more than just tease him with my slow touches.

"That's what you get for disobeying me. You should learn to obey me more often." I alluringly justified, propelling Federick to cock a perfectly shaped eyebrow at me in defiance.

"Now, where was I before the whole Damien thing?. . . . Oh yeah — how I don't wanna become a grandmother because you guys can't seem to keep it in your pants . . . Then you say girls are hormonal."

Well, damn me . . . I contradicted myself and kissed Federick on the cheek. Gradually smooching my way to his neck, I nibbled on his skin, leaving love bites all over his throat.

Reminding myself we were supposed to be talking like rational adults, not making out like teenagers, I reluctantly broke away. "You know what? Teo is so going to get it with me. Do you think it's acceptable for a boy of his age to be sexually active? Of course not!"

Giving me a weird look at my abrupt change in conversation, "Do you always think of other men while making out with someone?" Federick breathlessly quipped.

Ignoring Federick's witty remark and continuing to neck him, "Teo is the sweetest boy of the family, and I would have expected him to wait at least until he turns 16. But no . . . He had to start getting intimate with those bratty bitches. I swear, when I find out who he is screwing right now, I will make sure that bitch can't open her legs ever again. Taking advantage of my sweet baby boy like this is simply unacceptable."

Trailing wet kisses and love bites all over Federick's neck, shoulder blade and chest, tipsy me wasn't the slightest bit embarrassed. Au contraire, the idea of marking Federick to the point where he wouldn't be able to show his upper body to anyone for days, pleased me to a great extent.

However, when I began to unbuckle his suit pants, Federick firmly grasped my hands and shook his head 'No'. Pouting at being stopped, I was surprised Federick didn't instantly melt and let me do whatever I wanted; because trust me, pouting always got me what I wanted. Further astonishing was Federick's sweet smile, instead of his usual cocky 'I won' smile.

"Phoebe, I think this is enough for tonight. You need to sleep. But before I head out, tell me, are you drunk?" Federick stated with patience and consideration. One that I have never heard from him before.

"But I don't want to." Trying my winning pouting face, I whined.

His hard look, however, quickly compelled me to give in.

"All right . . . You won this time. I might be a teeny tiny bit drunk." Attempting to demonstrate how tipsy I was with my fingers as if I was holding a pinch of salt, I purred.

"Sure, I can see how *'Teeny tiny bit drunk'* you are. I should have known from the start you wouldn't behave like this if you were sober. But how much did you even have to drink? I could have sworn you had only three shots of vodka and one glass of wine during dinner."

Beaming at Federick like I had just won the lottery, "I did, but guess what . . . It wasn't any type of vodka. It was a Spirytus Polish Vodka 192 proof — the number one most intoxicating liquor in the whole world. And since being alone increases my anxiety and stresses all the nerves in my body, three shots instead of only one sounded like a fantastic idea. Are you satisfied now? May I return to my original task?"

"No, you may not. You need to drink a glass of water and go to bed. If you still wish to *'Return to your original task'*, you may do so tomorrow. Although I highly doubt this is going to happen."

Gandering at the elastic waistband of Federick's trunks slightly peering out of his half unbuckle jeans; I saw an opportunity. Hooking my forefinger on the waistband and pulling it towards me, I abruptly released it, filling the air with the sound of elastic slapping against the skin — immediately putting an end to whatever he was saying.

Earning myself a scowl, I pouted at his mean self, crossed my arms in front of my chest and remained seated on top of Federick, despite his meek attempt to get me off. Who was he to refuse me what I wanted? I am freaking Angel, for crying out loud! I always get what I want.

Ignoring my childish behaviour and logic. "Why the hell do you even have such a drink in your house? Especially one filled with growing teenagers?"

"Collection and fun." I simply concluded.

Dismissing his momentary silence and weird look, I looped my arms around his neck and attempted to resume my original task of marking him.

"**Phoebe!**" Was Federick's only warning.

"Why are you playing so hard to get!? We both know you've wanted to get into my pants since day one, so here . . . Have at it."

Detaching my lips from his neck, I vocalised with frustration.

"Well, I'm glad to hear what you really think of me."

Hurt flashing in his usual cold grey eyes, Federick thickly muttered before silently sliding me off him. Not giving me time to reiterate, he picked me up bridal style and carried me upstairs, in search of my room. Looping my arms around Federick's neck, I kicked the little sanity and reason I had out the door. Shoving the fact that I had just hurt him with my words, I took the liberty to smack my warm lips all over his neck, and shoulder.

"Phoebe, you need to stop now!"

Ignoring his pleading, yet rough tone, "Payback. Did you forget, you did the same thing to me in your office and at your parent's place? And that's leaving out the kiss you stole in front of my kids." Thinking I was winning this conversation, I added between sloppy kisses.

"Oh, really now! Glad you remembered Teo, Wyatt and Luke because they could walk in here at any time."

"Don't worry about them. They always come home after the curfew we settle on. They will probably be sneaking in at 3 in the morning, thinking I know nothing about it. But since they are teenagers who are constantly trailed by several bodyguards, I don't have to worry. Though, with Luke signing the adoption papers tomorrow and Teo being worried about what's going to happen to him, they are all probably going to be home by 1."

Sensing my body lowered on a soft bed, I realised Federick had just tricked me into stopping my sweet torture while he was searching for my room. Smiling down at me, Federick tucked me in and kissed me on the forehead. Astonished by his gentle, almost caring gestures, I swiftly grabbed onto his arm when he turned to leave and brought his attention back on me.

"Where do you think you are going?" I inquired as innocently as possible.

"Home, of course. It might not seem like it, but I'm only human and need sleep as well."

"I know you are no robot — not with that soft skin of yours." I teased.

"Look, Phoebe, I've had an eventful day, and I'm drained. Particularly after having spent most of my day and night getting angry, irritated, insanely jealous and hurt. I've had to refrain myself from having my way with you on several occasions in the past hour only, and your seducing has not been helping. I'm exhausted, and I'm sure you are as well, so please go to dreamland."

"Why do you have these negative emotions then?" With childlike innocence, I questioned.

"The fact that you of all people are asking me this question is ironic." Federick sarcastically added, which I effectively dismissed. — With the amount of time I've ignored Federick, I should have won an award by now.

"Why don't you just ignore those negative feelings? You will be less tired."

Suddenly concerned about Federick's health, "It's not good for your health, you know." Getting a grip over my sudden outpour of emotion, "And, no. You are not going to your place." I firmly stated.

"I am not ... Who said so?" Amused by my order and slight shake of the head, Federick defied.

"I said so." At this, he cocked an eyebrow but stayed otherwise quiet.

"Don't you want to see what will happen to my brats for what they did tonight? For keeping things from me?"

Full-on puppy eyes, I attempted to raise Federick's curiosity so he would stick around. Then again, in my drunken state, I wasn't sure if my puppy eyes had the same adorable effect it usually does.

"From what I saw today, I know tomorrow will be a hell lot funnier. But are you certain you want me to stay?"

"I would not be asking if I wasn't sure. Now would I?" I sarcastically commented.

"Okay, but let me get my shirt. I don't want you to freak out on me in the morning."

"If you don't want the dogs to chew on your damn shirt, just forget about it. Don't you think the blasted shirt is where it should be . . . All alone on the floor, while you are here with me, in my room, on my bed." I seductively articulated.

Pulling Federick onto the bed, I rolled over so his landing body wouldn't crush me to death, "Phoebe! Don't make me regret saying yes. There's only so much I can take and believe me it's not much. So you better behave, or I won't be held accountable for not being a gentleman."

"Okay, Mister. Bossy much . . . Gosh!"

Waiting for Federick to get comfy, I snuggled up on him and rested my head on his chest. Closing his arm around my shoulder, we were both comfortable and ready to sleep, but as usual, I had to open my mouth.

"You do realise I marked you like crazy, right?"

"No need to remind me, Phoebe. My big friend under the cover is a perfect and clear reminder of the latter."

"Are you mad?"

"No, I'm not."

"Why not? Shouldn't you be? I took advantage of you."

"Shut up and go to sleep, Phoebe."

"Okay boss, as you please, sir," I replied like an automated machine — as a perfect assistant would.

"Thank you for your support tonight, I appreciated, and . . . I'm sorry for what I said earlier. I didn't mean to hurt you." I lowly mumbled.

If not for Federick being here tonight, I wouldn't have taken the initiative to finally ask Luke to be my son. So yes, I was somewhat glad Federick ruined my perfectly planned dinner because having Luke as part of my family was far more important to me.

Kissing the top of my head as a response, I was engulfed by complete darkness in a split second.

CHAPTER 8
DINNER AFTERMATH

FEDERICK

'Get your shit together, dude! She nearly stripped in front of Damien, and all you can think of is her delicious mouth and how it will feel to have it on yours again.' Damn little annoying voice made its appearance again.

But my subconscious was right. Calling upon my usual coldness that can frighten a lion, I pushed down my hormones and concentrated on studying this version of Phoebe Smith.

Reckoning this playful and easygoing side of Phoebe was her true self. And the distant imperceptible version I usually deal with was a façade she wears for the world; I was more than convinced Phoebe was living her life protecting herself from whatever hurt her in the past.

Taking a gander at her relationship with her kids, it was clear she was more of a friend to them. However, as I recently found out, she will exercise her power as a mother — as the head of the family, when she deems it necessary. What stupefied me, however, was how casually she talked about her sons' sex life like it was no big deal. How she was cool with it and even instructed them on the many methods to get girls in their bed, but was still pissed at me for being a playboy. The unfairness in her reasoning hit me like a brick.

Then again, I soon discovered I wasn't the only one who had to face this discrimination. Teo was on a much worse boat. He not only had less liberty than his brothers. But was also **way** overprotected by his mom, and treated like he was made out of glass when he was clearly well-built for a boy his age.

Observing without judgement, I was once again proven right. Whenever Phoebe is shocked, stunned, happy, frustrated, irritated or simply angry, she would either freeze, ramble or exaggerate, without any care of who was around her.

But all amusement aside — **Who the hell was this girl I was falling in love with?**

Why did she need to hire bodyguards for her sons, let alone five of them? I knew she was loaded given her house and the car she was driving the last time I visited her, but how rich was she really?

At the same time, I knew both Phoebe and Damien were hiding something concerning the bodyguards. The brief look they momentarily share spoke volume.

'Maybe she was in danger. Remember how Wyatt mentioned it's only been a few weeks since their security detail increased.'

Okay, this voice in my head could potentially be going somewhere valid here. This theory would definitely explain her absences and mood changes.

Was this the real reason, though?

At that particular moment, I didn't really care. My worry for Phoebe and her safety overridden my curiosity. I swear this woman was going to be the death of me.

If I wasn't itching to punch Damien from the beginning of the night, by the end of it, I most definitely was. I was in utter disbelief by Damien's distasteful words. And the bastard wasn't even remorseful after hitting bull's eyes by insulting Phoebe's capability to be an effective mother.

How dare he chastise Phoebe about her ways of upbringing her boys? She had done a fantastic job with those boys. They loved their mother to pieces and were always so respectful to her.

It was Damien's parents who had failed at raising him right. Clearly, he was Teo's and Wyatt's father, yet he plainly denied it and looked at those boys like they were a curse.

But as Phoebe had told me from day one, she would rather take an insult upon herself than let her precious boys be insulted. The fury flaming in her eyes as she finally showed Damien his place was beautifully consuming. She was a lioness protecting her cub, and it was purely magical to watch.

Damien: 1 and Federick: 4

When Phoebe divulged, she was finally going to answer one of my questions; I was more than excited. However, what I didn't expect was for my whole body to undergo torture at the same time.

The sensation of Phoebe's delicate fingers against my skin, and her lips marking me like I was her territory was delicious torture. Straddling me, her hot breaths fanning over my neck, the sensuality of the moment increased to the point where my resistance dropped, and my desire to be inside her poked at her entrance.

However, when she mentioned Damien of all people, I was hauled back to reality. A reality where I was unnerved at Phoebe for making out with me while talking about another man. But with Phoebe playing with my senses while on top of me — like I've dreamed and desired for so long — regaining control proved to be complicated.

Detecting the slurs in Phoebe's words and her inability to say focus on one topic, it occurred to me that she might be drunk. And as alluring and seductive as she was, or however much I loved the control she was having on me, I had to get a grasp over myself. There was no way I was going to sleep with Phoebe in this state. I want us — our first time, to be memorable, not a drunken mistake.

Then again, Phoebe was a master of temptation. She could be the devil herself with how successfully she was tempting someone as impenetrable as myself. But, I knew Phoebe was no devil. She was my angel, my light through the darkness.

Aware I might regret my decision in the morning for staying the night with Phoebe — in her bed no less, I simply had to comply. There was no way I was going to leave my light alone in this big house by herself. Moreover, I wasn't going to give up the chance of sleeping and waking up next to the brightest star of my life. Next, to the one person, I have come to realise and accept as the second true love of my life.

Indeed, I was in so much trouble. My inability to resist falling for Phoebe despite my many attempts could prove destructive. Especially when this particular beautiful yet intricate woman was as infuriating and secretive as it gets.

In all reality, Phoebe has become like a drug I couldn't get enough of. And it might be killing me, but I was now officially addicted and hooked.

***

PHOEBE

Sensing the first ray of sunshine peeking through my curtains, caressing my face, I snuggled deeper into the warm and comfortable body beside me. The unpleasant pounding of my head hauling me out of the complete blackness I had fallen into last night.

Although the pain striking inside my head wasn't taking name to cease, I took comfort in the knowledge that my sons would be going through the same misery, if not ten times worse from drinking and partying all night long. Nestling closer to my personal source of bodily heat, the torment inside my head eased an inchmeal.

Too tired, lazy, sleepy and still a bit drowsy to make an effort to lift my head and see whom this comfy human male chest belonged to,

65

I fell back into slumber.

BEEP BEEP BEEP

Forcefully waking up at the screams of my alarm clock, I wanted to reach out and throw it at my wall. My reluctance to wake up, however, spur me to nuzzle deeper into my *'hotspot'*; hoping it will help reduce the noise and my headache.

"Tal, switch off that damn thing!" In a muffled tone, I demanded of the person I was now huddled on.

In spite of not remembering inviting my team over last night, I had figured the person I was laying on was Talon because let's face it. Xylan and Matt would already be shaking the life out of me by now, and if it were Damien, well . . . this darn alarm wouldn't still be beeping, much less even in one piece. Talon was the only one with whom I could sleep peacefully.

"Wakey wakey, Tal. Turn that damn thing off!" Gently shaking his shoulder, irked at having to repeat myself, I mumbled in an undertone.

Huffing an air of impatience at his "Hmm" as the persistent beeping kicked my sleep out the window, I was ready to take that clock and smash it on top of his head. The weird thing, however, the voice didn't seem to belong to Talon. This one was much sexier and alluring.

Deciding not to ponder over it with my throbbing head, I let it slide. It wasn't of any real importance to me anyway.

"Okay! I will do it myself." I mumbled, very much annoyed.

With half-opened eyes, I reached for the alarm clock on the bedside table beside him and hit the dismiss button before vertically sprawling on his bare stomach. Peeking through my eyelashes, the sight of the door welcomed me. However, as soon as my gaze dropped to the floor, I was hit with vertigo. Immediately shutting my eyes, I needed to regain my energy and full consciousness before I could start bashing on Talon for his ineffectiveness. Otherwise, I might just faint or worse puke.

"You're an ass, Talon," I uttered with exasperation.

"Making me wake up at —" Turing my head sideways, I glanced at the clock, "At eight on a Sunday morning." Having heard him pick up his breathing when I had shaken him, I knew he was well awake — that lazy butt.

"Sorry to disappoint . . . I'm not that Talon guy. The name is Federick Ashton Archer."

Waking up with a jolt, I sat Indian style beside Federick. However, quickly regretting my swift motion, I closed my eyes to ease the pain in my head and the dizziness that was trying to overcome me. Slowly opening my eyes, I was half expecting what I had seen or heard to be a figment of my twisted imagination. Just like the giant bunny, I thought I saw when I was a child.

Laying in front of me, however, was a pissed off Federick — looking like I had just hurt him.

"How? Why? What?" As if a thudding head was not enough, now I had several questions bombarding my already fuzzy brain. I swear I had sent him away last night, so what was he doing here — on my bed no less.

'My Gosh, did we do something we shouldn't have?' I internally screeched.

"Good morning to you too." Sitting up, Federick sarcastically greeted, the rudeness in him showing its face.

"What the freak are you doing here — on my bed?" As tempting as shouting at him was, I had to resort to hissing. I had to, after all, think of my drunken sons across the hallway and my pounding head.

"Is this your new way of saying good morning? Especially to someone you took advantage of last night, then called a different name the next morning . . . That's just great!" Annoyed, Federick hissed.

"Why are you even annoyed? I should be the one annoyed!"

Glowering at me instead of responding to my questioning tone,

I became acutely aware of our position. Pulling more of the blanket around me, more specifically in front of my chest, I tried to rid myself of the uncomfortableness of our situation. By doing so, however, I unintentionally pulled some of the covers off Federick, and one could say, I was dead-shock to find him not only shirtless but also without a pant.

"And that too with barely any clothes on?"

Although I wanted to speak in a firm voice, all that came out of my mouth was a mumble. I was left as a gaping statue. Eyeballing Federick's firm muscular eight-pack abs and well-built manly chest, no amount of screaming inside my head, demanding I pull out of it, was working. In front of me was one heck of a hunk. Sexy, hot and exceptionally sculpted, Frederick was the purest definition of a Greek God.

"Do inform me when you are done checking me out so we can finish this little conversation of ours."

"I wasn't checking you out. I was simply thinking, and you so happen to be in front of my eyes." In complete denial, I quickly responded.

"Now, get out of my room. I'll meet you downstairs; then you are going to explain to me why the heck you are even here!" I said in a firm yet low voice.

I needed to put an end to this headache — maybe splashing cold water onto my face would do me some good. With this in mind, I cautiously got off the bed and slowly threaded towards my bathroom, not once looking back at Federick. I couldn't afford to turn back to him when he was on my bed, looking so scrumptious — so lecherous and forbidden.

The pounding in my head not taking name to stop, I had no choice but to change plans and go for a hot relaxing shower. Stupidly believing Federick listened to me for once, I lost myself in my little world, giving my hungover brain a break.

Wrapping a small towel around me, and walking out of the steaming bathroom, the last thing I expected was to be taken by surprise — in what could be seen as my most vulnerable moment. Wincing and jumping at Federick's loud fake cough, I held harder onto my towel.

"What the heck are you still doing here? I thought I was clear when I asked you to leave my room and wait for me downstairs. And please, put on some clothes, for crying out loud." Annoyed at Federick and at myself for secretly loving how his eyes danced all over my barely covered and slightly wet body, I tried to maintain my gaze solely on his face.

Getting off the bed and slowly approaching me, "Well, at least, unlike you — who's barely covered with this short towel — I'm wearing my pants."

Like water over rocks, his comment went over my head. All I could think of as I openly ogled at Federick was how **God damn** tempting and inviting he was. He was a freaky Greek God. With his sexy bed hair, broad-shoulders and sturdily built physique, he left little to the imagination. Regardless of his pants covering his long legs, I had already gotten a glimpse of how toned and firm it was, just like his eight packs.

I was well aware Federick was an eye-catcher and every girls' dream, but **this much**. I had no idea. With how sexy, hot, handsome, and dashing he seemed in that moment, I didn't blame all these girls for throwing themselves at his feet. For worshipping the ground he walks on. They had seen in Federick Archer something I was now seeing — the guarantee of delicious sex that had the power of erasing the world around.

However, I knew better than to fall in his alluring web. I knew behind all these sexiness, and the promise of a taste of heaven was an arrogant son of a bitch.

"Stop gawking and drink this. It will help with the hangover and the bright light that's causing your head to pound." Federick uttered a bit too politely for my liking.

Snapping me out of it and confused as to why Federick was suddenly being helpful, kind and considerate towards me, when he is supposed to hate me, I was even more worried about what might have conspired last night. Pointedly and suspiciously scrutinising Federick, I snatched the glass of water and aspirin from his hand.

Washing down the pill and relishing in the cooling effect of the water, "Thanks."

"You're welcome. Go and change. I will be waiting here for you so we can continue our conversation."

Not taking advantage of this situation to poke fun at me or make one of his sexual comments, especially with how exposed I was, I was left astounded. Glancing up at Federick, I was hit with another bolt of lightning. Here, standing in front of me, Federick seemed ten times sexier than before.

What the actual freak was wrong with me?

I must be going crazy to even be admitting this to myself. However, I wasn't going to admit this out loud to this arrogant idiot. His head might just explode. And I wasn't in the business to clean up brain matter.

"Phoebe! I'm speaking to you. I know I'm sexy and all, but get a grip of yourself and stop staring at me like I'm the most delicious piece of meat you've ever laid eyes on. We both need to concentrate, and you are making it impossible."

"You are not the sexiest man I ever laid eyes on." Forgetting all about needing to get dressed, I blurted out for no apparent reason. Yup, I was definitely losing my marbles.

Confused as to why I made this comment, "Okay?"

Glancing anywhere but at Federick's face, my eyes landed on the redness on his body. Taking one small step forward, I scrutinised the love bites all over his neck, chest and collarbone. Sneaking a look at Federick's face and back down on the mountain of hickeys, I initially thought it was from his hundred dates this week, but I soon realised it was only a few hours fresh.

WHAT THE HELL!

CHAPTER 9
MARKED

PHOEBE

"**H**ow on earth did you get all of these?" Pointing at Federick's chest and neck, I pumped in pure confusion and bewilderment.

"You don't remember anything from last night, do you?"

"Well, I wouldn't be asking if I did, now would I?" Anxious I had indeed done the one thing I knew Alicia would not approve of, I sarcastically exclaimed.

"The hickeys are your handiwork, sweetheart. We made love last night . . . And, God, couldn't you keep your hands to yourself — but let's return to the main topic, we need to talk."

"We . . . I . . . I . . . did what!" Both outrage and stunned, I stuttered, my heart beating so fast I could hear and feel it pulsating against my template and the tip of my ears. I was so going to start hyperventilating.

"Calm down, Phoebe."

Pulling away from Federick when he reached for my shoulder

blade like he was a scorching fire ready to burn me alive, "Don't you dare touch me!" I firmly mumbled in shock.

"Hey, it's okay . . . It's no big deal. I actually loved it . . . Especially when you were screaming my name in bliss." Supporting his devious smirk, Federick took a confident step forward, like a predator, "Maybe we could do it again, what do you say?" Daring to wink at me, the king of assholes that was Federick made its full appearance.

"The fuck we are!"

Raising his eyebrows, Federick apparently found my reaction amusing. When, here I was, freaking out. The rules I lived by grumbling in front of my eyes.

'But is it that bad? Throwing away all those stuck up rules that denied you so much. Do you feel any different deep inside?'

Burying those dangerous thoughts in its own grave, "How could you do this to me? How could you, Federick Archer, stoop so low and do something so disgusting?" A bit saddened, I sensed my anger build up.

"Hey, don't blame me. I tried to stop you. But there's only so much seduction a man can take before finally succumbing. Especially when you kept kissing and sucking onto my neck and chest after I had pushed you away from me."

Wrapping my arms in front of my chest in a defensive mode, I glowered at the bastard.

"But since you don't remember the wonderful night we spent, with our bodies entangled in a hot mess, I could go into more details if you want me to."

"I DON'T BELIEVE YOU!" Infuriated, I bellowed.

"How can you stand here and blame me for what happened?" Striding towards Federick with fury exploding in my eyes, "I was drunk and vulnerable, damn it! You basically took advantage of me."

Instinctively taking some steps backwards, Federick's legs hit the edge of the bed, blocking his escape from my flame. "Hey, hold your horses! You are overreacting. I did nothing of the sort. I only responded to your persistent touches."

Standing face to face to Federick, my hot breath hitting his face, "I. Was. Drunk." I menacingly uttered.

Gulping, I bet Federick never imagined a girl wrapped in a small towel, could be so frightening.

"You could have controlled your freaking hormones. Instead, you dropped your pants as usual! And why the heck are you smirking?" Studying his face, it hit me. The asshole might just be joking in an attempt to torture my poor innocent soul.

"Turn around."

"Why?" Perplexed by my out-of-context question when I was about ready to rip his head off his shoulder, Federick inquired.

"Just do it, will you!" I demanded again, in a much firmer tone.

"No, I won't. We need to talk, and you have a **lot** of questions to answer."

"Shut it and turn, or else —"

"Or else what?"

"I'll make you."

"With only a towel on . . . Which, by the way, doesn't seem as tightly secure anymore."

Clearly underestimating me, I was all too happy to prove the arrogant bastard wrong. Stepping back, I took hold of his shoulder with my one free hand and roughly spun him around in a flash of light.

"Hey, easy there." Ignoring Federick's whining, I continued to check his back; and sure enough, there were no scratching or bite marks on his back.

"We didn't have sex last night, did we?"

Turning and towering over me, "How would you know? You

barely remember anything from last night." He tried, but his tone gave me all the confirmation I needed.

"First off, I'm not sore. Secondly, I was fully clothed when I woke up. Lastly, you don't have any fingernail claws or bite marks on your back."

"Fine, you got me . . . We didn't go as far as sleeping together. I knew better." Laughing a true to God belly laugh, Federick admitted.

"You jerk!" Smacking Federick on his chest, "You scared the living shit out of me!" Relief overcoming me, I vocalised.

"I apologise," Federick muttered between his fit of laughter.

"Will you stop laughing?" Blushing at my stupidity for falling into his trap, I gently shoved him onto the bed.

"Nope." The damn jerkface chuckled.

Not thinking twice about it, I straddled Federick, pinned his arms above his head with one hand and lightly thumped his chest with the other, in the hope he will stop his taunting laugh. I could have kicked him hard enough to shut him up or simply go inside my walk-in wardrobe to get dressed until he stops. But, no . . . I somehow ended up acting like a stupid girl who was around her crush.

Distracted by Federick's charming, almost alluring smile, I failed to notice him taking hold of my hands until he flipped me on my back. Hovering over me, Federick pinned both of my hands above my head, and instead of being mad at him for manhandling me, my breathing picked up. Feeling the wrap of the towel gradually giving away, I was glad I was now laying down, with the ending piece of the towel stuck between my back and the mattress.

I could just imagine how embarrassing it would have been if that dang towel had dropped and left me entirely naked while I was still on top of Federick. I would have never lived through it.

"You hit pretty hard for a small woman." A beautiful smile painted on his visage, Federick lightly mused.

Chuckling at the image of Federick's stun and petrified face if he ever witnessed me kill or hit someone with my usual force, "You don't want to know just how hard I can actually hit."

Little did Federick know he was pinning down one of the best ruthless assassins and spies. I bet if he knew it was Angel under him, he would be running for his dear life.

"Why are you chuckling?"

"Am I?" I calmly replied. My secret was locked, and my lips were sealed.

"What's with you scratching during sex? Are you a wild cat or something?" With a sweet smile, Federick teasingly inquired.

'Okay, what's with him being all mushy with me? Was it too early for him to act like his usual jerkface?'

"I've been told I like to leave my mark . . . Like a wild tigress." Dropping my suspicion about Federick's behaviour, I divulged more about myself despite the Angel in me, warning me not to.

Instantaneously releasing his hold around my arms, Federick planted his hands on either side of my head, caging me in. Closing observing him and how he covered his momentary lapse of anger and jealousy with a smile, my curiosity about the man that was Federick Ashton Archer was officially peaked.

"Oh, but you did . . . Look at my neck, my chest and my shoulder. I'm going to have to wear something to cover all those up, and since it's full summer, I'm bound to sweat to death."

"I guess I did." Lightly touching Federick's neck and trailing my fingers along the several love bites, lost in the action of my fingers, "I still can't believe I did all these." My voice in the far distant, I confessed.

Glancing up, my breath hitched. Federick's face was closer to mine, close enough for me to kiss. Noting his deep intake of breaths, worry overtook my desire to capture his lips with mine.

"Is something wrong? You don't seem fine."

Why was I even worried for Federick? He was his own person and could very well take care of himself.

"I'm okay . . . But you should probably stop what you are doing, particularly when you are barely clothed underneath me." Federick muttered with a low, almost strangled voice.

"Doing what?" Confused about his statement, I asked while continually mapping the marks on his neck. Other than being partly naked underneath me, I wasn't doing shit.

"Phoebe, sweetheart, I'm not going to be able to contain myself for too long if you keep playing with my neck, explicitly where the hickeys are. So, unless you want this towel wrench off your body and my mouth all over that delicious lips of yours before you could say *'What'*, I would highly advise you to comply with my request." Federick gutturally explained with as much patience and restraint he could muster.

Rapidly drawing my hands away from his neck, "Oh." Not knowing what to do with my hands that was itching to be in contact with Federick's skin, I kept them above my head, away from the temptation.

"Sorry, I guess I drank too much last night."

"You guess?" His tone filled with disbelief and an air of sarcasm, Federick mused with a smirk.

"I'm sorry for what I did to your whole upper body. I didn't realise it was causing you pain."

"Don't worry. You were not hurting me. It was the complete opposite."

"Huh?" This man definitely knew how to speak in cryptic language. "You are complicated. You realise that, right?" Staring into the complex depth of his grey eyes, I uttered.

"You're sure you're not talking about yourself, here, Phoebe."

Lightly smacking his chest, I couldn't help but giggle at his gentle teasing. Not making any effort to get Federick off me, I secretly loved this pleasant moment between us. It was rare, almost non-existent for

Federick and I to have a conversation or be in the same room without arguing.

But when the desire to reach up and kiss him surged through me again, I had to put some distance between us. Not wanting to fight with Federick, I gingerly pushed him to the other side of the bed and excused myself to go change into something more comfortable than a wet towel.

Smiling at me, Federick didn't argue back. Though, as soon as I passed by him, he took hold of my departing wrist, stopping me dead on my track. Curious as to what he wanted, I turned back only to see worry laced on his face. Either his bipolar side had returned, or he saw something that made him upset.

CHAPTER 10
BODY HEAT

FEDERICK

Lightly waking up at an early hour, I was granted with the most beautiful sight ever. Cuddling up on me, Phoebe peacefully slept, as if all her worries were non-existent. Stretching my arm further, Phoebe snuggled deeper to hide her face from the sunlight.

Ironically enough, my own ray of sunshine was hiding from the world's sunshine. With a broad smile, I gingerly pushed back a stray of hair from her face and kissed her on the cheek before going back to sleep.

I reckoned there was going to be some repercussion —such as a scolding — for staying overnight. But what I didn't expect was for Phoebe to call me another man's name the moment she fluttered her beautiful brown eyes. As if Damien was not enough to irate me, I now had to deal with this Talon. And let's not forget, Xylan and Matt, which I had conveniently forgotten about.

How many guys was my girl even currently seeing? — I was

in big trouble. But as the saying goes; karma is a bitch. And well, I was now paying the price for being such an infamous heartbreaking playboy.

However, despite my reasoning, I was still swirling in a turmoil of anger, happiness and confusion as I stared at Phoebe. But no matter how hard it was for me to stay mad at Phoebe and all her cuteness, I had to let her know addressing me another man's name after being so intimate with me, was unacceptable.

Nevertheless, I wouldn't deny taking great pleasure at watching Phoebe nervously shift under my intense gaze. Even more thrilling and confident-boosting was her gawping at me like she was last night; indicating a future for both of us was still possible.

However, desiring a serious future with Phoebe wasn't what confirmed I was whipped for her. Oh no . . . That confirmation came when I caught myself making excuses for her; reassuring myself that Phoebe wasn't at fault for calling me another guy's name since she was drunk and to actually go as far as to look for aspirin and water to help ease her pain.

To say I was flabbergasted and aroused when Phoebe strolled out of the bathroom with a small towel wrapped around her was a **big** understatement. If I could have jumped her right there and then, I would totally have.

What was funny, though, was that Phoebe had expected me, of all people, to follow an order, and was actually shocked when I was still in the room.

Having already accepted my true feelings for Phoebe, I saw no reason to keep my cold, impenetrable mask on. I was going to show her the real me — be it the bad or the good. She was going to witness the caring, possessive, and affectionate side of me. But before that, I had to reach her, and the only way I knew how to achieve this task was through her temperament. And what best way to get Phoebe riled up than to pull her legs and stay unfazed at the accusations and words spit out only to push my buttons.

Playing against Phoebe and poking at the stormy glint in her eyes,

I had to admit it was rather fun to watch her unravel. Her unconscious blurb of desire — despite her denial — her expression, attitude, disbelief and confusion was not only humorous but fascinating.

Although, when Phoebe demanded I turn around, it was my turn to be bewildered. *'Was she going to drop her towel and check her body to somehow see if I was speaking the truth?'*

But my query was soon answered when I found out that my sweet angel was a wild tigress in bed — further arousing me. On the flip side, however, I was also pissed and jealous at the knowledge that many men had passed before me and had seen Phoebe's wildness in action. Internally promising myself never to allow any other man to be intimate with her again, I realised I had a lot of work ahead of me. Especially when I knew nothing about Phoebe Smith.

My train of thought, however, was quickly diverted with Phoebe's cuteness, innocence and sweetness. Straddling me with pretty much nothing blocking her direct contact with the tightened material of my pants, I was secretly thankful her towel was playing the role of a barrier between us. At the same time, I also knew the towel around her wouldn't hold for too long, and when that dang piece falls, the probability of me keeping myself contained would be pretty slim.

Pinned underneath me, I was determined to have control again, but Phoebe had something else in mind. The one in control, her innocence despite claiming to be such a major playgirl, sharpened her temptress lash. Reckoning I would be pudding in Phoebe's hand if I didn't put some distance between her and me while she was making the Goddess of temptress proud, I reluctantly let her slide off me.

✳✳✳

PHOEBE

"What's wrong?" Tightening the hold of my towel in front of my chest, I inquired with inquisitiveness.

Maintaining his firm grip around my arm, Federick edges closer to me. Silent like a rock, Federick stared straight into my eyes. His soul-searching orbs of greys immediately giving birth to anxiousness within me. Imprisoned in his gaze, I felt more naked than I was, wrapped in my wet towel.

Sensing my anxiousness, Federick traded holding my arm for my shoulders and gently turned me around. Allowing him to direct my body without any fuss, "What are you doing?" I muttered with puzzlement.

Federick's lips still stitched together; he let his fingers do the talking and lightly trailed the side of my shoulder. Fuddled, I stood there, not knowing what to do or what was happening.

'Why was he doing this? Was there something on my back?'

Edging ever closer to me, to the point where his chest stuck to my back, his hot breath fanning the nape of my neck, the only thing I could concentrate on was his fingers mapping my back.

"I'm going to ask you something vital, Phoebe, and you are going to answer me. Understood." Federick mumbled against my skin, with an authority I couldn't for the life of me rebuke. All I could do was slightly nod in understanding with hitched breaths.

And dear me, was the Angel in me furious. She didn't like being ordered, much less following it without argument.

"Good." Wrapping one of his arms around my waist, Federick uttered with the same domineering power; almost causing me to release my hold on my towel. Gripping the front even harder, I gulped as silently as I could, not wanting Federick to know the effect he was having on me.

"How did you get this bruise on your upper back?" His fingers still fooling around the bruise, Federick demanded with a hint of anger.

Surprised that bruise had not fainted yet, "You don't wanna know?" Trying to brush off the question, I didn't want to remind

Federick how I had gotten it.

Tightening his hold around my waist, Federick pushed me further into his body. If I ever had any worry that being this close to Federick would be uncomfortable, it was now completely erased. Being held this firmly in his arms, a gush of warmth coursed through me and piled up between my legs.

"Oh, but I do. Now, spill." He yet again urged with the authority of an alpha.

Reminding myself that I have to, later on, find a way to fight back this specific potent and magnetic tone of Federick, especially when he is so close to me, "Remember that day when we were fighting in your office, and you shoved me against your wall? It's from then." Aware Federick would feel guilty and bash onto himself for being so rough and ruthless, "But, don't worry, the bruise is almost gone by now." I hastily breathed out.

Abruptly releasing his hold around my waist, Federick staggered back as if he had been burnt. Immediately missing his warmth and comfort, I was tempted to turn around and let him know it was okay to touch me. That I wasn't going to break in his rugged hands. His piercing, almost burning concentration on my faint bruise, however, left me rooted in place.

Astounding me with his slow and timid steps towards me, Federick once again lightly touched what was left of my bruise, as if it would hurt me if he pushed too hard.

"I am so sorry, Phebes. I was immensely upset that day, and I didn't realise how rough I was with you. Still, this shouldn't excuse my bruteness."

"Hey, it's okay . . . It didn't even hurt." I lied, cause God knows it hurt like a bitch. "It's just my skin type. I bruise easily and for a longer period."

"Shush. Don't . . ." Federick lowly requested when I tried to turn around to see his face. To cup his cheeks in my hands and let him know everything was alright.

I couldn't comprehend why all of a sudden, I was so nice to

Federick. All I knew was I didn't like the pain and sadness in his voice. His hurt at the realisation that he caused me pain pulled at my heartstrings in ways it never has before.

Taken by surprise when out of nowhere something hot yet wet and soft brushed against my back, where the bruise was, I turned into a statue again. With a gentle flick of his tongue, it dawned on me that Federick was kissing my back and shoulder — licking me like I was his most favourite ice-cream.

My breath hitched, a rush of warmth enveloped my body like a second layer of skin. My legs feeling weaker at the delicious assault of Federick's lips and tongue along my back, shoulder blades and the nape of my neck, my quavering hands let loose of the hold around the towel.

Wrapping his arm around my waist, Federick supported my weight and without once stopping, directed me to the nearby wall. Fire erupting inside of me like a remarkably active volcano, I slammed my hands on the wall for further support. I didn't know what was happening to me, all I knew was it felt amazing, and I didn't want it to stop. Not even when my towel finally drooped onto Federick's arm, leaving my upper body bare for him.

Those flaming and fiery butterflies twirling and pirouetting inside my belly, however, halted in their beautiful and intoxicating dance when Federick's hand slowly glided upwards to my breasts. At that moment, I realised if we continued this, it would go too far, and I couldn't possibly allow this.

But when Federick crouched and licked the bottom of my spine, gingerly kissing his way up to the side of my neck, my resolve to ask him to stop fondling my breasts died like the dry leaves in full-blown autumn. His touches leaving trails of electricity in its wake, the sultry swelling in my chest grew heavier. Sadly for the promiscuous heat exploding like fireworks inside me, when Federick grabbled my hardened nipple between his warm rough and soft fingers, my hands instantaneously flew up, clenching his wrist, stopping him from going any further.

Complying and not forcing me to go any further, I was more than appreciative and relieved. For one tiny second, at the back of my messed up head, the idea that Federick might just try to coerce me to go further, crossed my mind — just like the crooked men I was required to seduce and divert during several of my past missions often do.

But Federick didn't. He was respectful and even went as far as pressing my body against his chest while turning me around to face him, so I wouldn't feel as naked as I was.

Staring into my eyes, searching for something out of my comprehension, Federick didn't make any more advances. He just stood inches away from my face and kept searching. Biting my lower lip, I knew I had to step away, but I couldn't. The desire from before, still burning bright inside of me, I was confused about what I wanted.

Did I want Federick to go away? To never show me his face again so I would stop feeling those dang flaming butterflies? Or did I want him to take me in his arms and never let go? To use his lips for more than talking and giving orders?

Slowly leaning forward, after what felt like hours of simply searching my eyes, Federick's lips gingerly touched mine, as if testing the ground. To see if I was going to push him away and smack him again.

But even if I wanted to, I couldn't bring myself to slap Federick. Not when his lips were moving with mine in perfect synchronisation.

Flicking his tongue against my lips, Federick asked for entrance, and I knew I shouldn't have, but I willingly let him in. Sliding his tongue into my mouth, tangling, dancing and fighting for dominance, I was somewhat baffled. Here I was, for the very first time in my life, gleefully mouth to mouth with a man — one whom I was allowing dominance inside my mouth without any hidden agenda.

My lungs begging for air, I reluctantly and gently pushed Federick away, breaking this out-of-the-ordinary moment between us. Gasping and panting for breath, Federick rested his head on top of mine and locked his eyes on my brow orbs, not once looking down at my chest.

"This is wrong. I hope you know this." I managed to breathe out. The lust in my voice more than evident.

"Maybe for you love, but as far as I'm concerned, being here with you and touching you like no other man would, shouts right to me." Pulling up the towel that was still shamelessly hanging around my waist, Federick didn't once peek or stare down at my chest as others in his place would have.

Flushed at how gentlemanly Federick was as he wrapped the towel around my body, covering my most intimate parts from his hungry sight, my heart threatened to jump out of my chest and punch me straight in the face.

"Come on . . . If we stay like this any longer, I won't be able to control myself. Go and change, I'll be waiting." Touching my cheek with the gentleness of a paintbrush creating the most prized painting, Federick advised more than ordered.

Nodding, I started to make my way to the safety of my wardrobe only to have him playfully smack my ass as I walked in front of him.

"Bastard." I voiced out with a giggle and a genuine smile decorating my face.

Something was indeed wrong with me. I allowed all these to happen when never before in my life have I ever gone against so many of my rules and done something so impulsive. So out of character. So dangerously wrong, and delicious. Yet, here I was smiling instead of being furious.

***

FEDERICK

My intention to let Phoebe slide away from me for both our sakes instantly vanished the moment I noticed a faint bruising on her upper back, disturbing me to the core. I was fuming and had a burning desire to kill whoever was responsible for staining my ray of light with a spot of darkness.

On the other hand, what I didn't see making headway towards me like a crashing truck, was that I was the one responsible for such a horrific act. Staring at the disgusting chef-d'oeuvre stamped on the woman I so bluntly claim I love, a rush of anger and guilt overcame me. All I could do to keep a tight handle on my self-hatred was to take a step back and exhale.

Replaying the day I had shoved Phoebe against my office wall, I could now see she had hissed in pain. But I was too centred on my own pain to see hers. Hesitant for the first time in my life, I slowly approached Phoebe and gingerly mapped the bruise I had caused. I knew I shouldn't have been so intimately close to Phoebe after what I had done, but my emotions had taken the wheel, and I was left a spectator in my own body.

Despite being happy, ecstatic even, that Phoebe was finally accepting and responding to my advances, a part of me was hoping she would put a stop to all of it like she usually does. The last thing I wanted on top of having hurt her was for her to feel taken advantage of.

Surprised Phoebe was allowing me to go as far as I did, but not entirely sure how she truly felt about my advances, I slowed down to give her time to think. Taking in and appreciating every second of this rare moment, it was indeed a dream come true — to be able to freely kiss her senseless. To leave my mark on her neck. To have her respond so vividly to my every touch, every kiss and heightened breaths.

Although I was partly glad when Phoebe grasped my wrist to stop me from going any further, I had to fight my hormones and the scream in my head demanding me to continue. And even though Phoebe was making a poor attempt at completely stopping me, I realised going for more would be too fast for Phoebe. And, I will be damned if I didn't respect her choice.

Swiftly pivoting Phoebe, I pressed her against me so I wouldn't be tempted to peek at her beautiful firm bosom and do something I might later regret. Gazing deep into the depths of her brown orbs, I tried to find answers to my questions. To find out how she genuinely felt about me.

Alas, I was left searching. Phoebe was expertly blocking me out of her real feelings. Her walls were so high up; I couldn't even see the colour of her soul. Nonetheless, there was no denying the unidentifiable fight deep within her.

I wanted to reach down, to wrench out that fight from within her and comfort her till the end of days. What I didn't expect myself to do, however, was crash my lips against hers, especially when I was sure I had tamed my desires. Even more unexpected was Phoebe's passionate response and submission to my dominance.

Her hands moving to the back of my head, untangling in my already messy hair, Phoebe deepened our kiss as my tongue entwined with hers in a beautiful dance of soft melody. Enthralled and sucked in making-out, my body's begging for fresh oxygen was utterly dismissed. Thankfully for my own sake, however, Phoebe lightly broke us apart, putting an end to our very first most intimate moment. Even more intimate than when I was mapping a trail of kisses all over her back and neck.

Breathless after our kiss of passion and lust, we remain stuck to each other in utter silence. Intensely peering into Phoebe's mesmerisingly lascivious brown eyes, observing her facial expression, and listening to her heavy panting, I was surprised to be enjoying this innocent moment.

If she were another woman, my head wouldn't even be resting on her forehead, much less enjoying this air of passion and longing hanging over our heads. It would, without any doubt, be too busy doing something more physical. However, I respected Phoebe way too much to do anything overly sexual without a definite click between us.

However, the magic spell I was under quickly broke when Phoebe announced how wrong what we were doing was. But I had anticipated such comments from her. I knew once the flame of desire died down, she would go into denial and pretend this wonderfully magical moment between us didn't happen. Despite my reasoning, though, I took a chance and voiced my opinion about this whole matter without any fear and restraint.

I might not know everything about this woman yet, but what I knew without any shred of a doubt was that Phoebe was afraid of love and the relationship that comes with it. Smacking her away, I prayed for the almighty to give me strength and patience. Because God knows, I desperately needed it.

CHAPTER 11
THE BEAUTY OF PAYBACK

PHOEBE

Stepping out of the wardrobe, in the safe wrap of my clothes, I glanced at the clock hanging on my wall, "Gosh!" I all, but screeched.

"What's wrong?" Pouncing off the bed and rushing to my side in a blink, Federick inquired with worry laced in his tone.

"It's already nine o'clock." Doing my best to not be swoon by Federick's sweet reaction and genuine concern for my sake, I evasively stated.

"So?" Not understanding what the big deal was, Federick looked at me for an explanation.

"Follow me if you want to know, but put a shirt on." Smiling at what I was about to do to my sweet sons, I exclaimed to Mr Distraction.

Payback time was here, baby.

"I didn't hear you complain about my half nakedness a few minutes ago." Advancing towards me with a goofy smile, Federick jested.

A splash of blush creasing my cheek, "Shut it." I sheepishly uttered. "I'm off to the kitchen. Join me if you want — you might be of some help."

"You know I will do anything for you." With a wink and his award-winning smirk hanging on his face, Federick mused.

"Sure." Walking down to the kitchen with a devilish plan concocting inside my brain, I tried not to overthink Federick's words.

Filling up three glasses of cold water, I picked up three aspirins from the open medicine box on the counter; figuring Federick used this medicine box rather than the one by my bedside. Willing myself to stop ogling at his muscular self, I cast my concentration on the love bites his shirts were unable to cover.

"I don't think these marks are going to wear off anytime soon. Once again, I'm sorry. Perhaps, you should try scrubbing them with hot water to fade them out."

"Nah!" Slicing his hand through the air as if it was no big deal, Federick dismissively responded.

"It doesn't matter. I don't care how long it stays. The longer, the better, right." Federick cajoled with a sweet smile.

"If you say so." Nodding my head, I honestly wasn't sure how to respond to Federick's statement and smile.

I guess his type of chick doesn't mind another person's mark on the person they are sleeping with.

"Will you take these two glasses and three aspirins, please. I will take this one." Carefully approaching Federick, I pointed at everything on the table.

"No problem."

Noticing the glint of him wanting to talk about what had happened upstairs, I quickly walked past him and started on my way to Wyatt's room. Unlike Federick, I wasn't ready to talk about my lapse in judgement.

Keeping the air between us otherwise engaged, "Follow me, but if you have the urge to laugh, bottle it up."

"Laugh? Why would I have a sudden urge to laugh?" Federick asked, utterly oblivious of the devious plan cooking inside my brain. However, I didn't have time to explain, so instead, I halted and glared at his beautiful face.

Umm . . . I mean, annoying face . . . Definitely.

"Okay! I will refrain from my sudden urge to laugh. No need to give me those killer eyes so early in the morning."

"Good. Let's get moving then."

"Okay, Miss Smith. Got it, Miss Smith." Federick taunted.

"Please, I'm not that old for you to be calling me Miss Smith outside of the office, nor am I your General."

"Is this your official permission for me to call you, Phoebe?" With his infamously killer smirk, Federick mused.

"Sure . . . It's not like you really needed my permission, anyway."

Not with how he was addressing me upstairs.

Aware Teo and Wyatt tended to end in the same room after getting drunk from a party; I trudged into Wyatt's room with prudence. One could not even start to comprehend how the scene of them cuddling made my heart flutter with pure joy. But as my sick mind would have it, my thoughts began to flow in all different distorted directions.

The idea of what would happen if both of them got drunk with a girl; especially since they have the same taste for **everything**, I internally cringed at the image of both boys doing one girl at the same time. Immediately wishing my perverted thoughts away, I willed my brainpower to admire the sight in front of my eyes.

"Isn't this cute?" Pulling my phone out, I muted the sound and took several pictures of the boys.

My sons didn't seem to understand why I'm always taking

pictures of every sweet and cute moment, but this was a motherly impulse I couldn't bring myself to cease. Especially when I knew it sometimes annoyed them.

Surreptitiously wending my way to Wyatt's bedside, I snatched both of their phones without making a single noise. Retreating to where Federick was standing, I switched on their phones and was welcome with the same pattern for a lock.

"What are you doing?" Murmuring too close to my ears, Federick spawned my heart to kick at my chest.

"Can't you see? I'm about to increase their phones' ring." I retorted a bit too harshly, in an attempt to cease the weird feeling inside the pit of my stomach.

"But why? Plus their phones are password protected?" Brushing off my snappiness, Federick inquired with confusion.

"Since when do we need passwords to increase a phone's volume?" With pure sarcasm laced in my tone, I confidently and lowly spelt out.

"Well, **Miss Know-It-Al,** the phones in your hands are the most recent of its kind — with newly launched systems and programs. So yes, you need first to turn the phone on, enter the password, press the sound button on the side, then drag the small circle to the end you desire. The left end is to control the notification sound, and the right end is to control the media volume."

"Why do you guys even buy these expensive and complicated shit then?" I asked with irritation.

"Because of its capacity, apps and all the advantages it provides. It's a very efficient phone if you ask me, especially for teens."

"Money-eater, more likely."

Seeing as it was me who had to foot the bill for all these expensive 'EFFICIENT' gadgets my sons use, it was no shocker when only sarcasm came out of my mouth. Heck, I'm confident they don't even know the full price of their phone. They needed it and got it in a snap of their little fingers.

"How do you know their passwords?" Hovering over me like a persistent fly, Federick queried.

"Do you ever stop asking so many questions?" I responded with a hiss.

"When it comes to you, questions are the only things I have."

"Only questions, huh?" I unconsciously voiced out.

Smirking, his eyes glimmering with naughtiness, I immediately changed the subject before Federick could give me one of his unwanted comments.

"Before you say something, remember my sons should not find out I know their passwords."

"So they didn't give you their passwords, yet you know them. Dangerous . . ."

"Would you care to explain, how?" Federick murmured after I didn't respond to his taunting.

"Well, I'm their mother, aren't I."

"Doesn't mean a thing. My mom doesn't know my password."

"Cause she is not me and I like to keep tabs on my sons for security purposes."

"Isn't having so many security guards around them enough? — Why do you need so much security anyway?" Federick inquired; as if now remembering, he had a whole lot of unanswered questions for me.

"Not really your business." Keeping myself busy with the boys' phone, I retorted with attitude.

Detecting the boys shifting from the corner of my eyes, "Shhh! Let's not start arguing. Go quietly close the door and watch the show." Putting my plan into action, I quickly whispered before Federick could spit out another word.

"Okay. Until next time, then." Federick muttered as a promise before closing the door and returning to my side.

Opening up the sound mixer, I increased the volume to its higher pitch and placed both of their phones on the bed, near to their ears. Gently pulling their front window curtain, I had to restrain my devilishly chuckle. Turning on my much simpler and least expensive phone, I pulled up our group chat and called. Not even one second later, their lovely ringtones blared like the siren of an ambulance.

Alert! Alert! MOM CALLING!!

You better pick up the damn phone if . . .

If you care for your life . . .

Angry Mother-rrrr . . . Not good-dd at all-ll.

Delay for 5 minutes or less-ssss . . . . . .

You're sure to be grounded for life-eeeeee . . .

Aye Aye Aye Captain-nnnn . . .

You're-eee too-oooo late-eeee.

Alert! Alert! Your Mother is calling-gggggg . . .

She is infuriated-ddddddddd . . .

You better RUN for your dear life-eeeee . . .

Sorry-yyyyyy . . .

Your life is over-rrrrrrrrr

When she catches you-uu . . . . . .

"What the fuck is happening? — **OUCH!** My head." Wyatt clamorously shouted, immediately regretting it. Reaching for his phone, Wyatt successfully ended his *Amazing* ringtone for his lovely mother.

"Teo, you dumb ass. Silence your fucking phone before I do . . . Damn you!" Wyatt rudely whispered-shout at Teo, who just woken up, too busy holding his pounding head to reach for his phone.

"Oh, crap! Who opened the curtains? I was sure I closed it before hitting the bed." Squinting and trying to hide the sun rays with his arm, Teo grunted.

"Good morning, Wyatt. Teo." Holding onto my laughter, I loudly made my presence known, aware my high pitch was pissing them off along with increasing their headaches.

"God! Mother. Lower your voice . . . I have a killing headache here."

"Really? . . . I wonder why?" Making the right call to not glance directly at Federick as he was attempting to hold his laughter, his eyes glimmering with amusement, I rowdily taunted my sons.

Hissing at me in response, I couldn't help but chuckle. Their current misery well deserved after what they pulled last night.

"Payback is a bitch, sweetheart. One would think, living with me all these years, you would know this by now." With a playful smile, I stated in a 'duh' tone.

"Yeah, one would think we would be used to it by now." Teo lightly uttered with sarcasm.

"Watch it, boy who shouldn't be having sex at this age." I casually responded, letting Teo know he will be facing the consequences of his actions later on.

"I'm very sorry about this one. I was actually trying to find the appropriate time to talk to you, but we've all been so busy that the right occasion never seemed to come up." Teo responded in a low tone.

"Right!" Expressing my disbelief, I wasn't about to fall for this one.

"Just bring me a grandchild, and I swear I will either kill the girl or completely disown you. Then we'll see how a pretty ex-rich brat like yourself will make a living to feed three mouths." Gulping and nodding his head, despite his killing headache, Teo carefully weighed the seriousness of the matter and my tone.

"Bring it elsewhere, you two! I have a major migraine. So please, leave me alone to sleep." Wyatt cut in, a bit too loudly for his liking, and winced once more, the high pitch of his voice causing him pain.

"Oh, stop whining. Get your little ass off the bed." Sitting by Wyatt's side, "Here, take this." Handing him the glass of water with the pill, he had no choice but to toughen up.

"Federick, will you please?" Directing my eyes towards Teo, I asked.

"Got it." He responded with a smile before giving Teo the *'I'm sorry for you'* look.

Slightly relieved after having taken the medication, Wyatt, in comparison to Teo who had laid back down, suspiciously surveyed Federick. The question as to why Federick was still here with yesterday's clothes clear on his face. It took no genius to recognise Wyatt was slowly gathering his energy to start questioning both Federick and myself. Thankfully, though, Wyatt did not yet notice the love bites stamped on Federick's neck. And I will be damned if I didn't try to keep it that way.

Taking advantage of Wyatt's fuzzy and tired brain, I kept talking, so he wouldn't have the chance to fully register everything happening around him. It was an efficient tactic to compel Wyatt to save up his energy to concentrate on what I was saying.

"Okay boys, Luke is next. If you wanna tag along, you better get up." At this, both boys began giggling like little girls who had been offered a truckload of candies.

"Wouldn't miss it for the world." Wyatt and Teo simultaneously expressed their excitement.

CHAPTER 12
A FAMILY DYNAMIC

PHOEBE

"Luke lives here?" Federick inquired with astonishment.

"Of course, he does! Where else would he go?" I stated in a *'Duh'* tone. It should have been evident after last night.

What did Federick think? I would take in a complete stranger as my son.

Heedful of the questions about to sputter out of Wyatt's mouth, I quickly grabbed Federick's arm and dragged him out of the room, running away from my sons' interrogative and suspicious regards. Any other day, their furrowing and narrowing gaze wouldn't affect me to the extent where I refuse to meet their eyes in fear of saying something I shouldn't, but after this morning, staying clear of their interrogation was my best option.

"Doesn't Luke have his own apartment?" Federick mumbled next to me on our way down the hallway; where Luke's room currently was.

"Stop being dumb." Keeping my voice down, I exclaimed.

"How am I being dumb? I wouldn't be asking all these questions if I knew at least some truth about you and those around you. For crying out loud, Phoebe, I had to research for hours on end where you, my Executive PA, really live!" Federick whispered-yell, the coldness in his tone spiking.

"Keep your mood swings to yourself." I retorted back with as much annoyance.

"Mood swings and me, ha! You must be looking at your reflection in a mirror, love." Sarcasm laced in his every word, Federick gibed.

"Stop using endearments when you are talking to me, especially when my sons are behind us."

Halting in my track, I pointedly glared at Federick and directed my eyes behind us, to where my sons were. Clearly, these two seemed very interested in trying to hear what we were discussing. Being considerate of my sons' presence and not blowing up, as usual, Federick bit back whatever rude comment he was about to spit out.

Instantaneously washed with guilt for being so rude to Federick when he had merely asked a simple question, my mind shouted back at me, cursing me for my insensitivity and for testing the patience Federick has been investing in me.

Staring into his pool of greys, "Sorry." I lowly mumbled before continuing on my original path.

"To answer your question. Yes, Luke has an apartment, but given he's my sons' best friend, he often crashes at my place. And since this house has a lot of vacant rooms, I gave him one." I gently explained on our way.

Provided Luke was an agent; the chances of being detected were higher. Being stealthier than before while opening his door and entering his room, I almost toppled over when I saw his sleeping figure. But, thank God, I was able to refrain myself from ruining my payback plan.

'Why was Luke even on the receiving end of my payback plan?' Having

no actual answer to this question, I came to the conclusion that I was simply doing it for fun.

Sleeping sideways and snoring away, Luke was sprawled on his stomach with only his boxers on. Half of his upper body hanging out of the bed, his head was dangling in the air, with the covers barely covering him.

Given how Luke was sleeping, I bet his neck and shoulder would be crying in pain later on. What was he thinking? The air would keep him afloat.

Doing the same to Luke as I did to my other two sons, I snapped several pictures of him before snatching his phone to increase its volume and placing it close to his ear. Treading backwards till the door, with the skill of a ninja, I was surprised when my back collided against Federick's chest right in the middle of the room, preventing me from moving any further.

"So you know Luke's passwords too?" Federick lightly whispered next to my neck, aiming for only me to hear.

Though, what Federick didn't realise was that being in this exact position reminded me of this morning. The images of those memories flashing in front of my eyes, I couldn't help my breathing from momentarily hitching. Biting down on my lower lip to prevent any sound from escaping, I slowly nodded 'yes', instead of responding like a normal human being.

Fully aware of the effect he was having on me, Frederick mischievously smirked over my head before taking a step back. Able to breathe properly again, I thank the lord for Federick's distance as I slowly regain power over my crazy bodily reaction.

Pressing the call button, nobody would have ever guessed how ridiculous Luke's ringtone for me was. Of course, the music was related to my Angel side. Heck, even his password pattern was the Agency logo — this boy was sure having a lot of fun being an agent.

I'm a Barbie girl, in a Barbie World

I'm the hottest and Sexiest of all - lll. . .

Others en-vy me-ee

They- they are jea-lous-ss of me-eee . . .

It's na -na-tural . . .

But . . . But . . .

I'm a hot-ttt bad-bad-ass Barbie girl-lll . . .

A Barbie-ee Girl-llll

A Barbie Girl in a fucking Barbie World-ddd

Kicking asses . . . . . .

Kick .. . . . Kick . . . Ass . . . Asses-sssss . . . . .

Kicking asses and- and- and remains hot-ttttt . . . . . .

IF NOT HOTTER-RRRRRR

Barbie Girls makes guys hard-ddddd . . . . .

HARD WHAT!!!!!

Hard . . . . .Hard . . . . Hard-dddddddd

For her-rrrrrrrrr

Beautiful Barbie Girl . . . . .

Then all we heard was a crash as Luke grabbed his phone and flung it at the wall in front of him, ending this awful song for me. Loudly grunting, Luke brought all of us out of our momentary daze. Well, this was undoubtedly disturbing and embarrassing. Federick's raised eyebrows confirmed that much.

But hey, at least, I now know I am a badass Barbie girl. Though, I wouldn't say in a Barbie world; it would more likely be in a crazy, full of psychopaths and liars world. Dropping my gaze to Luke's phone, on the floor, laying in pieces, I was so thankful I was out of the way.

"Ouch, this must-have hurt. I'm happy I'm not your phone." I stated in a normal tone, not even bothering to raise my voice as I did with the other two.

His eyes still closed, he repositioned himself and snuggled deeper against the pillow beside him. "Mom, my sleep. Respect, please." Luke stuttered out loud.

"Ouch! Ouch! Shouldn't have screamed." Luke moaned, causing me to let out a small laugh. He was being so stupid and lovable. I would bet he was the one who drank the most, last night.

"Continue screaming like a bitch, of course, it would hurt, stupid." I jested.

"Mom . . . Voice lower . . . please."

"Okay, got it, baby boy. But, you gotta wake up. We have some business to attend to this afternoon."

"Nooo. My head is about to explode. I'm so going to die before my time. Now leave. Let me die in loneliness." Luke whined like a baby, being his overdramatic self.

Chuckling, I sat by his side, despite his constant whining and over-exaggeration. Passing me the glass of water along with the pill he's been holding onto all this time, Federick indicated to give Luke his medication.

Telling myself, I've seen a cuter smile than Federick, "Thanks." I mumbled while massaging Luke's head to help reduce his pain. Nodding in response, Federick didn't say much. It was like he was a ghost only I could see.

Luke's soft moans capturing my attention, "Sweetheart, have these aspirins, it will help. I'm not going to sit here all day and massage your head."

"Hmmm . . ." Came his only response.

Yes, Luke was not paying any attention to one word coming out of my mouth. I could literally feel him going back to dreamland. Removing my hand from his head in the hope he would wake up, Luke immediately reached for my hand and held it on top of his head; not ready to say goodbye to his free massage.

"Fine. I will do it for a little longer, but then you have to wake up, drink this water and put on some clothes. Deal."

"Deal," The pillow muffling his voice, Luke was the epitome of funny and cuteness.

Turning around, I shrugged my shoulders at the three guys behind me, letting them know, I simply had to comply. Both Wyatt and Teo leaned on either side of the threshold, with their arms crossed over their chests, their patience evaporating with each passing second. At the same time, no matter how much I was trying to avoid Federick's piercing stare, I couldn't for the sake of me advert my eyes from him. It was like he was attempting to solve the biggest puzzle of his lifetime.

Luke's loud moan, however, instantly broke mine and Federick's searching gazes.

"Didn't you have enough of moaning last night?" I jocularly inquired with a mischievous smile. Instead of replying, Luke shook his head 'No', way too invested in his head massage to majorly care.

"Oh well, you picked the wrong girls to do the job, then."

"Mom!" Both Wyatt and Teo screeched, forcing Luke to wince and stare coldly at them.

"Ouch . . . If only looks could kill, you both would be six feet under right now." I joked, gently laughing, so I wouldn't disturb Mr Luke and his sensitive head.

"We don't care . . . Do we, Teo!" Wyatt responded with a playful attitude.

"No, we don't. Absolutely not."

Raising my eyebrows at both of them, "You don't, huh."

"No. Luke got what he deserves. Especially after picking up most of the striking-looking girls, leaving me with a bunch of the lame ones. Can you believe that happened to me? Me of all people!"

"Oh, poor Wyatt . . . Did Luke bruise your monstrous ego?" I teased in a baby voice.

"Yes, poor me. And now, you are rewarding him by massaging his head. Why don't you just hand him the damn pill as you did to us? — Why is he even getting a massage to begin with? Did you even hear the lame ringtone he has for you? Ours was way better and cooler." Wyatt whined like the spoiled brat he was.

"Hey! Not my ringtone. Don't insult my creativity." His chin on top of his pillow, Luke glared at them.

"Jealous much?" Cocking my head a little to the left, with a playful smirk, I taunted Wyatt.

"And someone else seems too amused for my liking." Glancing at Federick, I compelled him to swallow his upcoming roar of laughter.

Finally registering Federick's presence in the room, curiosity took over Luke's face. Thankfully for my sake, Wyatt decided to jump in before Luke could bombard me with his questioning.

"Jealous . . . Me! — As if. I'm just annoyed Luke took this one sexy chick, despite knowing I wanted her first. I swear mom; she was so damn hot. Hotter than the rest at that party. Especially with her red tight short dress, specially made for her incredible figure — God, I would have loved helping her out of it and those breasts —"

"OKAY, OKAY! I got the picture. She was the dream girl. No need to be so descriptive about her. Go drool over her in your room, not in front of your mother." Seemingly snapping out of his daydream, Wyatt blushed like a ripe tomato.

"Yeah! Go drool over her in your room; imagining how she must be in bed. Because guess what . . . I don't have to imagine it. I already had her in all possible ways. And, perhaps, I will even call her later on, just to annoy you and have some fun at the same time . . . Imagine me tasting and touching her all over again . . . Her big round firm breasts, her sweet red mouth all over me and those pink and soft — **ouch!**"

Lightly slapping Luke on the head instead of continuing to massage it, I effectively shut him up. "Okay Luke, we got you and the picture very well. I don't want to hear any more about this gorgeously divine girl that has both of you smitten and so wrapped up around her fingers."

"Ouch! Mom, headache, remember." Luke whined before slamming his face back on the pillow.

And, here I thought he was already fully awake.

"I remember quite well, but if you guys insist on making my poor innocent ears and brain suffer from your more-than-descriptive sexual competitiveness nonsense, I won't care any longer. My poor ears . . . I'm sure they are internally bleeding from all those dirty words. My poor babies, I would probably need to go wash them with holy water."

"Innocent, my ass." Federick lightly whispered beside me, propelling me to glare at him harshly. Then again, the only thing I managed to accomplish was succumbed to the power in his mischievous smirk and gleam in his eyes. Blushing, I had no words for Federick.

"See, Mom, this is what I was talking about. He is going to rub it on my face now." Wyatt complained in his soft, cute voice. One that 99 per cent of the time gets him everything he desires.

"He won't, sweetie." I reassuringly stated.

"Will you, Luke?" Giving Luke a pointed look, I posed.

"Me . . . Of course not. How can an innocent face like mine do such an awful thing." Luke responded with a smile.

"That's what I thought." Even though I knew he didn't exactly mean it, I simply didn't want an argument so early in the morning. It was barely 10 am, for crying out loud.

"See, everything is settled. Now, Luke, get your drunk ass off the bed and meet us in the kitchen. I'm going to make breakfast."

"Okay, but I'm so sleeping in tomorrow."

"Sure," Chuckling, there was no way he would be able to sleep in tomorrow. Not unless he wants to bunk school, and the latter is not happening on my watch.

"My God, you have one funny and amazing family, Phoebe Smith," Federick commented after Luke nestled his face back into the bed; a vain attempt to have a quick five-minute rest.

Unsure if there was an underlying meaning behind Federick's words, "I will take this as a compliment and say thank you."

"It was a compliment, Phoebe." Nodding, I got off the bed.

"You're coming?" I uttered on my way to the kitchen.

"Of course, love. How can I possibly refuse you." Making his way beside me, Federick replied with a sweet smirk, instead of his usual arrogant one.

Mischievous as usual, Wyatt and Teo followed behind, repeating mine and Federick's words in an annoyingly sweet voice while making kissing and gagging noises. Having had enough of their mocking and on my last nerve, I turned on my heels and pinned them with one of my infamous sterns glower, challenging them to continue.

Lowering their hands from mimicking kissing gestures, and looking everywhere, but at me, it was safe to say they picked the right option.

"Good choice, boys," I muttered and continued towards my destination.

Federick chuckling beside me, I let it slide given he was not accustomed to our ways of behaving towards each other. Nonetheless, I was glad that he, at least, was not judging me, but instead seemed to be making an effort to understand me, my kids and my life in general.

This simple action of his pulled at my heartstring and compelled me to be intentionally considerate towards him. To see him in a new light, rather than just an arrogant playboy who only thinks about himself.

Then again, I still wasn't absolutely confident if I could completely trust him. Federick was, after all, a cold, calculating tycoon — feared by so many other business moguls.

CHAPTER 13
BREAKFAST

PHOEBE

"**W**hat's on the menu, chef?" Luke inquired as soon as he stepped foot inside the kitchen.

"What do you think there is, Luke?" Minding my own business while trying to figure out what was wrong with me for inviting Federick for breakfast, or for allowing myself to do what I did this morning, I vocalised as calmly as I could.

"Something to do with flour since your face is covered with it. And my brilliant brain tells me it is your famous pancake." Luke proudly responded, cutting my train of thought short.

"Well, tell your *Oh so brilliant brain* what I'm making is pretty obvious. I always make pancakes on the Sundays I'm home — now, go have a seat."

"Okay. Why insult my brilliant brain so early in the morning?" Luke whined while Wyatt and Teo snickered at him.

"Whatever." Chuckling, I continued with my task.

"You make your own batter?" Federick interjected, propelling Luke to once again fully acknowledge his presence.

"Sure, I do." I stated in an almost 'duh' tone. Thankfully, I stopped myself just in time from being too rude when Federick was still being friendly.

"Oh, hey, Federick." Luke waved, a bit puzzled.

Sharing a questioning look with Teo and Wyatt, they both shrugged their shoulders in response, their confusion as to why Federick was here this early in the morning sparkling like diamonds.

"Good morning, Luke." Completely ignoring their questioning and puzzled look, Federick answered with a beaming and truthful smile, surprising all of us in the process.

Awkwardly smiling at Federick, my sons instantaneously turned to me for answers. Disparatively shrugging my shoulders, I ignored their looks and suppressed the urge to blurb out anything incoherent. The uncomfortableness in the kitchen raising, I anxiously peeked at everyone through my eyelashes while patiently cooking my pancakes. If anyone wanted to break the silence, they were more than welcome too. It just wasn't going to be me.

"So. . . How did last night go?" Stressing his every word, I could tell Federick was trying to be careful with what was coming out of his mouth.

"Good." Sharing a knowing look between themselves, all three boys simply answered.

All I could do at this point was, watch — as if I was watching one of those stressful drama shows that eventually makes me bite my nail with nervousness and anxiousness.

"Okay. So who won the bet?" Federick tried again after a few seconds.

Federick was definitely trying hard to make small talk with the boys so the atmosphere would be less awkward. And although I appreciated it, I was also worried about how it will all go down.

"I did," Wyatt commented with a smile, but then, just as quickly, a strained look took over his demeanour.

"Shouldn't you be happier if you won? I would have been." Seeming more at ease and more real as he went with the flow, instead of trying too hard, Federick posed with intrigue.

"I am happy. But I would have been happier if someone — I won't say who — didn't steal the one girl I wanted more." Further relaxed with talking to Federick, Wyatt whined while shooting daggers at Luke.

Oddly enough, a wave of relief coursed through my heart when Wyatt, of all people, started warming up to Federick. It was weird. I should be more concerned with them warming up to Damien, not Federick freaking Archer.

"Well, all I can tell you with your overprotective mother around is —"

"Hey, I'm right here, you dumbass." I cut through Federick's professional tone as soon as I heard him mentioning me.

But, unlike his usual hard stone-faced demeanour, Federick gave me one of his winning smirks in response. I would have been further surprised, but despite still being annoying and arrogant on certain occasions, I was slowly getting used to this new kind and more humane side of Federick.

"Ignoring your mother, I would like to say you shouldn't worry too much about that one girl. There are lots of bigger fish out there, and I guarantee you will find way better. You should take advantage of your win and make Luke suffer the consequence," With a wink, Federick advised Wyatt.

"Hey!" Luke interjected at the unfairness.

"Oh, no worries, I'm already concocting something." With a devious smile, Wyatt responded, or rather threatened.

"Don't be too harsh though; it's only one girl." Federick pointed out.

"I know. I will never do anything to hurt my brother — blood-related or not — for one girl; as sexy as she might have been." Wyatt seriously propounded.

Cooing at Wyatt's maturity and reasoning, my cheeks instantly burnt like hot lava as everyone spared me a curious and funny look; especially Federick.

"What!" Covering up my minor embarrassment, I defensively uttered.

"Oh, nothing." All of them replied way too quickly.

"I can't help it if my baby sounds so grown up with his wise words." I blurted out under their gazes, to only have all four of them chuckle at me.

Turning off the stove, "Whatever." I once more defensively exclaimed.

"So, Teo, how did your night go?"

Taking Teo by surprise, "Uh . . . Umm . . ." Teo trailed, unsure of what was happening.

Worried, he might have done something wrong, "Why do you seem so shocked?" Federick asked.

"Um — it's . . . just that . . . I wasn't expecting . . . you to speak to me . . . all of a sudden." Stammering, Teo messily ran his hand through the back of his head.

"Sorry, for some unknown reason, Teo has been acting very shy these past few months. He used to be a blabber-mouth, but now he only speaks when brought into the conversation or when he is with his dear brothers."

"Like you like to blabber." Federick jokingly added.

"Haha . . . So funny — I barely talk to your sorry ass." I stated as a matter of fact.

"I've noticed," Federick whispered when I passed by him while serving everyone their food.

Not wanting to stir any unwanted topic, especially in front of the kids, I turned a deaf ear to his comment. "What are you three whispering about?"

Discreetly taking hold of my wrist as I tried to head for the farthest seat from him, Federick stealthily pulled me towards him. But as I was writhing my hand, about to escape his clasp, my sons turned towards me, compelling me to swiftly comply with Federick's wishes. Quickly sitting down beside a smirking Federick so the boys won't see his hold around my wrist, I glared at his stupid face, wishing death upon him.

"Oh, nothing much. Just wondering why your boss is still wearing yesterday's clothes and has a fresh hickey on his neck?" Wyatt responded after silently discussing with his brothers.

My brain scornfully screaming at me for forgetting the whole hickey situation, I tried to concoct a quick answer. However, this attempt of mine was made near impossible. Smirking at me, Federick took advantage of the table separating us from the kids' view, and placed his hand on top of my knees. Glaring at him, wishing I could shout at him; or better yet, kill him, I discreetly attempted to swat his hand away.

"Well . . ." Stuck in my vain attempt to find a good enough lie so quickly, I had to admit; it was getting more and more difficult to lie to the people I care about. I now understood exactly how my father felt and why he had given up on lying to me after I became a teen.

"Well?" All of them pressed — even damn Federick.

"Well . . . Seeing as it was already late when you guys left with Damien, Federick decided to crash over, just in case. How he got those stupid things on his neck, I have no idea — maybe he invited one of his many girlfriends over while I was sleeping, who knows?"

Squinting at me, clearly not believing a single word coming out of my mouth, my attention was redirected when Federick slightly glided his hand upward and tightened his hold on my thigh. Nearly jumping in surprise, I couldn't care less that the boys didn't buy my lies. My fear of being caught with Federick's hand so close to my intimates pinned me in place like a piece of cloth on a washline. Even the most powerful wind could not have moved me.

"And you expect us to believe you?" Wyatt suspiciously asked.

Lightly groping upward and downward, his long fingers, acting like hot droplets on my flesh as he unashamedly stroked my thigh, all I could do was furiously nod my head in agreement to whatever Wyatt was spurting out.

"Then how do you explain the hickey on your shoulder and the back of your neck?" With a smirk, Luke shocked the life out of me.

Moved by a storm and not believing what I just heard, "A what now!"

"A huge red hickey on your shoulder and back of your neck," Wyatt repeated.

My hand instantly flying to the back of my neck, I turned my furious gaze towards a smiling Federick. Vexed he marked me, and didn't care to notify me beforehand, I was ready to explode. Thankfully for Federick, the presence of my kids were keeping him safe and alive.

"I was so drunk last night; I don't remember anything. But go ahead, ask Mr Federick Archer. I'm sure he will have an answer." Given it was Federick who put me in this mess in the first place, I left it up to him to figure something out.

Finally stopping his torture on my thigh, "Are you sure you want me to tell them what happened?" Federick uneasily asked.

"Oh yes, go ahead, Mr Archer. Explain to my sons how I got this thing on my body because I sure don't remember." Wiggling my eyebrows at Federick, I sweetly encouraged.

This was good revenge. Matching Federick's death glare with a satisfied smile, I patiently awaited his answer.

"If you guys are done playing the *'It's not me, it's him'* game, we are still waiting." All three looking back and forth between Federick and myself, Wyatt impatiently stated, like a devious lawyer.

Shaking my head 'No', I pointed both my gaze and forefinger at Federick, "Federick is going to answer because I was too drunk to remember what happened." I stated with a childish stubbornness.

At the same time, though, my regard told Federick I didn't want my kids to find out the actual truth of what might have conspired or what stupid thing I might have done in my absolute drunkenness. Understanding my unspoken words, and my delicate situation, Federick devilishly smirked at me.

Suddenly, I wasn't so sure proposing he concocted a lie was the most fabulous revenge plan. I had more to lose than him.

Swiftly and discreetly placing my hand on top of Federick's thigh as he was about to open his mouth, I tightened my hold and pleaded him with eyes to not say anything stupid. Deviliously smirking, Federick discreetly slid his hand down and peeled mine from his lap with great ease.

"Well, if you insist so much . . . But don't complain later and tell me I didn't warn you."

"I —"

"No, it's okay. I got it." Cutting in and not giving me the chance to speak, I slumped my shoulders, anticipating the worst, knowing I was officially screwed.

"No need to look so worried, babe. It's not that bad." Purposely stretching on the word 'babe', Federick sent my head flying back with frustration.

"Stop calling me those names. I am not your babe." I warned through gritted teeth.

"You guys done yet? We want answers as to why both of you have hickeys. Are you two a thing now?" Clearly not having a lock on his mouth, Wyatt demanded. Damn overprotective kid.

"NO! We are so **not**!" I exclaimed a bit too loudly.

Not liking my answer, Federick further tightened his grip on my thigh and gave me a look — one that appeared almost sour. A feeling of guilt poking at my insides, I felt weird. These new emotions and reactions sticking their heads out in the company of Federick, or even when I am merely thinking about him didn't make sense at all. But, damn . . . Was I unable to get rid of it or purely ignore it?

"As your mom said, no, we are not." Federick patiently uttered.

"Then care to explain." Luke cut in this time. It appears Luke and Wyatt were the only ones who had taken vows to pester us. Teo was too busy quietly enjoying the show playing in front of him. Unlike me, who was a nervous ball.

"Well, after you three went with that Damien guy —" Not liking the way Federick mentioned Damien in front of the kids, I shot him an exasperated look, instantly cutting him off.

"Let me correct myself. When you guys went to the party with Damien, your mom's childhood best friend."

Stretching out the last part, for some reason hating speaking nicely of Damien, when dear Damien has been nothing short of a gentleman, my two brats smirked approvingly at Federick's dislike. Despite itching to scold them on their reaction towards my poor Damien, I bit down on my tongue and satisfied myself with disapprovingly glaring at all of them.

"She started drinking more than she should have, and from there, everything went downhill. I tried super hard to stop her, but she wouldn't take no for an answer. And you guys know, Phoebe gets what she wants once she sets her mind to it. She will literally do anything to achieve her goal."

Federick might have hoped to break the ice with his last comment, but as the boys seriously stared at him after breaking into a chuckle for a beat, it was evident there was another layer that needed cracking.

"After much persuasion, however, Phoebe was able to get what she wanted."

Pausing for dramatic effect, I was stupefied that Federick, Mr Cold face, could speak dramatically, instead of being his usual direct and blunt self. My heart already beating faster in anticipation, Federick was hugely successful in leaving all of us hanging.

"And?" Teo pressed, speaking out for once in a long time.

"Curiosity killed the cat!" I tried cutting in.

Waiting for a few beats, his devilish smirk indicative that my interruption didn't hinder him, Federick's build of anticipation was eating away at me like acid on flesh.

"And she dragged me to a freaking strip club." Federick declared in a higher notch.

"She what!"

"I what!"

The boys and I screeched in shock and utter disbelief.

"I so didn't do such a thing." I quickly defended myself. Federick was, for sure, being absurd.

"And how would you know? You were drunk out of your mind, remember." Federick pointed out with a smirk.

"And that's how kids, both me and your mom got hickeys. I could go into more explicit details on how she got it from one of the strippers, but that wouldn't be appropriate. Would it now?" As we all continuously gawked at Federick with disbelief, my sons, unlike me, were unquestionably buying his devious fake story.

"Mom dragged you, her boss to a strip club." Teo and Wyatt simultaneously exclaimed with a chuckle before breaking into a full laugh.

"Don't let your minds run too wild now, weirdos. Finish your breakfast; it's getting cold." Force gearing away from this crazy subject, I directed the boys to the plate of food in front of them.

"Oh, we won't, trust me. We want to keep as sane a mind as possible." Wyatt jokingly responded, propelling me to stick my tongue out at him playfully.

CHAPTER 14
PANCAKES & INTERROGATION

PHOEBE

"**A**re you going to spend the day?" Breaking the comfortable silence that had been surrounding us, Wyatt asked Federick.

Stealing glances at me, "I'm not sure. It depends."

After his sick joke of an excuse for the hickeys, the jerk better not be sure about his own survival, let alone if he could stay over the entire day.

"You are welcome to stay, you know." Surprising both Federick and me, Teo blurted.

Shifting my attention to Wyatt, I was further astonished to discover he too was supportive of this idea. The idiot went as far as genuinely smiling at Federick. Now, if this wasn't a clear encouragement, I don't know what was.

"I would love to stay and have the opportunity to know all three of you even better, especially you, Teo," Federick added with one of his rare heart-stopping smiles.

I guess it's a morning full of rare smiles and emotions then.

"But . . ." Already sensing the *'but'* in Federick's phrase, Luke interjected.

"But . . . Much to your mom's displeasure, I have already crashed in yesterday's dinner, and I don't want to intrude any more than I already have." Disappearing as quickly as it appeared, the tint of sadness in Federick's voice could have been easily missed.

"Oh, it's okay. What matters is that we finally got to witness you and our mom interacting, where you are not senselessly kissing her or being pissed off by some confusion." Teo stated with reassurance and humour.

"I see someone has gotten their voice back. Must be from all those screwing around you've been doing." I sarcastically chimed, earning myself a well-deserved blush from Teo.

"No. I think it's because he likes me far better than he does you." Federick jokingly offered.

"Ha . . . You wished. I bet your ass they hate you but are simply being nice." Sticking my tongue at Federick, I playfully mocked him.

"Well, mom, you just lost. We don't hate him. It's actually the opposite." Finishing his breakfast, Wyatt announced with a smirk.

"That's true . . . It's easy to talk to him — not that it isn't with you." Teo swiftly covered his ass.

"Don't you have anything to add?" Turning to an awfully quiet Luke, I directed my sarcasm at him.

"Naha . . . I'm just trying to enjoy my breakfast. Plus, tuning you guys out is doing a great deal of help to my aching head."

"Oh, how sweet of you. I can feel the overwhelming love from here." I added with sarcasm laced in my every word.

"I guess you lost your bet then." With a smug, Federick teased.

"You're feeling very proud of yourself right now. Aren't you?" I bite back with annoyance, already regretting inviting the smug-face over for breakfast. Yet, a small part of me was glad he was here. And it was this small crazy part of me that was ecstatic my kids had taken a liking of Federick.

"Oh, don't be jealous. I can't help it if I'm so likeable." Discreetly applying pressure on my lap, Federick exclaimed with an annoying smile.

Doing my very best to ignore the heat oozing off from his hand and onto my body, "Arrogant much." I added with a scowl.

"No need to be mad at me, I'm sure they still love you more than anything else." Brushing off my light swat on his hand, and oozing of confidence, smugness and reassurance, Federick uttered with a sweet voice.

Giving up on removing Federick's hand from my lap, "Oh, I know this."

"Now, who is being arrogant," Federick interjected with sarcasm.

"I'm sure they are going to dislike you once they discover the real you." With a smug and a smirk, I revealed.

"I doubt that." Teo gently added, swiftly cutting through Federick's upcoming argument.

Huh. I guess Teo has taken a great liking of Federick. Sadly, I know Federick will only end up disappointing him. But, as the good mother that I am, I didn't want to shatter my baby boy's hopes; especially when he had just started to act like his old self again.

"Sure, sweetie." Neither encouraging Teo nor discouraging him, I softly added as an afterthought.

Still, this didn't flatten my glare on Federick. A glare strong enough to make Federick understand that if he hurt my child, I will shred him to pieces.

"You guys are funny when you are together." Having finished a vast majority of his plate, Luke finally chimed with a broad smile. "I like you." Turning his full attention to Federick, Luke added as an afterthought.

"Yay, me too." Wyatt and Teo simultaneously exclaimed, earning themselves a proud smirk from Federick.

At this, I knew I was royally screwed. But hey, they seemed to have found a new friend, even if this one was not as responsible as I would have preferred. This day was indeed turning out to be more than astonishing.

"I like you guys as well." Sincerely smiling, Federick compassionately and genuinely revealed.

Aware I won't be seeing this sweet and humane side of Federick anytime soon, I revelled in this rare moment. However, just when I fully immersed myself in the beauty of this unfamiliarity, my phone hauled me back to the present, like a truck hauling a drowning car from the depth of a lake.

"Sorry I have to take this."

"Sure." Curiously looking up at me, all four were itching to know who was calling.

Glancing down at the phone screen, I hoped to the high God that it wasn't from the agency. The last thing I needed was to find a quick enough excuse for my disappearance for 'Work' when Federick was sitting here with us. Upon realising, it was merely my lawyer, I huffed a breath of relief, thanking God for saving me this time around.

But then, it caught up to me like a whirling fire.

Why the hell was he calling me when he was supposed to already be on his way here with all the papers ready to be signed? Did something go wrong? Was my perfect plan for a typical family going to get ruined **again**?

"Is something the matter?" Concern, Federick's questioned, interrupting my crazy thoughts.

"No. It's nothing." I lowly mumbled, "Everything's good." I tried to reassure myself more than him.

'Yes, it could be a courtesy call . . . maybe Kenneth is just calling to let me know everything is fine and going as planned.' My inner voice reassuringly chimed in.

'Ha, you are being nice all of a sudden . . . Where did all your crazy bitchiness go?' I sarcastically retorted.

'Hey, I'm merely your long lost and forgotten consciousness. No need to chastise me.' The little voice barked back at me.

Gently squeezing my thigh, Federick dragged me out of my distress once more. Appreciative of Federick's gesture, I reassuringly smiled at him before walking to the far end corner of the kitchen. The last thing I needed was for them to listen in on my conversation in case things were to get dirty.

'Just relax the ish up, will ya.' The nagging voice retorted.

Making sure my voice was worry-free, "Kenneth, is everything fine?" I asked with gentleness.

"Given how long you took to answer the phone, I should be the one asking this question."

"Sorry." I instantly breathe out.

"It's okay. And don't worry, everything is fine. I only called to inform you I will be running late. The paperwork is taking a lot more time than expected to fully process."

With a lightness I recognised *oh too well*, I let out a sigh of relief. The image of Kenneth nervously rubbing the nape of his neck, encouraging me to smile. Similarly to Alicia and Joseph, Kenneth was a good and loyal friend of my father and had supported me during my worst time. More than just a business advisor and family lawyer, he was my confidante and personal therapist when I was in desperate need for help.

"Phebes, you're still here?" Kenneth loudly inquired.

"Yeah, sorry. I zoned out." Cognisant I could be one hundred per cent honest and truthful with Kenneth, I sheepishly divulged.

"Glad to know I hold this much importance to you." Faking hurt,

Kenneth sarcastically joshed.

"Oh, you know how much I love you."

"Sure." Allowing my childishness to take over me, I stuck my tongue out at his short answer despite knowing he couldn't see me.

"Real mature, Phebes, real mature," Kenneth added with a light chuckle.

Trying my best to deny that I knew what he was referring to, "What! I don't know what you are talking about. I didn't do anything."

"You sticking your tongue at me, even though I'm not there, you crazy one."

"Ha, sometimes you know me way too much, Kenneth."

"I wish it was all the time. It would have certainly made my job a hell lot easier."

"Sadly, it's never going to happen. Anyways, what paperwork problem do you have? Can I help in any way to speed things up?"

"No, it's fine. Just some governmental procedures that I, your lawyer, am here to do." Kenneth replied with passion.

"No need to go all possessive on me about your work." Conscious Kenneth is one of those who put their heart in their works and detest it when people bug in; I jokingly pointed out.

"My work. I'll be as possessive as I want." With the attitude of a ten-year-old, Kenneth stubbornly exclaimed.

"And they say I'm a workaholic." I mused.

"Whatever. I will be at your place later on during the day. And Phebes, next time you want something this important done, please give me at least a day's worth of notice. You know how legality likes to take its sweet time."

"Yes, sorry for this one. It was a spur of the moment thing."

"No kidding," Kenneth stated with full-blown sarcasm.

After a short beat, seriousness laced in his voice, "So . . . You are certain about this?" The wise and cautious soul in Kenneth asked for confirmation.

Stealing a glance at the kitchen table, where everyone was happily talking among each other, **"Very."** Matching Kenneth's serious tone, I was more than confident that what I was doing was the right thing.

"Good, I'm glad for you." Kenneth sincerely assented.

Overjoyed Kenneth didn't disapprove of my decision; I could only hope everyone else would take it as lightly as he did. Especially Alicia and Joseph.

"Thanks, this means the world to me."

"No problem, kid. I will leave you alone now. Someone finally decided to show up." With a tint of annoyance at the end, I softly chuckled at his impatience.

And they told me **I** had to master my patience.

"Finally! I was beginning to think you got murdered back there." Most probably scared of Kenneth's powerful pissed-off tone, a lady lowly apologised for her delay on the other side of the line.

"Bye, Phoebe." Bringing his attention back to me, Kenneth's harsh tone mellowed down.

"Bye Kenneth, don't be too harsh to the poor lady."

"Sure." With yet another undertone of sarcasm, Kenneth ended the call.

Turning around to see everyone expectantly looking at me, "Kenneth." I simply replied.

"Oh." All three boys went back to their conversation.

"Another one of your boyfriends?"

Choking on my juice at Federick's abrupt accusation, I found it difficult to breathe. His demeanour swiftly changed from annoyance to caring, Federick fully turned towards me and patted my back to help me regain steady breathing.

"Asshole." Dangerously glowering at Federick's smirking face, I retorted the very moment I was able to speak.

"What? Only asking a simple question."

Discerning Federick's hint of irritation, I was confused. Other than assuming his bi-polar side has returned, I couldn't come up with a reason for his sudden mood change.

"And you are not even sorry about it, you prick."

"It's not like you would have died." He sarcastically replied.

"I could have."

"Not on my watch, sweetheart." Federick gently added with a wink that pulled at my heart and made me feel a strange kind of good and warmth.

"Jerk." Doing my best to stop this insane reaction his mere words were having on me, I quickly retorted.

"I would be less of a jerk if you would simply answer me." Federick stated in a 'Duh' tone.

"He is my lawyer, you idiot." Instead of responding, Federick let out a sigh of relief.

Surprised how he can be happy, annoyed, irritated and relieve all in a matter of minutes, "You and your bi-polar side are going to send me to an early grave."

"As I've said before, Phebes, you are seeing your own reflection."

"As if." I retorted in a mocking tone.

"You are!" With the stubbornness of a five-years-old, Federick exclaimed right back.

"Kids, if you are done fooling around, mind telling us why uncle

Kenneth called?" Saving Federick from my comeback, Wyatt interrupted us.

"Something about running late because the paperwork and procedures are taking a hell lot more time than expected."

"Oh." Both Luke and Teo said in unison.

CHAPTER 15
BUDDING FRIENDSHIP

PHOEBE

"This is why I don't like the whole business ordeal." Trying to get away from my decision for his profession, Wyatt countered. Unfortunately for Wyatt, no matter how much he whined about it, I wasn't going to back down.

"And that's why you are going to take your college business classes more seriously." Full-on mother mode, I sternly asserted.

"But it is so boring and long. Plus, I'm the youngest in that class."

"Because you are simply more intelligent and capable." I retorted with stubbornness.

"Still!" Wyatt complained like a toddler.

"I don't care how boring you find it; you are going to take this course seriously. My decision is final." I asseverated with a tone that told Wyatt to not mess with me.

"So . . . How come Wyatt attends college when he is only 16? I was certain he goes to high school." Saving Wyatt from another scolding, Federick swiftly interjected.

"Right! That's what I've been trying to tell her. I'm only 16 and already taking college classes on a subject I hate."

"You are not going to start again, are you?" I asked gravely.

"But mom . . ." Being observant of my fiery glare, Wyatt stopped mid-sentence.

"Please, do not refrain from answering my question." Saving Wyatt's ass yet again, Federick sarcastically interrupted.

"I enrolled him in an international business college class at the start of the school year. I want Wyatt to have at least a business diploma by the time he finishes high school."

"I'm pretty sure by the end of high school; I'm going to have more than just a diploma." Wyatt moodily added.

"Huh, and here I thought it was all fun with you."

"Well, you thought wrong, Mr Archer. My kids' education is essential to me." With a hidden smile, I revealed.

"Will you be so kind as to clarify how you managed to do such a thing?" With a smile and curiosity sparkling in his eyes, Federick inquired.

"The head of the college board owed me a few too many favours. All I did was remind him of one of them. Plus, Wyatt's 'A' grades helped a lot." I casually responded, as if it was no big deal.

Slightly taken aback by the new information, "You're an 'A' grade student? I thought you held the title of the infamous playboy."

"Oh, I hold the title, alright. If not possibly more. But this ain't an excuse to let my grades drop." Wyatt smugly responded.

"I'm impressed." With utmost pride, Federick vocalised.

Making this moment, all the cuter with his blush, "Thanks." Wyatt mumbled.

Sensing more questions brewing within Federick, "I'm going to start the dishes." Picking all the plates, I instantly put a stop to the interrogation.

"Mom, we are going to the playroom. Shout if you need us." Luke announced to my departing back.

"It was nice meeting you, Federick. We'll see you later." Teo tacked on with a smile.

"Sure. It was a pleasure to meet you too." Federick bade Teo goodbye before he left with his brothers.

As if the flashes of what had happened this morning was not torturing enough, the anticipation of Federick closing in was slowly killing me.

Standing behind me and reaching for the plate from my slightly quivering hands, "Here, let me help." Purposely breathing on top of the hickey he stamped on the back of my neck, my breathing intensified, and I swear I could have fainted right there.

"Thanks, but I will do it." Hoping Federick would comply so my breathing would return to an average human pace, I softly mumbled.

Taking the plate from my hands, "I owe you this much, Phebes." The combination of him being so close to me while calling me by my nickname propelled my heart to jump, bringing me to a loss.

Slowly turning me around and capturing my gaze, "Especially after such a wonderful dinner and breakfast."

"Sure." Averting my eyes from his piercing ones, I turned back to the sink, forcing myself not to be influenced by his low murmurs or closeness.

Pointing at the hand towel with my chin, "You can dry the dish-es."

Nodding, Federick stood way too close to me, in all his glory as he silently wiped the plates clean. My inside churring, I couldn't stop myself from stealing small glances at Federick. Those damn eyes of mine had a mind of its own.

Catching my not-so-discreet-gaze once again, "You can openly ogle at me, you know. No need to be sneaky about it." Federick chuckled.

"Whatever."

'Huh, he is turning soft.' My inner voice made its grand comeback.

'Shush!' I internally scolded myself.

'Oh, don't shush me. You know I am right.'

'Maybe he was always like this deep down. He did say the world only knows what he portrays, not the real him.' I tried reasoning with myself. Indeed, with the rate this was advancing, I could turn crazy any moment now.

'Just like you, then!' The little voice stated as a matter of fact.

'Just like me.' With a sadness trying to envelop my racing thoughts, I mentally repeated.

"Phoebe!" Federick called out a bit louder than necessary.

"Yes?" Fully in the here, I asked.

"You zone out on me again. Didn't you?" Blushing at Federick's gentle smile and question, I didn't need to answer.

I was utterly confused as to why my body was reacting this way whenever Federick was in the picture. Was it possible for a human being to be allergic to another human being all of a sudden? Maybe the kiss brought up this allergy? — I could tell I was being beyond stupid, but Federick and my body were driving me **nuts**.

"You're probably not going to like this, but I do have several unanswered questions."

Ready to interrupt Federick with some form of lame excuses, he beat me to it.

"Look, I recognise it might be difficult for you . . . Even for my simplest questions. But being in the dark is killing me here."

"Curiosity killed the cat, you know." Throwing in a little humour, my attempt to change the conversation was left unsuccessful.

"**Phoebe.**" With complete seriousness, Federick sternly exclaimed.

With the way, I was going, especially with my lame attempt at excuses, my credibility as a professional liar was soon going to get expunged.

"Why don't you go home and freshen up." I tried one of my diversion tactics.

"This is not the answer I am searching for." Federick voiced out with exasperation.

However, before he could act on that frustration, my phone rang, saving my behind once more. Huffing an air of annoyance when I explained I needed to take the call, Federick was left with no choice but to do the dishes all by himself.

'Well, he did propose to help . . . So, here he is, helping.'

Throwing the wiping cloth on the counter, "Kenneth." I greeted.

"Hey, Phebes, I'm almost done at the courthouse. I only need a few more signatures, present it to the judge, then I will be on my way to your place." Sensing Kenneth's bright smile while he was updating me, I couldn't help but smile as well.

"You are the best."

"I know I am Mr Perfect." With a playful snicker, Kenneth smugly added.

"Overconfident much."

"As if . . . Anyway, I will ping you when I'm close to your place."

"Okay, bye."

"Your lawyer?" Startling me, Federick interjected beside me.

"Yes." Getting over my initial shock, I stated in a matter-of-fact tone.

"You guys seem awfully friendly." Arching a brow, Federick suspiciously pointed out.

"Yes, Mr Bipolar, we are. Kenneth is family and has always been there for me."

"Family, huh . . . In what way exactly?" Federick asked with incredulity.

"Don't tell me you're still with that boyfriend crap?" Swallowing my urge to hit his head on my beautiful wall, I was indeed bewildered by Federick's odd theories.

"What if I am?"

"Are you dumb? — Didn't you hear my sons call him uncle."

"This didn't stop anyone before. Plus, with the way you guys talk, it's clear you are not related."

Do. Not. Hit. Him. I keep telling myself. He is just plain out dumb and impossible.

"Blood is not the only thing that defines a family, Federick. If you should know, Kenneth holds the same place in my heart as your mom and dad."

Even after my explicit explanation, Federick continued to stare at me with a questioning and searching gaze. As if trying to discern if I was lying.

"Come on, go home and clean up. You've been in the same clothing since yesterday." Instead of acting out my frustration, I tried reasoning in a gentle tone.

"I have more questions," Federick stubbornly pressed.

"I have things to take care of before Kenneth's arrival, so maybe later." I effectively lied.

"Things, huh. Like what?"

"Like legal, business things." I evasively revealed. "Now, go."

"You seem to be in a hurry to push me. Why is that?"

Toning down my heavy pressing tone, "It's not like this. I only want us to be productive."

"Sure, you do."

"Will you please comply with my request."

Acknowledging a change of plan was needed, "I will try to give you some of your answers later on." Not really meaning it, I suggested.

"Even though my gut is telling me not to believe you, I will. Because I know that you, of all people, wouldn't break a promise." Federick was trying to guilt-trip me, and damn was it working.

Taking me by surprise, Federick pecked me on the cheek before making his way to the playroom to bid boys goodbye. Blushing from the cuteness of Federick's action, I remained glued and watched Federick casually walk out the front door.

Realising I had to take some time to ponder over what had happened between us, I was grateful Federick didn't bring up the subject of this morning or last night. However, there was no escaping the reality that we will soon have to talk about it. Refusing to answer his questions was becoming all the more difficult with how close he was getting to me.

As Joseph had pointed out, Federick does deserve to know some of the truth, just like my kids do. However, I also had to keep all of them safe and away from the mere shadow of Cole Vanderwill. And if it means continuously lying to them, then so be it. It has proven to be the safest option so far.

***

FEDERICK

Following my several missteps, combined with the hickey on both mine and Phoebe's neck, I was astonished when Wyatt, Teo and Luke offered me their friendship instead of being tough on me. Particularly after how hard they were on Damien, who unlike me, the unsupportable boss — Phoebe's words, not mine — was their mom's childhood best friend.

If someone were to ask me though, I would have loved to point out that I have been more than supportive and patient towards Phoebe, explicitly with all her disappearing acts. But who wants to hear my opinion.

"So will you stay the day?" Sensing my uncomfortableness at once again being left alone with them, Teo came to my rescue.

How pitiful of me . . . The Great Ruthless Federick Ashton Archer was intimidated by his assistant's kids. Then again, there was no assistant like Phoebe Smith. Plus, I was in love with this particular one.

"I —"

"Lower your voice." Proving my theory that this family has a disease of cutting through people's conversation, Wyatt slyly glanced at his mother talking on the phone.

"I would love to stay, but knowing your mom, she will push me out of here the moment you guys leave this room." In a lower voice, I sadly explained.

'But not before getting my answers out of her.' My brain reminded me.

"You will figure something out, but just in case, give us your personal number." Wyatt effectively broke through my train of thoughts.

A bit taken aback, "Okay."

"Thanks." All three of them responded as Phoebe made her way back to us, with a bright smile caressing her face.

Jealous and envious this Kenneth guy could bring such a sweet smile on my angel's face, my suspicion on who he was to this family rose back up. It was crazy of me, but I knew I had to meet this exceptional lawyer of hers personally. If not for my own curiosity, then for my peace of mind. In fact, peace of mind was exactly what my brain has been demanding out of me, but knowing Phoebe, this wish of mine was not going to be accomplished anytime soon.

Heck, even after all the surprises and shocking news that has been dropping on me for the past few weeks, I still wasn't immune to its effect when Phoebe announced Wyatt attends college as well as high school at the young age of sixteen. Even more astounding was the fact that Wyatt was to graduate high school with a college business certification in hand.

Having seen Phoebe with her kids, I would have never imagined she would be one of those parents who pushes their plan for a career on their children, whether they like it or not. At the same time, in comparison to those stuck up parents, Phoebe lets her sons enjoy life and is relatively easy on them. Honestly speaking, the chemistry Phoebe has as a parent was quite weird but also balanced.

Despite not understanding why Phoebe was so insistent on Wyatt becoming a businessman within a limited timeframe, a sense of pride overcame me when Wyatt revealed he was an 'A' grade student as well as the famous jock and playboy of his school. It brought back wonderful memories of my high school years. And even though I had to work harder to keep my grades this high up, I could see myself in Wyatt's shoes.

Gradually learning more about Wyatt, Teo and Luke, it dawned on me that I wanted to know them better. Not just because they were Phoebe's kids or my parents' supposedly grandkids, but because I was genuinely interested and curious. They were fascinating and cool kids, and I couldn't wait to know them on a more personal level.

Silently advancing towards Phoebe after the boys had left the kitchen, the big elephant plopped back into the room, increasing the heaviness in the air around us. Phoebe's body slightly shivering as I approached her, it was clear she was remembering this morning but was also desperately trying to push back the memories. Conscious Phoebe was not going to purposely bring up what had happened between us; it fell on me to have that talk with her. No matter how much I knew, it would hurt to yet again be rejected by her. I recognised I was behaving like one of those clingy women I hate, but this was who Phoebe turned me into.

Striving to lighten the atmosphere before draping Phoebe in my mountain of questions, I played my arrogant yet seductive card while helping with the dishes. And when she furiously blushed, I knew I got her. Oh, so I thought . . .

Alas, Phoebe can never go easy on me. Oh no, why would she when she gets a greater deal of pleasure into torturing my poor soul.

As if not answering my questions straight up wasn't bad enough, Phoebe was now openly pushing me away to 'Freshen up'. I understood she couldn't, or, rather wouldn't tell me everything simply because the Great Federick Archer always gets his way, but my frustration was getting the best of me. Particularly when her dismissiveness was killing my resolution to be patient and give her the time she needed to answer my questions.

Phoebe could have at least pretended to give me the chance to properly ask my question, or better yet, attempt to answer a few of them. But no . . . We have to play by her damn stupid playbook all the freaking time. To make matters worse, the whole world seemed to have some unresolved grudges against me. Her lawyer called at the precise moment we were discussing, giving Phoebe the perfect excuse not to answer my questions. Without any doubt, this lawyer of hers had lousy timing.

Not despairing, I pretended to comply with Phoebe's request after a small innocent argument. I needed her to feel safe and not anticipate what I was planning. Kissing her goodbye, my speculation was proven. Under Phoebe's strong and cocky demeanour, there was a shy woman when it came to romance.

Walking into the playroom to bid my goodbyes to the boys, I was left stunned. Instead of a simple teenage cave, the room was the literal dream playroom for any guy of any age group. Plastered on the front wall, a smart curve LED 4K ULTRA HD TV with a shade of blue on all four corners took almost half of the wall space. Proudly standing beside the Tv were two huge stereos with the same shade of blue. And in front of them laid the newest brand of Xbox.

At my right, a large white cupboard decorated with tints of blues was half-opened, and from the looks of it, sheltered their Wii, PlayStation, game consoles and disks, among various other cool gadgets and games. Comfortably sitting on a large sea-blue retractable sofa, the boys were gleefully playing Apex Legends in their gaming laptop — trying to beat each other.

A pool table and a football table claimed its space behind the couch, and on the far left, a tennis table occupied a section. With small bean bags laying around the entire room, this place could easily fit two master bedrooms.

For someone who is rarely stunned and has absolute control over his emotions, I couldn't help but to continually gawp as I took this picture-perfect playroom.

Noticing the full snack bar and a coffee table beside a closed door, I remembered just how much Phoebe loves nibbling on snacks at every opportunity she gets. Giving the entirety of the room another once-over it dawned on me that Phoebe heavily uses this room as well.

"Hey boys, I was wondering . . . What's behind the locked door?" Bringing attention to me, I posed.

Paying me little to no regard, "Oh, just the entrance to the sports side of the house." Winning the game, Wyatt responded.

"Sports side?" Not entirely satisfied with Wyatt's answer, I pressed for more.

"You know; the gym, basketball ground, volleyball ground, tennis room, inside pool, sauna and mom's private practice room." Teo clarified with a gentle smile.

"And before you ask, we don't know what's inside mom's private practice room. It's always locked, and none of us is allowed in." Slightly creeping me out with his mindreading, Luke took the words out of my mouth.

Unsure if I should question him, I bid my goodbyes and promised I would be back to hang out after I *'freshen up'*. I swore I would get my answers today and no one was going to stop me. If I had to wait a few more hours, then so be it. Besides, my waiting would only be advantageous. After Luke signs the adoption paper, Phoebe would be much happier and more inclined to answer my questions.

CHAPTER 16
REVELATION

PHOEBE

"Luke, come to my office," I hollered from my office threshold.

"Coming." Luke voiced out from the playroom right after Wyatt and Teo wished him good luck.

Returning to my seat, patiently waiting for Luke, I narrowed my eyes at Kenneth, hoping it will stop his obsessive need to rearrange all of his documents — all over again.

My nerves getting the best of me, "Dude, relax."

"Don't you dude me, young lady." Kenneth promulgated in a fatherly tone.

"Old man, then." I joshed.

"Take your nervousness somewhere else and let me do my job."

"Wow, you are so good at pep talk." Dismissing Kenneth's scowl, I sarcastically mused.

"And this mouth of yours is going to bring you so far." His attention undivided from his stack of papers, Kenneth bantered with sarcasm.

"Whatever."

"Mom," Luke announced himself.

"Come on in, and close the door behind you." Nodding, Luke did as told.

"Where are your brothers?"

"Still in the playroom."

Pointing to the seat across from me, "Good, take your seat."

"Kenneth." Luke acknowledged before taking a seat beside him.

Nodding his greetings, "So, let's get started, shall we?" Kenneth excitedly announced.

Commanding myself to kill my nervousness, "Sure."

"Before we sign the papers, we need to get a few facts straight."

"Go ahead." I anxiously interrupted Kenneth.

"Without interruption will be better," Kenneth stated in a business tone. Ascertaining Kenneth was in full-on business mode; my best option was to comply without argument.

Turning on the video recorder, "I will be asking questions I might well know the answers to, but you will still need to respond for the record. It's the procedure." Casting a professional glance between Luke and me, Kenneth enumerated.

"The recorder?" Pointing at the object with his chin, Luke inquired, not fully understanding why we needed it.

"I record everything for every case as a precautionary procedure. We never know what we might need for evidence in the future. But to begin with, Luke, do you know who your real parents are?"

Luke stiffening the instant the question was asked, I was ready to lash at Kenneth; however, one look at his sternness, I bit down on my cheek. It was necessary; his heedful eyes told me that much.

"No, I don't." With sadness laced in his every word, Luke finally spelt out. Instinctively arching forward, unable to do much, I placed my hand on top of Luke's for moral support.

"Do you want or intend on finding out who they are after signing the adoption papers?"

"I won't mind." Not being able to shut it any longer, I interjected.

"**Phoebe!**" Kenneth reprimanded.

It was twice now that my name has been used in this manner in a matter of a day, and believe me when I say I don't appreciate being shut up. Kenneth was lucky we were so dang close, or his shoulder would have a hard time supporting his neck.

"I have no interest in finding out anything about my blood parents." With determination, Luke sternly exclaimed.

As much as I didn't want Luke to hate his actual non-existent parents, I managed to keep my lips sealed for the time being.

"Good. As you know, you are approaching 21, which means, even if your biological parents show up, you have every right to object to them. As soon as you sign these papers, they will no longer have any control over you. Rather, it's Phoebe who's going to have control as your mother."

"I understand," Was Luke's direct yet straightforward answer.

"Then, there's nothing for me to add. Unless one of you has something to ask?"

"Nope." Both Luke and I simultaneously responded.

"Okay, then. If both of you agree to the term of this agreement, I'll be the witness while both of you signed those four papers. Luke, you go first, then hand them to Phoebe."

"Gladly." With a smile, Luke responded.

Shaking Luke's hands, "Congratulations, you are now officially Luke Smith." Kenneth congratulated with a broad smile and embraced us in his tight hug, "I am so happy for both of you."

Filing away the documents and switching off the recorder, his demeanour more relaxed, "The next process is to change your will, so think well about it. The necessary documents are already being worked on, but be mindful that it's going to take a while. So please don't rush it, and if at all possible, write your own rough draft first. It will speed things up."

"You are so prepared." I complimented Kenneth's efficiency.

"Well, raising a small brat as yourself doesn't come easily unless one is prepared."

"Insulting me again, I see." I pouted at Kenneth's teasing.

"Cheer up, baby girl. You have a new kid, and I have a new nephew to spoil." Messing with my hair, Kenneth cheerfully proclaimed.

"I'm going to tell Joseph you were rude to me, or better yet, Alicia." Childishly pouting, I grumbled.

"You do that."

Arching my eyebrow at Kenneth's smugness, I pinned him with silence.

"I will prefer Joseph, though." He uttered as an afterthought.

"Alicia it is then," I countered with a smirk.

"You are ruthless, little one."

"I'm not little. I have three grown-up kids." Folding my arms in front of my chest, I stubbornly responded.

"Oh, sweetheart, you will always be Joseph's, Alicia's and my little girl." Messing with my hair, "For now, I have to go prepare myself for the masses of paperwork you poured over me."

Hugging us a final time, "I'm sure you two have a lot to discuss." Bidding his goodbyes, Kenneth closed the door behind him.

"Before we bridge the topic I need to discuss with you; I want to show you something." Walking towards my large bookshelf, I announced.

"All right." Standing up, Luke followed.

Cheerfully smiling at him, I removed one specific book from the shelf. Flipping it open to the hollow middle, I pushed onto the small button. Soon afterwards, a small section in the wall, where the book was, sank and a handprint biometric scanner appeared.

"A secret passage," Luke exclaimed with excitement and a knowing smirk.

"Yes, and this book is the first key." Waving the book in front of Luke, "Our handprints is the second." Setting the book in its original spot after the shelf slid open, I divulged.

"Is it going to recognise my handprints or do I have to wait until you have it programmed?"

"Your handprints, as well as Wyatt's and Teo's, are already programmed in the system. And in case of an emergency, any of you guys can open whatever secret door you want. However, your brothers are not aware of the concealed passages and shouldn't come to discover it unless they are facing life-threatening danger." Nodding in understanding, Luke remained at the threshold while I walked inside the room.

"Come on in." I softly encouraged.

Studying Luke as he gawked at the design of the room, clearly amazed with his surroundings, "As you may have guessed, this is my secret office. But tell me, do you find anything bizarre in here?" Testing Luke and his perception capabilities, I questioned.

"Well, if we account for the fact that this is not only your secret office but also your lair, a lot is missing here. Then again, the silver painting on the wall is concealing what appear to be sealed steel doors." Still observing around him, Luke efficiently responded.

"Good observation. This room is merely an office and the main entrance to several other secret rooms within this house, including the actual lair under the house."

"Ha, I would have expected no less from you." Luke extolled in awe as he continued to admire the place.

Pushing on the button beside me, "In case of an unexpected attack, the primary weaponry compartments are on your right."

Pressing on another button on the wall panel, a section of the floor opened up, and a steel rack filled with even more weapons appeared. "And this here is the second compartment of this room."

"Wow!" If Luke was amazed by this amount of weapons in my office, he should definitely visit the weaponry room behind the door on his left. He would be left panting with elation.

Walking towards me, "And all these buttons?"

"Each button opens the door to a different chamber or compartment."

"This is amazing." Luke marvelled with an excited glint.

Lightly slapping Luke's hand away from the side control panel, "Hey, don't go around pressing each button now." With a laugh, I mused and purposely ignored his sweet pout.

"Don't be a baby. You will have every opportunity to explore and play around later on. Plus you will have to go over the protocols of what to use and when with Talon. For now, however, we need to discuss something of equal importance."

Not happy to leave this room yet, "Alright." Acting like a five-year-old who was forcibly being dragged out of a candy store, Luke declared.

"How come the other doors are not fingerprinted?" With curiosity laced in his every word, Luke inquired.

Closing the secret passage door, "Oh, they are. You just haven't noticed it. Each doorknob is preprogrammed with a fingerprint recognition software, and the crucially important rooms have an eye scanner for added protection."

"Sneaky, I like it. What are the other things we need to discuss?" Taking his previous seat, Luke questioned.

"Wyatt and Teo."

"What about them? I haven't told them the truth yet."

"Well, this is what we need to discuss."

"Okay?" Confused, Luke stated.

"You know we cannot tell them the complete truth yet."

"Sadly enough, I do." With a hint of guilt, Luke answered.

"Well, to appease your guilt, and for you to create a stronger bond with them, I have reached the conclusion that you are going to let them in on some of the truth."

"Some?" Interested and perplexed, Luke waited for me to elaborate.

"For starters, how about you reveal your real age. And if things don't escalate too badly, you can even tell them about the bodyguard matter."

"What if they end up hating me?" Clearly afflicted and tormented about their reactions, Luke asked with distress.

I too was worried, but I couldn't allow these emotions to affect my decisions and actions. And if Luke was to take my place in the future, he too should start training to handle his feelings.

"Look, I recognise this is difficult and that I'm the reason for your despair. But, don't you think it will be better if they find out now, at the beginning of your relationship, rather than later, from someone else? Particularly from someone who wants to destroy us."

"You do have a point. But I'm still nervous about this."

"Don't trouble yourself too much. Everything will be just fine. We will make it work; you simply have to be patient."

"If you say so." Luke spelt out after a few minutes of silence.

However, I knew he was not convinced. Heck, I, myself was not convinced. So, how could I possibly expect him to be?

"I say so, now go, I'm sure Teo and Wyatt are impatiently waiting for you." With a reassuring smile, I encouraged Luke to do what was right and necessary.

"Besides, there is a high chance they will end up hating me rather than you." Aware Luke will have a higher chance of being forgiven if I didn't tag along, I exclaimed with a sad smile.

"No matter what happens or what you do, they will never hate you. We all love you way too much for this." With fire in his eyes, and his tone suggesting that me even thinking this was nonsense, Luke enumerated.

"Right. . ." Not convinced of Luke's encouraging words, especially after Cole Vanderwill's proclamation when he made his reappearance, I returned Luke's hug before he left for the playroom.

Now I just had to wait and see what would happen — if I will need to be a referee to avoid bloodshed between brothers or just be a helpless spectator. Whatever the situation, I sure as heck was going to be dreading every second of the wait, particularly with Vanderwill dancing around my head as if he had already won this battle.

CHAPTER 17
BET

LUKE

Over the moon, my lifelong dream of having a family I could call my own had finally seen the light — and what better family than Phoebe's.

At the same time, there was no denying I was petrified about revealing certain truths of my real identity. Not knowing what Wyatt and Teo's reaction would be, scared me beyond imagination.

Will they hate me? — Will I be the causation of bitterness within this sweet loving family?

In spite of all these doubts, Phoebe was right; I needed to tell them myself before they discovered the truth from someone else. Plus, it's not like I will be able to hide my actual age from them for too long.

Inhaling in a deep breath, I prepared myself for the worst, stretched my lips into the biggest smile I could muster and entered the playroom.

"Hey bro, what took so long?" Pausing his game and fist-bumping me, Wyatt questioned.

"Oh, you know, paperwork." Internally convincing myself every-thing will be just fine, I stretched with a slight grin.

"So how did it go? You seem a bit pale for someone who should be dancing in excitement." Fist-bumping me, Teo concluded.

"It's nothing." I expressed.

"Okay." Sharing their infamous look only these two could under-stand, Teo and Wyatt exclaimed with uncertainty.

"Come on, let's continue our match." Wyatt declared after a beat of awkward silence.

For a slight second, it seemed like Wyatt and Teo knew something they shouldn't. As if they were aware, I had something important to say but preferred not to press. But it couldn't be. Deeming my insane thoughts as irrational and a trick of my nervous mind, I switched gears and joined their match.

"Dude! You're barely paying any attention to the game!" Throwing their controllers on the couch, tired of me losing for the fifth time in the past half an hour, Wyatt and Teo simultaneously exclaimed.

"Are you sure you two are not twins?" Their ability to share the same thoughts at the same time still sort of freakish to me, I jested.

Sharing another knowing look, "No doubt." They both responded.

"I'mma have to dispute it."

"If you wish. But what I wanna know is why you are so distract-ed?" Wyatt perplexedly voiced out.

"Yeah, I would have thought you would be so excited, you would be talking our ear off." Teo divulged with slight confusion.

'Tell them now!' My brain shouted with exasperation.

Taking a deep breath, my shoulders slumping, I let out a sigh of exasperation. "Actually, I have something important to tell you guys." I finally managed to utter. This was step one, right.

"It seems like it." Taking his seat on the couch and looking expectantly at me, Wyatt articulated.

"But you guys have to promise you will give me a chance to explain myself and not interrupt until I'm done," I revealed in an almost quiet tone.

With a small smile plastered on Wyatt's face and curiosity on Teo's, as if they knew where this conversation was going, I was further on edge.

"Sure." They both agreed.

"So, you remember how we first met?"

"Obviously. It was in the alley outside a club."

"Well, what you don't know is that this particular club does underground street fighting, and when we first met, I was trying to get out of that life."

"Wow. . ." Receiving a nasty glare from Wyatt, Teo's interruption was cut short.

"It's not as cool as it sounds . . . Anyways, two weeks after we befriended, I coincidentally ran into Phoebe while readying myself for one of my fights." Stopping to take a deep breath, I took the opportunity to observe their faces.

"Naturally, I didn't know she was your mom. So, I flirted with her and invited her to watch my fight to impress her further. But, she apparently already knew all about me and that we've been hanging out."

"We told her a week after meeting you." Teo calmly clarified.

Wyatt's disgust drowned in his fit of laughter, "Dude, you flirted with our mother!"

Blushing with embarrassment, "Not funny . . . Anyways, remember how you only started seeing me at your school two weeks after we became friends."

"Yes. You said you got expelled from your previous school for punching the science teacher. So, you moved to ours because we were your friends." With a small smile caressing his lips, Teo disclosed.

"I still don't buy that excuse," Wyatt exclaimed his disbelief.

"You would be correct."

"What was the real reason then?" Teo and Wyatt simultaneously inquired.

"I never got expelled."

Puzzled, "Huh?" Staring at me like I was a box of mismatched scattered puzzles, they both vocalised.

"You're both probably going to hate me after this, but I need to come clean . . . . . I am actually 20, nearing 21, and have already graduated from high school. The only reason I'm attending your high school is that Phoebe hired me to be your undercover bodyguard." I revealed in one hasty breath.

Sensing Wyatt about to say something, I pushed aside the relief that washed over me as I spilt the beans on this secret.

"I am so sorry for lying to you guys for so long. You're both awesome and don't deserve this, but Phoebe offered me a life out of street fighting — I'm not saying Phoebe is responsible because she is not. She is a wonderful mother who only wants her sons to be safe. It might not make any difference, but you should know I have truly come to love you two as brothers and Phoebe as a mother. But I couldn't go deeper into our relationship with this lie hanging over my head." Abruptly hugging me, Wyatt and Teo cut my blabbing short.

"FINALLY!" Tackling me to the ground, both of them vociferate.

"Huh?" Expecting punches, hate comments or angry shouts, I was taken by astonishment and confusion when they lovingly hugged me instead.

"We've known for a while now." With a genuine smile, both clarified.

"But how? . . . When? . . . And why didn't you mention it before?" Confused was not the word I would have used to describe my feelings — I was far beyond that frivolous word.

"Bro, give me some credit here. You seriously thought I wouldn't have done my research before inviting you in our lives as our brother — before encouraging my mom to act on her idea of adopting you." Wyatt proudly divulged.

"You have a point."

For a split second, the idea that Wyatt might have come across critical secrets during his research crossed my frenzied brain. However, I quickly realised the possibility for the latter was near to impossible. No one outside or inside the agency, except the ones at the top knows my real identity and aliases — one of the many perks of working for Angel. Absolute identity protection.

"But why did you let me lie to your face for so long? You could have confronted me." Bewildered, I questioned.

"I know how persuasive our mom can be. But most importantly, I wanted to give you time to reveal everything on your own. Plus, it was fun watching you struggle to give us perfect excuses whenever you neared getting caught." With a smile, Wyatt snottily claimed.

"How about trust, then? How did you know I could be trusted when I was lying to your face?" Still trying to fully digest the information, I spoke my mind.

Here I thought I would be the one astounding them, but no . . . It was the other way around.

"Honestly, when I first found out I was beyond pissed. I wanted to confront you right away and beat the living shit out of you. But after discussing the situation with the voice of reason, alias, Teo, we concluded that we would give you time and silently observe you."

"Oh!" I interrupted.

"Yes, oh. We spent months intensely studying you, but even then we were unable to figure you out completely. On the other hand, we were able to figure out when you are or are not lying."

"Did you now?" Disbelief laced in my words since deception was part of my job description, I was finding it hard to believe a pair of teenagers could figure me out.

"As much as you try to hide it, whenever you lie there's a light muscle strain under the left side of your chin." Teo clarified.

Okay! I was flabbergasted. How did they do this?

"It was challenging at first, but Teo noticed it when we were evaluating if you could be trusted. Actually, you should be extremely thankful to Teo. He's the only reason you are standing here today, as our brother." Noticing my confused look, Wyatt explicate.

"How did you do it?" I directed my question to Teo.

"Power of observation and reading human microexpression based on different situations. Basically, neuroscience." Teo divulged with a blush.

"You are good," I stated, amazed by his exceptional ability — one that would undeniably be beyond useful to the agency.

"Thanks."

"See, I told you, your obsession with that brainy stuff would help us a lot in the future." Lightly bumping Teo on the shoulder, Wyatt mused.

"So this is the secret obsession you've been trying to hide from me?" Surprised I didn't notice this talent before, I asked for clarification.

Glaring at Wyatt for spilling the beans on his secret, "Yep." Teo confirmed.

"What? Luke is family now. He has the right to know." Wyatt vocalised.

"Does Phoebe know?"

"Obviously not!" Teo responded with unnecessary force.

"But why? It's pretty cool."

"Because I don't want her to know just yet. Which means, you are going to keep your lips sealed."

"Okay," I responded with uncertainty.

"He is serious, man. Mom can't know. The last time I pushed for this idea, he got pissed and didn't talk to me for a whole week."

"Alright, then." I reluctantly complied.

Having already jeopardised our relationship by lying to them about my real motive behind getting so close to them, I had no other choice but to comply. It was a harmless and innocent request.

"Good." Teo and Wyatt simultaneously responded.

"So you guys are not mad at me?" I inquired for reassurance.

"Of course not. We are cool."

"I was already expecting you to divulge this secret of yours once you signed the adoption paper." Wyatt pompously claimed.

"You must be feeling exceptionally confident of yourself right now." I mused with sarcasm.

"You have no idea. But I also had faith in your judgement. You seriously wouldn't keep lying to us once our bond grew stronger." Wyatt continued.

"Keep me out of it. I wasn't so sure you would." Teo finally added his piece.

"Thank you so much for the vote of confidence you have in me. Who knows where I would be without it?" I sarcastically jested Teo.

"Cannot blame a man for being too careful." Not affected by my tone, Teo stated in a *'Duh'* tone.

"You are right. Sorry, Teo."

"It's all good now that you've told us the whole truth."

Momentarily freezing at the mention of *'The Whole Truth'*, my level of moral culpability rose to a new height. The realisation that I was still technically partly lying hitting me. Thankfully, I somehow managed to keep a constant smile on my face.

"Let's put all these secrets behind us." Extending his palm towards Teo, Wyatt encouraged.

Slowly removing a hundred dollar bill from his pocket, Teo handed it over to Wyatt with a grim expression. Most certainly unhappy to lose his money.

"I can't believe you guys betted on me?" Regaining full control over my guilt, I exclaimed with disbelief and humour.

I had no right to feel bad. I was merely doing my job. And if I wanted to be as good as Angel, then these things shouldn't affect me. I had to fight it.

"Of course we did. We couldn't agree on whether you were going to reveal the truth today itself. I had faith in you, while my dear little brother didn't — which cost him 100 bucks." Patting his pocket, Wyatt exclaimed with a prideful smirk.

"Unbelievable." I voiced out more to myself.

"Now tell us what happened with the underground fighting. How did mom get your ass out of there?"

"Well, it's a funny story," I stated in an amused low tone. One would think I was bemused, but in reality, I was anxious.

"We don't have the whole day." Unable to take my stretched pause, Teo pressed.

"Hey, isn't Federick supposed to be here? He told us he would be coming back." Mimicking an *'Oh, I just remembered'* tone, I quickly tried to change the topic.

"You're right. Maybe he forgot, or he's with mom?" Discerning I purposely changed the train of the conversation, I was thankful Wyatt didn't push for more. Instead, he showed his understanding and patience.

"Federick and mom seem to like each other." Sharing a quick, silent look with Teo, Wyatt continued.

"As friends." I quickly pointed out to Wyatt.

"No, stupid. In a romantic way." Teo clarified.

"NO WAY!" I exclaimed in disbelief. This was an absurd theory.

"Tell me you're kidding right now!" Wyatt declared with shock.

Shaking my head in denial, I couldn't believe they think Phoebe, aka, Angel would ever have romantic feelings for someone so ordinary as Federick. Heck, Phoebe was incapable of having a romantic relationship with anyone in general.

"Come on, don't tell me you didn't notice the longing glances between them last night and this morning?" Wyatt stated as if it were the most normal thing to say.

"Plus, didn't you notice the irritation and annoyance radiating off Federick when that Damien guy was here? Or, how about the jealousy on Federick's face and action whenever Damien or any other guy's name were mentioned." Trying to back up their theory, Teo added after his brother.

"You guys are seeing things. Sure, Federick is a nice guy, but he is mom's boss." My brain rejecting this far-fetched idea, I pressed with utter disbelief.

"This hasn't stopped anyone before." Wyatt declared in his utmost 'duh' tone.

"But this is mom we are talking about. She is an extremely professional person, with all these rules. One of which is not to get involved with someone she works for." I tried to convince them and myself at the same time.

"Are you sure you are 20? Because you sure act and sound like a kid to me."

Sticking my tongue at Wyatt for his unnecessary comment, I took a moment to reflect on their suggestion.

"Nope. I can't imagine it."

"There ain't much to imagine, Luke. They clearly slept together last night. You can't deny the hickeys on both their necks. And you can't seriously believe in their lame-ass excuse." Wyatt pointed out.

"There must be another more logical explanation for those hickeys. There's no way they are together." Denial taking over me, I expostulated.

"They might not be a couple yet, but there's definitely something cooking between them. I can feel the electricity in the air." Wyatt countered in more detail.

Slightly shaking my head, "You're wrong."

"Wanna bet." Teo challenged.

"On?" I asked for more information.

"I bet you a month of allowance that mom and Federick are going to end up together." Teo clarified.

"If that's what you want. But considering it is two against one, let's change the rule a bit." I proposed after a beat.

"Like what?" Both of them asked with curiosity.

"Let's have a deadline."

"What do you exactly mean by a deadline?" Confused, Teo inquired.

"Well, since there are two of you, I could potentially lose two months of allowance. So, I propose we give them two months to become a couple."

"Challenge accepted. In 2 months, Federick and mom will be together." Sharing their confirmation look, Wyatt and Teo simultaneously responded.

"Wait. Are dirty tricks allowed?" Wyatt asked as an afterthought.

"Hell ya!" I exclaimed with excitement.

If we are going to bet on something as such, we are bound to make these two months interesting and full of unexpected tricks.

"I'm so going to win this." Shaking their hands to seal our bet, I declared with confidence.

CHAPTER 18
TRUST

FEDERICK

Covertly standing behind Phoebe's mid-open office door, I was dumbstruck and speechless when I heard Phoebe *'Advised'* Luke to inform Wyatt and Teo about his truth. I shouldn't have been so shocked; I had my doubts about Luke's actual age. But what in the world was the *'Bodyguard'* thing?

This family was so full of secrets, and my parents were somehow part of this insanity. Yet, I was left in the middle, utterly oblivious of my surroundings with growing frustration that was getting harder to bottle in with each passing day.

Their conversation turning further absurd by the minutes, it dawned on me that from now on, I have to prepare myself for the worst and weirdest case scenario wherever Phoebe was concerned.

I came here to know Phoebe, the people around her better and to get the answers to my several questions. In that sense, I had to embrace the bombshell that came with this decision.

Picking up footsteps approaching the threshold, I swiftly turned around and hid behind the nearest pillar in the hallway. Walking towards the playroom with a long face, it was evident that Luke was internally struggling. And as much as I wanted to lend a helping hand, I recognised I couldn't intrude. This was a delicate family matter. All I could do was hope Wyatt and Teo won't take the revelation of his secret too hard and punish him for it.

Allowing a few minutes to pass, I barged into Phoebe's office and locked the door behind me. Startled, Phoebe's hand flew under the table. Realising it was only me, she let out a sigh of relief and allowed her body to relax.

Brushing off her incoherent grumbled, "Was expecting someone else?" I satirically demanded.

"Was expecting silence and quietness." Both surprised and annoyed by my presence, Phoebe retorted.

Fortunately for both of us, I was getting better with reading this woman. If only I were given the opportunity to read her eyes more often, without her trying her best to block me out, I would do a better job at understanding her. It was a difficult task, but not impossible. I just had to counter her persistence to block me out.

"Hey, there! Did you just space out on me?" Phoebe voiced out in disbelief.

Reckoning I was the first person to have ever spaced out on her without feeling the tiniest bit sorry for it, "That's you getting a taste of your own medicine." I nonchalantly enumerated.

"What are you even doing here? Shouldn't you be at your place?" Suspiciously eying me, Phoebe demanded in an accusatory tone.

"Your sons invited me over when you were busy talking to your lawyer. Besides, you did promise to answer my questions after I freshen-up." I simply summarised for Phoebe.

"And it's now you decide to inform me you've been invited."

"I wouldn't have gotten to see your startled face if I did. Now, would I?" Dismissing the ire in her tone, I quipped.

"You are truly impossible! One of these days, you are going to get yourself seriously hurt for popping out of nowhere." Phoebe reprimanded with seriousness as if she was scolding one of her kids.

It was cute, but I was no kid. I am the Federick Ashton Archer. Nobody would ever dare mess with me if they valued theirs and their family lives.

"What? Are you going to kick me again for startling you? That would be so *seriously hurt.*"

Huffing in response, I discerned Phoebe was trying to be patient, but so was I. I have been trying for weeks now, if not years.

"Why in the world did you lock my door?" As if now realising we were in a locked room together, Phoebe wearily asked.

"Oh, I was hoping to have a repeat of this morning." Slowly closing in, building the anticipation and tension like a predator towards its prey, I lied.

"You better back off right now." Propelling her seat backward with a push of her leg, Phoebe exclaimed with seriousness.

Ignoring her warning, I continually approached her until the chair hit the wall, trapping her.

"That's not what I remember you saying this morning. Actually, if I remember correctly, you were throwing yourself at me and purring like a hungry kitten at my every caress and kiss; about ready to do whatever I ask of you . . . I can make you feel the same way all over again. All you need to do is ask . . . And if you are nice enough, I will happily take you higher." Lightly grazing the back of my fingers along Phoebe's arms, I huskily muttered, loving how heated, flush and troubled she got within seconds.

Cornered, Phoebe tried to get up to escape our closeness. However, I was having way too much fun at her expense. Her virgin-like innocence was insanely adorable. A side of her I didn't know existed until this morning in the kitchen. Placing my hands on her shoulder blades, I lightly pushed her back into her seat.

"You are sick. This morning was just a spur of the moment, plus I had a hangover." Once again using her trick of looking at my nose to emulate staring into my eyes, Phoebe stubbornly claimed.

Instead of being hurt by her words, I had the urge to smile and continue my teasing. It was clear Phoebe was going into defensive and denial mode, but I wasn't going to give her the satisfaction of seeing me react the way she wants.

Holding onto the armrest of Phoebe's chair, I slowly crouched forward, further trapping her. "Just like in my dad's office was a spur of the moment." Maintaining my usual controlled arrogant face and hiding my smile, I seductively sledged.

"Yes!" Glowering at me, Phoebe managed to utter a response.

"You seem to have a lot of these '*Spurs of the moment*'. Should I be worried, sweetheart?" Intentionally letting my hot breath hit her face, I huskily breathed out.

"No need to worry about me. I can very well control myself. Worry about yourself." Trying to regain control over her breathing and the situation at hand, Phoebe bit back a bit too fiercely. Discerning Phoebe was not used to being teased and riled up in this specific manner; I had officially found my new favourite past-time.

"Are you sure about that, sweetheart? I think we should look into these '*Spurs of the moment.*' I'm an excellent doctor for these types of problems . . . It could get dangerous, you know." I faked a sarcastically sweet and concerned tone.

"No, thank you. Take your doctorate somewhere else. Moreover, it only happened twice, so get over it and shut up." The sexual air getting to her, Phoebe exclaimed with frustration.

"Do you want it to happen more than twice? I will be more than pleased to grant you this wish." I husked with a cocky smirk.

"Of course, you would." Hinting at my reputation of sleeping around, Phoebe responded without humour.

"Is this a yes?" Completely ignoring Phoebe's indirect insult, I inched closer to her face.

"What will it take for you to get off my back and stop this new nonsense of yours?" Both annoyed and defeated; Phoebe broke our small-lived silent stare.

"Accepting defeat already?" Tempting my luck, I jested.

"Really!" About ready to push me back with force, Phoebe exclaimed with irritation.

"Okay, sorry." I apologised.

Straightening my posture and crossing my arms over my chest, I towered over Phoebe's petite figure. "I want some of my much-deserved answers." I quickly declared before she could take back her offer.

"Really! You're still walking around with this question and answer shit." Huffing a breath, Phoebe expostulated.

Taking hold of her chair's armrests, I dragged Phoebe and the chair towards the table. Sitting on top of the table, I positioned Phoebe in front of me.

"Yes, I am. I deserve some answers, Phoebe. Look at it from my perspective. Please. I work with you every day. Still, it seems I know nothing about you. To make matters further unbelievable, you and my parents seem to have known each other for a hell of a long time without my having any clue. Wherever I turn, I'm stuck in a circle where I'm the only one who's constantly left out and lied to."

"It's difficult." Phoebe cut in.

"Don't you think I know this! You may think I'm stupid, Phebes, but flash news — I am not. I may be dense concerning you or your situations, but even this is gradually changing. Can't you see, I need to be able to trust you completely. To be able to truthfully say I know you — at least a part of you to start with." I opened my heart to Phoebe, frustrated with how she was treating our situation.

"Is this a new form of torture to get your answers out of me?" Phoebe asked with pure seriousness.

"How can you say such a thing with such seriousness? Here I am, going out of my comfort zone, divulging my heart's pain to you, and you are making a mockery out of it — out of me." I spelt out with pain and an inkling of anger.

"I'm not making fun of you. I'm merely asking a question, and I am sorry if it pains you. But as heart-warming and sweet as what you've said is, I still don't understand why you need to trust me completely. Nor why you have to tell other people how much you know about me?" Phoebe cautiously explained.

"Trust is a necessity for me, Phoebe. If not everything. Excluding my parents from this conversation for now — which mind you, is an essential aspect — I need to trust you, so we were able to work properly together. Tell me honestly, Phoebe, do you or do you not trust me?"

Hoping for an immediate '*I do*' the instant the question left my lips; I was left baffled at the indecision in her beautiful brown eyes. Reading her like an open book, my chest constricted at the sight of her internal struggle to answer this simple yet crucial question.

"Well, I didn't expect this." Readying myself to get off the table and out of this room, I uttered in a sour mood.

As much as Phoebe's look of indecision hurt me, I didn't want to hurt her back with harsh words. Words, I would certainly regret later. So, getting my answers would have to wait another day.

✳✳✳

PHOEBE

Overjoyed Luke was finally an official part of my family; I couldn't wait for his training as the heir of my agency to kick off. At the same time, I was dead worried about how Wyatt and Teo would take Luke's truth.

Ruthless as ever, the Angel in me was advising me to treat this situation as a ground test in the event that Wyatt or Teo learns the truth about me. Be it directly from me or someone else.

Self-preservation being a significant part of Angel's personality, I understood this calculated mindset. Nonetheless, this didn't stop me from hating this insensitive part of me when it affects my kids.

Engrossed in my emotional turmoil, I failed to notice the shadow of someone slipping into my office. My brain and consciousness still locked onto the killer in me; I immediately went for the gun under my table.

Facing the intruder, I had no clue who to expect. Perhaps one of Vanderwill's men . . . Then again, Vanderwill doesn't know my real identity or where I live. Even after ten years of us playing hide and seek, the knowledge that Vanderwill still knew nothing about Phoebe Ziva Smith provided my troubled life with some peace of mind.

Realising it was only Federick freaking Archer, I let out a breath of relief, glad I didn't shoot his ass just yet. It will, after all, be a shame if I were to shoot Federick because of a misunderstanding. I'd rather shoot him fair and square right between his cold eyes.

The question now was, what in the world was Federick doing here when I specifically ordered him to go home? Besides annoying me, being an asshole and torturing me to no end, I couldn't find a better excuse as to why he would bother coming back.

Federick being the first person to ever dare space out on me and not be begging for my forgiveness or fearful of missing out on the next sunrise, I was stunned. Comparatively, no matter how much I was pissed at Federick, his arrogance or his annoying attitude, I was impressed that he managed to get himself invited by my sons; especially Wyatt.

On the other hand, I didn't much appreciate Federick's sexual teasing or any comments that brought up what had happened last night and this morning. I had no clue what type of game Federick was playing, but this new tactic of torture was without any doubt working.

Reddened and unusually heated, I felt cornered. To make matters worse, my harsh words didn't seem to flatten his smile. Instead, it further fueled him. And as much as every part of me hated to admit it, when he called me sweetheart, I didn't mind it — not one bit.

Infuriated at the latter realisation, I was left with no choice but to accept defeat to put an end to Federick's sweet torturous talks.

Glaring, I took note to add this new method of extracting information in my torture handbook for later use. Maybe against Cole Vanderwill himself. What wouldn't I give to see his despicable, murderous self squirming and accepting defeat as I was right now to a simple guy, with no knowledge of spy interrogation techniques.

A guy who despite his arrogance and jerkish manners has been surprising me since last night with his out-of-character behaviours.

For instance, when I finally gave in to his demands, I was more than confident Federick would demand something along the lines of *'I want to get into your pants'*; given his constant blunt advances these past days. I had already planned out how to forever kick him out of my house after giving him a piece of my mind. However, what I wasn't prepared for was for Federick to speak his heart while making a perfectly reasonable point.

As stupid as it was of me to be jealous of Federick for having the luxury to be so carefree, I envied his capability to open his heart to a stranger like myself, without any concern in the world. I ached to be so open. Unfortunately, unlike Federick, I didn't have the luxury of a choice. I couldn't openly express myself. Perhaps, this was one of the reasons why I have always been rude, heartless and cold towards Federick. I unconsciously envied what he exhibited.

Heedful of the hurt in Federick's voice and look; I realised I had to tone down my negative attitude towards him. It wasn't his fault he got to live a normal life. Besides, I love being a spy — I couldn't imagine my life without my agency. It was a definite part of my identity; a part I would never trade or give up for anything in the world.

With the impact of a wrecking ball, Federick's question shook my foundation. At a sudden loss, I didn't know how to respond to Frederick's dreadful question. All I knew was, I didn't want to give Federick false hope or lie to his face about something so real. Because, as much as I was denying it, I care for him, a lot more than I probably should.

Plunging myself into Federick's deep pool of greys as he searched the depth of my browns, I discovered my indecision hurt him. Sour face and tight lips, the softness and gentleness caressing his features evaporated. Being the king of granite-face, Federick masked all his emotions in a blink. His once warm grey eyes turned cold as the north pole.

Sharply staring at me with arms crossed over his chest, his body stiff as a statue, Federick straightened himself, ready to walk out. Suddenly upset, hurt and unsettled about Federick leaving in such a state and so soon, I had a gut-wrenching clarity.

The question now was; will my stubborn, proud self admit it out loud or try to turn the conversation around? Whatever my decision would be, I knew sooner or later Federick's burning questions about the mystery that was me would need answering.

If not because of his frustration about always being openly left out, then because of his parents. The latter connected both of us on so many levels; I couldn't bypass it even if I wanted to.

***

FEDERICK

"Wait!" Reaching out and placing her hand on top of my thigh, "I'm sorry, I was thinking over something important." Phoebe muttered in a soft tone.

In any other situation, I would have loved how Phoebe had tried to stop me with such a sweet yet simple action. However, I was hurt and striving not to let her inconsideration affect my already broken heart.

"So what conclusion did you reach?" Trying my best to ignore the distress flickering in her eyes, and the electric jolts coursing through my veins from her simple touch, I coldly retorted.

Relentlessly searching Phoebe's eyes to see if she felt the same electricity between us, I was yet again confronted with the invisible black curtain hiding her actual emotions.

"Well." Unable to take it any longer, I brushed her hand away from my thigh and impatiently demanded an answer.

"Stop behaving as such, will you!" Clasping my flying hand between hers, Phoebe huffed.

"As what?" A bit vexed, I sharply retorted.

"As a complete jackass, you jerk! Can't you see you're being childish." In a taut tone, Phoebe finally uttered.

"Am I really being the jerk here?" I exclaimed in disbelief. I can't believe she called me a jackass when she was the one being both childish and a jerk. I was the only one being reasonable here.

Gripping the edge of the table like my life depended on it, my knuckles turned white. "Just tell me. Do you or do you not trust me?" Allowing Phoebe to rest her hand on top of my knuckles, I pressed in a rough penetrating tone.

"I do, okay!" Phoebe loudly huffed, clearly frustrated she had to admit it openly.

"See, it wasn't that difficult." Holding onto my smile, for the time being, I calmly responded.

"Happy now!" In a tight voice, Phoebe exclaimed.

"Very." Relaxing under Phoebe's touch, I allowed myself to smile.

"Good for you." Breaking our silent stare, Phoebe affirmed.

Bringing her chair closer to me, I stretched my legs either side of her chair. Withdrawing her hand and relaxing her back on the chair, I could have cared less if our position seemed inappropriate. As long as Phoebe didn't mind sitting between my legs, I was content with our closeness.

"What do you want now?" Evidently unhappy, she had to admit the truth out loud, especially to me, Phoebe asked with a glare.

"Clarifications. I'm glad you finally admitted you trust me, but I still need my answers."

"Does this mean you don't trust me?" Folding her hands in front of her chest, Phoebe almost moodily catechised.

"Believe me when I say I would love nothing more but to completely trust you, Phoebe. But sadly, sweetheart, I can't allow myself to venture into such an important emotion until I know more about you. I can't have myself wondering each day how you are precisely connected to my life, or if what you are saying is indeed the truth."

"In other words, you don't," Phoebe stated with a gloominess behind her raised tone.

"Trust is earned, Phebes. I can't exactly magically hand it over simply because I care for you. So no; at least, not completely. You've yet to earn it." My every word filled with unusual emotion, I carefully explained.

Quickly covering the hint of sadness, maybe even regret, behind her wooden façade, my heartstring tugged for her.

"So will you for heaven sake answer some of my questions?" I pleaded.

Stunned, since I've never pleaded for anything before, it dawned on me; I was so immensely in love I was even ready to try new things. Searching my eyes for something unknown to me, Phoebe gave my request a proper thought.

"If you truly trust me, you would trust in me with some of your secrets and free me from worrying myself to death with crazy theories." Conscious Phoebe was close to caving to my insistent demand, I further pressed.

"Okay."

Brightly beaming at Phoebe, I could have kissed her for finally accepting and indulging me.

CHAPTER 19
INTERROGATION

FEDERICK

"But," Phoebe exclaimed before I could say or do anything.

"Let's be real for one minute. We both know I won't be able to answer all your questions. So, I will be avoiding them to stay true to my promise to you. Hopefully, this will prove I trust you and earn your trust in return."

"As long as you answer truthfully, without making a joke out of me and clear at least some of my confusion, I'll take any bone you throw my way." Beaming at the face of this new beginning, I was aware it would have been surreal for me to expect Phoebe to reveal everything in one day.

Refraining from giving in to my desire to do a happy dance and make a complete fool out of myself, I held onto Phoebe's hand.

"Well, are you going to get to it already? Or continue staring at me as if I just offered you a candy shop?" The depth in her eyes screaming anxiousness, Phoebe covered it with a sarcastic smirk.

"Oh, yeah . . . The questions . . . Give me a minute." Still wrapping my head around finally having my wish, I incoherently mumbled like an idiot.

Way to impress the girl you love!

"Let's get started then, shall we?" I enthusiastically uttered.

"Shoot," Phoebe responded with resignation and fake excitement.

"What's yours and your kids' real relationship with my parents?" Not giving up on the opportunity to stay close to Phoebe, I maintained my hold on her hands and started off easy.

"As you have surmised, I'm neither Alicia's nor Joseph's kid. But they took it upon themselves to be my guardian after helping me through a rough and dangerous path that could have destroyed my kids and myself." Releasing a small breath to maintain control over her emotions, Phoebe searched my eyes for proof she could trust in me with her life stories.

"I am sorry for whatever you had to go through, but I'm glad my parents were there for you." I sympathetically articulated.

"I am too, and thanks." With a small smile, grateful I was not pitying her, Phoebe responded.

"This still doesn't explain how you know each other to begin with. Especially for you to trust them to play such a significant role in your life. Plus, I've never seen you at my place until recently?" Searching my memories for a younger Phoebe at my place, I found 'Nada'.

"My dad and Joseph were best friends. In that sense, your parents knew me from birth."

"Were? Where's your dad now?" Sensing Phoebe was leaving something out; I set out to clear my evident confusion while trying to not come off as too demanding.

God only knows how Phoebe manages to answer my questions and still be evasive to the point of further confusing me.

"Remember when I said I hit a rough patch ten years ago?" Slightly nodding, I waited for Phoebe to continue on her own time.

Casting her gaze to the sidewall, "Well, my dad getting murdered because of me was a big part of it." Sadness coursing through her every word, Phoebe revealed.

Gently hooking my forefinger under her chin, I slowly turned her head back towards me. "I would love to reassure you and say everything is going to be fine, but we both know it won't be true. What I can tell you though, is once you stop blaming yourself for whatever you did or didn't do back then, things will get a bit easier for you." Letting my guard down, I showed Phoebe pure sincerity.

Slowly leaning towards Phoebe, "Then again, knowing you, you won't stop just yet. I hope you'll let me in on why you feel this way, but I understand it's too early for this question. I'll do my best to let you tell me on your own terms — however, I don't promise I'll be able to keep my words for too long."

"Fair enough." Gradually lessening the distance between our faces, "Thank you for being patient and compassionate. I appreciate you not trying to give me false hope as others have done." Phoebe breathed in a low voice.

Hot breaths gently caressing our faces, the realisation of what was about to happen hit me. Unhurriedly sitting straight back and faking a light cough, I plastered a reassuring smile on my face.

"I'm only being truthful, Phoebe." Granted I would take practically any opportunity to kiss Phoebe, right that moment didn't seem appropriate; especially after she had revealed something so close to her heart.

"The reason why you didn't see me at your parents is that I had my own place, with two kids to look after. Plus, I was absorbed in my own world — besides, back then, you were away to college. Not to mention the one year you vanished from the map." Realising what could have happened if I didn't show superhuman restraint, Phoebe swiftly changed the topic, shifting the atmosphere around us to a lighter one.

"You mean you weren't living with my parents? Because I distinctly remember my mom saying otherwise when she was scolding you." Purposely ignoring Phoebe's statement of me vanishing from the surface of the earth for a whole year, I smiled and teased her instead.

"You think you are so funny, huh." Flushed, Phoebe mused with a real and genuine smile.

"I like to think so. But don't let my fun and amazing self stop you from answering my question." Relishing this moment of being free with Phoebe, I joked.

"I lived there in the beginning, but then I had to get on with my life. I would take my kids with me around the time you would visit — and since you were gone for several years, it was easy for us never to cross paths."

"You mean you were hiding from me?" I jocularly rectified.

"One could say so, but it was mostly because my kids were on vacation too and wanted to spend time with me." Phoebe clarified, surprising me in the midst.

How could I not have noticed somebody else was living in my parents' house while I was away?

"Don't be mad at what I'm about to ask. It's only an observation I've made from what you've told me and what I've seen, but, feel free to correct me." As if walking on eggshells and the slightest high octave would crack its foundation, I cautiously enumerated.

"Go on." Phoebe encouraged.

"You are 26, yet Wyatt is 16 and Teo 15, so logic dictates you adopted them. How did this happen?"

Sucking in a deep breath, it was clear it was a sensitive subject for Phoebe. However, she had to know I would want to clarify this point.

Massaging small circles on the back of her hand, I gave Phoebe her time.

"I adopted them after a tragic accident." Phoebe finally divulged in a croaky tone.

"Both of your kids are extremely intelligent, so I figured they know they are adopted. My question, however, is, do they know who their real parents are and what happened to them?"

"My boys are indeed wise; which is why they understand we are not to discuss their blood parents. They know enough to help them continue with their lives as normal teenagers. For them, I am and always will be their only parents." Her tone rising in defensiveness, Phoebe locked gaze with me; the depth within them demanding I stop right there.

As weak as I currently was to Phoebe, I silently complied.

"Not to sound accusatory, but given the bond your sons and you share, I would have never pictured you as the mother who would leave her kids at their grandparents for days. Did they know back then that my parents were not their real grandparents?" Doing my best not to offend Phoebe, I carefully posed.

"They've always known, and as far as your statement goes, it was months, not days, but whatever." Phoebe clarified as if it was no big deal.

But the pain in her tone was more than evident. Once again, I was dumbfounded by not only Phoebe's statement but the mystery that was her.

"Despite having taken the responsibility of adopting them, I was alone, sad, angry, lost and depressed. As much as it pains me to admit it, I hated their presence, blamed them for what I had lost and was unsure if I could trust them. So, I pushed them away from me. Thankfully, Kenneth, Alicia and Joseph knocked some serious sense into me. And for this, I will forever be in their debt." Perceiving my dumbfounded expression, Phoebe recounted with a humourless snicker.

Despite empathising with Phoebe and her hurt, I was still beyond shocked to learn Phoebe, of all people, once hated her kids to the point of leaving them with my parents for God knows how long.

"You promised you wouldn't lie to me and I'm going to take your word for it. So, if I ask why you felt this way towards them, will I get an honest answer?" Weighing each word, I inquired.

Silent, Phoebe searched my eyes and thoroughly studied my face.

"Their father. This is the only answer you will get from me." Phoebe firmly pointed.

Recognising I wasn't going to get any more detail on the subject, I complied with a nod even when Damien's face popped into my head, taunting me. The last thing I wanted was to press and lose the opportunity to have my other questions answered. I will eventually get to Damien and find out how he exactly fits in the picture. The best strategy at that moment, however, was to shift gears.

"Would you mind telling me who Talon, Matt and Xylan are to you? I've already met Logan and his fiancée, so I'm not worried about him." Aiming to scratch off the other guys' names off my list, I blurted out part of my thoughts about their close friendship.

"They are my best friends. Have been for the past nine years now." Not clearly understanding the motive behind my question, but curious, Phoebe answered with a hint of cautiousness.

"Best friends you sleep with?" Not entirely believing her, but doing my best to cover the jealousy and annoyance in my voice, I briskly expressed.

"Where do you get these insane ideas from?" Phoebe questioned with bewilderment.

"Where do I? . . . Where do I, indeed . . . Let me think? . . . Oh yeah, you yourself told my mom." Sarcasm in every word, I voiced.

"Are you crazy? I told her I spent some of my night with them, not sleep with them. They are my best friends for Christ's sake!" Withdrawing her hand from mine, Phoebe exclaimed.

"You didn't deny it either when I accused you otherwise."

"Gosh! Do you want me to deny and clarify all your accusations now?" Frustrated, Phoebe demanded.

"It isn't a bad idea. It will most definitely help me a lot." Ignoring her exasperation and utter disbelief, I thoughtfully stated.

"Great. Just great." Studying my face for a hint I was fooling around, Phoebe retorted.

***

PHOEBE

Weirdly enough when Federick admitted he didn't trust me, a wave of hurt washed over me. Especially after I had accepted and voiced out my trust in him, right to his stupid face. Then again, I shouldn't have expected less. Not when I have consistently and openly lied to his face and hid things from him.

Perhaps it was the fact that I didn't like the lack of trust he had in me or the fact that he admitted to caring for me, but as I agreed to his questioning, I promised myself to answer as truthfully as possible. To stop the lying as a whole, unless it was a matter of life or death. Nonetheless, the idea of being interrogated by Federick and imagining how he would take my partial answers where necessary churred at my inside.

Reminiscing about the past ten years; about what I have done, about what has been done to me or about the people gone from my life, was hard. Thankfully, I managed to keep my emotions intact — to keep Pandora's box chained.

I was expecting to regret my decision of saying yes to Federick, but that asshole was basically a gentleman. He knew when not to push too hard, and his *'Know-it-all'* attitude was non-existent. But most importantly, he didn't show pity or judge me after I revealed some of my defects.

If I were in his place, I would have heavily judged myself. Particularly after learning, I had taken the responsibility of two young kids, whom I call my own, and left them with two perfect strangers — which Alicia and Joseph were to them at first. I didn't comprehend why Federick was so patient, loving, compassionate, supportive and truthful, but I appreciated every bit of it.

Despite Federick's overbearing crazy self, I had to admit; I was enjoying this 'Q&A'. Granted, some questions were frustrating, troublesome and borderline crazy, but with the two of us in the picture, I wouldn't expect any less. I simply hope this little game of ours doesn't cause some serious damage, because at the end of the day, I couldn't, or better yet, wouldn't allow Federick to learn about my spy life — about the dangerous and dark side of me.

***

FEDERICK

"Do you have any more questions?" Her patience tested and slightly irked, Phoebe demanded.

"No need to be upset with me. I'm only looking for a better understanding between us. Don't you get it! The more I know about you, the better it will be." I patiently explained.

"I would beg to differ." Phoebe tenaciously declared.

"Very well, then. Answer this next question."

"Which will be?" Itching for an argument to avoid further questioning, Phoebe brusquely cut in. Unfortunately, for Phoebe, I was onto her little trick.

"You mentioned your dad owns two successful businesses, as in the present tense. So why are you working for me, instead of continuing what your father had started?"

"Are you implying you don't want me working for you anymore?" Trying to push my button, Phoebe humouredly posed.

"What I'm implying is, why in the world do you not control your business? And as far as your question goes, you and I fully know nobody can do as splendid of a job as you. You are practically irreplaceable, and I would be an utter nutcase to ever let such a precious piece of diamond as yourself slip through my fingers."

Not taking the bait, I genuinely praised Phoebe. Being her cute self, Phoebe instantly burned up. Her hair falling like a dark curtain in front of her face, she attempted to cover her noticeable blush.

"No need to be shy about it. It's the truth. Not only are you tempting, confident, sexy as hell, but you also have incredible brainpower. Losing you would be a disaster for me and the company." Gently pushing Phoebe's hair back, I tucked it behind her ear. Flushed and tomato red, Phoebe was a mesmerising sight for sore eyes.

"Thanks, but this still doesn't mean I will answer your every question." Attempting to hide how much my compliment affected her, Phoebe essayed to be as toneless as possible.

"You are welcome. But I had no ulterior motive behind my compliment. It's sincerely how I feel and think of you. Nonetheless, will you please answer my previous question?" Surprisingly patient and not offended she thought my compliment was a form of manipulation, I softly stated.

"I'm still carrying on my father's legacy. But after what happened ten years ago, I needed some time off."

"And ten years is not enough time off." I quipped with humour.

"It really feels like you want me out of your company." Phoebe jested.

It was surprising how we will go back and forth from sensual, uncomfortableness, upset, happy, joking and easygoing. This unique flow of emotions in a matter of minutes was what I call a **Phoebe-branded** experience.

"Not one bit. If I could, I would steal you from your own company and keep you for myself." Collecting my racing thoughts, I responded with a winning smile.

"Oh, you already have."

"Uh?" Confused by Phoebe's statement, I blankly stared at her.

"Let me reiterate." Breathing in, her smile took a dive.

"When my father died, all of his businesses got passed down to me. However, back then, I was weak, and I compromised both the companies with my harsh, rash and impulsive decisions. Particularly within the first year of the incident."

Sucking in my desire to cut in; to tell Phoebe she was not weak, but instead strong for taking a step forward, I let her continue.

"Having had enough of my self-pitying and erratic behaviours, specifically towards my sons — Joseph, Alicia and Kenneth —intervened and gave me some much-needed advice. Even though, back then, it practically felt like forced advice. According to them, I had to take a few months off to rethink my actions and what I would do for my family's future. Only then could I come back and choose to concentrate mostly on one business until I was ready to manage both."

"I gather you took their advice?" I chimed in after a few beats of silence.

"I didn't have much choice. Plus, I quickly recognised I was a complete mess. So I agreed on the condition that I won't be forced into therapy." Phoebe concluded.

"Therapy, huh . . ." I repeated as a reflection.

"Yep, do you believe them! A shrink and I in the same room were so not happening." Phoebe recounted with disbelief.

"I couldn't even begin to imagine such a horror." Hiding my smile, and imagining Phoebe laying on a couch all pissed off at being compelled to divulge her deepest darkest secret, I faked an outrageous tone.

"Yeah, I can discern the *'Not imaging it'* look on your face." Phoebe sarcastically quipped.

"Thank God you chose to rebond with your sons; otherwise, they would be lost." I truthfully confessed; earning myself a genuine smile from Phoebe.

Pondering over it, I too, like many other males, desired Phoebe from the moment I laid eyes on her. However, witnessing her motherly side and the genuine love between her kids and herself was what made me fall head over heels for her.

"Best decision of my life." Phoebe voiced out more to herself than to me, and I couldn't agree more.

Disentangling Phoebe from the ties of her memories, "What happened to your businesses in the meantime?"

"Well, after much research for one of the companies, we employed a long-time associate as acting-CEO for whenever I am away. As far as the other company is concerned, I didn't have much to worry about."

"And why is that?" I briskly cut in, my interest to its highest peak.

"The second company is co-owned. My dad and his partner constructed it together; as such, I left it to the other owner to take care of the company." Phoebe divulged as a matter-of-fact.

"So if I'm getting this straight, you are currently controlling one of your businesses on a part-time basis and given this *'co-owner'* full control over your other business." I reiterated with disbelief.

"Pretty much," Phoebe responded as if it was no big deal.

"Wow! I don't want to come off as rude, Phebes, but this is downright stupid. Please tell me you at least check on this co-owner's work or that you are a hundred per cent sure you are still a part of this aforementioned company."

"Calm your horses, will you." Phoebe mused with a small laugh.

"You do realise that we, businessmen, are devious, greedy, competitive and ruthless. I thought I taught you better." I lectured with utter seriousness.

How could she be so at ease? For all we know, that co-owner has already stolen her company right from under her nose, and she wouldn't discover it until it's too late.

"You did teach me plenty. However, I recently realised I trust him. Yes, he is young, a playboy, a jerk, cold and ruthless, but he would never play such a dirty trick on me. Besides, every now and then, I check on him and his work." Phoebe declared with confidence.

"I really wonder about you sometimes. And I hope for your own sake that you are right. But you should check on this guy's work more often. . . I don't want you to go bankrupt now, do I." Praying Phoebe was right, I added with a hint of seriousness and jest.

"It's funny how you seem more worried about my companies than I do."

"Well, someone gotta be the bigger and more responsible person. Especially when you are so laid back about something so crucial."

It may seem like I was overreacting, but being one of the most ruthless tycoons in the country, I knew the business world and its dirty tricks from the inside-out.

"Bigger and more responsible person, huh?" With humour glistening in her beautiful brown eyes, Phoebe repeated with a chuckle.

"I'm not kidding, Phoebe. Business is serious. It's not all sunshine and rainbows."

"I know. I work for the most ruthless, cold, impatient and jerkish business tycoon in the entire States, remember." She joked.

"Thank you for all the praises." I mocked. "I just don't know how to take it."

Tittering at my sarcasm, "Don't worry, Federick. I trust this guy. I'm confident beneath all the bullshit he shows everyone; there lies a nice person." Phoebe extolled with reassurance.

"Should I be jealous of this guy?" I suspiciously inquired.

Confused by my question, "Why would you need to be jealous?"

"You seem a bit infatuated with this guy. Maybe you like him." I pointed out a possibility that didn't sit well with me.

"Yuck, no! He is too much of a prick for me to like him in this way."

Not entirely convinced, mainly because of the discomfort behind Phoebe's eyes, "If you say so . . . Yet, this doesn't mean you shouldn't occasionally check on his work."

"I will. Happy now."

"Very. Maybe you could even start taking full control of all your companies."

No clue why I was feeling possessive and protective of Phoebe's companies when I didn't even know a single thing about them, I blamed it on my love for her. At the same time, I knew I had to try connecting with her business.

"It would mean I would have to stop working as your PA . . ." Letting her sentence hang, Phoebe jested.

Yet, I didn't find it one bit funny.

"We will have to reconsider our options, then." Pensively stroking my chin, I thoughtfully announced.

"Indeed, we do. I enjoy working as your PA way too much, anyway." Phoebe enthusiastically answered, compelling me to smile back.

"Speaking about you being my PA, you could have a higher position, or better, own a share. So why are you stuck to the title and pay of my executive personal assistant?" I curiously asked. Surely enjoying working as my PA with all the daily arguments and pressure isn't all fun.

"If I desired a higher title, Federick, I would have simply taken official control over both of my companies, don't you think so? Besides, as unbelievable as it sounds, I go through all your bullshit not just because being your PA is sometimes fun, but also because it's less stressful and demanding." Phoebe spelt out her unbelievable logic.

"I don't understand. Working for me means you have three different jobs. How is it less stressful?"

"Because unlike you, I only supervise the heads of my companies; which means, I don't have as much paperwork as you waiting for me at the end of the month." Cocking a perfectly shaped brow, Phoebe pointed out.

"Well, at least I have your help. Sometimes, it seems you are mostly supervising my work than actually working under me. And weirdly enough, on most occasions, we behave as business partners; especially with all those arguments." I blurb out.

Taking note of Phoebe slightly shifting her gaze towards the wall behind me, everything that came out of my mouth fully registered.

"What are your businesses about again?" Hoping and praying what went through my brain was wrong, I suspiciously demanded.

I one hundred per cent knew I was the sole heir and owner of Archer & Associate. However, after quickly re-examining everything that escaped both of our lips and her personal connection with my parents, the doubts were starting to set in.

CHAPTER 20
UNNERVING Q&A

FEDERICK

Up to her old trick again, Phoebe avoided looking directly at me, "Why?" She hesitantly asked.

And here I thought we were finally reaching an understanding, I internally mocked with sarcasm.

"I'm curious, and you promised to answer my questions. And this time, do try to look me in the eyes instead of fixing my nose." I clarified, letting Phoebe know I was onto her infamous trick.

"I also specified I would only answer those I can and avoid the ones I can't." Returning her fierce gaze onto my calm ones, Phoebe professed.

"It's a simple question, Phoebe — unless it somehow has something to do with my company." I declared with suspicion.

"Pssh! It has nothing to do with your company." Phoebe dismissively purported.

"Answering shouldn't be a problem then." I firmly stated.

"It's about finance." Huffing an annoyed air, Phoebe ultimately gave in.

"Both of them are?" Not entirely believing Phoebe's word despite her promise to not lie to me, I pressed.

"More or less," Phoebe commented.

And people say I speak in short sentences. They should definitely meet Phoebe Smith.

Straightening my back and folding my arms over my chest, "Is this your form of a proper answer?" I inquired with a raised brow.

Dismissing the flicker of hunger in Phoebe's lingering gaze as she followed my every movement, I concentrated on our situation and my scepticism.

Slowly raising her eyes from my chest to my lips, Phoebe showed more self-control than me. "Yes. I can't tell you more than I already have. This is the easiest and sincerest answer." Gulping and holding my gaze, she voiced.

"Is it like classified or something?" I jocularly added to ease the tension. Then again, it died the moment recognition flashed into her eyes.

Taking into account Phoebe's timid and unsure smile, "You're kidding me, right!" Perplexed, I demanded.

"What? I didn't say anything." She defensively exclaimed.

"Yes, but your eyes tend to speak volume, and right now it ain't making any sense whatsoever." I pointed out in a matter-of-fact-tone.

"Well, maybe you misread it. You wouldn't be the first one." Phoebe retorted with withstand.

"And you are comparing me to somebody else again. You do realise I'm my own person, with my own personality, right? Besides, stop trying to change the subject." I firmly and harshly snapped.

"Can we drop it, please? You promise you wouldn't push if I answer your question to the best of my ability. And I'm doing exactly that."

"Fine. But remember, I will be expecting some more clarifying answers soon." Taking a few deep relaxing breaths, I complied for the time being.

"Sure."

I was aware Phoebe didn't really mean it, but sadly for her, I will eventually get the whole truth. I only have to be further patient and earn more of her trust.

"So . . . You, Matt, Xylan and Talon are definitely not sleeping together?" I returned to one of my previous questions, which was evasively answered.

"For Christ's sake, Federick! I told you already. We are not." Propelling off her seat, Phoebe incredulously screeched.

"Come on, sit down. I just wanted to be sure."

Holding onto her arms, I directed Phoebe back towards me. Huffing an air of exasperation and locking a resigned gaze, Phoebe allowed herself to be dragged back onto the chair.

"Are you satisfied now?" Glaring with impatience, Phoebe spoke out.

Further unnerving Phoebe with my bright smile, "Very."

Pausing and pulling my serious face, "Do you, however, intend to have sexual relations with Damien Ambrosh?"

"Are you serious right now!" Disbelieving my query, Phoebe exclaimed with force and brusquely stood.

"I am extremely serious." Gently laying both hands on her shoulder blades and gingerly pushing her back down on the chair, I responded with calm and earnestness.

"Obviously I'm not!" She irked out a bit louder than necessary.

"I am happy to hear this." Doing my best to keep a blank face when all I wanted to do was smile, I studiously searched Phoebe's eyes for any sign of deceptiveness.

"What's with you putting all my best friends and myself in the same sentence as sex? — Better yet, where did your sudden interest in my sex life surge from?" Stumped and searching my gaze for an explanation, Phoebe demanded.

"I'm curious . . . and largely because all your best friends seem to be men who sleep in the same bed as you, and you seem single." I clarified with a gentle delicacy I never found useful until today.

"You are impossible. Friends of opposite gender sleeping on the same bed don't necessarily mean sex is on the table." Her eyes full of humour, Phoebe stated as a matter-of-fact.

Completely forgetting my other questions; even my witty comment about how people or friends of opposite sex sleeping on the same bed most definitely means sex in the ordinary world, "You are single, right?" I abruptly asked.

"Very much like you." Slightly shaking her head, Phoebe confirmed.

Unsure if I should be happy about this response or worried, given my status as a major player who sleeps around, I was almost tempted to demand she shares more details.

"I don't understand why, all of a sudden, you are so interested in my non-existent romantic life. But as the words themselves state, I have none. So will you please move to another subject?" Phoebe expressed with amusement.

"I'm pleased my distress is the reason for your amusement." I sarcastically mocked.

"Why on earth will you be distressed? My *'Romantic life'* is mine, not yours." Phoebe jested.

"How can someone so intelligent be so clueless, it boggles me." I spelt out to only earn a confused **"Huh"** from Phoebe.

Taking note of my lingering eyes on her full lips that I had the pleasure of tasting last night and this morning, Phoebe let out an **"Oh"** as the meaning behind my words and actions fully registered in her thick brain.

"It appears you finally discerned the reason behind my curiosity towards your *Romantic life*," I exclaimed with effect.

"I did, which is why I'm going to tell you again . . . These moments that have been occurring between us are not going to repeat itself. So please, stop. You will only end up hurting yourself." Weighing each word coming out of her sweet mouth, it appeared Phoebe didn't want to come off as too rude. Still, it hurt to hear her say it out loud.

"We'll talk about this particular matter later on." I tried postponing the inevitable conversation, which would potentially cause me heartache.

"I don't want you getting hurt because of me, Federick. Try to understand and consider this for future reference." Gently squeezing the back of my hand, Phoebe firmly stated.

***

PHOEBE

The query about my businesses was a given. What I wasn't expecting, however, was Federick showing he cared and revealing how much I was worth to him.

Sensing a tug and a weird churning inside my chest, I realised I had to keep Federick at arm's length. My rude comments, however, didn't seem to faze him any longer.

Why in God's name did I have to let information about my companies slip my gigantic mouth?

Despite my better judgement, I recounted and shared details of my personal life, and some aspects of my businesses. In all reality, I could have told Federick the mere minimum and be done with him. But no . . . I had to open my big mouth and divulge more than necessary. Then again, as much as I wanted to deny it and maintain my wall high-up, I had to admit; opening up to Federick was relieving.

I appreciated his restraint, his concern and kind words towards my situations and kids. At the same time, I was getting a real kick out of his distress for my businesses. Particularly the one that was co-owned. Notwithstanding, I found Federick's theory about me being infatuated with the co-owner purely absurd. Even with our little recent history, I was sure I didn't like the guy as such. It just couldn't be.

What I feared would happen, came knocking down my door with fervour. Our fun discussion had turned dangerous and having given my words to Federick; I couldn't lie — not if I wanted to gain his unwithering trust.

Albeit Federick was joking at first, I instantly discerned the look of recognition flashing in his eyes. The room engulfed in suspicion and awkwardness; I concluded it would be wise to give Federick the half-truth. After all, this was what Joseph wanted — to bring his son in some of the truth.

As a matter of fact, my agency is known to the public eyes as a high-profile-only finance company. A change my father would not be fond of if he was still alive. Alas for my father's value, the anonymity of my agency was crucial to me. Hiding my agency in plain sight when I gained full access over my agency, I increased both its popularity and standing amidst the companies and people that matter whilst ensuring my agents and my agency is protected. Unknown and unidentifiable to the world.

As the saying goes, change is vital for evolution and success.

Nowadays, I'm in collaboration with all of the law enforcement; with them unofficially working under my agency, and side by side with the Department of Defense. As many have realised while running for their lives, we are everywhere.

In all reality, being grilled by the non-agent, Mr Federick Ashton Archer, I could have sworn he was one of us — probably as my competitor or my best interrogation expert. Not only was Federick able to rip answers out of me, the **Great Phoebe Smith**, aka, **Angel**, when Cole Vanderwill himself could not, but Federick's theories were also surprisingly close to reality, if not to the point.

It was worrying how Federick was successfully reading me or my lies. Yet, what I found further disturbing was his ability to utterly distract me with the mere flexing of his arms under his tight-fit shirt. Knocking some sense into my clouded mind so I would cease my stupid gawking of Federick, like the rest of the women population who throw themselves at his feet, does, I regain some control over this strange sensation inside me.

I should have done a better job at hiding the look of recognition on my face when Federick questioned the link between my company and Archer & Associates. Still, I was so taken by utter surprise; my poker face pulled a vanishing trick on me. Baiting Federick by pushing his buttons as a solution to divert his attention so he would change the subject, alas, showed no success. The jerkface had learned my technique to avoid conversation and manufactured a way to counteract it. Resorting to my last solution, I dug into my pool of politeness and straightforwardly asked Federick to back off. Gratefully Federick agreed. Then again, from the expression on his face, it was clear his agreement was only temporary, and he would continue to persist until he got all his answers.

Unbelievably enough, Federick returned to his early absurdity of me sleeping with my best friends, despite my already denying it. As exasperated as I was with his foolish questioning, the most stupid and ludicrous one so far was his query about Damien Ambrosh and me being in a sexual relationship.

Irked at Federick's seriousness about his line of questioning, I couldn't believe this was how he chose to approach the subject of Damien. I knew one way or the other, it was going to happen, but this. . . He had intentionally put Damien and me in the same context as romance just so he could observe my reaction and form an opinion to serve his own unknown, and most probably selfish purpose.

Unable to comprehend why Federick was so adamant about learning more about my personal life or better yet, my *'Romantic life'*, I searched his unusually warm eyes for an explanation. Alas, I was left pondering.

Following the slow trail of Federick's eyes, it finally clicked in my thick brain. For one second, one beat only, I was petrified — for him and myself. The thought of what would happen to Federick and me after I break his heart by rejecting his undeniable attraction to me, chilling my blood.

Why? — I couldn't begin to understand, and I wasn't sure I was going to find out any time soon. What I was sure of, however, was that Federick had to stop feeling this way towards me. It was not only dangerous but also unhealthy and forbidden — this morning itself proved it.

Weighing my words carefully, I attempted to explain the situation to Federick, to convince him he had to stop whatever he thought he felt for me.

Then again, despite the slight flicker of hurt in the depth of Federick's eyes, I recognised my little speech wasn't much of a success. His answer and change of subject proved the latter. And as much as I wanted to make sure he understood my point, I welcomed the change of subject with a smile — up until it started bothering me again.

It was clear this day had just gotten started, especially with the *'Hidden'* look of determination inside Federick's eyes when he had stepped foot inside this office. Even though patience wasn't one of my strong suits, I convinced myself to make an effort and go out of my way to be patient with Federick — especially after having broken his heart.

CHAPTER 21
TWENTY QUESTIONS GAME

FEDERICK

"You won't hurt me, Phoebe. Trust me." Not taking Phoebe's words lightly, I truthfully exclaimed.

"I do trust you, it's me whom I don't trust," Phoebe uttered with a hint of sadness.

Curling a finger under Phoebe's chin and directing her conflicted gaze towards the warmth of my grey pool, "Don't say this about yourself."

"Believe me, I somehow always end up hurting those who are close to me, especially those I care about." Phoebe pressed as if this was a fact that I had no choice but to accept.

Dismissing the inkling that her words had a double meaning, I weaponised myself with humour to bring Phoebe back to me. "You mean, I'm close to you, and you care for me. This is so sweet." I teased with a mischievous smirk.

"You are so full of yourself. I wonder how you even walk through the door without bursting your head open." Breaking into a small chuckle, Phoebe jokingly retorted.

"Don't worry about my beautiful and awesome head, sweetheart." Lightening the atmosphere, I joked back.

"Are we anywhere done with your twenty questions game?" Gently swapping my hand away from her face, Phoebe inquired with a never-dropping smile.

"Sorry, sweetheart, I'm nowhere done with you. Do indulge me some more." Acting as if her brushing off my touch didn't bother me, I stated in a happy tone.

"Come on, Federick. Did you come here with a list of questions? Because if it's the case, just hand it to me. I will answer the ones I can, scratch the ones I can't, and we'll be out of here in less than twenty minutes." Phoebe conveyed with those puppy dog eyes that tugged at my heartstrings.

"There's a list, alright; it's all in my head." I professed with a straight face.

Disbelief washing over Phoebe, "Really, Federick! Are you putting me under investigation?"

"Even if I were, you wouldn't know." Killing my joke with a shrug and a *'Don't be so sure'* expression, I had to backtrack for a beat.

"Don't tell me you've been under investigation before?" I muttered with scepticism.

"I'm not saying anything else, detective. I will be lawyer-ing up now." Phoebe mused, clearly attempting to divert my attention from the actual craziness at hand.

"Why is it that every time I jokingly pitch a crazy and surreal scenario, it turns out you might actually be part of such circumstances?" Not ready to drop the subject yet, I suspiciously inquired.

"It's all in your messed-up head, Federick, how will I know?" Insulting my brain, yet again, Phoebe acted as if I didn't just suggest something that's seen as crazy and unreal in the actual world.

Why do I even love this woman?

"Thank you for taking a few seconds of your precious time to insult me. I feel special already." I articulated with sarcasm.

"Why you are more than welcome."

As much as I loved easygoing and playful Phoebe, I also realised I would never get to my other questions if we kept at it. Time was flying by too fast.

Internally sorting through my list to remove the unsafe questions, I accidentally voiced out my uncertainty about what I should ask next. Phoebe being her usual sassy self just had to chime in. After all, how could she resist an opportunity to insult me?

"How will I know? I'm not inside your brain." Her infamous *'duh'* look plastered on her face, Phoebe stated in her matter-of-fact tone. Little did she know, she had just dung her own grave.

"You wish you were, though." Completely ignoring her sarcasm, I shoved Phoebe inside her self-made grave.

"Ha, only in your dream!" Phoebe retorted with a slight tint.

Gingerly trailing the back of my finger on her cheek, "This reddish-pink tint on your soft cheeks tells me a different story."

Blushing harder, "F . . . you." Smacking my hand away, Phoebe riposted.

Laughing at Phoebe's childish yet insanely cute reaction, she was six feet deep.

"Such an unladylike word from such a lady." I playfully chastised.

"Will you just shut it?" Phoebe flung back with a pout, immediately melting my hardened heart.

"How will I ask more questions then?" I mused in a sweet voice.

"Yet, asking questions isn't what you've been doing for the past ten minutes." Phoebe clarified with a hint of smugness.

"Point taken. Tell me how you know your kids' passwords then? And why do they have so many bodyguards around them? Because even I don't need as much." Figuring if I get an answer for this one, I won't need to ask what my mom meant when she let it slip that Phoebe might be in danger, I posed in a serious tone.

"Well, you don't own and manage two crucially important businesses now, do you?" Phoebe sarcastically countered.

"You are doing it again. Before you ask what, rethink what came out of your sweet little mouth." Masking my emotion, I exclaimed with a straight face.

Voicing an *"Oh"* and a *"Sorry"* after reconsidering what she had said, I was glad Phoebe was acknowledging her mistake and not blaming me for something I didn't do. This indeed was progress.

"Good. Now spill." I spoke in a clear tone.

"I'm a concerned mother, plain and simple. And unlike you, my sons are the heirs of two million-dollar companies — companies which may make their life dangerous and difficult if precautions are not taken." Weighing each word, Phoebe explained with renewed patience.

"Now you've risen my curiosity about your businesses to a new level. Surely finance businesses aren't so dangerous." Perplexed by her statement, I posed.

"Then kill that curiosity, it will only endanger you . . . I'm extremely serious about this, Federick." Taking hold of my hands, Phoebe strongly emphasised.

"Unlike the common notion, many might have, finance companies like mine are highly targeted. And before you ask why, it's because of our high profile clientèle." Lightly squeezing my hands and searching my eyes to see if I would comply, Phoebe explained.

"From the looks of it, this is the only answer I'm getting, aren't I?" Studiously observing Phoebe, I questioned.

"Yes," Phoebe concluded in a flat tone.

"Okay. I will change the topic once more. But Phebes, I will need more answers soon."

"You are feeling quite strongly about that, aren't you?" Phoebe voiced after a lapse of silence.

Nodding, "See, we are already getting to know each other better." Wiping away my serious face, I avered with an amused look.

"If you say so," Phoebe added with a genuine smile.

"How did your kids get those cool ringtone? Striving to relax Phoebe further, I inquired.

"It's a funny story, actually. But you would have a hard time believing me."

"I'm all ears." Absorbing Phoebe's contagious smile, I smiled back at her.

"Remember when I took some personal time off two months ago . . . Well, I flew to Italy to search for a very well known software engineer the boys heard from some friends. The next day, I barged into his place of work and paid him to come to the State to configure the boys' phone ringtones with their own words and music. Crazy, isn't it?" Phoebe chuckled after recounting this far-fetched story.

"You're pulling my legs, aren't you?" I exclaimed beyond belief.

"I told you, you wouldn't believe me. But it's the truth." She affirmed with the same smile.

"It's confirmed; you are crazy. Who goes off to another country, pays some guy to travel all the way to New York City just for a ringtone?"

"A cool ringtone, though." Phoebe mused.

"Woman, you make me wonder sometimes."

"What! It's not like I couldn't afford it. Plus, the boys can be pretty convincing when they desperately want something. It was a simple and innocent request." Phoebe clarified as if it was no big deal.

"Well, since Luke broke his phone, you will have to go back." Aiming to damper her smile because this was pure craziness, I pointed out this morning's incident.

"Oh, it's nothing. I convinced the man to sell me his program so that I could use it anytime I wanted, and not have to make the same trip each time Luke or Wyatt break their phones. Believe me; it's not the first, nor the last time these two have broken their phones."

Further surprised, "How exactly did you get the guy to agree to your every term?" Suspicious and hoping Phoebe didn't sleep with him as a way to convince him, I dug.

"I have an inkling of what you're thinking, and before your imagination gets the best of you, let me inform you that I didn't do such a thing. I should be mad at you for even thinking so little of me, but as you've mentioned, you don't entirely trust me yet, as such, I can't expect much from you. Still, I would appreciate it if you would stop thinking so low of me. I respect myself too much to use sex as a weapon on innocent men to get what I want." A bit vexed, Phoebe cleared.

Acknowledging my jealousy had taken over me, I realised this time; I was at fault.

"I'm sorry. I don't know what I was thinking or what went through me. As you mentioned, I have a messed-up head." Ashamed for thinking such a disgusting thing about Phoebe, I apologised and cracked a joke.

"A very messed-up head," Phoebe added with a smile.

"To answer your question, it's not only you who know how to charm people." After a few beats, Phoebe playfully disclosed.

"Does this mean I have charmed you?" I flirtatiously posed.

"I didn't say anything about me. I said 'People'. Plus I was implying I charmed the guy into accepting my terms." Phoebe divulged with another smile.

"You mean lead on." Chuckling, I jested.

"Pretty much."

"And you are proud of it." Smiling, I couldn't wait until Phoebe tried to use her charm on me.

"Of course! But what's important is that I got what I wanted."

"What Phoebe wants, Phoebe gets. Right." I playfully quoted the same phrase she used to mock and insult me with during my first year in my company.

"You still remember this." Recognition flashing in her eyes, Phoebe posed with bewilderment.

"It's hard to forget anything which has to do with you, Phoebe. Especially when it involves our first big argument." I reminisced with a grin.

"Yep, I remember that day. You made me so mad. I was seconds away from punching your cocky face so hard it would have been difficult to recognise you."

"Thank God, you restrained yourself. Otherwise, God knows what would have happened to my gorgeously charming and sexy heartthrob face." Returning her smile, I mused.

Being her cute childish self, Phoebe stuck her tongue out at me in response.

"Why did we argue again?" I posed, not remembering the exact topic behind our argument given arguing is what we do almost every day at work.

"You thought I was a controlling, conniving, mannerless bitch." Phoebe replied with a constant smile.

"No, really." I tried again, not believing her.

"Hey, I'm only quoting what you called me after I successfully convinced the board members to reject your idea for 'Development'. If we had gone through with your plan, we would have lost some of our old but crucial clients and investors." Phoebe clarified with a smug look.

"Don't blame me. It was the first time my plans were put into questions by my executive PA — that too in front of my whole board. How do you think it made me feel?" I asked, remembering what had happened. Now that we are talking about it, it sounds funny, but back then I would have begged to differ.

"Well, it was a dumb idea, and I just couldn't agree with you after I had already sacrificed so much for the company."

"Sacrificed so much, huh! Care to elaborate?"

"Time and brain." Phoebe quickly explained.

Taking a calming breath to kill the suspicion that arose from Phoebe's answer, I concentrated on my next question.

"Phoebe, I realise you're going to be infuriated and probably hate me for asking this, but it's important you give me an honest answer . . . Although, I also recognise you are probably going to be evasive about it."

Baring herself for whatever was coming her way, "Okay, shoot." Phoebe prepared herself for a possible explosion.

"Is Damien your sons' father? I've speculated he is, based on your words and behaviours, but I need to hear it from you. And if he is . . . Are you going back with him?"

Baring my soul, my heart and myself for the harsh truth I knew was going to slap me in the face, I carefully questioned. Fixating my gaze onto Phoebe and waiting for her answer, I watched her breath hitch; which didn't one-bit help calm my already overworked nerves.

"Look Federick, I truly appreciate you being patient, but trust me, you don't want the real answer. Plus, I've gathered you are trying to construct a healthy, truthful and real relationship with all three of my sons, and the complete truth might ruin this budding relationship." Phoebe spelt out with a distressed look.

"This still doesn't answer my question, Phebes." My eyes pleaded to please give me an answer because it was crucial for me — for us.

I wanted to shout, to tell Phoebe I needed to know she wouldn't get back with that asshole. Alas, all of it was stuck at the back of my suddenly dry throat. The only thing I could do was internally yell at myself and gawk at Phoebe like she was the sacred water denied to my parched self.

"All I can tell you is to continue trying to develop a relationship with my sons." Phoebe formulated each word carefully as if there was an underlying meaning behind them.

Letting Phoebe's words sink in while studying her with puzzlement, I was left stranded amid her cryptic phrase and its possible double-meaning. Deciphering and decoding her intriguingly complex sentence was out of my hands. I desperately wanted to shout; to demand a clear answer. Alas, all I managed to accomplish was intently stare and sit with my mouth agape like a puff-fish. Thankfully, Phoebe's phone rang and jolted me back to reality.

Hesitatingly breaking eye contact with me and picking up, "Hey Tal, I'll call you back in a few. I'm currently occupied with . . . something important." Phoebe announced in an almost low tone.

"Everything is fine, don't worry." She concluded before hanging up.

Even though I was internally grinning, and content Phoebe chose me and our conversation over Talon, I maintained my natural stoned-face. A stony face I've perfected to warn people to not mess with me.

"You're not going to explain yourself anymore, are you?" I propounded after a beat.

Searching my face with a cautious gaze, trying to figure out my emotions, Phoebe crashed against the protective layer that expertly hid my real feelings — just as her walls of protection that keep me at arm's length. However, what Phoebe hasn't realised yet, was that her eyes were windows — windows to her soul. One that was unfortunately often fogged up, preventing him from clearly reading her.

"I'm genuinely sorry, but I can't. Still, if you take the time and ponder over what I told you with a clear, fresh and open mind, you might find your answers in my statement."

Unsure of my real emotions about the matter at hand, or of my upcoming reaction, Phoebe carefully breathed out. I was mad for sure, then again, I had expected her to shut me down at some point. Heck, I'm surprised we even made it this far.

"Okay," I replied in a flat tone.

"Okay?" Baffled with my simple one-word answer, Phoebe posed with precariousness.

"Yes, okay. I'm not stupid, Phoebe. I know you will shut me down if I push too much." I concluded without any emotions.

If Phoebe wasn't going to provide me with a straight answer, I might as well show my displeasure towards her actions — or in my case, her inaction.

"This is quite intelligent of you."

Cocking an eyebrow at Phoebe's attempt to crack a joke, I was taken by her audacity to huff an air of annoyance at me when it was mainly her fault I was acting this way. If she had simply answered my question in proper English, I wouldn't be behaving as such.

Not a friend of the awkward silence weighing on us, "Was it Talon who called?" I asked the obvious as a way to make small talk.

Nodding in response, "I don't know what Talon wanted. I ended his call to answer your unending questions." Phoebe swiftly declared, bringing a small smile on my face despite my attempt to hide it.

"We are reaching an understanding already." I bemusingly stated.

"It was obvious, given your curious side and suspicious eyes." Phoebe pointed out with an amused grin.

It looks like I have to do a better job of keeping my emotions in check. I certainly wasn't aware I had suspicious eyes while inquiring about Talon.

"Good observation. Your next question; what did you mean when you asked Luke to reveal his real age to Wyatt and Teo." I blurb out in a serious tone to only have Phoebe's eyes bulged out of its socket.

If this were another situation, I would have definitely laughed my ass off. However, at that moment, I needed to retain myself, be severe and cold

CHAPTER 22
PEEKABOO - IT'S ANGEL

FEDERICK

"**H**ow? Wh . . .a . . .t?" Dumbfounded and in shock, Phoebe incoherently stammered.

"I overheard Luke and you talking on my way here." I passively replied as if it were no big deal. Yet, from her facial expression, it appeared to be a huge deal.

"How much did you hear?" With distress behind her voice and eyes, Phoebe tried asking in a calm voice.

"Calm down, will you," I uttered in a relaxed tone.

"Answer my question." Phoebe pressed in a superior alpha tone interlaced in an authoritatively commanding intonation that surpassed her usual bossy, domineering, challenging and imperious attitude. As outrageous as it sounded, this different side and tone of hers flat out turned me on.

"You know, I explicitly asked you to calm down, not the other way around." I taunted in hope to hear this assertive tone of hers again.

However, Phoebe seemed to have realised her change in demeanour and tone. Inhaling and exhaling small breaths, "Will you simply answer me?" She asked again, her eyes pleading for me to comply.

"All I heard was you telling Luke he should reveal his real age and explain the bodyguard thing to his brothers." I sincerely divulged.

I realised I could have further teased Phoebe, or even lied about what I had *'Heard'* to amass more information. But those cute innocent pleading puppy eyes of hers got me big time. I swear those eyes could literally make me do things I would otherwise not do. A part of me immediately wanted to remedy this weakness, while the other part of me couldn't give a flying rats' ass.

"Thank God." Phoebe lowly muttered in relief.

Puzzled and aware I wasn't supposed to hear her, I didn't let anything show on my face. However, my curiosity was very well alive and kicking.

"So, are you going to answer me or push back again?" I sharply inquired, bringing Phoebe back to reality.

"Look, I'm not purposely ignoring you or denying you an answer. But I just have to sometimes."

Staring at Phoebe as if her explanation didn't matter to me, I was cold, like my usual self at work. And as much as I wanted to be warm, I had to be tough to get a response out of her stubborn rear.

"Fine! Luke is 20, approaching 21. I met him about a year ago. Two weeks after he befriended my sons. As the overprotective mother that I am, I made it my job to research Luke's background. There were mostly satisfactory results, but what caught my attention was that he was a professional street fighter."

"Well, this explains his posture and structure." I interrupted without meaning to.

"Huh?" Phoebe voiced in confusion.

"He has the body of a fighter. Acts and stands as one too. But hey, don't let me stop you. Go on."

Nodding in understanding, "Since I don't want Wyatt and Teo to have anything to do with fighting or violence, I was determined to end their new friendship. My research indicating there was only one legit street fighting club in the area Wyatt and Teo frequent, I asked around to find out which night Luke was fighting. However, while I was discreetly looking for Luke, he personally introduced himself to me. No idea who I was, he invited me to watch his fight. Realising, it was the perfect opportunity to observe him closely; I accepted."

"I thought you were determined to end their friendship. How come you even consider giving Luke the benefit of the doubt?" I injected with pure curiosity, for everyone knows it's practically impossible to change Phoebe's mind once it's made.

"His charm." Bewildered by her answer, I blankly stared at Phoebe.

"Don't ask me how or why, but I've met a lot of fighters in my life. And Luke was, without a doubt, different. He not only stood out from the rest, but he was actually sweet in comparison to other fighters. He had a jolting innocence in him. In fact, Luke was too sweet to be a real danger, and this got my full attention. The instant I saw him fight with near perfection; however, I was in awe and knew I had to have him work for me. And him already being friends with my sons was a plus."

"How did you manage to convince Luke to give up everything to work for you?" Curious to know what method she used this time to get what she wanted, I inquired with interest.

At the same time, the fact that Phoebe knew a lot of fighters to the point of distinctively knowing their behaviours was a bit disturbing and worrying. For me, on the other hand, it was normal. I usually train in combat and fight in my spare time. But how does she know?

Perhaps she too trains in fighting? Still, this wouldn't necessarily explain how she knows which fight club is legit or not.

Maybe some of her friends told her — yes, this must be it. This would explain her surreptitious expertise.

"Funny thing, Luke wanted out of the street fighting world," Phoebe confessed, breaking my silent rampage.

"At first, I was stunned and puzzled, given his talent. You should have seen him fight. He was not only astonishing but also radiating with confidence and moving with jaw-dropping expertise. Even someone as particular as me was beyond impressed, especially given his young age." With a dazed look and mesmerising smile, Phoebe recounted.

Faking a cough to bring Phoebe's attention back on this earth, I stared at her with curiosity.

"Sorry, it's just . . . If I were Luke, I wouldn't in a lifetime ever consider leaving fighting, not with his natural abilities that people train hard to achieve. Anyways, I proposed to get him completely out of the street fighting world, plus provide him with an education in exchange for his services. At first, he obviously didn't believe me, but after I held onto my end of the bargain, Luke immediately agreed. So the next day, we registered him at Wyatt's and Teo's high school."

"And the school board didn't make a fuss about it?" Recalling how uptight high schools were with their rules, especially given Luke's actual age, I suspiciously questioned.

"It's a private school, Federick. Plus, Luke was registered as an undercover bodyguard. Nobody outside the school board, your parents and the people close to me knows about it." Phoebe concluded in a *'duh'* tone as if I were to know all these tiny details.

I only recently found out about her kids, let alone her being so close to my parents — so I think she should give me a break.

"How exactly did you manage to get Luke out of such a life?" Instead of handing Phoebe the lovely opportunity to retort back, I swallowed my sarcasm. The last thing I needed was to personally hand Phoebe the rope to strangle me.

"If I tell you, I would have to kill you." She declared with a slight smile.

"I'm being serious." Noticing my disbelief expression, Phoebe continued.

I was about to say *'Ya right'*, but the humourless glaze in her eyes told me she wasn't kidding. I sincerely didn't know what to make out of it, but I took her word for it and back off for the time being. Specifically, after she was able to get Luke out of such a dangerous life — after all, I did love my life.

Perceiving my somewhat strange and conflicted expression, Phoebe took it upon herself to *'Reassure'* me.

"The look on your face is one of the reasons why I said, the less you know about me, the safer you will be. Your disbelief and curiosity are clear as daylight, but I need you to back off a bit." If this was supposed to *'Reassure me'*, then she did a miserable job at it.

"And here I thought you liked me." Aiming to lessen the tension and awkwardness of our situation, I cracked a joke.

"I care for you Federick; there's no doubt about it. Which is why, I need you to stay as far away from me as possible — at a much safer distance." Phoebe stated with utter seriousness. Yet, her admitting out loud she cared for me was the only phrase that stuck in my lovesick head.

"You care for me, huh." I suggestively repeated, yearning to hear it once more.

"Yes I do, but only as a friend. Nothing more."

As fast as a firing bullet, Phoebe's words hit my heart with an unpleasant pang. I was cognisant she would friend-zone me as soon as the opportunity presented itself. Still, the pain from hearing her say it out loud was here, no amount of precognition could have lessened the hurt.

"Just as a friend, are you certain?" Doing my best to hide the sadness oozing inside my heart, I pressed. I had to be stronger to earn Phoebe. Maybe it won't happen right away, but in the end, Phoebe would be mine.

"I realise I haven't officially asked you to be my friend given our usual unpleasant encounter at the office, but this is what I consider you. A friend." Emphasising on the friend part, Phoebe explained.

"So I will do both of us a favour and ask you directly . . . Will you be my friend?"

Phoebe's words acting like a verbal punch on my already broken heart, I watched her bring forth her hand, awaiting an agreement handshake. As if her words alone were not enough, she had to rub salt on my wounds by officially asking me to agree on something I had no desire to comply with.

"Sure, why not? Let's be friends." With reluctance, I reciprocated her handshake as if I was finalising a business deal.

As much as I wanted to reject her proposal, I couldn't for the life of me bring myself to say no. Not with her sweet face and puppy dog eyes. Plus, if I had denied, it would have destroyed what we've already built and ruined any chance I might have in the future.

"However, I have a condition. I don't ever want to be lied to. I expect only the truth from you." Keeping my domineering attitude in check, I asserted with a slight force.

If I was going to be friend-zoned, I might as well take full advantage of it. Then from there, slowly progress to a much higher relationship status. I didn't battle with myself, my emotions, my ego and made an effort to accept my true feelings for Phoebe to only be a *'Friend'*. **NO**. She was mine, and I'm going to make sure everyone knows Phoebe Smith solely belongs to Federick Archer.

"Of course. Still, us being friends doesn't mean I'm obliged to reveal everything about myself to you. The situation between us is to remain the same. I will only tell you what I can. Also, our relationship at work is going to stay professional. We are going to discuss matters we don't agree on and behave as usual. I don't want people to have the wrong idea, especially Nadiya and Logan."

"Makes total sense to me," I replied with a fake smile.

However, I had a strong feeling Phoebe saw right through me but chose to ignore it when her phone once again vibrated.

"Sorry I have to take this call. I pushed it as long as I could." She explained with a hint of remorse.

"It's good, go ahead, take it." I nonchalantly replied.

"In private, please."

"And here I thought we were friends," I commented with sarcasm and an unamused glint in my eyes, challenging Phoebe to say otherwise.

"Please." Restraining herself from saying anything harsh which could disrupt this already rocky new friendship, Phoebe pleaded.

"Since you've said please for the second time now and your sons are probably waiting for me, I will comply. Though, this doesn't mean our questioning session is over."

"Okay. Do inform me if they are fighting about the whole Luke thing. And if at all possible, calm them down until I get there."

"Ordering me around already." I joked.

Plastering a small smile, "It's a request Federick . . . Plus, as their new friend, you can do as much."

"Got it." Internally shaking my head at her swift tactics, I got off the table.

Halting by the threshold of her office, an interesting but absurd thought knocked at my door. "Out of curiosity, did I personally know you as a kid? Since your dad and mine were best friends, it's only logical I would have seen you or at least known of your existence."

"Wouldn't you like to know." Teasing, Phoebe winked at me.

"Phoebe."

"Close the door on your way out, please and thank you." Ignoring the order and exasperation in my tone, Phoebe refused to give me an actual answer.

"Anything for you, boss."

Dropping my insane and most probably impossible theory, I faked a bow and slowly closed the door. Letting out a small laugh, Phoebe waited for me to completely close the door before taking the call; putting an end to its unending vibrating.

Unbeknownst to my logical senses, as soon as I closed the door, a cloud of curiosity overtook me like a monster overpowering its victim, and I couldn't resist pressing my ear against the door — the notion of heading to the playroom a far-away thought.

Albeit Phoebe's conversation wasn't completely clear, I could still make out some words, further jumbling my brain. As if finally getting some of my answers wasn't enough to make me happy, I was now searching for more complicated questions.

Way to go Federick, I mentally scolded.

"Why do we need to please him?" Her voice laced with an undeniable frustration towards the guy they were talking about, Phoebe brusquely demanded.

"He does realise there are several other excellent teams at his disposal, right?"

"Oh, lucky me!" Phoebe sarcastically uttered after a space of silence.

Standing by the door, I was certainly glad to discover Phoebe wasn't plain out sarcastic to just me, but actually to every individual.

"Tell him I'm busy and already have my hands full." Clearly not wanting to comply, Phoebe concocted an excuse.

"I heard wrong. Please tell me for his sake that I heard wrong!" With an unknown danger oozing off her words, Phoebe exclaimed with murder in her voice.

Bewildered by this sudden tone and character change, a cold chill ran down my back. And from the power her words carried, I was sure Talon felt it too.

"I don't give a fuck who he is! He has no right to get involved in my case. Cole is MINE ONLY! If he doesn't immediately back away, Talon, I won't be held accountable for what happens to him in the next twenty-four hours." Phoebe viciously spelt out in the same Alpha tone she used on me earlier.

Except, this time it was more than just ordering, it was deadly and venomous. I have a strong feeling that whatever this man did, pissed Phoebe off beyond fury. However, what further caught my attention was the name, Cole.

I wouldn't have given much care to this name, but the animosity, hate and hint of obsession in her voice grasped my attention by the neck. I only hope this obsession angle was a figment of my over-imagination, and Cole was simply a business gone wrong. Or God helps me; I would have an additional problem on my hand. For the moment, however, I needed to find out who this Cole was and what connection he has with Phoebe. Not to forget about the guy who was asking for Phoebe and her *'Teams'*.

Beyond a doubt, something fishy was happening, and her *'Businesses'* were at the epicentre of it — which is why, despite my better judgment, I found myself having no other choice than to start my own private investigation on Phoebe. It was clear she wasn't going to reveal anything significant anytime soon.

"Okay. But inform him we are going to have a serious talk. Also, everything will be on my terms. He will not interfere at any cost." Phoebe finally agreeing to whatever they were discussing brought my attention back to her conversation.

"Forward me the address and inform him I'm on my way." Taking a deep breath, Phoebe flatly instructed in a professional tone she has never used around me before.

It undoubtedly seems like there are many facets of Phoebe I still don't know. Though, I have full intention of learning more about each piece of her.

Loudly opening and closing a drawer, it was clear Phoebe was pissed at the situation and the person meddling into her business. Heedful of Phoebe's stomping towards the door, the anger apparent in her every step, I stealthily hid behind the same pillar as before, making sure she didn't notice me. Otherwise, I would be royally screwed.

"Boys, I have some business to take care, and might be late, so don't wait up." Locking the door, Phoebe called out in a normal tone. As if she wasn't just pissed off and about ready to spit acid on someone's face.

"Okay." All of them responded in a monotone tone like they've gone through this particular surreptitious attitude of Phoebe's on several occasions already.

Noticing my voice wasn't among them, Phoebe halted, but fortunately for me, shook it off when her phone rang. For once, I was glad her phone had lousy timing; otherwise, I would have been busted — ending my investigation before it even had the chance to take off.

"I'm coming, Xylan, be patient. Some people have a life on a Sunday, you know." Phoebe snapped.

"Sorry, it's just this new director seems to have found an ingenious way to get on my nerves." Phoebe apologetically explained as she passed by me, oblivious of my inquisitive self.

"Sure, I will bring you some apology-candies. Happy." Phoebe added after a few beats before ending the call with a nod.

"I should have never agreed to Talon's merging idea. Now I have to deal with politics and its prying uptight people." Keeping her phone in her pockets, Phoebe bit back.

"*I want the best, so get her to come.*" Phoebe mimicked a snotty man's voice, nearly cracking me up.

"I will show him what the best means. He will regret ruining my Sunday and sticking his nose where it doesn't belong." Making her way to the garage's inside entrance, Phoebe moodily mumbled.

Losing sight of Phoebe when she stepped into the garage threshold, I got out of my hiding spot just in time to see her breeze by the front of the house in a much different car than the first two previous times. How many cars does she even own?

CHAPTER 23
UNWELCOME MEDDLING

PHOEBE

"**H**ey Tal, did you garner any new details on the location we received from Xylan's source." Having dealt with Federick, I expectedly inquired, assuming Talon's insistent calls brought good news.

"I've put together a team to verify the validity of the information. Unfortunately, there's been no confirmation that it's Vanderwill's current whereabouts. However, they are securing the surrounding of the location as we speak. We should expect some updates by tomorrow."

"Thanks for the report. But I'm curious why you called my emergency line when you still don't have an actual update?" Striving not to come off harsh, I gently posed.

"Well, you might have forgotten, but Blair Artic, the new NSA director, is moving in the Alpha base this week and he specifically demanded our team's assistance on a consequential case. Since it's one of his first official cases as the director, we have to make a good impression by providing our best services, so our merger remains intact. Additionally, we need to help him gain the respect he deserves, meaning, letting him take full credit of this case upon completion."

My frustration getting the best of me, the notion of keeping my voice down was long forgotten. "Why do we need to please him?" I partly whined and partly demanded despite already knowing the answer.

Granted my agency is the primary funding, weaponry, and technology supplier for the military and government branches such as the NSA, CIA, FBI and Interpol, it doesn't give them the right to dictate me. Explicitly when the primary purpose of the unification agreement we signed eight years ago was to lower bloodsheds and increase profits through taskforce partnership.

What all of them haven't figured out yet, though, is that Archer & Associates also plays a significant distributing role. However, it wasn't due to a lack of trying. Oh no! Big-league monied people involved in the world of espionage, similar to the previous NSA's director, had their suspicions about Archer & Associates. Alas, each query turned out to be an utter failure. Then again, not much could have been expected from their investigation. My influence and connection as Angel have no limit, especially with the trading key of finance and weaponry in my fist.

A vitally powerful and prime key that would end in Luke's fist after me — which leaves me no choice but to throw Luke into a fierce, cruel, harsh and vigorous training.

Plus, with the Great cold-hearten, sovereign mogul Federick Archer as the face of Archer & Associates, nobody dares to question him, thus protecting the import and export I undertake in the dark.

"Because, dear Phoebe; Angel is the head of the agency, and as such, she has to ensure the unification treaty she signed years ago remains intact. To put it differently, do your best not to piss off the director of the NSA." Probably waiting for my stubbornest to peek its ugly head, Talon briefly explained with patience.

"He does realise there are several other excellent teams at his disposal, right?" I briskly stated more than asked.

If Blair had asked my team's assistance a month back, I wouldn't have been so difficult. However, the reality of the matter was different. I couldn't or better, shouldn't concentrate on another case other than my own. Otherwise, I might lose the only lead I currently have on Vanderwill. And under no circumstances could I afford to let Vanderwill slip through my fingers again — not even with the unification treaty on the line.

"I tried to explain our situation, but Blair wants our team's name stamp on this case, specifically yours, Angel. I quote; *'I want the best, so get her to come.'* He even spoke in that snotty tone when he isn't even that old to be talking as such." Talon reiterated while making fun of the new director.

"Oh, lucky me!"

"Phoebe, I don't need sarcasm. I need confirmation."

"Tell him I'm busy and already have my hands full." Hoping to elude the matter, I tried again in a more serious tone.

"I didn't want to do this over the phone, but you leave me no choice. Blair said to inform you he stumbled upon some acutely interesting information on Vanderwill. He is ready to divulge his findings in exchange for your help with his case. Now, before you start exploding like hot lava out of a century-old dormant volcano, you have to remember Blair is the director of the NSA. Meaning, you can't go around in a killing rage, planning his assassination simply because he offered a helping hand. I need you to please take some deep breath for all of our sake."

Talon's revelation hit me hard like scorching water scalding my skin. My blood was boiling to the highest degree possible without self-exploding. Fuming with utter rage by the time Talon finished, I was thankful the thought of other people currently occupying my house crossed my infuriated mind. Otherwise, my fury would have destroyed this office; like a deadly hurricane on a defenceless island.

At the same time, the realisation that someone other than my team having some information on Vanderwill didn't sit well with me. Luckily Talon was able to reach my sane side with patience, facts and explanations.

Going down the same path as I did in the past was not an option. I had too much at stake. I couldn't risk going on another killing spree simply because the new director and his men decided it would be fun to fiddle with my business and *'Stumble'* onto some important detail involving Cole Vanderwill.

I am bloodthirsty, yes. I will openly admit it. But what I'm not, is stupid. The question of how Blair got unique up-to-date information on Vanderwill, while I don't, needed to be answered. Particularly when ten years ago Cole's case was sealed and redacted to all, except to my team and I.

Another substantial question Talon's warning and reasoning brought up was what Blair was even thinking, messing around my classified case. Me, Angel, of all people. Intending to find out more about Blair, to confront him face to face and gouge all information out of him, I complied with the case *'Request'*.

Ending the call and inhaling deep breaths to calm the roaring storm inside me, I ripped open my bottom drawer and took out my favourite gun — a custom-made LEM-triggered, double-stacked, DA HK 45 Compact-Tactical (v3).

Realising I forgot my all-access badge inside the new black 2020 Dodge Stealth I'm supposed to gift Wyatt, I carefully tucked my gun between my pant's waistband, hiding it under my top, and locked my office.

As weird as it was for Federick to not respond to my goodbye after continually nagging me for the past days, Xylan's call didn't give me time to ponder over it. All that occupied my mind was the crime scene I didn't want to go to and Blair's audacity to meddle with my business.

CHAPTER 24
CONNECTING

FEDERICK

Bearing in mind Phoebe's murky comportment and cryptic responses, my next best solution was to have her boys authenticate her story. Albeit, a part of me was worried I would create a rift between Phoebe and her family by mistakenly revealing something the kids don't know. Although, given the special bond in this family, I was ready to take a chance. It was low of me, but my love and curiosity were blindfolding all common sense.

"Hey, you just missed our mom." Lounging on his couch, Wyatt voiced the moment I walked into the playroom.

"And her scolding." Luke snickered from his bean bag.

Teo, on the other hand, simply greeted me with a smile before returning to the online game Luke and him were playing.

Joining Wyatt on the couch, "Ah, her scolding . . . That's the one thing I've dodged while interrogating your mom for the past hour." Throwing a sly glance at Luke, I divulged with a tender yet cocky smile.

"Is this what you adults call having sex nowadays?" Wyatt taunted with a knowing smile, leaving me open-mouthed.

I swear, this family has a habit of enkindling reactions within me that I would have never imagined possible.

"Not everything is about sex, young man." Emulating Phoebe's parenting tone, I surprised myself all the more.

I couldn't believe it. Me, Federick Archer, the heartthrob of the city, the one-night-stand-type-of-guy, was acting and speaking like a parent. Further mindboggling was that I actually uttered out sex wasn't everything.

What in the world was happening to me!

"Sure, it's not, father." Wyatt jested with satire.

"Really, Wyatt." Corking a brow, I challenged Wyatt to try going down that road with me.

Casting his inquisitiveness towards me, "How did your questioning go then?" Teo intentionally spoke with divided attention.

"Any success?" Mischievously arching his brows, the connotation of his words as bold as a black sharpie on a whiteboard, Wyatt proved once again that he was the naughtiest one of them all.

"Or has she been shutting you down for the past hour?" Stifling a laugh like the rest of the gang, Luke jocularly pinched in with an underlying meaning.

"You guys think you are so funny, don't you? Well, guess what . . . As shocking as what came out of your mom's mouth were, I did get most of my answers." I proudly proclaimed, as if I had just climbed to the top of the Himalaya.

"Did you now? Do let us on it." Clearly thinking I was pulling his leg, Wyatt gaunt.

"How about my *'Executive Assistant'* is a millionaire and owner of two companies on the down-low. Oh, let's not forget the reason behind why you, Wyatt, are taking college-level International Busi-ness class at such a young age. I feel sorry for you, buddy. According to what Phoebe said and her reaction when you tried to escape your online courses this morning, you are stuck on becoming a remarkable successful businessman. There's no getting out of it."

"I'm aware, but riling my mom is way too much fun. Besides, I love the idea of becoming a businessman and taking over one of her businesses. It's a legacy I'll happily fulfil."

Surprisingly appeased that Wyatt loved the career path Phoebe chose for him, I found myself drawing closer to the boys.

"What else did you find out?" Fixating his game, Teo probed.

"How about . . . Luke is actually twenty and your undercover bodyguard." I dramatically revealed, stunning Luke to the point where his character instantaneously died, making Teo the winner.

"Why on earth would mom tell you all this?" With disbelief, Luke cautiously questioned.

"Umm . . . I don't know . . . Perhaps to convince me to forgive all her lies and indiscretion, so she'll prove she trusts me and gain my full trust in return." In a calm yet sarcastically serious tone, I explained.

"Ouch! There must have been some serious shit going on in that office." Wyatt pinched in, his expression matching Teo's *'I am sorry for you'* look.

"Why would Phoebe, of all people, do all those things? It makes no sense. She has nothing to apologise for. Everything she does has been to protect her sons and nothing more." Bewildered and suspi-cious, Luke voiced out his confusion. The idea of Phoebe's sudden out of order character not sitting well with him.

"Well, dear Luke, you will have to ask Phoebe this question personally. However, what I would like to know is why Phoebe needs so much protection around Teo and Wyatt? I already got her side of the story, but I want to confirm it with you. Surely as their personal bodyguard, now brother, you should have a better idea than any of us here."

"Sorry, but I'm not allowed to discuss the details of my assignment with anyone, especially not in front of the people I swore to protect — at least not without Phoebe's permission. What I'm authorised to say, however, is Phoebe's work and the influence she has among extremely powerful people can bring about dangers in her life."

"How about explaining how Phoebe managed to get you out of underground fighting then?" Hoping I would get a more definite answer out of Luke, I tried again.

"Sorry, but this is classified as well. I guess you will have to make do with Phoebe's answer."

Despite not obtaining the full answer I was aiming for, I now had a better idea of how far Phoebe's influence extends. Which definitely helps explain why I couldn't access her full bio on the internet or my company database. Based on Luke's answers, I can now safely presume Phoebe uses her powerful influence to acquire whatever she desires. Be it for an intricate business deal or getting Luke out of the underground fighting world.

"That's the best answer you will get out of Luke, dude. We tried to dig for more, but he wouldn't budge. Not even guilt-tripping him worked." Wyatt declared as Luke, and I continuously stared, as if challenging one another.

"No worries, I got what I needed." Breaking eye contact with Luke and turning towards Wyatt, I proclaimed with a small smile.

"How are things between the three of you anyway, especially after the bombshell Luke dropped on you two?" Remembering Phoebe's request, I changed tune.

"We already had an idea about Luke's real identity so we can't hold a grudge. Teo can read micro-expression." Wyatt nonchalantly summarised as if it was no big deal.

"You do realise this isn't the most normal thing in the world?" I voiced my stupefaction.

"We know, but you gotta admit, it's pretty handy," Wyatt responded.

"For example, we know you are romantically attracted to our mother." Mirroring Wyatt's smirk, Teo pinched in.

"You forgot to add his perceptive ability isn't always accurate." Luke immediately tacked on, buying me time to compose myself from the shock and embarrassment of being caught.

"Oh come on, even a blind man can see the attraction and chemistry between them." Teo counter-attack.

"I'm sorry to disappoint, but I'm on Luke's side this time. Your mom officially asked me to be her friend; there's no attraction or chemistry there."

Despite not believing my own words, I backed Luke to cover my actual feelings. At the same time, I knew Phoebe had feelings for me. No matter how much she suppresses her real emotion, her eyes said it all.

Supporting a winning smirk, "You've just backed up our theory." Wyatt claimed as if he won the lottery.

"Oh, really. How so?" I defied with confidence.

"We are talking about our mom, Federick. If she officially asked you to be her friend after years of continually complaining about your jerkish behaviours. I assure you it's because she's starting to have romantic feelings for you. We all know it's part of her defence mechanism." Teo proudly stated.

"Oh, so you are a shrink too now?" Luke provoked with an attitude.

"Got any problem with that?" Teo fires back with the same attitude, completely shattering the image of the shy quiet boy.

"Okay, let's not start arguing please." Given they don't have any father figure in their life, I demanded in a low tone as an attempt to not sound too fatherly.

"What do you think of Damien?" Wyatt inquired out of the blue.

Taken off guard, I breathed in my dislike for Damien. Least I needed was to give Phoebe a reason to accuse me of instigating her sons against a man who could be their father, particularly when she only expects the worst out of me.

"I don't think anything of Damien, except that he's a business associate and your mom's childhood best friend." Keeping my tone in check, I diplomatically responded so I wouldn't give away my disdain for Damien.

In all reality, I don't actually hate Damien. What I hate is his guts, his connection to Phoebe, the way he treats her and the thought of him being with her. The love of my life.

"Yet, your eyes say something utterly different. It's screaming the truth. You hate the idea of Damien being close to our mom, as much as any of us does." Teo announced after a few beats of silently studying me.

"Hey, don't include me in your list, bro. I have nothing against the guy." Luke promptly stated, earning himself a deadly glare from Wyatt.

"It's okay, Wyatt. Luke is mom's perfect little soldier; it's obvious he will take her side. Not trying to be rude, Luke, but the truth is you would blindly do anything, and everything mom says without asking a single question. And I don't know how you do it, but I guess that's why she thought you would be the perfect bodyguard for us."

Silently observing the boys, I attempted to discern if I would have to break up a fight. However, I was left astounded at Luke's slight smirk, as if Teo praised him instead of insulting him.

"We all have our special ability, bro," Luke concluded with pride.

"You boys are quite something," I commented after a while of peaceful silence.

"Got that from our mom." Handing me the game console for the next match, Wyatt jested.

"If you don't mind me asking, who was the boss you mentioned the day I first came to this house?"

"You mean the day you were a major jerk to us, kiss our mom, got slapped and kicked in the balls?" Acting as if he now remembered the hash event of that day, Wyatt jocosely taunted.

"Don't be a smarty-pants, Wyatt. And, Luke, all guys get a kick in the nuts at least once in their life, so I'll stop snickering if I were you." Slightly flushed for being called out as such in the open, I retorted with sarcasm.

"The boss was you, of course. Didn't you call her moments before coming into the house?" Tea stated with confusion.

"I did." Feigning reminiscence, and covering my spill, "Sorry, I thought you might have been talking about someone else. Never mind." Quickly brushing off my inquiries, I solely concentrated on our video game — on the special bond forming between us.

Freely laughing at our boyish stupidity and sportfully arguing about our scores, I was having the fun of my life. It was unbelievable how relaxation coursed through my bones to the point where my usual coldness was non-existent. Incredibly so, the boys exhibited a magical effect similar to the one their mother has on me.

All good times, however, come to an end. Out of nowhere, a conservatively-dressed older, tall, caucasian grey-haired lady stepped into the playroom. Instinctively standing with my back to the boys, I was ready to attack despite my momentary astonishment.

Demanding she introduced herself with my infamous icy death glower, I grew edgier when she audaciously and suspiciously stared back instead of cowering and complying. Dismissing the conspicuous tensed air between this stranger and myself, all three boys ran to-wards her and greeted her with a lovingly endearing hug.

"You are?" Treating me as an intruder, the older lady demanded in a harsh tone.

The glint in her eyes, however, indicated she had an idea of who I was — then why the act?

Swallowing my confusion, "Federick Archer. Who might you be?" I demanded in a much higher tone.

"Maria. I work here." Mimicking Phoebe's tendency to answering in short sentences, Maria concluded.

"Maria has been taking care of our family for centuries now. She started when mom was still a toddler." Teo shared with a smile.

"So you are practically family?" Trying to clear the air, I toned down the authoritarian in me.

"I sure am. Then again, I wasn't aware Phoebe had started to bring her boss home."

Reckoning I didn't make a first good impression, I rolled with the turn of events. "Phoebe didn't bring me home, as you've put it. Last night's dinner ended later than expected, so I crashed here."

"Oh, so you stayed the night as well. Where is Phoebe, anyway?"

Getting the sense, Maria was more like Phoebe's second mother than just her kids' caretaker; I was hit with a pang of nervousness. Clearly, if she was secretly interviewing me for potential son-in-law material, I failed.

"Out. Mom had to take care of some business." Slicing his hand back and forth under his chin to signal for me to stop talking, Wyatt swiftly answered from behind Maria.

"Okay. By the way, congrats, Luke. Kenneth told me the news on my way here." Maria congratulated with a genuine smile.

"Are you and Kenneth together?" Taking Wyatt's advice and changing topic, I curiously inquired.

Watchfully examining me, "No. Kenneth is my best friend, and since he picked my husband and me from the airport, he dropped me here." She cooly summarised.

"Ah, this explains why I haven't seen you during my previous visits." Like an imbecile, I prepared my own noose and hung myself.

Cocking her eyebrow, "So, you've been dropping by and crashing over on multiple reprises for the past months?" Maria judgingly posed.

Strangely abashed and mortified at Maria's judging tone, "Oh no! — Last night was the first time I crashed here . . ." Holding onto the lasso I wrapped around my own neck; I tried to save my own skin. Unfortunately, my high-pitched jumpy answer didn't ease Maria's scrutinising look.

"Maria, I'm dying of hunger." Teo immediately exclaimed, saving my sorry ass.

"I'll make some snacks for you all. Meet me in the kitchen when I call."

Quietly nodding in agreement, we returned to our respective place — with me acting like I didn't just shoot myself in the foot.

Bringing my sorry post-derriere to reality after Maria left, "I don't think she likes me."

"Well, you have a special talent of screwing up and making people suspicious of you." Luke voice in a *'duh'* tone; strongly tempting me to give his sassy ass a fitting answer.

"Don't worry, you don't always give the first good impression, but knowing Maria, she will give you a second chance. She is nice that way." Giving Luke the evil eye, to which he simply shrugged, Wyatt worked at reassuring me.

"In fact, I'm sure inviting you for snacks is Maria's way to observe you closely. So you better ace it if you want a future with our mom." Stressing me even more with this supposition, I didn't even bother correcting Teo this time around.

Highly aware of Maria's scrutinising, I was thrown back into my teenage years. This time, however, I was experiencing the upheaval I always taunted my friends with while they met the girlfriend's parents. And I got to admit; it wasn't any fun.

If a simple maid who had taken care of Phoebe since her childhood, technically representing her mother figure can make me feel nervous and uncomfortable. I completely understood why my friends were always such a nervous wreck when it came to **'The Meeting'**.

Sitting at the counter working on warming up Maria to me until the aloof look in her eyes disappeared, I pitied all the guys I taunted.

Despite loving the growing connection between the boys and myself, I still couldn't stop the arrays of questions running a thousand miles an hour inside my head. Not knowing where Phoebe was; what she was doing; who she was with; or why she was not home yet, was silently and slowly killing me. Most disturbing of all, however, was the mysterious way she left as well as the perplexed call she received before kicking me out of the office. The words *'Director'*, *'Team'*, *'Case'* and especially, *'Vanderwill'* among others kept torturing my already over-confused brain.

I needed to know more — to start my own investigation. But, I also didn't want to pry and break the promise I made to Phoebe. And that's where my quandary lies.

If Phoebe were to find me snooping in her life or attempting to force information out of her when she was not ready, I would forever lose her.

I can't believe that me, Federick Ashton Archer, of all people, was going to say this, but patience and love were my only useful weapons against Phoebe.

"When you're done daydreaming about our mother, do let us know. Maybe then, we can return to getting to know each other better." Teo's voice pierced through my thoughts, bringing my attention back on him and his brothers.

"Sorry to disappoint, but I wasn't daydreaming about your mother. I was simply attempting to find a way to lessen my confusion on the person that is your mother, because if this continues, I'm going to be living with a permanent headache." Not even considering lying, I clarified for all three. Phoebe herself told me to continue constructing a healthy truthful relationship with her kids, so I'm only fulfilling her highness orders.

"Well, good luck with that dude, cause none of us had been able to accomplish this miracle yet." Wyatt teasingly challenged, aware of how intricate his mother was.

"No worries, Wyatt. I will find my way. Haven't you heard your mom say; What Federick Archer wants. Federick Archer gets." Quoting Phoebe, I exclaimed with confidence and a smirk.

No matter what happens or how long it will take me, I'll eventually find the complete truth about Phoebe and her eerie life. That was a promise to myself.

CHAPTER 25
DELTA SPECIAL INTELLIGENCE

PHOEBE

With only one hour to spare, I breeze through the road like a madwoman. I still couldn't believe I was wasting my Sunday investigating the disappearance of a priceless artefact when I could be doing something far more substantial. That Blair Artic . . . I couldn't wait to kick his behind once I saw him at the museum.

"Ma'am, this section of the museum is closed to the public." About to cross the police tape, I halted at the grouchy tone of a security guard.

Already in a bad mood, I had no desire to speak with anyone other than my team. Sharply challenging the guard's audacity to stop me, I swiftly unclipped my badge from my side and shoved my credentials at his face. With furrowed brows and tensed body posture, a chill ran down his spine.

Quite frankly, I was pleased I hadn't lost my ability to ignite fear in people to the point where they squirm in place, petrified by my mere glare. Federick really had me doubting my coldness with his recent attitude change. It's like my cold and stern look doesn't affect him as it affects others.

The hair on his arms standing to attention, the guard loudly gulped his own spit, "I'm sorry Agent, but, please do indulge my ignorance. What does D.S.I mean?" The obviously frightened, confused and low-ranked guard timidly inquired.

Not wanting to explain myself for the second time today, I allowed my daggered glare and vicious, cold scowl do the talking. Since this guard was already unknowingly wasting the little amount of time I had, making him shit his pants for my own fun seemed like the right thing to do.

"It stands for **Delta Special Intelligence,** and the woman you are currently questioning is the head and owner of this highly prestigious organisation." Talon flatly cut in, saving the guard from being sliced into multitude little pieces from my glare alone.

Lifting the yellow police tape and holding his hands out for me, "Come on, we've wasted enough time with the introduction." Talon resonantly stated.

Placing my hand on Talon's, I stepped behind the *'Do not cross'* barricade and looked for anything that jumped at me at first sight. Being drilled not to be caught or leave any evidence behind, getting into the criminal's mind was elementary for spies and assassins of my agency. Fundamentally, acute observations were a critical and essential process in theft cases, especially within such highly secured places.

Neat and well-kept, the massive white hall of the museum was filled with exquisite and unique paintings at every corner. If not for my previous visits to equally grandiose museums, I would have been too awestruck by this glamourous art maze to pay any actual attention to where the multi-million painting once was.

Halting behind Talon, I stood still under the gigantic pure black crystal chandelier. Tuning out all outside noise, my attention was fixated on its details. Shining like stars on a pitch-black night, the black diamond cut and black raindrops stone proudly hung on the high roof, in the middle of the bright hall. Bringing life to this place, this breathtaking and magnificent chandelier screamed its unwithered significance.

Sweeping my investigating regard past some of the handcraft sculptures, towards the folk of uniforms, I deduced it was the crime centre-point. Spotting Matt and Xylan questioning the museum's staff, I continued to study my surroundings silently, to get a better picture of the thief or thieves entry and exit point.

"I don't give a flying rat's ass what your director said. I want you to hand over all your research and current full reports concerning this case." Locking horns, Matt gave the museum manager a coloured piece of his mind.

"What seems to be the problem here?" Approaching my team, the manager, a few of the officials and museum's personnel, I frigidly demanded in a sharp, clear voice.

"This uptight manager is refusing to hand over the complete report of his so-call investigation." Showing his displeasure, Xylan folded his arms over his puff-up chest.

"Did you identify yourself as an agent from the D.S.I taskforce?" I flatly inquired for confirmation.

"I sure did." Throwing killer daggers look at the manager, Xylan proudly stated.

"So." Glowering at the manager for a valid explanation, I urged in a penetrating tone.

"We've already taken care of the problem, ma'am. The case has been filed, and our detectives are working on retrieving the lost painting as surreptitiously as possible." Gulping, "We do appreciate your help, ma'am, but the owner of this painting is one of our best clients, and we need to ensure he stays with us despite this recent tragedy." Nearly cowering with fear under my threatening glare, the manager hesitantly clarifies.

Turning an annoyed and irritated glare towards Talon, "Can you explain why the director of the NSA, of all organisations, wants me on this when it's already been taken care of? — Better yet, where the heck is he? Wasn't he supposed to meet us here?"

I had no time to lose, and this right here was a perfect example of a major waste of my precious time. This Blair guy was honestly vexing me and begging to be beaten up to a pulp.

"He called before I met you outside to inform me he had a personal emergency and couldn't make it. He apologised, but he suspects this theft has something to do with several other similar unresolved thefts and forgeries across London, Paris and Canada. If the preliminary data from the detectives' unbiased investigation matches with our findings, your observation and conclusion, I'll bring you in on their ongoing case." Talon professionally explained.

"I have no idea what you people are searching, but this is clearly a classic case of art theft." The manager annoyingly chimed in.

Zeroing my frosty glare on the manager, "Brief me on this ongoing investigation of yours."

Still fuming that Blair ditched this meeting after practically dragging me here against my will, I allowed the manager's statement to slide for this once. Nevertheless, I hope for Blair's sake that his *'Personal reason'* has nothing to do with getting into some girl's pants. Or God, help me!

Not only did Blair ruin my Sunday, put his nose where it doesn't belong, but also managed to further piss me off by forcing this stupid case down my throat. As though Federick alone wasn't enough, now I had to handle Blair, Damien and the *'Lovely return'* of dear Vanderwill.

"Well, upon perusal of our sterling security, we've concluded at least two people were involved in this awful transgression." The manager proudly summarised like an old-age detective.

"Have you done anything other than pure speculation during your investigation?" Cognisant of how one person with the right type of training could steal this aforementioned painting, I boldly demanded in a professionally sarcastic *'Duh'* tone.

Cruising an analytic glance around, the design of this museum hall proved to have a few evident blind-spot and opening point to the professional eye.

"We suspected the thieves worked with an insider to case this place. Alas, after questioning everyone present during the time of the theft, our theory didn't pan out. But we anticipate the thieves will be trying to get all attention off of them as soon as possible. So, we resorted to tracking the painting by planting a C.I with a reputation of buying expensive stolen paintings on the black market." Unsure what detail I would find more appealing and useful, the manager was less confident than before.

"Yeah, right. Look around, despite all these equally priceless paintings, only one was taken. Did it occur to you that the thief had a client list in hand? Or better yet, working for a particular client who demanded this specific painting." Cockily smirking, Matt sarcastically pointed out.

Hiding a ghost of a smile, I warningly glared at Matt, cautioning him to behave more professionally and less like Xylan. Perusing the tidiness of the scene around me, I was determined this theft was a job of only one man — someone who screamed of control, precision and determination. To put it simply, the culprit knew precisely what it wanted to steal, thus not letting itself be tempted and distracted by other priceless artefacts in this very hall.

Based on the profile I've gotten on this individual so far, I wasn't surprised to detect the hidden yet deafening message of overconfidence. It was clear, the mastermind behind this theft wouldn't be as easy to capture, especially when taunting the lead investigator with cryptic clues was this crook's favourite hobby.

"How is your security system in this section of the museum?" Determined to better profile this criminal, I posed.

"If you must know we have an impeccable top-notch security system. It's nearly impossible to tamper with." The manager haughtily summarised.

"Talon." Locking eyes with my right-hand man, I voiced my command. Nodding in silent understanding, Talon headed to where I wanted him.

Suspicious, confounded and curious, the manager questioned

Talon's departure. His befuddlement and stress line decorating his forehead greatly amusing me.

"He's going to your control room to inspect every single component of your top-notch security system and see if anything jumps out at him." Hoping this stubborn manager would leave me alone, I briefly informed.

"Why? I already informed you our security system is working perfectly. We even did a thorough system inspection as a precautionary step. The only reason the alarm delayed during the theft was that the robbers used the latest cutting edge BlackBox specifically designed to circumvent our security system. We found the blasted device on the wall during our investigation." Raising his voice, the manager's tone carried a hint of annoyance, only serving to irritate me further.

"Lister, Mister. You've done your job, but this is our case now. So I'll strongly advise you to let us do our job as we deem appropriate and necessary." Xylan jumped in with equal irritation and annoyance towards the man.

"Despite all the inquiries you've done, we still believe there has been a breach in your system. This isn't a two-person job, but a one-person job. So, if you want, continue your never-ending search, but I'm going to do my job my way." Reminding myself I was running point on this investigation, I filled my lungs with some fresh air and frigidly disclosed.

"Now, walk back to your office and prepare to hand over the security tapes for the past month, last night included, along with all your reports — written, recorded or otherwise. Plus, I want everything you documented, used, discovered together with a list of all your employees and detectives working this case. Everything should be sent to my office by tomorrow." In a flat tone, I directed my order to a speechless manager.

"I could call your director if you wish. Though I can't promise the safety of your job afterwards." Matt threatened in a booming voice, enjoying the power he had over the manager and the position he put him in.

"No need too. Everything you need will be sent to your office by tomorrow night." Gulping and nervous, the thick-headed manager finally agreed and left.

"Matt, collect all the important reports and crime scene photos from the officials and have them send everything else tomorrow. Xylan, snap pictures of this place. Don't miss a single corner. We'll compare them with the detectives' pictures afterwards. I'll be in the control room with Talon." Listing my instructions, I marched away without losing any more of my precious time.

"Found anything valuable yet?"

Either Talon didn't hear me, or he simply turned a deaf ear to my inquiry. Approaching him to discern what he was doing, I was left scratching my head in confusion.

"What!" Receiving a glare from *'Mr Do-Not-Disturb-Me'*, I exclaimed with innocent eyes.

"You're hovering." Talon simply stated before returning his attention to his work.

Well, I wasn't aware that attempting to see or figure out what the heck he was actually doing was classified as hovering in his stupid dictionary.

"If you would care to explain what you are doing, then maybe I wouldn't be *hovering* as much." I satirically retorted.

"Do tell me, what have you gathered from your *observation* so far?" Arrogantly cocking his brows, Talon teased.

"That's what I thought." Talon mocked in a matter-of-fact tone.

Pink and flustered, "Whatever. Just tell me what you got."

"Well, if you would stop pestering me, I could actually get some work done here." Talon sardonically concluded.

Throwing my hands up in surrender, "Okay, got it! I'll sit down and wait for you to be done." Taking the seat behind him, I left Talon to his intricate work, filled with cryptic code and wording beyond my comprehension.

"By the way, congratulations." Breaking the lengthy silence, Talon almost monotonously congratulated.

"Huh?" I mumbled with puzzlement.

"Luke finally becoming a Smith." Acting as if this wasn't an actual big deal, Talon maintained a straight tone.

"How? — Oh, Kenneth." Nodding, Talong confirmed Kenneth, his dad, had already spread the news.

Partly disappointed since I wanted to surprise my best friends with the good news tonight when we would meet-up at my place, "Do the others know?" I verified.

"It's not my surprise to give away, Phebes. I'll give you the honour of informing them." Talon concluded before resuming his work.

Left with my racing thoughts, it dawned on me that Federick might still be hanging around my place. The most sensible part of me was praying Federick would be gone before Matt, Talon, and Xylan drove to my house. The other unsensible part of me, however, couldn't help but wonder what Federick would think of my best friends and me after seeing us together.

Would he think less of me? Conclude I'm way too crazy of a person and run for the hills? Or would he stick around long enough to get to know each one of them personally? To try and understand our unique friendship and accept it?

Disturbed from my train of thoughts and the weird spinning sensation in the pit of my stomach at the image of Federick, I couldn't start to comprehend what I should do next. My lips stretched into a smile as mine and Federick's interrogation flashed in front of me like an HD quality 5-star movie, I was almost sure I went bonkers.

What was wrong with me? Why was my brain so focused on Federick freaking Archer? There were so many people that should be invading my mind, right now. Take Damien for example, nobody knows of his return yet, and I should be investing all my brainpower on concocting a plan to ease-in Damien's arrival announcement. Particularly with Alicia and Joseph. Given the last time I attempted to take Damien's side, they were crystal clear they wouldn't hear a word, and pointedly explained how Damien ran away, leaving me alone with two toddlers when I most needed him.

Given their love for me, it made sense why Alicia, Joseph and all my four best friends hated Damien's gut. They were eccentric and came to the absurd conclusion that Damien's desertion subconsciously scarred me.

But after seeing Damien again after so many years, I was even more positive, all of them were wrong. Damien's return only stirred up happiness and wholeness within me. There was no feeling of abandonment or resentment.

Coming up with an idea, I texted Damien, inviting him to my place later on that night. Forewarning Damien I was working on tackling the announcement of his return, one step at a time, I made him promise to behave. Personally, Damien wasn't necessarily the problem. The problem was the anger the others had for him.

Updating my schedule, I left a note for Nadiya to clear half of my day tomorrow and invite Mr and Mrs Archer for dinner at my place after lunchtime. I was determined to get this whole ordeal over with as soon as possible. And with the announcement of Luke becoming a Smith, I had a winning card in hand for when they would get mad at Damien or me. Surely, the news of becoming a grandparent all over again would trump their aggravation.

"I knew it!" Talon loudly bellowed. "Their system has been hacked." Dragging me out of my endless thought by force, I jumped off my seat in surprise and alert.

"Can't you be a little bit quieter?" I reprimanded with a murderous look.

"Daydreaming again, I see." Cockily smiling, Talon taunted again.

"Yeah, daydreaming about the different ways I can torture the person who ruined my Sunday before going for the kill." Keeping a straight face, I sarcastically declared.

"Oh, how can I forget . . . Killing is your favourite sport."

"It's one of them," I confessed, giving more weight to Talon's comment.

Pondering over it, I try my best to do good. To eliminate those who deserve it along with helping those in need. But the fact remains, I'm a sadistic and sociopathic person. I enjoy the kill and have never felt remorseful, embarrassed or shameful about it — which was one more reason why Federick can't, under any circumstances, fall for me. He needed to stay as far away from me as possible. Whether he likes it or not.

"What did you find?" Partly dreading and partly hoping my earlier theory about this case was right, I questioned Talon with mild anticipation.

"It's been hacked, but not by any type of hacker . . . Oh, no. It was a first-rate savvy one. All bases were covered, and almost every trace of anyone messing with the system was erased. No one had an inkling someone was snooping around the museum's digital infrastructure. Then again, I'm one of the best at what I do, and I'll be damn if I don't discover this hacker's plot." Talon exclaimed with confidence and a hint of excitement.

"In this case, I'm sure you realised there's more to this case than meets the eyes." The Angel in me taking over, I stated with confidence.

I knew damn well that Talon was intelligent enough to have noticed this significant development and the discrepancy in this case. In fact, I would bet he's already scheming something to get to the bottom of this matter.

"Which is why I introduced a special bug into their framework devised to give me remote access to their entire network from the agency's connection. I'll have to dive through their system to spot any digital breadcrumbs left behind by the hacker and possibly figure out what the thief was looking for in a museum's network. I'll also work on tracing the IP address of the attacker. Either way, if I find anything worth looking twice into, I'll send it your way."

"Of course you can do all this. Taking control over other's digital information like it's no big deal. Remind me never to let you near my computer ever again." Impressed by Talon's ability and talent to control modern technology like no other, I noted with a hint of sarcasm.

"Whatever, let's get going." Beelining for the exit, Talon muttered with humour.

Striving to keep up with Talon's long stride, "Xylan and Matt texted, they left for my place five minutes ago."

"I'm driving then," Talon announced before dashing my car.

About to race Talon, it dawned on me I couldn't run or exert myself. Not with the silky chiffon scarf neatly wrapped around my hickey-covered neck. A special embarrassing gift from the master of assholeness himself. If Talon or the others saw it, they would tease me to death, not to mention the endless questions . . . God, no! . . .

"Woman, I have no idea why you're blushing, but hurry up." Opening the passenger door for me, Talon shouted from the car.

"Just drive us to my place, will ya." Buckling in, I purposely ignored Talon's comment.

About ten minutes away from my place, we caught sight of Matt's silver Porsche a few cars away from ours. Unlike Talon, who was driving like he was in a mad race, Matt was calmly driving and enjoying the warm scenery as if he was on a long romantic drive.

Given the childish and competitive nature of my team, Talon persistently honked to get Matt and Xylan's attention. Overtaking their car, we mocked them and hightailed out of there. At this, Matt pressed onto his gas pedal, starting a ten-minute race to my house.

"Losers!" Heading towards the threshold of my porch with a laugh, I jested.

Making mocking faces at Talon and me, Matt and Xylan took their loss with a smile.

"So, you guys found anything new?" Trailing behind us, Matt inquired with curiosity.

"Yep. But we'll do some profiling groundwork first; then I'll let Talon brief us about this famous thief. Afterwards, we'll go into more detail about what we found. What we suspect and what we should do next." Closing the main door behind me, I debriefed in a mildly low voice.

"What's with the new director by the way? He asked for you, then didn't even bother to show up. How rude of him." Following my lead, Xylan pointed out with disapproval.

"Yeah, right. How dare he stand me up?" Still pissed at Blair for not showing up, I wholly agree.

Then he says he needs my help! Who did he think he was?

"Who stood whom up?" A distinct loud masculine voice I've learnt to recognise *oh to well* demanded from the dining room. Momentarily shocked, I knew I was screwed.

CHAPTER 26
EMERGENCE OF EMOTION

PHOEBE

"Hey, mom, Talon, Xylan, Matt." Wyatt's warm yet cheeky welcome momentarily pried me off Federick's interrogative gaze.

Sitting at my kitchen counter with an air of undeniable impatience instead of being out partying, as usual, Federick recaptured my confounded gaze. Noting my unresponsiveness, Talon faked a cough beside me. Alas, I was too focused on the oddness of Federick's presence in my house, this late at night, to take heed of anyone else in the room.

"Sorry for Phebes' bad manners. We're still trying to teach her how to be more ladylike." Xylan jested to clear the air.

"I'm Xylan Ivailo, on my right is Matt Gregor and the hard, non-smiley face beside Phebes, is Talon Carver. Who might you be?" Stretching his hand towards Federick for a handshake, Xylan inquired with a smile.

"Federick Archer."

Dismissing Federick's flat tone, I exhaled a breath of relief when Federick returned Xylan's handshake instead of glaring at his out-stretched hand like it was an insect. It was apparent Federick had realised all three men were my best friends, yet, it didn't seem to have wholly relaxed him. Reserved, his cold unreachable wall was still set up high.

Having a light bulb moment, "Oh, **THE** Federick Archer. I see it now." In an *'Awe'* tone, Matt sent Xylan a knowing look.

"Pleased to finally meet you. We've heard a lot about you." Mischievously smirking, Xylan gleefully announced.

"The pleasure is all mine. Although, I can't say I've heard about you guys as much as you've heard about me." Glancing at me, Feder-ick voiced in his usual professional tone.

I wonder if Federick could speak to others in a normal and cheer-ful tone instead of always being so professional and politically correct. It would be a nice change to see him let go around the people I care about. Then again, this was a weird wish in itself, given moments ago, I wanted Federick gone.

"It's not surprising. We are talking about Phoebe here." Dismiss-ing my presence in the room, Matt commented with an amused grin, earning himself a smack on the head from dearest me.

"I'm surprised you even recognise our names." Less cheerful than the rest, Talon's suspicious tone reminded me I forgot to tell my best friends I talked with Federick earlier today.

"Federick overhead us talking when I was at Joseph's for dinner, and explaining some details to him was the only way to shut his annoying mouth."

Pitching in, I was thankful Talon nodded in understanding rather than questioning me. Especially when Federick quirked his eyebrows at me and my comment, leading to my cheeks reddening and the annoying voice in my head teasing me about how much I really liked Federick's *annoying* mouth.

"What are you still doing here, anyway?" Taking the first escape route by the throat, I inquired with puzzlement.

"Oh, you know, just keeping your sons' company since you decided to vanish without any specific reason." Federick cockily responded.

"Well, some people do have important work to take care of instead of simply hanging around like you." Not about to take shit from Federick, I retorted with my own sassiness.

"Work, huh . . . That's some type of work you have, where all your best friends end up at your place at this hour of the night." Sarcastic and suspicious, Federick's hard look connoted his distrust in my word. In me. Even after I gave him my words, I wouldn't lie to him.

"Well, thank you so much for not doubting my every word." I sharply snapped, hurt Federick still didn't trust me after I've divulged more to him than to anyone else in this room.

"All of them work together in one of her company. Didn't you already know that?" Wyatt exclaimed with a hint of confusion.

'He would know if I had mentioned it to him.' Shifting my gaze between Wyatt and Federick, I inwardly jeered.

"Talon is her right-hand man." Teo volunteered more information after his brother.

Standing with my arms folded over my chest, I raised my left brows, silently challenging Federick's accusation. To my satisfaction, a sheepish shadow coated Federick's face.

"Besides, not all her best friends are here. Logan is missing. Where is he?" Luke pitched in, prompting the realisation that I was failing as Luke's handler.

Since Luke was Wyatt and Teo's unofficial bodyguard, he wasn't at Logan's farewell party, as such it was my duty to keep Luke informed. Alas, I've been too distracted to inform any of my sons about Logan.

"Logan will soon be getting married, so he transferred to Archer & Associate as the company's president."

Surprised at first until the connection between the two companies dawned on him, Luke nodded in silent understanding.

"I can't believe Logan gets to watch you and Mr Federick argue all day long. We are definitely missing out on the fun." Xylan childishly complained. And as the grown-up that I was, I stuck my tongue out at him.

"Did you guys see who his fiancée is?" Matt inquired over mine and Xylan's childish behaviour.

"I did." Aware none of them except Federick personally caught sight of Nadiya, I immediately bragged.

"No! Not fair. I was supposed to see her first." Clearly preferring acting like a child instead of the adult he was, Xylan groused.

"What can I say . . . I'm Logan's baby sister, after all. But if you want, you can see her tomorrow. She's working as my PA at Archer & Associate." Giving in their child-like behaviour, I gloated with a wide grin, further annoying Matt and Xylan.

Catching a glimpse of Talon scrutinising and observing Federick like he was a criminal, I couldn't put my fingers on Talon's weird behaviour towards Federick. Then again, I didn't really want to know.

"She's such a rude person. How do you even put up with her?" Directing his question towards Federick, whose eyes were glimmering with amusement despite his *I don't care* facial expression, Xylan whined.

"It takes a lot of arguing, but I manage. Although . . . I recently found an efficient way to shut her up for at least a few minutes." Hinting to his morning, Federick professed with a devious smirk.

Blood rushing to my face, it took an enormous deal of robustness to hide my visible blush. Unable to meet the gaze of the staring audience, I ferociously glunched at Federick, letting him know I was displeased at the innuendo in his declaration.

"Might I know what this new way of yours is? It surely would be of great help to us."

Swiftly pivoting towards the source, utter silence blanket the room, up till Federick's whispered swearing broke everyone from their jolted state. Discerning Wyatt and Teo's disapproving demeanour along with Luke's neutral air, Matt and Xylan's confusion turned into curiosity.

"Dam, you made it." Ignoring everyone, I rushed to Damien and welcomed him with a hug and bright smile.

Reciprocating my hug and pecking me on the cheek, "Maria, let me in." Damien informed.

"Damien Ambrosh? From ten years ago — the supposed best friend who has the worst timing to disappear." With an intense hint of burning disapproval, Talon venomously berated.

Given it was only Talon and Logan who knew Damien, Matt and Xylan's exclamation of surprise was well-expected. All eyes focused on me, a mixture of confusion, astonishment and anger pirouetted within the confined space of my living room.

"Oh, Talon Carver, why the hostility towards the man who freely handed you the honourable title of Phoebe's right-hand man? Shouldn't you be immensely grateful to me?" Sneering with sarcasm, Damien earned himself an aggravated growl from Talon.

"Unlike what you might believe, I worked hard to earn this title rightfully. And if you think I'm hostile, you have another surprise coming, **buddy**. I can't wait until Logan redefines your meaning of hostility once he's made aware of your return and it's mysterious yet suspicious timing. Isn't it just ironic how you have to face the same demons you've run away from several years ago?" Murderously and bitterly glouting, Talon mimicked Damien's sarcastic tone.

Unable to do much, we were silent spectators witnessing two grown men throwing blazing daggers at each other and about ready to jump at each other's throat — without caring that Wyatt and Teo would witness their violence.

"I don't think Logan Virgo will be doing much, dear Talon. Last I heard, he left to work for Archer & Associate. And for what? For his nuptials with an Italian girl who's here on a work visa. Ironically speaking, he's doing the same thing he has been accusing me of."

Damien scoffed with his own disdain.

Momentarily flummoxed by Damien's explicit knowledge of Logan's private life when I never mentioned a thing, I was a bit concerned. Particularly when Damien hasn't stepped foot inside the agency for the past ten years. Equally disturbing was the hint of threat in Damien's words when he spoke of Logan's love life and Nadiya. But that couldn't be. Surely, I was overreacting and letting my imagination run wild as Federick does. **Yes, this had to be it!**

Damien would never in a million years purposely hurt one of my friends, especially one who was a part of the agency and literally like my big brother. I just needed to give all these males some more time to deal with each other decently.

"Oh, Damien, Logan is far from doing what you did. The man has honest intentions and unlike you . . ." Regarding Damien like he was a vile insect, "Logan is still here for Phoebe and ready to offer his continuous support, no matter what. Now, unlike you, I don't fancy disappointing Phoebe, so I strongly suggest we drop this banter for the time being before we start a fight in front of everyone." Talon cockily scorned with a finality that evinced he was indeed the second-in-command to one of the greatest empires around.

Gandering between the two tension balls in the room, I was pleased Talon was making an effort to refrain himself, rather than fulfilling his nine-year-long yearning to pounce on Damien for a nasty roll in the mud. But I wasn't out of the hole yet. Logan and Damien's encounter was going to be far more explosive. While Talon knew Damien from a distance, Logan and Damien often collaborated as a team on special cases, and that unmatched bond was going to be my downfall. Keeping watch of the ever-increasing daggered glare between Talon and Damien, I was further sure of my diagnosis.

"Well, this was some intense discussion . . . Anyways, that's Matt." Pointing at Matt's studious face, his defences palpable, "And I'm Xylan. Glad to finally meet you." With his usual contagious cheerful smile and attitude, Xylan treated Damien like he was an A-lister celebrity and excitedly shook his hand.

"I can't believe I'm actually looking at the first of Phebes' life." Like a major idiot, Xylan didn't even bother to control whatever was coming out of his mouth.

"What do you mean by first?" A hint of jealousy flashing in his eyes, Federick inquisitively and suspiciously demanded.

"Forget about this. I invited all of you here to make an announcement — if you're all done being at each other throats, that is." And just like that, it was my time to butt in.

Deliberately brushing off Federick's intensely frigid, near murderous scowl, I stepped further into the centre of the group.

"Federick, Talon and Damien already know. Nevertheless, I wanted Damien here because he was surprise number one. So yeah — surprise. Damien is back." I sheepishly exclaimed, aware it wasn't a great surprise to some. But since it was for me, that's all that mattered.

Directing my gaze at Talon, "And I expect all of you to behave appropriately towards Damien, as well as, treat him with the respect he deserves." I pointedly asserted.

"The second surprise is . . ." Holding my team's gaze for dramatic effect, "Luke is now officially a Smith!" Barely keeping my heels on the floor, I near screeched in joy. "He signed all the required legal documents earlier today, and I'm pretty sure Alicia will be throwing a celebratory party after I tell her the good news."

Jumping with excitement, Xylan and Matt hugged me before hightailing to a beaming Luke. Grinning from ear to ear, I was overwhelmed with joy and peace. However, the instant I glazed over at Damien I instantaneously regretted it. The urge for him to give me his input about adopting yet another child from the streets was clear as crystal. But, I refused to let Damien damper my rare blissful mood. My decision was made, and his opinion could take a backseat.

In the meantime, a more pertinent mystery needed to be solved.

Giving my teams and kids time to catch-up, I stealthily slid beside Federick for a little chat. Surely such a cold-hearted, indifferent, arrogant, chauvinistic playboy and business tycoon like 'The Great Federick Archer' wouldn't be hanging around my kids just because I 'Vanished' and left them unsupervised for a few hours. He must, without a doubt, have some ulterior motive — there's no other explanation for his strange and irregular behaviours since last night.

"Why are you still here, really ?" Not even attempting to hide my disbelief, I whispered with utter suspicion.

"Unlike someone, I actually don't make it a habit of lying to the people I claim to care about. So when I said it's because I was keeping the boys' company, I meant it. I didn't want to leave them alone in their predicament. It's called being considerate."

Frowning with evident confusion, I couldn't figure out what the matter was with Federick, his mood swings or the hint of accusation in his tone. Poring over at me through his peripheral vision, Federick maintained his silence and returned his blank gaze towards the group of people in front of us.

Once again letting his accusation about me lying slide, "What predicament are you talking about?" I mumbled.

Despite the buzzing around us, the deafening silence between the two of us was the only sound I could hear. Inferring Federick was upset and mad at something or rather at someone — aka, me — I still couldn't figure out why. As far as I'm aware, I've done nothing wrong since the last time we spoke.

"This is a celebration and bonding moment, Phoebe. You took Luke in, which was great. But right afterwards, you had him dropped a major bomb on Teo and Wyatt all by himself, without even considering its rippling effect. Do you realise your decision combined with your absence could have potentially destroyed Luke's existing relationship with Teo and Wyatt? Instead of being here with your sons for support and explanation after Luke was done; up you go to some weird business meeting. Didn't it once occur to you that they might need their mother? And whether they admit it out loud or not, that your action might have hurt them." Enumerating in a low soft voice, Federick's attempt to subdue his harshness miserably failed.

Federick's raw words and his honest-to-God concern pulled at my heart's string. At a part of me, that wasn't usually touched or even acknowledged.

"They did understand, didn't they? Plus, they are used to this. I'm sure it didn't bother them as much as you think it did." Smothering the rise of guilt in my stomach, I slapped Federick with facts that would prove his points wrong.

Regretfully, one look into the depths of Federick's pool of greys, an unidentifiable force yanked at my inside, compelling me to reflect upon his words. Locking eyes, it dawned on me Federick was right. If I'm not overprotecting Wyatt and Teo like I would my most priceless and fragile asset. I'm treating them and their emotions like I would my prized agents — expecting them to understand without any proper explanation and not be hurt by my unsympathetic actions. But the reality was, Wyatt and Teo were no agents. And while it's true Luke could take the hit of my insensitivity because he knew the truth behind my every disappearance or erratic behaviours, Wyatt and Teo were left standing in the dark.

Although it's true, I needed to be more sensitive and a real mother to all three of my sons, I also knew Wyatt would call me out on it if I were being too inconsiderate. Not to mention, their grandparents, Kenneth, my best friends, especially Logan, who was like an uncle to them, would knock some sense into me. Nevertheless, it was still impressive how Federick made such a valid observation in such a limited timespan.

And here I was, assessing Federick as an agent when moments ago I admitted I needed to ease on my insensitive Angel side when I'm around them. On the other hand, keeping my emotional numbness from thawing has kept my kids and me alive so far, and with Vanderwill's return, this was what I needed.

"As much as I hate to admit it, you are perfectly right, and I'm genuinely sorry. I'll make it up to them. But Federick, you got to understand, my work is extremely important, and if I have to '**Up and go**' as you've put it, I don't have any other choice but to." Making sure my voice was down, I sincerely responded.

"Phebes, we have some business to take care of. If we are done here, shall we head to your office." Supporting an impatient look, Talon interrupted mine and Federick's little chat.

Inferring being in the same room as Damien was taking its toll on Talon, my conversation with Federick had to see a premature end.

"Sure, we've got a meeting to resume. Why don't you take the guys to my office and I'll follow behind."

"Is Damien joining us too?" Innocent like a child, Matt curiously propounded.

"Obviously not! He's not part of our team anymore." Talon coldly hissed before I could utter a single word.

"Don't you think you're being too harsh on the guy?" Trying to discern what the actual matter between Talon and Damien was, Xylan scrutinised both men.

"Me, too harsh! You're kidding me, right." Talon exclaimed with bitter sarcasm. "I can't believe this!" Storming off, Talon oriented towards my office.

"Don't be jealous, Talon. I'm not going to steal your precious team even though I could if I wanted too." Damien mockingly voiced out, his grin growing when he heard Talon's departing growl.

"Wipe that smug off your face, will ya." I reprimanded Damien with mild authoritativeness after Talon was gone, to which he dared respond with a mere shrug.

"Head to the office, I'll be joining in a few." Directing my order to Xylan and Matt, I gave them their time to shake Damien's hand and bid their goodbyes to everyone else.

Focusing my full attention on Damien, "You really shouldn't be going through all this because of me. I apologise for your discomfort, and the disdain Talon has grown against you." Resting my hands on his chest, I expressed my regrets.

"It's fine. But, you do realise it's only going to get worse when everyone else finds out." Placing his hand on top of mine, as if to say he understood, Damien explained with little to no emotion.

Yet, I knew deep down all the unwanted nasty comments and reactions affected him. How could it not? Damien once was the most respected male figure within the agency. He was admired, looked up to, had a promising career ahead of him, and every male dreamt of being him. The man was so prideful of all his achievements that it sometimes irked Mia and me. But now, because of me, Damien was destroyed and left with nothing.

Adding fuel to the fire was returning to this very city after a decade and still having Vanderwill freely roaming around. I couldn't even begin to imagine how demanding, exhausting, wearisome, or even hellish all this was on Damien.

Alas, for my dear friend, tomorrow wasn't going to be any easier. I, at least, have my kids as my anchor, but Damien . . . He eviscerated that anchor when he left years ago. All he has are his several cases and loneliness.

Leaping forwards without any warning, I tightly hugged Damien. I wasn't sure who really needed this hug — him or me. But I relinquished his firm embrace and the magic of this moment.

"You remember you once promised me that if we have each other, we can get through any difficulties life throws our way? Well, if you want me, you still have me. And I promise we will get through this together." Holding onto his shoulder blades, crushing the sparkling fear that Damien might not be true to that promise any more, particularly after what had happened, I expectantly promulgated.

Pecking me on the cheek with a smile, Damien confirmed we were still true to our promise. Relief washing over me, a natural smile caressed my visage.

"I really need to get going. You know how work can be. And Dam . . . Even though I wish you would spend the night, you can leave if you want too. I don't want to pressure you more than I already have. Just for me, though, stay a bit and spend some time with the boys to get to know them better. As far as Federick goes, he will soon be heading to his place." Glancing at Federick for confirmation, he pulled his jerk card and shrugged his shoulders in response.

"Anyways, if I see you when I'm out of the office, I'll be more than happy. If not, I'll be saddened, but I'll understand and not hold it against you." Kissing Damien on the cheek, I turned to my boys, not particularly wanting to hear Damien's answer to my request.

"I don't believe I'll make it out of the meeting for dinner, so enjoy whatever Maria has prepared. I'll catch up with all of you later." Hugging each one of my babies goodnight, I left for my office.

CHAPTER 27
MEETING THE BEST FRIENDS

FEDERICK

"**Y**eah, right. How dare he stand me up?" A pissed-off female voice I could identify with close eyes originated from the living room.

"Who stood whom up?" I assertively demanded to none other than my dear Phoebe.

Last I heard she went to handle some sort of business at either her finance company or the one whose name was not to be mentioned. Yet, here she was. Late. With three well-built men following her and speaking about being stood up by another mysterious guy. As if this particular scene wasn't enough to stem a fume of anger and jealousy within me, Phoebe added salt to my wounds by ignoring me and my questions.

Peeling my eyes off of Phoebe, I studiously observed her three best friends. Taking into account Xylan and Matt's bubbly mischievous personality, I reckoned they were of no danger to my agenda of courting Phoebe. They were actually nice and amusing people.

Talon's wariness of me, however, threw him in my competitor list.
His tone when speaking to me and his evident protectiveness towards
Phoebe had me wonder if he was in love with Phoebe. Or if he and
Phoebe were a thing.

I recognised I sounded like a paranoid clingy boyfriend, which
was so unlike me. But I honestly didn't know what to think anymore.
Phoebe has and still was hiding so many secrets from me that I
couldn't help but doubt everything.

Then again, when Wyatt clarified my apparent disbelief about
why Phoebe's best friends were here at his hour, part of me was glad
to be proven wrong. The other part of me, however, was definitely
embarrassed. And Phoebe's quirk eyebrow challenging me for doubting her words didn't ease my sense of abashment.

My surprise upon learning her best friends worked for her, and
Talon was her right-hand man, however, surpassed my embarrassment. Who would have imagined, 'The Great Phoebe Smith', my personal executive assistant had her very own right-hand man. Definitely
not me.

Further staggering though was learning that Logan, who now
holds the largest shares in my company, worked for Phoebe too.
This situation and the way Logan earned his title as the President of
my company without my immediate knowledge definitely sounded
fishy and suspicious. But this was Phoebe we were talking about. She
would never commit corporate crimes or even dare to betray me in
such a malicious manner. She knew how much Archer & Associate
meant to my family and me. As such, even thinking about Phoebe taking over my business and backstabbing me was out of the question.
Yes, Phoebe was still hiding something from me, and perhaps it was
my love for her that was blinding me, but I'll be damn if I didn't trust
her on this particular matter.

Sensing Talon's intense scrutinising stare, the absurd theories
roaming free through my head immediately dissipated. Standoffish,
I glued my lour on Talon. Perhaps, Talon seemed so protective of
Phoebe because he was her right-hand man and best friend. Yet, I
couldn't shake the feeling that there was something more to Talon
than met the eyes.

UNMASKING

My gaze falling on Phoebe on its own accord, it appeared arguing and attempting to annoy her best friends were Miss Phoebe Smith's favourite pastime. A fly on the wall, I silently observed Phoebe in her natural habitat, her true free self only increasing my love for her. There was no doubt; I had eyes only for Phoebe. For her beautiful shining self that was teaching me how to love and be patient. How not to be my cold, selfish, calculating and arrogant self.

What made the evening further engaging was Xylan's baby voice when he complained about Phoebe's lack of manner. Having found an opportunity to tease Phoebe without letting the others know what had been happening between the two of us, I grasped the chance with a confident smirk.

As I had envisioned, Phoebe's face and ears instantly glowed like Christmas lights in a dark frosty night despite her attempts to hide her blush. Riled up and ferociously glowering at me, Phoebe made this moment all the more memorable for me.

You know how sometimes it feels like the whole universe has something against you; as if it can't bear your happiness. Well, add this feeling with how you would feel if someone suddenly poured a cold bucket of ice water on top of you while you were having the best dream of your life. This was precisely how I felt upon hearing and seeing Damien in Phoebe's house so late in the evening.

As if the mere appearance of Damien wasn't enough, Phoebe had to dig the knife deeper. Way too cosy with Damien, she proudly announced she had personally invited him over after our special moment together since last night. Despite hating Damien's presence near Phoebe, Talon's sudden outburst, as confusing as it was, aroused the realisation that something important could be learned; compelling me to stay put and quietly observe the scene.

The train of conversation between Talon and Damien was more than insightful. Not only did I learn two of Phoebe's best friends hated Damien more than I did, but also that Talon got promoted as Phoebe's right-hand man after Damien's departure ten years ago. A time where she most needed Damien by her side, to help her take care of Wyatt and Teo while dealing with the death of her father. A period where her life went downhill. Despite all these discoveries, the main question still remained.

Who were the two boys' birth parents? From what I gathered, Damien was the dad, but Phoebe also clarified she wasn't the birth mother. Then what really happened ten years ago? And what was the actual relationship between Phoebe and Damien?

The whole situation, the seemingly underlying meaning of their words and the tensed air in the room, sprung up more curiosity about Phoebe and her life. Be it her life ten years ago or the present where I'm personally involved. Amidst everything unfolding, what truly disturbed me was Xylan's slip about Damien being Phoebe's first. The green monster inside me got much more difficult to tame or contain.

The first what? First boyfriend? First business partner? First right-hand man? Or the first guy Phoebe slept with?

Catching sight of my cold murderous stare demanding an answer, Phoebe dismissed me. Dismissed my bleeding heart and the hurt she was inflicting me with her indifference. Instead, she preferred to make sure dear Damien was properly welcomed and treated respectfully, even if some of us had a completely different opinion of Damien and how we really wished to welcome him.

Focusing on the cheerful smiles between Talon, Matt, Xylan, Wyatt, Teo and Luke, I calmed myself down. Being openly jealous and mad wouldn't serve any purpose. Control and silence were my best weapon. At least up till Phoebe left Damien's side to accuse me of lying despite being the one who was doing all the lying.

Smothering the lure her closeness had on my body, I gandered at Phoebe through my peripheral vision and hoped my harsh yet honest words stirred her. What I wasn't expecting, however, was getting caught on the hop.

Benumbed on the one hand, and delighted on the other, Phoebe's confusion when I pointed out the obvious was an eye-opener. Phoebe was not purposely indifferent to my feelings. She had a problem identifying and showing her emotions.

Truthfully, I wasn't an expert on the emotion area either, but I at least knew how to identify and show my feelings based on a situation. Some might call it manipulative, but I saw it as conservation of resources. Only the most-deserving merited a sight of my real emotions and Phoebe definitely qualified. Being here with Phoebe and considering what we've gone through so far, I reckoned with enough love, direction and push from all of us; Phoebe would hopefully be able to unhesitantly express herself and accept the love we are all offering her. If we are lucky, she might even grow enough sympathy to stop lying and hiding information from us.

As if the world wanted to inform me I had taken the right initiative concerning the love of my life, Phoebe, of all people, sincerely apologised. And for the first time ever, uttered out loud that I, Federick Archer, was right. That in itself was a big step and proved Phoebe had a beating heart instead of a stone inside her chest.

Despite not appreciating Talon interrupting mine and Phoebe's little chat, I quickly got over it at the mention of the word *'Team'*. Even Damien used the same word while taunting Talon. Yet, no one had found the use of such a term for Phoebe's businesses a tad bit intriguing or unusual. Surely the use of the word team, particularly the way their tones seemed to insinuate wasn't common in the finance world, indicating that all of Phoebe's best friends worked at her second company. The same company she didn't want to talk about. And this my friends, ensued my determination to find out what her other business was all about.

Hearing Phoebe apologising to Damien for absolutely no real explanation reminded me how much I despised it whenever Phoebe continuously asked for his forgiveness when she never before asked anyone for forgiveness — even when she was wrong. As if I wasn't unnerved enough with the whole situation, Phoebe had to literally throw herself at Damien, not caring if her sons or I were watching.

Evidently unnerving me wasn't enough for Phoebe. She had to up her game and be all lovey-dovey with Damien. Declaring her promises to always be there for him no matter what happens. I couldn't believe how Phoebe couldn't see how pathetic she was being by offering herself so easily to Damien, especially when he had no remorse about abandoning her ten years ago. The way Phoebe was acting along with talking was making me sick to the stomach to the point where my inside began churning and boiling with rage.

"If only looks could kill, Damien would be six feet under right now." Wyatt teasingly whispered close to my ear so only Luke, Teo and I could hear.

"You have no idea, Wyatt. No idea at all." Attempting to calm the green monster moments away from breaking free and hulking out, I lowly and frostily growled.

How on earth could Phoebe not see the look in Damien's eyes when she invited him to stay the night and spend time with the boys. I was personally confident he would jump at the first opportunity to leave. Yet, there was this flicker of hope in Phoebe's eyes.

"Don't worry about him, Federick. Trust me. He's not going to be a problem for long. But first, you need to calm down before you ruin the small chance you have with my mom." Maintaining his smile so he wouldn't raise Phoebe's suspicion, Wyatt calmly and quietly contended.

Then again, I didn't think Phoebe would have noticed even if Wyatt were to spew or make scaring faces. Her sole focus was Damien — okay, maybe I was over-exaggerating, but this guy was genuinely getting on my last nerve.

CHAPTER 28
NEW TEAM LEADER

PHOEBE

"I can't believe you guys actually think Damien is some sort of impressive dude. He's a coward who didn't even think twice before leaving Phoebe — our **BEST FRIEND** — when she most needed him. With two kids no less. What would you think of me or anyone among us if we acted so pathetically?"

Standing in front of the half-closed door, Talon's words against Damien shouldn't have surprised me. Yet, it pained me to know how much hate Talon has cultivated towards the one person he once looked up too.

"Tal, I'm not excusing Damien's lapse of judgement. We all agree he was wrong. But you gotta remember he was hurting too. Phoebe lost her best friend who was like a sister to her, but Damien eventually lost more. He lost his fiancée, the one and only love of his life. Now, tell me, how can we essentially scale who was hurting more when we weren't even there. Let alone ever went through the kind of heartbreak they did." Careful not to stir a major fight and for once behaving maturely, Xylan explained with great patience.

"How can you stand here and defend that bloodsucker? You never even met the guy until a few minutes ago!" Talon defensively expostulated.

"I've known Damien far longer than you, Tal, and I would second Xylan in a heartbeat. I'm sorry, but you're being unreasonably harsh on Damien. At the very least, try to give him another chance. I would have had if I was in any of your places." Closing the door behind me, I walked to my table.

"But, Phebes —"

"Look, Talon, I reckon you're trying to look out for me. As you should, given you're my right-hand man and a part of my family. But Damien is a part of my family too, and you need to learn to accept him. Damien loves me just like you do — like many of you do. He simply has had a rough time. I already have my work cut out for me when I'll have to convince and appease Logan, Alicia and Joseph, so will you please at least attempt to make it a bit easier on me. I would greatly appreciate it." Dropping my authoritarian attitude, I explained with a pleading look.

"Fine. But this doesn't mean I'm okay with him. The less time Damien and I spend in the same room, the better." Huffing his aggravation, Talon agreed.

"Great." Depositing the stack of files we acquired earlier on top of my table, "Shall we get back to our new case then?"

Quirking an eyebrow at Matt's impatience to start this case, "Alright then. Matt, Xylan, prepare two different crime boards. One for the pictures you took and another for the pictures the detectives handover. Talon, keep searching through the museum database for any valuable intel."

Taking notes of the stacks of folders in front of me, pique, the reality that I was now one man down hit me hard. "I'll study these files for insights on what we are actually dealing with and what our next move is going to be."

"You know, this will be a great opportunity for Luke to start his training. Besides, we will get a helping hand." Finishing inspecting my first file, Talon's voice caught my attention.

It was like the man had read my frustration and came up with the most fantastic plan. Matt and Xylan nodding in accordance, the vote was cast. The sooner Luke starts his field training, the better.

"Mom, Maria said you asked for me?" Immediately closing the office door behind him, Luke questioned with puzzlement.

"Yes." Directing my gaze to my right-hand man, "Tal."

Without needing further explanation, his face straightening, emotionless like a rock, "As you're aware, officially becoming a Smith means automatic integration into the Elite Team. Not to mention being next in line after Angel, on top of remaining Wyatt and Teo's primary undisclosed bodyguard. You are talented, intelligent and an exceptional fighter. The main reason you were approached and handpicked by Angel, herself. All these are your advantages, Agent, but you are still a newbie. You've yet to attain the credential and experience necessary to be a part of this team. As such, your training is going to be harsher, more severe, intensive, bone-wrenching and on most occasions, unannounced. Each member of this team will train you as they deem fit, but I'll be running point in your training, whereby I'll make sure you face your every single fear. I hope you've considered all these factors before signing the adoption papers. If not, you still have 48 hours to get out of it." Talon noted in a calm, professional straight tone, sparing me the duty of having *The Talk* with Luke.

The words Talon spoke seeping into him; Luke studied Talon with firmness and brawniness, "Of course, I considered all these conditions when I signed the papers. Besides, I agree with you. Just because I'm one of Phoebe Smith's sons doesn't mean I automatically deserve becoming Angel's successor. I need to earn the position and status on my own." Luke responded with utmost confidence, delighting me even more and reassuring me I've made the right decision concerning him.

"Good. We are going to kick off your training with detective work. With your IQ, it should be easy and basic. Throughout this investigation, you will be expected to contribute like any member of the team. Have any questions, ask. Want to make a point, go ahead with confidence or shut up. Have any ideas, share it without hesitation. It might be wrong, but in an investigation, the right type of questions that help move forward is often the most blatant point voiced out loud." Concluding with a glance towards me, Talon returned to fixating his monitor, leaving me to take over.

As the team leader, the head of the agency and as Angel, it was on me to direct Luke on what he should do next. Conscious Luke had little to no experience with the sort of detective work we do; it seemed wise to start him off with something I could easily supervise.

Teaming Xylan and Luke to construct the crime scene boards, I shared the pile of folders with Matt. Occasionally and surreptitiously flicking my attention from my files to Luke, it was a pleasure to see his training from the Agency débutante basecamp was paying off. Going through my last few documents, I was safe in the knowledge that Luke was going to make me proud.

Associating the insights pulled from the reports with the photos filling the board like pieces of a case-tête, Talon's briefing on this infamous thief was the centrepiece of this puzzle. The determiner of how far this investigation will go and whether I'll have to personally see to it that this criminal's wings are chopped. Especially for impelling me to lose my time and resources on his kind of scum when I could be spending my days and time on trying to catch Vanderwill.

"The person who stole this painting was definitely hired." Pinning the last picture on the board and taking a step back, Luke proclaimed.

"Other than the obvious, what else were you able to deduce?" Leaning back on my leather chair, devoid of any emotion, steepling my fingers under my chin, the Angel in me, alive, I professionally inquired and waited for Luke to give the board another once-an-over.

"This work was meticulous, suggesting the perpetrator is or was an experienced treasurer." Fully twisting towards me, Luke observed.

"How did you come up with this conclusion?" Talon demanded in an equally distant and professional tone.

"Well, a closer look shows the stolen painting was in an area filled with other equally expensive much-accessible artefacts. Yet, only one was taken. Strengthening my point is the painting in the centre of the gallery." Pinpointing the specific colourful abstract art, I would depict as a rainbow puke rather than actual art, "It's more precious and priceless than any art in this part of the building. This dictates that the stolen painting was targeted and not chosen at random." Luke professionally explained with the confidence of a man who has been investigating art theft for decades.

"Been studying arts a lot?" Xylan playfully poked fun at Luke's extensive knowledge of arts.

"School project." Luke simply noted and returned his gaze on me, awaiting instruction.

"Do you have any other points?" Indirectly urging Luke to think more about certain weird factors that didn't make sense in this case, I propounded.

With a long and thoughtful regard, "Analysing these pictures, I can't help but hit a bump every time I ponder over the BlackBox. There's something weird about it. Like it's the key to answering most of our questions — it's just a feeling, though."

With uncertainty and confusion washing over his face and words, I slightly smirked at the fact that Luke was starting to ask himself the right questions. Realising this case would allow Luke to shine, to prove himself and show the agency his worth by capturing this famous, untouchable thief, this whole investigation didn't seem like a waste of time anymore.

"Talon, does this correlate with the MO of the thief, Blair mentioned?"

Nodding in confirmation, it was clear what I had to do.

"Luke, since you seem to know more about art than any of us here, along with heading towards the right direction, this case is now officially yours. My advice, keep questioning those weird feelings. Ask yourself, why do you have them? — Then find the answers that would shake the confusion off."

"You're not joking, are you?"

Quirking my brow, "Did my professional tone and regard hinted

I was joking?" My voice holding a sterner tone than before, I demanded.

"No, of course, not . . . Thank you so much." Luke rambled, still in
awe.

Nodding to welcome Luke, it was understandable why his excitement had left him open-mouthed. Leading your own team and case
for the very first time was a significant deal in our world — a time
of major celebration. Encircling Luke, the rest of the group openly
expressed their excitement and congratulated Luke on his first detective case. Glad my unit quietly agreed with my decision instead of
rebelling against me, especially when Luke was still green and this
case was for Blair, I internally rejoiced.

"Provided this is your first time as a leader, that too for a high
profile priority case, I'll see to it that tonight's meeting is short. This
should give you enough time to celebrate and think about our plan
of action. Not to forget, ploy a clear strategy on how to capture the
culprit as well as récoupe the painting."

Luke excitedly nodded, his wide contagious smile plastered on his
face.

"Talon, tell us more about this famous thief." Giving Talon my full
attention, followed by the others, I waited to hear about the causation
behind why this case was stuck on my team.

"Not just any thief, Phebes, but a master in his domain. Despite
being on the FBI and Interpol most wanted list, they only have his
side profile as a form of identification. He's practically untraceable.
As per Blair's intel, he's in his mid-forties, always in a 4-piece suit and
loves collecting all things illegal. He's an excellent forger, suspected
of a variety of bond forgeries, the artist of several embezzlements
and theft in numerous countries. He single-handedly robbed diverse
high-class museums of their priceless antiquities. He's a man of many
talents, over-confident, enjoys teasing the detectives investigating his
cases with intricate clues and weirdly enough, has a gentleman-way
of doing business."

"Why does Blair think this is the mighty handiwork of Mr Gentleman thief?" Slicing my hands over the scattered files on my desk and

pointing at the boards of pictures, I propounded.

"The pattern of events. *'Mr Gentleman thief'* as you've put it is known as *'The Fox'* and follows a specific pattern, part of his gentleman charade. We've determined the person who stole the painting was an expert and hired, which matches the beginning pattern to the other cold cases *The Fox* is suspected to be involved in. The conflict here, however, is that *The Fox's* work is clean. He never leaves anything behind, not even a body count. And this BlackBox left in the open for anyone to find, has Blair doubting. Then again, it's known he doesn't personally commit the thefts. He strategises and always employs different people to do his dirty jobs, which could explain this sudden irregularity."

Exceptionally attentive to Talon's briefing, it was crystal clear Blair wanted to bring this famous *'Fox'* guy to justice. Winning this case during his first year would be a career-maker. But the question still remains. Did Blair's form of justice constitute killing the guy, or bringing him in front of a court?

Aware I couldn't be overly protective of Luke, letting him run free on this case seemed fair and right. Then again, protecting my family always comes first, and if this case gets too messy, I'll have to take over. As my asset and son, I couldn't allow any harm to befall him. But, for now, Luke shall lead and prove his competence. Turning my gaze on Luke, I hinted for him to jump in.

"Did you find what you were looking for in the museum database?" With confidence and professionalism, Luke questioned Talon.

Sitting back, with a hidden grin, I watched Luke take control of the case. Stealing a few glances at me to confirm he was behaving in the manner expected of him, the leader within Luke grew. Paying close attention to Talon's point on the irregularity left behind by the thief, there was no denying hacking the whole museum system with such professionalism and carefulness was unnecessary.

Why go through all these troubles when the target was a mere painting? And why leave something behind that could be traced, yet go through the entire museum's database with such stealthiness?

"You know, perhaps the painting wasn't the only item stolen?"

Luke took the words out of my mouth.

"The painting could be a cover-up, and the real target was something completely different." Matt pitched in, giving all of us something fundamental to work on.

"Like covering a murder." Xylan mysteriously quipped, clearly enjoying his theory better.

"Xylan, stop making fun of this case. We are serious here." I chastised the joker of the team.

"What? This would explain the weirdness of this case. Frankly, which idiot leaves the weapon of their way in and out of a crime scene they've prepared so much for unless it was on purpose." Laying back on his chair with his arms behind his head, as if he has just cracked the case open, Xylan sarcastically retorted.

"Nice theory Xylan, except for the murder part. The cops did their jobs, and there's no indication of foul play."

Turning to Talon since he was the only one who spoke to Blair and knew 'The Fox' complete bio, "Have this form of diversion been used by The Fox before?"

"So far, no. Nonetheless, we have to consider the possibility he changed his M.O given his habit of switching thieves for each part of a heist." With an 'I will find out more later' look hanging on his face, Talon briefly explained.

"Let's work on this theory for now. Talon, I think you should keep looking through their system for any anomalies and tomorrow visit the museum to check their internal hard-drive for further information. Maybe for something that might have been deleted or erased? If there's a mere possibility we can recover whatever the hacker destroyed or retrace its steps, we should give it a try." Recognising Luke had a point about the hacker attempts to destroy evidence of its presence; Talon nodded at Luke's request.

"As for the rest of us, I suggest tomorrow evening we go through everything the museum sent to the headquarter." Stacking his notes, Luke proposed.

"Notify your dear Blair; I accept his case. I want the information he promised me on my desk by tomorrow night. And inform him, we'll soon be having a serious talk in person."

My years of training tells me I should be on guard since I haven't met Blair yet, but I also trusted Talon's judgement. Talon would have never even brought up the idea of taking Blair's case if he felt there was something shady about Blair or his proposal. Besides, as long as Blair doesn't touch a hair on Cole Vanderwill's head, I can certainly cope with the fact that he *'Stumbled'* onto some new intel on my target.

"Sure." Talon simply responded before giving me a hug, followed by Matt and Xylan.

"We'll see you tomorrow." All of them except Luke bid their goodnights.

"Luke, we need to talk," I called out before Luke could walk out with the others.

Looking at me, Luke nodded, before closing the main door and heading back to his seat.

"You know I love and value you, right?" Not stomping down on my Angel side yet, I waited for Luke to nod his agreement despite not understanding what I was hinting at.

"Then, you also need to seriously grasp the reality that you're next in line to hold the keys of the trading world."

Federick's words playing in the back of my mind, I considered Luke's feeling and slightly tamed my authoritative tone. "Meaning, you can't afford to be overly friendly and kind. You need to be firmer in your actions and speech. Words like; Maybe, Perhaps, I think, or I suggest, can't be used so casually while leading a group. You can occasionally get away with Talon, Xylan, Matt and me, but when working with others, this type of behaviour will not be acceptable. You're required to show strength in your demeanour and in what you're doing, even when deep down you're freaking out or totally unsure of yourself. You need to have more faith in your gut, and when you are stuck or afraid you're going to make the wrong decision, you can always ask for help. However, be sure to carefully phrase your words so you remain in control as the alpha you ought to be."

Looking at me like a wounded animal, "I understand, and I'm sorry I'm unable to perform as you expected of me."

Luke's apologies hitting close to home, I slightly shook my head and devised a new method to prompt Luke to behave more like a leader. Wholly implementing Federick's advice, it was high time I started treating Luke more like a son rather than a mere soldier.

"Luke, sweetheart, I recognise you're a naturally kind and caring person, but sweetie, you can't be apologising for no apparent reason, especially when you haven't done anything wrong. I understand all of this is extremely new to you, and you're still in the learning stages. But, I also know for a fact that if anybody can do this, then it's you. Which is why, in addition to Talon's training, I'm going to prepare a list of other basic training designated for the heir of the agency that you will have to follow to the letter, or there will be severe consequences that even I won't be able to stop." Formulating a tone and attitude supporting the combination of a mother and a severe teacher, I informed and warned Luke.

As much as it pained me to destroy Luke's rare hint of innocence and cheerful, optimistic personality, it was practically impossible to preserve his sweetness and gentle character in our dangerous and secretive world. I hated having to bring darkness in Luke's life, but becoming more like me was his only way to survive.

Cutting short the vacuum of silent reflection between us, Luke squared his shoulders, indicating he was ready for whatever I was going to throw his way and nodded in understanding.

Having sent Luke back to whatever he was doing after finishing up the discussion of our possible future plans, I got into clearing my desk of all essential documents. That is until my phone vibrated beside me, weirding me out since all the kids were home and nobody else texts me so late at night on my personal number.

An involuntary smile crept up my face as I read Federick's text, informing me he was leaving and wishing me a good night sleep. Itching to leave my office to bid Federick a proper goodbye, I forced myself and my confused mind to stay put. Satisfying myself by responding with a simple goodbye text, I continued to stack my papers. But as seconds turned into minutes with no response from Federick, a wave of agitation coursed through my bloodstream. And no amount of phone-checking could bring me down that rollercoaster.

But why was this bothering me so much? We were, after all, just friends. Then, why on earth was I, Phoebe Smith, a fearless killer, experiencing this weird unexplainable emotion? Rethinking if I made the right decision not to bid Federick a proper in-person goodbye, I hated Federick for making me question myself again.

"Phoebe, it's late. You should head to bed." Stepping into my office, Maria voiced in a low tone, as she used to when she was my nanny.

Stealing a glance at the clock hanging on the wall in front of me, I couldn't believe I was spending my late night hours trying to figure out why Federick hasn't texted me back yet. Questioning if it was because he was mad at me or because he was too busy with one of his many flings to answer back.

Briefly squeezing my eyes shut in an attempt to erase the image of Federick with another woman from my mind, I swallowed the sour taste in the back of my throat. I couldn't comprehend why I was thinking and feeling the things I was, but I knew it had to stop.

Taking a deep silent breath, I compelled myself to get Federick out of my head and concentrate on Maria's curious look.

"Thanks Maria. I'll head to bed right away. Is Damien still here?"

"Sorry, sweetheart, he had some business to take care of. Something about a meeting tomorrow morning." Maria added with sympathy.

Well, at least Maria wasn't talking crap about Damien like everyone else has been doing so far and I was immensely grateful for the latter. Dismissing her, I locked my office and headed to bed, mentally preparing myself for tomorrow's undeniable eventful day.

CHAPTER 29
APPROVED & WELCOMED

FEDERICK

Left alone with Damien and the teenagers, an undeniable awkwardness hung over us — so palpable, I could poke at it with a knife. In that instant, I realised I had to kill the possessive teenager inside me and act like the collected, grown man that I was.

Taking the first step, with the neutrality of a slab, I invited Damien to dine with us. Aware Damien was working on finding a proper excuse to leave; I silently studied him. His fleeting eyes. His fake smile. The tension weighing down his shoulders and his feigning interest in the boys. I would even go as far as concluding Damien found interacting with the boys to be a nuisance.

Ten minutes or so after Luke was suspiciously called into Phoebe's office, a sense of triumph overcame me as the moment I was impatiently awaiting finally came. Using the grand excuse of suddenly remembering he had to prepare for tomorrow's meeting, Damien left.

Either he had forgotten or was plain out stupid, but both Phoebe and I were going to be in the same room as him for tomorrow's meeting. And the only thing Mr Damien needed to do was show up and listen to the several proposals we'll be throwing at him.

Regardless, I was more than happy Damien punked out instead of staying the night with my girl. Perhaps dear Damien Ambrose hasn't realised the harsh truth yet. But I, Federick Ashton Archer, do not ever, I mean **ever**, share what's mine. And Phoebe Ziva Smith was all **mine** from the day I laid eyes on her.

Unwilling to leave until all of Phoebe's friends were gone, I got into gaming with Wyatt and Teo. Then, it dawned on me. These two boys probably knew of Phoebe's companies and what it's all about. I simply had to ask the right questions, and unlike earlier, Luke wasn't here to stop them.

'One key factor you've obviously overlooked is that Phoebe, the love of your life, will forever hate you for using her kids behind her back to satisfy your nefarious curiosity. Then bye-bye your chance with her.'

Sometimes I really hated that nagging voice of reason, but it was once again right.

'Oh come on, without me you are a manipulative, bitter, frozen and unbreakable iceberg.'

And that's what I get for being nice to my exceptionally arrogant inner voice.

Listening to my trusted gut, I suffocated the whole espionage urges and focused on developing a healthy bond with Wyatt and Teo. Time flying by with each virtual combat, I only noticed how late it had gotten when Luke flumped onto the couch beside me with a huge smile.

Scoring a 10-8, effectively pulverising Wyatt's score, "Did your girlfriend send you a sexy picture of herself or what?" Puzzled by Luke's unfazed smile, I quipped.

"No. Why?" With one eyebrow raised in confusion, Luke countered.

"Then why are you grinning so wide?" Turning my full attention onto Luke, I posed.

"Because I'm now a member of mom's Elite team." With a glow in his eyes and a genuine grin, Luke excitedly announced.

"Elite Team?" Unashamedly pushing for more, I didn't even try to hide my suspicion.

The colour draining from his face, with an **'I just got caught red-handed'** expression replacing his earlier glimmer, Luke's slip spoke volume. It was clear he shouldn't have divulged a word about his new job.

"Besides, someone like me can't have a girlfriend." Sensing my uproar of questions, Luke effectively jumped ship. However, I wasn't in the mood to humour him and play along.

'Have some self-respect, dude. Remember your earlier rant about keeping your promises.' The wiser and more sensible part of me reprimanded as soon as the thought of pushing Luke beyond his limits crossed my mind.

Acting this rashly and impulsively would violate Phoebe's trust in me, especially with her kids. I would undeniably get all my answers, but Phoebe's kids won't be a pawn. I won't allow it. Either be it by Damien or me.

"You could have a girlfriend if you weren't so adamant and freak out by commitment like mom." Wyatt pitched in. "Right, Teo."

Mischievousness gleaming in Wyatt's eyes, his tone suggestive, I glazed at those two brothers with suspicion. Elbowing Wyatt on the side, Teo had my full attention. They were hiding something, it was clear as daylight.

"Firstly, there's nothing scary about commitment. There's up and down, but that's life. If you are with the right person, it's magnificent and beautiful, but if you are with the wrong person, it's hurtful and painful. Either way, you should be bold and strong enough for the adventures, and the changes relationships bring with it. And Teo, why on earth did you elbow Wyatt?"

"Oh look who has already taken their role as our step-father seriously. I'll advise you to slow your roll, cowboy. You've yet to make a decent move to seduce our mother." Wyatt jested.

"Especially with Damien dancing around her. You should start making your move, or she's gonna slip." Teo added his piece with an equal hint of amusement.

"Do you have your part to add, Luke?" I sarcastically inquired.

"Don't look at me. I know for a fact you and mom will not work."

And he was actually truthful. No wonder he has no real longterm girlfriend yet. It's not commitment issues that Luke has; it's being unsympathetically too blunt.

"Thank you for your vote of confidence, Luke. I feel so much better already."

"Oh, you are more than welcome," Luke responded with the same amount of sarcasm.

"Anyway, I apologise. I shouldn't lecture or scold you, boys. I have absolutely no right."

There was no doubt I was being too fatherly towards them when they weren't even my kids. But I couldn't stop myself. It was beyond my understanding, how someone as cold and affectionless as myself could care for the wellbeing of three teenagers I barely knew.

Why on earth was I being such a softy? The cold standoffish arrogant, selfish playboy that is Federick Ashton Archer hasn't felt or acted this way for a long time. So how has Phoebe Smith been able to change me to such an extent? And why was I suddenly being so considerate towards complete strangers?

"Federick! Are you still with us?" All three called out for me.

Forcibly pulled out of my troubled thoughts, "Sorry, you were saying?" Returning to the present world, I asked no one in particular.

"I was saying; you don't have to apologise. You are our friend and soon to be the love of our mother's life. So yes, you have every right to act like the father we never had. Just don't go all authoritarian on us." Teo's words and his brothers approving glances melted my heart, instantly dissipating the various questions flowing through my confused mind.

"Thank you so much, boys. You have no idea how much your guys' acceptance of me in your family means." Hugging them, I showered them with appreciation.

"Okay, let's not get too cheesy now. You still have to win our mother over, and as far as I can see, you're not exactly winning." Trying to get out of our hug, Luke pointed out.

Unfortunately for Luke, instead of slapping him with the fact that I was winning by three points over Damien, I tackled him to the ground with the help of Wyatt and Teo. And guess what? Dear Luke wasn't immune to tickling, not a single bit.

"Okay, Teo, you still haven't answered my earlier question. Why did you elbow your brother without any reason?" Laying on the ground, our laughter subsiding, I questioned once again.

"That's a story for another time, Federick. We have school to-morrow, and it's time for us to head to bed. But thank you for your advice. One of these days it will certainly be of great use." Standing to his feet, Wyatt stated with a slight grin.

Suspicious of Wyatt's grin and Teo's nervous glint, I dropped the issue for the time being and bid them good night. Taking the time to text Phoebe good night, I awaited her response, hoping for her to bid me farewell. I probably shouldn't have done it. But I did it anyway. Hanging about in the living room, I was left waiting and disappointed when Phoebe responded to my sweet loving message with a simple goodnight text. Rather than replying back, though, I silenced my phone, took my keys and drove home. I sure as heck hoped my action, or better, inaction affected Phoebe and made her realise her mistake.

I reckoned it might have been a mistake to allow myself to feel so easily and openly after the horrid incident with Veronica. It was hard for me to love romantically with all my heart — at least the pieces left of my broken heart — when years ago I had sworn I would never again venture in this path of possible destruction.

Then again, when I see Phoebe and how she interacts with her family, my eardrums muffle the alarm bells. She's the firestorm that set me ablaze with an indescribable passion. She's the reason the bitter and harsh memories of Veronica's words had stopped haunting me.

But now, as Phoebe's indifference hit at my core, all those memories swept over me with fervour. With an intense desire to hunt me down and burn me to crisp like a wicked witch's curse.

CHAPTER 30
BAD BLOOD

PHOEBE

"Good morning, Phebes." Walking alongside me with two cups of coffee, one for herself and one for me, Nadiya greeted.

"Good morning, Nad." Smiling at her vibrant face and accepting the cup she handed me, "Thanks, but you don't have to bring me coffee. It's my secretary's job, not my personal assistant." Glad Nadiya was finally here after a hard and successful training; I politely reminded her.

"I know, Phebes, but pampering you is my sister-in-law's duty and right, so you better get used to it. Anyway, what brings you here so early?" Intrigued, Nadiya inquired with a smile.

The reason behind my sleepless and worrisome night flashing in front of my eyes, I internally groan. Who would have imagined a man's action or rather — inaction — could affect me so much? Not me.

"I couldn't sleep, so I figured working would be better than tossing around for hours." Divulging half the truth, I smothered the causation of my migraine.

"Well, this triple shot should help you stay awake in case your sleep deprivation decides to catch up with you."

"Thanks, I appreciate it. Also, call Alica Archer after lunch, please. Inform her that she and Joseph are invited for dinner at my place, tonight. Her private number is in my contact book." Recalling the notification for the upcoming dreadful event, I summarised for Nadiya.

"Sure. What should I tell Mrs Archer if she asks the reason behind your invitation?" Nadiya inquired with both confusion and inquisitiveness.

I guess anyone in their right mind would wonder why a mere executive assistant would invite the parents of *'The Great Federick Archer'* for dinner. At her place, nonetheless.

"Simply inform her I have two surprises for them. Oh, and make sure Federick doesn't find out about this dinner." I calmly instructed Nadiya before returning to my stack of papers.

"Okay." Nadiya uncertainly uttered.

Taking my silence as her cue to leave, Nadiya nodded and returned to her desk.

"Miss Smith, a certain Damien Ambrose, is here and wishes to meet with you. Shall I send him in?" Nadiya buzzed after twenty minutes or so.

"No. Inform him I'm coming out," I stated in the same professional tone.

Given Damien somehow already knew Nadiya was Logan's fiancée, I collected all the necessary documents and rushed out of my office as quickly as possible. In view of Damien and Logan's bad blood, making sure Damien doesn't hang around Nadiya for too long seemed like the best play — at least, until Logan was made aware of Damien's presence.

At the same time, it would be stupid of me not to presume Logan already have a clue of Damien's presence. Particularly after Talon's attitude last night. As calm as Talon was during stressful situations, he was even more hot-tempered when pissed. And last night, that man was beyond irked.

"I wasn't expecting you here so early." Dragging Damien away from Nadiya's desk and closer to the threshold of Federick's office, I tried to get away from prying ears.

"Good morning to you too, sweetcheeks," Damien muttered with a playful grin.

Smiling and hugging Damien, "Sorry. Good morning to you too." I mumbled in his arms.

✳✳✳

FEDERICK

"You will never be truly loved!"

"If not for your money, you are a worthless and sad person."

"You are a plaything, Federick. You'll **always** be used."

Waking up with a start, my body soaked with cold perspiration, Veronica Silver's vicious and ferocious derides continued to haunt me. The tortuous nights, where my dreams were invaded by memories of Veronica's actions and relentless harsh words had returned. Sadly this time, Phoebe was the reason behind this devil's reincarnation.

Getting a grip over myself, I stepped under the cold waterfall of my stainless steel thermostatic shower panel, its body jets serving to further relax my nerves. God knows how much I needed it. Especially if I were to continue dealing patiently with Damien and Phoebe

Whilst there was no denying the chemistry between Phoebe and

269

me, there were major roadblocks to overcome. Damien being the main obstruction. And Phoebe's overly-supportive or loving attitude towards him being the second colossal obstacle. Not to mention Phoebe's inclination to defy the attraction between us. At the same time, I had to deal with my aptitude of allowing Veronica to scare me away from love.

The road ahead was definitely hard and volatile, but my guts tell me, it would be well worth it.

"Hey, Federick, wait up," Logan called out as I was about to push the button to close my personal elevator door.

Impatiently tapping my feet on the steel floor, I held open the metallic door, waiting for Logan to reach me and spit out whatever he needed.

"You're heading to your office, right?" Still in a disgruntled mood, I swiftly nodded in affirmation.

"Cool. Do you mind if I tag along?"

Stepping inside my private elevator before I could refuse, unfazed by my dirty and cold look, Logan made a bold and dangerous move. Taking a deep, relaxing and silent breath, I selected my floor number, hoping this trip to my office will end already.

"So . . . I heard you met the rest of the gang last night. How did it go? What did you think of them?"

Evidently, Logan wasn't going to shut up. Even after I made it crystal clear, I didn't want to talk or be disturbed. Either he was completely oblivious of the dark aura oozing off me or was simply ignoring my grumpy mood.

"It was quite an interesting group, and the guys seemed cool. But, Talon. . . Either I unknowingly pissed him off, or, there is something seriously wrong with the guy. He just couldn't stop scrutinising me." Finally giving up on my silence, I recounted as we left the elevator.

"Oh yeah, Talon is just . . . How do I put it . . . Hmm . . . Overpro-tective of Phoebe."

"If by overprotective you mean jealous and in love with Phoebe, then yes." Reaching for more information, I interposed my earlier speculation.

"Nah, Phoebe considers Talon a brother. Just like I consider Phoebe as my spoiled baby sister."

"Phoebe might see Talon as a brother, but this doesn't mean Talon feels the same way." Unwilling to give Logan the chance to change the conversation, I counter-attacked.

"Well, Talon is — **Fucking hell**. Tell me I'm not seeing Damien fucking Ambrose in Phoebe's arms right now." Stopping dead in his track, Logan stentorianly expressed his outrage and fury.

Halting beside Logan, "Unfortunately, yes. It's him." I stated in my usual standoffish manner. But the reality of the matter was that I was seething with green jealousy and anger.

"No. Fucking. Way!" An appalled Logan sneered between grinding teeth.

Breathing roughly than usual, Logan curled and uncurled his fists before speed-walking towards the two lovebirds. Like a lion would move towards its prey prior to going for the kill.

***

PHOEBE

Out of nowhere, a large firm hand grappled my arm and yanked me back with force. Swift like a lightning rod, a fist went flying onto Damien's face. So hard, he stumbled backwards and fell butt-first onto the tile flooring. Frozen like an iceberg behind the shadow of the attacker, shock oozing off Damien and me, we attempted to get a grip over ourselves and what had just happened.

"You should have taken my warning seriously and stayed away. Because unlike you, I keep my promises." His body posture ready for a fight, his usual playful eyes colder than the north pole, viciously throwing fire daggers at Damien, Logan spat with venom.

Gawping between a huffing Logan and an injured Damien, "Wh—at? . . . Why? . . ." Stunned and baffled, I all but stuttered.

Instead of an appropriate answer, though, Logan shifted his leering from Damien to me and grabbed my wrist in his insanely tight clasp. Without a word, he dragged me to my office and slammed the door shut behind us, the vibration shaking the oak door framing. Logan's muscle jaw flexing and his breath slow. Deep and rasp. Fire blazing in his pool of greens, anger and disappointment oozed off of Logan like smoke from a flaming gas station.

Snatching my hand from Logan's death grip and twisting away, "What the fucking hell, Logan?" Standing still in front of Logan, not caring if the entire floor could hear us, I shouted in a high pitch tone with anger rolling off me.

"What the fucking hell, indeed? . . . Um . . . Let me think . . . Oh, wait. I remember! What in the fucking world is fucking Damien doing here? Or better yet, what are you doing hugging him?" Logan's sarcastically shrilled.

"If you must know, Damien is here on business. Regardless, you didn't have to go to such an extent to show your disdain for Damien. For fuck sake, why can't you simply accept and be happy that Damien is back!" Equally pissed off, I admonished.

"Oh, how sweet. Damien is back." Deriding, like an asshole, "Do you want us to throw a welcome-back party for him? Oh, wait . . . First, do you know how long he's gonna stick around this time?" Logan scoffed with a high tone of sarcasm.

"Will you stop being such an unsupportable ass!" I berated with exasperation.

"This still doesn't answer my question." Unfazed by my attempt to insult him, Logan raucously asserted.

Holding Logan's fervent stare, my defences eventually crumbling, "I don't know okay!" I stridently professed.

"So what? Be happy Damien is back, and then when he decides to make himself scarce for a second time, you'll break down into multiple pieces all over again. Because believe me, Damien is **not** going to think twice before vanishing the instant the situation gets too complicated for him." Slowly advancing towards my struggling self, Logan declared with a hint of irony and confidence.

"I'm not the same girl anymore, Logan. I'm not stupid." Accepting Logan's closeness, I defended in an almost weak tone.

A part of me knew Logan was right, but the other part of me — the past that was filled with guilt — was doing a damn good job at defying the logic of the situation. I didn't want to accept the reality where Damien would eventually leave. Plus, they were wrong on one point. Damien wouldn't vanish on me. When it's time for him to go, he will inform me, and I will accept it like a grown-up.

"I'm not saying you are stupid, Phebes. I'm not an insensitive prick, but let's be realistic. We both know Damien will pack his bag the instant the pressure of everything that's happening gets too hard for him to handle." Holding my cheeks between his palms, "I've always treated you as my baby sister because that's what you are to me. My baby sister whom I love with all my heart and would readily die for. Because of this, and so much more, I would hate to see you go down that road again because of this jerk." His kind, loving, protective big brother tone washing over me, my anger dissipated like the fog that has been struck by the first rays of sun.

Locking eyes with Logan, my demeanour laced with love and truthfulness, "I understand."

"You think you do because you are the invincible Phoebe Ziva Smith, but you honestly don't. We've made it a long way, and if this asshole does anything, I mean remotely **anything** at all, I swear to you, I won't spare him this time around." Studiously reading my eyes, Logan stressed out each word before pulling me into a bone-crushing hug.

"I love how you care for me, but you have to understand Damien is hurting too. You can't really blame him for leaving, especially when back then I too was a mess. Just please, stop bashing on Damien. I love him, and you all will eventually have to accept this truth."

I mumbled in Logan's arms, utterly oblivious of someone else's presence in the room until a fake cough caught mine and Logan's attention.

CHAPTER 31
MISCONSTRUED

FEDERICK

Watching the scene unfolding in front of me with contentment as Logan executed one of my long-awaited desires, I could affirm with certainty that Talon wasn't kidding when he claimed Logan would redefine Damien's meaning of hostility. Logan was a wild and impulsive animal, with an unforgiving fire dancing in his pool of greens.

As blissful as witnessing the stunned look on Damien's smug face was, I didn't appreciate Logan's roughness towards Phoebe. Yes, I was still mad at Phoebe, but my protectiveness for her wellbeing exceeded my irkness at her indifference towards me.

Overhearing shouts coming from Phoebe's office, I took a chance and twisted her office's doorknob. Alas, the door was well locked. Unable to stand the odd incomprehensible low mumbles seeping from Phoebe's office, my curiosity and protectiveness overrode my desire to respect Logan and Phoebe's privacy.

"Where do you think you're going?"

Turning towards the audacious source, I bore my glare onto Nadiya's curious look while she helped Damien to his feet.

"I didn't realise I needed your permission to enter my own office." Eager to learn more about Phoebe and possibly her relationship with Damien, I retorted.

"Your office. Yeah, right! You're more likely going into Phoebe's office through yours." Nadiya alluded with a smirk as I reached my office's threshold. This girl was definitely getting ahead of herself, but right now, Phoebe was more important to me than dealing with a mouthy assistant.

"Of course, he is. Why wouldn't he? After all, he's been glued to Phoebe's ass for weeks now."

Letting Damien's words roll off of me, I momentarily closed my eyes, took a deep calming breath and slowly unclenched my balled fist. God only knows how much I wanted to knock Damien out. Thankfully, I was able to control my growing fury and walked away.

"So what? Be happy Damien is back, and then when he decides to make himself scarce for a second time, you'll break down into multiple pieces all over again. Because believe me, Damien is **not** going to think twice before vanishing the instant the situation gets too complicated for him." Logan's confident and booming voice asserted as I stealthily stepped foot inside Phoebe's office.

Leaning against the casing of Phoebe's and mine connector door, I silently and studiously observed them. Observed how Logan's words affected Phoebe and her resolution to fight the logic behind his words. I swear if I hadn't spoken to Logan before, I would have fooled me by the scene unfolding in front of me. Their closeness and Logan's sweet overprotective words made it seem like they were a couple. Thankfully, Logan considered Phoebe as his baby sister and luckily for me; I was on Logan's good side in comparison to Damien — one more point for me.

But then, out of nowhere, I was whipped me off my high horse at the greatest rate ever. Hearing Phoebe openly admits she still loved Damien despite everything he did, shattered my barely healed heart. My hopes and dreams for true happiness flew away in front of my eyes in a matter of seconds.

I guess the dream I had this morning was a harsh reminder of what I couldn't have. Why I should continue to protect myself from this inexplicable form of love I feel for Phoebe. The reason why I needed to keep my walls up — no matter how strong the pull between the two of us was.

Then again, giving Phoebe up or the possibility of love so I wouldn't get hurt again seemed wrong. I was at a loss, and nothing seemed to make sense. All I knew was I needed to calm down and think logically with less anger coursing through my veins like poison.

In the meantime, however, what I could do was put an end to this whole debate about how important Damien was to Phoebe.

***

PHOEBE

Lips tightened. Eyes narrowed into slits. Throwing icicles at me. Federick stood against our connecting door with his arms crossed over his puffed chest. Clearly, he didn't get the memo that I required privacy.

Oh, no . . . He ignored it Federick-style.

Matching his cold blank grey eyes, my mood still spoilt, "You should really learn to take the hint when not to disturb me. Most importantly, respect my privacy."

"Why? You're worried someone will overhear just how much you love Damien Ambrose?" Marble-faced, Federick fired back with sarcasm and a hint of venom.

Exhausted by this whole Damien situation so early in the day, I forcibly swallowed my urge to yell at Federick for once again rapidly speculating without any basis or hard evidence. Instead, I disparagingly shrugged my shoulders, effectively dismissing Federick's rudeness.

Stony-faced. Flame blazing in his usually emotionless eyes. The stress line in his cheekbone became more pronounced as he silently ground his teeth. Evidently infuriated by my dismissal, the frostiness in Federick bored into me.

'Why does he care, anyway?'

He didn't care last night when he didn't bother responding to my text — not that there was much to respond to, but still.

'And why the hell was his inaction upsetting me so much? It was just a stupid text, Phoebe. Get a grip of yourself for Christ sake!'

Not understanding why I was suddenly experiencing this insane tsunami of emotions over such a small matter, I mentally scolded myself.

"We have a meeting to get to — let's get moving," Logan stated in an attempt to dodge the invisible thundering electrical storm building up between Federick and myself.

Reading the uncomfortableness in Logan's eyes, I darted one last sharp glare at Federick and nodded my head in affirmation.

Walking back to the lobby, I was thankful someone was kind enough to have tended to Damien's bloody nose. However, upon real-ising the good samaritan was none other than **Lucy Braton**, I instantly took back my word. Holding an ice pack to Damien's face, that leech's big chest was way too close to Damien for comfort.

"I got it from here!" Holding my hand in front of Lucy, I gravelly and frigidly demanded the ice pack.

"It's okay. I'm already doing it." Battling her fake eyelashes, Lucy voiced in one of her fake sweet sickening tones.

"Lucy, I was being polite. Back off from him." Plastering a fake sweet smile on my otherwise straight-face, "Please." I honeyedly threatened.

"You better give the lioness what she wants before she pounds on you for lurking around her territory." Federick satirised.

"You're right. We don't want her to start biting everyone's head off so early in the morning." Roughly handing me the bag, Lucy sassed and stomped away as the drama queen she was.

Further infuriated by Federick's taunting, I focused my attention on Damien before my killer instinct propels me to do something I would later regret. Squatting in front of Damien, I gently set the ice pack on his wounded face to ease the pain once again caused by me.

'Will you stop blaming yourself for everything that happens!' My inner voice popped out of nowhere in a reproaching tone.

'Look, Mrs Inner Voice put a lid on it! I already have a lot on my plate because of the others, and I don't need to be fighting with my inner self — besides, I'm merely taking responsibility for my mistakes. And Logan punching Damien is no doubt my fault.'

Shaking off this insanity of questioning my actions and fighting with myself, I hightailed out of my troubled thoughts.

Giving Damien my full attention, I didn't think twice about Lucy; assuming she was far gone by now. But, oh, boy, I couldn't have been more wrong. Within minutes of leaving me alone, that bloodsucking vampire jumped on Federick Archer — her favourite prey.

Instead of pushing Lucy off him, Federick openly welcomed her advances and annoyingly honeyed, sickening and revolting voice. Going against the words he spoke in my office, Federick embraced Lucy's approach and flirtiness without an ounce of hesitation.

Standing so close to Federick, her fake boobs puffed out of her half-opened blouse to the point where it could explode. Now, that would be a show worth watching.

Witnessing Federick's never-ending whoring behaviour, I couldn't believe I kid myself into believing someone like Federick Archer could change in a good way. He was still the same arrogant overbearing, annoying and overconfident playboy I grew up knowing. The only difference was that Federick's cold, indifferent, standoffish and whoring manners have somehow managed to affect me.

'For God sake! Why was the picture of Lucy in Federick's arms pissing me off so much?'

I wasn't this annoyed when Lucy was throwing herself at Damien.

Oh no, at that moment, I had the extreme desire to smack Lucy so hard she would need another plastic surgery to straighten her face. Throwing daggers at Lucy, I was strongly starting to doubt my sanity. Either I had gotten a blow to the head without my knowledge, or I was finally losing it.

"You are supposed to be helping with decreasing the pain. Not increasing it." Taking the ice pack from my grip and attending to his own wounds, Damien jested with a grin.

"Well, if you would stop looking for a fight, you wouldn't be hurt." I harshly snapped, earning myself a few raised eyebrows from my audiences.

"I apologise. I'm just disgusted with the double-standard, fakeness and shamelessness of some people in this room." Glancing around the room, I left out the part where I wanted to rip Lucy's pretty little blonde head off her neck.

"You could speak directly to this person, you know. Especially since I can picture someone else in this room which is shameless, fake and has double-standard." Federick voiced out from across the lobby.

Federick was clearly looking for it. First, he ignores me. Ruins my sleep with his constant bizarre behaviours, acts out, then flirts with the office most popular bitch right in front of me. As if all this wasn't enough, he was now openly challenging me with his firing glare.

Well, he was going to get it with me.

What does he think! Because I let him close to me — to my family — and opened up to him during the weekend, it gave him the right to trample over me? Oh no, he had something else coming his way. I was going to show him; Phoebe Ziva Smith doesn't take crap from anyone — not even from **'The Great Federick Archer'**.

"I'm glad you were able to identify yourself based on my *'Not-so-vague'* description. But please, don't let me interrupt your whoring. I'm sure Lucy is already feeling under-appreciated from your absence of attention." If my tone wasn't rude and bitter enough, then my blazing and infuriated lour finished the job.

"You . . . Little —"

"Guys —Guys!" Nadiya exclaimed in a high pitch.

"What!" Both Federick and I unintentionally snapped at her.

"I don't mean to interrupt or disturb you two, but you are all late for the meeting." Seemingly unaffected by our foul attitude and firing scowl, Nadiya calmly stated.

"Thank you."

Federick and I once again uttered at the same time, propelling us to challenge each other in another timeless round of ferocious glare. One that I had no intention of losing.

"Ahem." Loudly clearing his throat, Logan hauled Federick and me back into reality.

Choosing to be the bigger person — yet again — I moved past this tension-filled atmosphere and smiled at Nadiya in appreciation of the reminder. Then again, it seems mother-nature decided the mere presence of Miss Lucy was still too little to annoy me. Damien had to be part of the equation.

"Sweet fiancée you have there, Logan. Where did you pick her up?"

Intentionally picking a fight, Damien pushed his luck for an opportunity to punch Logan back. And what better way than to target the one person for whom Logan left the Agency. The woman he plans to marry and promise to protect and love unconditionally.

"You better stay the fuck away from my fiancée." Logan's defences further rising, he spat with utmost disdain.

With a smug smirk, "Is this a death threat?" Enjoying unnerving Logan way too much, and playing the fool, Damien sarcastically jeered.

Silently observing Logan and Damien, I readied myself to intervene in case they break into another fist-fighting. There is no way I was going to let their animalistic rage and pride destroy my company's lobby.

Stepping closer to Damien and me, "It's a threat, alright!" Logan fired back in a booming voice.

"Both of you, stop this foolishness right away." The Angel in me taking over, "That's an order." I interjected, aware they won't have any other choice but to follow their leader; their boss and Alpha's orders.

As much as I hated ordering my best friends — particularly, Logan — in my *Angel tone* outside missions and the Agency, these two left me with no other choice. They were creating an unnecessary scene in front of everyone. Which unfortunately also consisted of Lucy — the company's head of gossip.

Intently staring at me, drowning the room in deafening silence, Logan and Damien reluctantly cowered down and uttered a *'Fine'*. Overlooking the two men with a flash of disappointment, I couldn't comprehend why everyone still had such a high level of hate towards Damien. **It's been a decade.**

Yes, I was deeply hurt and devastated when Damien left right after my dad's funeral, but I got over it. I recognised and understood why Damien had to take the decision he did. He had no other choice.

He was a mess, and I was a much bigger mess. Not to mention, there were two unwanted toddlers asking for their mother and father, and jumping around to the point of decimating our patience.

Regardless, both of us have recovered from that unfortunate time. We now have a better understanding of our situation and the decisions we have to make.

"You must honestly have a death wish to intentionally be taunting Logan." Leading the way to the meeting room with Logan and Federick following behind, I muttered to Damien.

"Nah . . . But teasing Logan is too tempting and fun." With a goofy grin, Damien dismissively responded.

The happy memories of when Damien and I were playful and would intentionally pull everyone's legs just for the heck of it flashed in front of my eyes. Matching Damien's amusement-filled eyes, it hit me.

Damien would definitely be continuing this bad habit of his; meaning, he was going to drag me down with him — like he used to.

CHAPTER 32
BIRTH OF HOPE

FEDERICK

Shot through the heart and clouded with anger, the only card I could play was returning to my indifferent, unemotional and stand-offish demeanour.

Seething and watching Phoebe tend to Damien's wounds; it was more than evident that I needed to keep my distance from Phoebe. At least, until I figured out what to do next.

Thinking being distant towards Phoebe would be difficult, I discovered I was only fooling myself. Phoebe's disrespect and disregard towards me along with her sardonic rudeness made the job less burdensome — that is until I noticed the fire of jealousy dancing in Phoebe's eyes at the sight of Lucy sticking to me like glue.

The venom in her words, or, the troubled and conflicted glimmer in Phoebe's usual composed and neutral eyes were as real as the burning sun in the middle of summer. This was definitely not a figment of my imagination. Phoebe was starting to develop feelings for me. And from the looks of it, doing everything in her power to fight it like it was a nasty bug.

Unfortunately for Phoebe, Cupid had already shot his arrow, linking her and me. Nevertheless, I wasn't easily going to forget what she told Logan — oh no. She will have to work for my forgiveness. Phoebe needed to be shown that despite my love for her, I wasn't going to take any crap from her or anyone else.

I wasn't going to be played again.

With everyone fixating on Damien and Logan as they unashamedly taunt each other, there was no point in keeping up my flirty appearance with Lucy. Nor did I have to continue supporting her body weight as she clung onto my arm like she was incapable of standing on her own.

"I'm not your lifeline, Lucy." Shaking my arm out of her vice-grip, I frigidly whispered. I swear her damsel in distress act was getting old.

Silent and practically invisible, I watched with awe as a unique power oozed off of Phoebe as she used that same rare '*Alpha tone*' and ordered the two hot-headed men to stop. Without even a peep, they retreated — further bewildering me. It was like she was their leader, and they were her pack.

Heading to the board meeting, my thoughts were all over the place. Lost in all I've gathered so far, the strangeness surrounding Phoebe and her friends' relationship was eating at me.

Why was it that they never question or defy Phoebe whenever she uses that peculiar '*Alpha tone*'? Something was up, and I was going to solve this mystery.

"I can't wait until your parents find out Damien is here." Curling his lips, the malevolence clear in his words, Logan whispered beside me as we followed a mumbling Damien and Phoebe.

Digesting the news that my parents personally knew Damien, "So. . . my parents don't like Damien either?" I muttered with curiosity lacing my every word.

"Oh, heck, no! They've always known there was something shady about Damien. But since he was Phoebe's best friend and like a son to Phoebe's father, there wasn't much they could do back then. But now. . . Oh. . ." Grinning like a maniac, "Your parents are more in charge and can change a whole lot."

Refraining myself from jeering something along the line of *'Only best friend or more?'*, I took in the new information that would undeniably help piece together the mysterious puzzle that was Phoebe's life and the people in it. There was no denying the weird and strange connection between Phoebe, my company and everything else around her — meaning a professional investigation was in dire need.

***

Marching into my office like she owned the place, Nadiya disturbed the quietness and peacefulness I had worked hard to nab after ending that God-awful meeting. I swear, one more hour in the same room as Damien and Phoebe, I would have committed a murder. I was about ready to strangle Damien and throw all the chairs at the shareholders' faces just to let out some steam.

Blankly staring at Nadiya's smirk, "You might not need to knock when you enter other people's offices, but I require all my employees to knock and wait for my response before stepping foot inside my office." Reminding myself Nadiya was the fiancée of my biggest shareholder, I took a deep calming breath and flatly stated.

"Oh, I'm sorry, your majesty. I merely wanted to check how you were doing."

It appears falling in love with Phoebe drastically transformed me. In any other situation, in the past, if anyone remotely dared to behave the way Nadiya did, I would have made sure that person would think a hundred times before ever daring to act as such ever again. Instead, here I was, fighting to not crack a smile at Nadiya's fake bow and poor imitation of a British accent. Channelling my inner coldness, I quirked an eyebrow at Nadiya, challenging her to keep fooling around.

"Seriously Federick — if you don't mind me calling you Federick, that is. But how are you feeling? Especially after what you heard between Phoebe and Logan."

"You have some major gut for someone new." Comfortably leaning back on my black mid-century high-back designer leather chair, "Now I get why Phoebe likes you so much." I professed in a controlled, amused tone.

"Does this mean you are fine with me addressing you by your first name?" Nadiya persisted in a chipper tone, which only served to increase my headache.

Carefully observing Nadiya, I had to agree with my gut. There was something refreshing about Nadiya Amatore.

"As long as it's not in front of my clients and you are respectful, we won't have a problem."

"Great." Nadiya voiced in such an excited tone; one would think I just offered her a million dollars.

Then again, she might as well have. Despite being a mere assistant, Nadiya had just gotten permission from 'The Great Federick Archer' himself to address him by his first name. A privilege even the highest-ranking member of the society rarely had.

"If this is all, I would really like to have some 'Me' time."

"Oh, come on, don't be such a spoilsport. You can have all your 'Me' time in your home. Now, fill me in. How did the meeting go? I heard it was like a pressure cooker in there."

Cocking an eyebrow with interest, it was definitive. My love for Phoebe has softened my hard shell. Instead of being annoyed by Nadiya's persistence, her overly cheerful smile and puppy-dog eyes, I was amused and charmed. Reading the curiosity and defiance in Nadiya's eyes, I pitied Logan, who has to continuously and personally deal with the tenacious yet appealing side of her.

"Shouldn't you be interrogating your fiancé or Phoebe, instead? Or better yet, doing something productive?"

"Phoebe is still out, and it's almost impossible to get Logan to spill the beans whenever Phoebe is in the picture. So, you are the next best option. Plus, being productive is over-rated at this point."

"Before you say anything else about your work capabilities, let me remind you, I'm the owner of this company — making me your boss' boss. Also, given my reputation, what gave you the idea, it will be any easier to get what you want from me." Steepling my fingers under my chin, I imprisoned Nadiya's gaze and waited to see what she would do.

"First off, Phoebe hired me for my exceptional high-speed work capabilities. So when I say, productivity is overrated, that's because I have already done what was asked of me and much more." With confidence and pride, Nadiya asserted. "Secondly. Please. Pretty please." She singsong with an amusingly pleading look.

"You're quite the charming woman, Nadiya Amatore. If you weren't already engaged to Logan, I would have sworn you were trying to hit on me."

"Eww and Yuck! How's that for an answer." With a playful glint, Nadiya gagged at my comment.

"A common response from women who die for my attention but gets none." Completely relaxing and letting a smirk hang on my lips, I joked back.

"I'll let you know, in my eyes, my fiancé is a much more delicious hunk than you. So instead of concentrating on my non-existent attractiveness for you, why don't we focus on your love for my future sister-in-law."

It's not often someone catches me off guard and causes my eyes to pop out of its socket with surprise. But Nadiya easily achieved this task with her comment and *'Know-it-all'* smirk.

My defences rising back up, "I have no idea where you came up with this absurd theory. But I suggest you have your head check. Preferably before your wedding." I exclaimed in complete denial.

"Federick, I'm not stupid. It's pretty obvious you guys have the hots for each other."

"Well, I'm sorry to destroy your fantasy, but from what Phoebe told Logan, she is still very much in love with Damien." I was hoping my fierce look would shut Nadiya up or at least compel her to drop this conversation. Alas, it appears she didn't get the memo.

"Don't be ridiculous and so oblivious, Federick. We all saw the jealousy in Phoebe's eyes when you and that Lucy chick were in each other's arms. Plus, if what you are saying is the entire truth, then you won yourself some points by making Phoebe snap at Damien in front of everyone."

About to respond with a *'Duh! Obviously, I thought about this'*, I stopped myself from being a total jerk to Nadiya as a surge of hope birth inside me.

"You might be right, but I'm not going to force my love on Phoebe. Especially when she has already picked her side." Reasoning with my stubborn inner self and this new surge of hope, I calmly stated.

"Oh, please, give me a break. We both know Phoebe is waiting for you to make your next stupid mistake, so it will justify why she needs to keep fighting her real feelings for you. So man-up, Mr Federick Archer." Nadiya retaliated in a firm tone.

Taming my amusement, "You do realise with whom you are talking, right." I stated in a straight tone.

"With a sexy yet extremely arrogant, stubborn, oblivious, hot-tempered, mistake-prone and ice-cold man, who just doesn't seem to know how to properly get the love of his life. Which is why I'm going to prove to you that Phoebe Smith does have romantic feelings for you."

Actually taking pride in her *'Insulting'* description of my character, I let it slide. "How exactly are you planning on doing this, genius?" With a raised brow, I satirically exclaimed.

"You just watch. But for now, I need you to take a break and temporarily distance yourself from Phoebe. You want her to miss you so bad she would voluntarily come to you. And since I don't want to be a constant pawn in your guys game, do not involve me in your plans. I'm willing to advise you, but I'm not jeopardising my friendship with my future sister-in-law for you. I only need to prove that Phoebe has feelings for you, then I'm done." Nadiya calmly and boldly explained.

Her demeanour indicated she already had a plan.

Meeting Nadiya's assertive stare, knowing we were both walking on eggshells with this crazy alliance, "Okay, I'm in." I confidently accepted her conditions.

"Cool, I gotta take your leave now." Standing to her feet, "FYI, Logan asked me to inform you that you two are having lunch at this famous French restaurant downtown."

"Aren't you any more interested in hearing all the juicy details about what happened?" I mockingly questioned.

"Nah. I only came here to make sure you realised Phoebe does love you — deep down. You will need it when Logan interrogates you, along with test your worthiness at lunch. As you may have observed, Logan is an extremely overprotective big brother — besides, once Phoebe is back, I will get all my juicy information out of her."

"Good luck with that." I bid to Nadiya's departing figure.

Grabbing my car keys, Nadiya's words played in my head like a broken record. Despite having broken my heart this morning, a ray of hope for mine and Phoebe's future rose, ready to bud.

It's true. Deep down in her walled-up heart, Phoebe did have feelings for me. I have personally spotted it in her eyes. The question though was; how deep down was it?

"You're aware you can't order or oblige someone to have lunch with you — particularly me." Taking my seat in front of Logan, I bluntly stated.

Sipping on his cocktail and waiting for me to place my order, "Yet. Here you are." Logan responded with a smirk.

"Didn't have many choices now, did I. Nonetheless, next time an invitation would be much appreciated. One that preferably doesn't involve using your fiancée's charms on me."

"What? I needed reassurance you wouldn't try to hit on my future wife if the situation ever presents itself."

"I'm so fortunate to have such a trustworthy associate like your-self." Swallowing my food, I responded with pure sarcasm.

"You can't blame a man for being too careful these days. Especial-ly when the temptation in question is *'The Great Federick Archer'*. The man every girl would die for." Logan mused with a playful smirk.

"Rectification; most girls. Not all of them. We have two of the exceptions working for me."

"Oh, come on. We both know Phoebe has feelings for you. And I know something happened between the two of you this weekend that spurred her to tap into her emotions. Her jealousy explosion this morning proved it all."

Taken aback by Logan's blunt statement, my first reaction was to deny everything. But one glance into his green eyes had me recon-sidering. Reading me like an open book, he could see past my lies. Trusting my gut, as usual, I nodded my head in confirmation.

Relaxed and truthful to myself, I let Logan make most of the conversation. To test, observe and seize me up like Nadiya warned he would. In the back of my head, however, I was alert and gathering as much information as possible.

"If I've passed your little test, can you now tell me what the real deal between Damien and Phoebe is? What are my chances?" Cutting the pleasantries short, I redirected the line of conversation.

Fist balling, it was clear I had touched a hot spot. Sadly for Logan, I wasn't one to back down. I thrived in others' discomfort. Firmly and frigidly outstaring Logan, he had no choice but to huff out his instinct to close up and push back.

Taking in a calming breath and complying with my interrogation, "As tempted as I am, this isn't my story to tell. Nevertheless, I can confirm that despite the special connection between Damien and Phoebe, you still have a pretty high chance. But, you need to be **really** careful of Damien; he's hellishly cunning, conniving and manipula-tive."

"I can take care of Damien Ambrose. What's most important is knowing I have a fair chance." I asserted with a rush of determination.

"You realise there's a high chance Phoebe will involuntarily hurt you and break your heart, especially with all her secrets. You might be blinded by love right now, but you should keep in mind that being with Phoebe would be challenging." Indicating for the waiter to bring the check, Logan concluded in one of the most serious and composed tones I've heard him use so far.

"And here I thought you were team Federick and Phoebe." I mused.

Cocking his head to a small degree, Logan responded with a *'Really, dude'* look.

"I'm aware it's not going to be all *'The sky is pink, and the air is purple'*, Logan. No matter how surreptitious, confusing, frustrating, close-up or eerie Phoebe is, there's just — something unique and special about her that drags me in." I honestly confessed.

"Phoebe is all that and much more. But you should know, I won't think twice about harming you if you hurt Phoebe. I won't allow anyone to break her heart **ever again**. So if you insist on pursuing Phoebe, I need you to think twice about whether you can handle all the secrecy and surreptitiousness that comes with her — I need you to make sure you are strong enough to handle the complete truth when it does come out. Most importantly, ask yourself if you can stick by Phoebe's side regardless of what you discover about her. No matter how crazy or surreal it might appear to you."

Searching my eyes for any sign of weakness or dishonesty, "Only then can you become a part of my baby sister's life." The threat and warning clear in Logan's words and tones, I knew better than to take this lightly.

"Look, I will be honest. It's true Phoebe's attitude and behaviours continually test my patience, and up until this afternoon, I was ready to give up on us as a couple. But after her jealousy scene, Nadiya's speech and your confirmation about my chances, I'm more than determined to fight for our love. Even if it means I have to occasionally be mean and crude towards Phoebe — as far as sticking by her side goes, it will be my honour to stand by the woman I love."

"If that's the case, all I can do is welcome you to the family and wish you a heck lot of good wishes. You'll need it to remotely get a decent date out of that woman." Making our way out of the restaurant, Logan jocularly concluded.

"Do you know Wyatt and Teo's father?"

Gaping at me in utter astonishment, like I had demanded one of his kidneys, the laugh was snatched right out of Logan.

"Unfortunately, I do. But I can't tell you anything about him. And if I were you, I wouldn't ask Phoebe this particular question anytime soon." Logan warned in an alarmingly cautious tone. Little did he know I had already asked Phoebe this question but had gotten no answer.

Puzzled by Logan's sudden peculiar behaviour, more questions about the father of Phoebe' sons arose. It was clear Logan was no longer going to reveal anything significant. My only choice was to go around the pot as I did with Phoebe.

"That's cool. I will get all my answers about Phoebe's personal life in due time. But for now, let's talk about you, my company and Phoebe's companies." Approaching the valet area, I stated with utmost seriousness.

"Let me guess; you wanna know how I got the V.P position without your knowledge or consulting?"

Giving Logan the chance to explain himself, I swiftly and professionally nodded in response.

"The previous V.P was a very close friend of mine and Phoebe. But he owed Phoebe a big favour. And since he was looking for a way out and I was hunting for a more stable, constant and safe job for my new life with Nadiya, Phoebe saw an opportunity to solve our problem. She played the right cards so I would legally inherit Danny's position and shares. You didn't find out because it was done on a personal level."

"Thanks to her famous and grandiose influence, I take it." Leaving out the part where I was planning on buying Danny out so I would have more power and shares, I commented in a matter-of-fact tone.

Nodding, Logan left me hanging. Apparently, he too wasn't going to explain Phoebe's influence.

Reaching for more, "Since you worked for Phoebe, what can you tell me about her two companies?"

"Trying to get corporate secrets out of me, Federick." Jeering, Logan effectively avoided answering my question. But he had something else coming his way.

"Ha Ha, you are so funny. Now do try to actually answer me." I concluded with pure sarcasm.

"Fine, Mr Grumpy. It's nothing special. Just a successful finance firm that only serves notably high-socialite clients."

If I were anyone else, I would have believed Logan. However, the struggling glint flickering his pool of greens was telling me a whole different story.

"So, you are telling me it's this non-special firm that made your life feel so in danger you had to change not only your job but your career path." Waiting for the valet to bring our cars, I scornfully voiced my disbelief.

"More or less. But frankly, Federick, as much as I want to answer your every question, I seriously can't. You got to understand and accept it's Phoebe's story to tell, not mine. All I can do is provide clarification to a certain degree."

Ignoring Logan's pleading look, I took my chances and pushed further.

"Clarify this for me then! What's Phoebe's other company that none of you dares to speak of?" I upheld in a fierce and final tone, indicating he better give me an appropriate answer before I blow up. And believe me, no one wants 'The Federick Archer' to blow.

"It's a private, sort of classified company. But seriously dude, stop pushing your limits to find out everything about Phoebe so hastily. Your recklessness will only put yours and others' lives in danger. And if something happens to you because of her, Phoebe would never be able to forgive herself." Logan's quizzical behaviour all but tempted me to try and find out the mysteriousness encompassing everyone in Phoebe's life.

"You realise you just increased my curiosity and determination to try and find out the truth," I stated with a smirk.

"Regretfully, I do. But remember, it's Phoebe who's going to end up hurt if anything remotely bad happens to you. She may not realise she loves you yet, but I assure you, Phoebe does recognise she cares for you. So be extremely careful with your future actions, particularly when Phoebe is someone who detests being vulnerable — and you, my friend, are exactly that vulnerable point in her life."

"I understand, and I'll make sure to not get into any trouble." Not exactly sure how I felt about being Phoebe's vulnerable point, I aimed to put Logan's mind at ease.

"Good. I gotta get going now. Thanks for responding to my lunch invitation." Jumping into his car without giving me the chance to respond, I too made my way to my car.

Albeit, I didn't amass all the information I was looking for; I was fortunate enough to have learnt more about Phoebe's real feelings towards me. Receiving that confirmation from more than one person who was close to Phoebe killed my doubts and glued together most of the shattered pieces of my heart.

Once again hopeful, it was confirmed — this woman was doing some serious damage to my solid firm wall. Somehow she was slowly melting away the hard shell encasing my heart and enveloping it with love and tenderness.

In spite of the warning bells hammering inside my head or the pain from the sour memory of Veronica and the lessons she taught me, I couldn't stop my soul from connecting with Phoebe. It was like we were interconnected and have known each other forever.

Determined to take what's mine; there was no way I was going to let anyone snatch Phoebe from me.

CHAPTER 33
MESSING WITH MY HEAD

PHOEBE

"**P**hoebe, Mrs Archer, confirmed she and her husband would be at your place by seven, tonight," Nadiya informed as I passed by her on my way to my office.

With a growing migraine and too spent to talk after that excruciatingly Godforsaken meeting, I nodded in response.

Today's meeting was supposed to be simple, but no. . . Not with Damien, Logan and Federick. All that was left for them to do in that meeting was to pull out their members and measure — **typical males**.

Popping an Advil and gulping down a glass of water, I let the freshness and coldness cool my nerves mainly caused by Logan and Federick ganging up on Damien and me. I swear, if looks could kill, I would be dead, revived then dead again by now.

Signing and lightly massaging my template, I was thankful for our board members. They were my saviours. If not for them, an agreement between the two companies wouldn't have been settled on.

Much less the miracle of postponing the rest of the meeting for next Monday.

"What are you doing?" Allowing herself into my office, Nadiya inquired.

"Texting my sons and Maria to inform them of tonight's plan." Texting away and returning to my comfortable mid-century designer high back white office leather chair, I dismissively informed.

"Maria?" Claiming one of the beige curvaceous leather Everly Quinn Penney Task Chair in front of my table, Nadiya queried.

She sure was getting comfortable — but who could blame her. We were now family and friends, and I needed to treat her as such. Not any less.

"Maria is the family domestic, but to me, she is so much more than my housekeeper. She's family. She looked after me until I was a teenager, and now she is looking after my kids." Slightly smiling, I recounted as the memory of my childhood with Maria played in front of my eyes.

"So. . . Are you going to explain what exactly happened this morning?" Breaking the momentary silence, Nadiya's inquiry compelled me to lay my phone on the table and give her my full attention.

"Didn't Logan clarify the situation for you? Besides, you saw first-hand what happened." The professional and cautious side of me instinctively rising, I pointed out.

"No, he didn't. He told me to ask you for the explanation personally. So, tell me exactly why my fiancé abruptly turned into a brute."

Fierce, the protectiveness for her fiancé and question in Nadiya's eyes spoke volume. She wasn't one to back down. A characteristic I could see Logan fell for.

Aware Federick wasn't in his office, and other employees didn't occupy the floor, the only concern was whether I should tell Nadiya everything, only part of the truth, or nothing at all. Taking into account everything that Logan sacrificed for Nadiya; his trust in her and the budding relationship between Nadiya and myself, my decision was made.

Nadiya deserved to know everything except my spy life.

Stressing the importance of keeping everything I told her a secret, I made Nadiya promise with her life she wouldn't utter a word of what I was about to divulge.

If Nadiya detested Damien by the time I was done explaining why her fiancé decided it would be a great idea to be a complete ass this morning, she did an incredible job at hiding it. Reading her face like she was a poem full of hope, I was relieved when there was no sign of disgust whenever Damien's name was brought up in our conversation.

"So. . . Damien is pretty much the perfect definition of a complete jerk, but you still love him because he's one of your first best friends. At the same time, you feel responsible for what happened to him. To make matters worse, everyone around you despises Damien with an extreme fervour because of his decision to leave when you most needed him." Nadiya summarised in an almost 'Duh' tone and the right amount of sympathy.

Reading Nadiya's demeanour, I was an open book to her studious eyes. Somehow, perceiving I dreaded being looked at as weak and with pity, Nadiya supported me by remaining her usual rational, confident and sassy self. My devastating past never changing her view of me.

"Pretty much." Letting Nadiya know her inquisitiveness didn't bother me, I confirmed with a smirk.

"Ouch. I wouldn't want to be in your shoes."

"Wouldn't even fit you." I teased with a wide grin.

There was definitely something about Nadiya that puts me at ease and brings a genuine smile on my face. Unfortunately, not as much as Federick does on occasion, but that's a problem for another day.

Pondering over the one person I shouldn't, I couldn't stop myself from wondering where the heck he was. He didn't have a meeting or lunch date with one of our associates — so where did that master of rudeness disappear to?

Most importantly, why on earth was the fact that we haven't adequately spoken since yesterday afternoon bothering me so much? Heck, we barely spoke a word to each other today, let alone make proper eye contact. And here, I thought we were good — especially after what happened this weekend. Alas, it turns out I was wrong.

All I was awarded was his ice-cold glare instead of that warm, comforting and captivating regard he was supporting the entire weekend. Either Federick was actually bipolar, or I've missed out on the information that there were two of him.

One who was loving, sweet, comforting, charming, sincere, trustworthy yet flirty, sarcastic and responsible. And another who was borderline arrogant, standoffish, cruel, a playboy, flirtatious, annoying, irresponsible and so forth.

"He's on a lunch date," Nadiya uttered out of nowhere.

Taken by surprise, I tumbled back to planet Earth with a "Huh".

"You keep glancing at Federick's door, so I figured you were wondering where he is. He told me earlier that if needed to, I should inform you he went on a lunch date with one of his lady friends." Nadiya clarified with a smile. Yet, I didn't find anything funny in what she said.

"Oh." Giving in to the unknown sensation of my heart tightly squeezing inside my chest at the mention of Federick being with one of his many girlfriends, I almost blank out all of Nadiya's words.

Almost.

"Wait. What does he mean by *'If needed'* to? I'm not one of his bimbos sitting on my hands waiting to be made aware of what to do when **'Need to'**! And why did he tell you instead of me? I'm his personal executive assistant for crying out loud! — Besides, since when did you become such good friend with that double-standard, bipolar, arrogant bastard?" Hit with a varying spectrum of annoyance, Federick's sudden detachment combined with his inconsideration to inform me where he was going frustrated me to no end.

"And here I thought only Federick gets jealous." Nadiya calmly vocalised, as if my sudden blowout didn't bother her when it was so unlike me to behave so erratically.

"Federick Archer doesn't do jealousy, Nadiya. And neither do I." I responded with as much coolness and composure as possible.

I certainly was not jealous. How could someone like myself be jealous? Especially for someone like Federick Archer. No way! Nadiya was definitely mistaken.

"Of course, you guys don't. Although, from your little rambling, it seems you are missing him pretty badly." Teasing me, I couldn't help but profusely blush.

"Obviously, not! My curiosity about Federick's whereabouts is purely professional. What if someone important calls and asks for him? As the company's Executive PA, I'm required to have an accurate answer — and as far as my rambling goes, it's simply because Federick's inconsiderate behaviours frustrate me to the point where I want to wring his neck." Trying my best to fight the redness covering my cheeks, I quickly defended.

Nadiya's smile broadened, "Sure, that's the only reason." With disbelief in her voice, she mumbled before leaving me alone to my racing thoughts.

What other reasons would there be for me to miss Federick Archer? There was nothing special about that jerkface. Not the unique twinkle in his pool of greys whenever he genuinely smiles. Nor the warmth in his captivating gaze that weakens my grips around my deepest and darkest secrets. Nor his cold, intense stare that drags me deeper in its depth — capable of searching my soul. And especially not his sturdy warm sexy body that screams *'Come cuddle with me'*. Or worse, *'Come mount on me'*.

It was definitive. I wasn't missing Federick. Particularly not his delicate warm, soft and hard lips on top of mine. And beyond any doubt, I was not yearning for his tight embrace and the way he could affect my senses by pushing me against a wall. And his habit of yanking me towards him with the power of an Alpha was not something I pined for. Moreover, the notion of me longing how secure and wanted he made me feel whenever he gripped me with passion in his strong arms, was absolute rubbish.

No, not even his charming ways could make me miss any of these aspects. I was a rock and unbreakable.

BING

Talon's text yanking me out of my illogical rambling, I was forced to return to real life. One where Blair was finally handing over the new details he has on Vanderwill. Information that was for my eyes only until I decided otherwise.

Notifying Talon to let Luke know to keep this precious file on top of my home-office desk after he picks it up after school, I made sure Talon understood the file shouldn't go through more than two people's hands.

Breathing out my worry that the data might get into the wrong hands, my gut was screaming something big was a door away.

"How are my handsome boys doing?" Walking into my living room, I cheerfully greeted.

Sparing me a few seconds of their precious time, they greeted back with a welcoming smile before returning their attention to their thriller robot film. Evidently, their movie held more importance than their poor, hard-working mother.

Slouching on the couch and keeping my sarcasm to myself, I threw my head back and rested my eyes.

"Hard day?" Teo gently inquired.

'Oh, so now you acknowledge my presence.'

Reminding myself not to take out my work stress on my kids, I breathed out my sarcasm.

"Beyond tiring. Your uncle and new friend decided it would be fun to gang up on Damien and me all day long." Massaging my template, "It was a mini-war."

"Juice or tea?" Considerate as ever, Wyatt offered.

"Tea, please." Nodding, Wyatt headed to the kitchen where Maria was most probably busy preparing tonight's dinner.

Sipping on my steaming hot Chamomile and lavender tea while scrutinising their movie — filled with guns and an evil computerised intelligence ordering all the ugly little robots to go on a deranged killing spree, I gave up on trying to figure out the name of the movie.

Turning to the experts besides me, "Okay, I give up. What are you boys watching?"

Snapping their necks towards me, all three gawked at me like I had grown two enormous heads. Pausing the movie, all three started rambling on about the storyline and validity of the film. One would think they would do me the honour of merely summarising the movie. But, oh no. . . They had to go into great detail. Pausing and un-pausing each scene, since it was such a horror that I haven't watched this specific film.

Explaining — or better yet — arguing which part of the blasted movie was the best or worst, I cursed myself for asking the boys. As if the arguments at work weren't enough, I now had to listen to my kids bickering over a freaking movie. A movie!

Why the heck did I even bother asking them the name of that movie? I should have just kept my big mouth shut.

"I'm heading to the shower," I announced loud enough to break their argument. "Your grandparents would be here shortly." I quickly informed and escaped before they once again entangled me in their on-going bickering.

Well, at least the idea of ripping their heads off didn't sound as appealing to me as Federick and Logan's head did at the meeting today. In comparison to those two grown-ups, my sons' sibling-bickering was innocent. For sure, it increased my headache, but their squabble was cute and unintentional. Their behaviours as childish as it was, only intensified my love for them.

There are times I take my boys for grants, but the facts remain — without them in my life, I'm lost. Alicia and Joseph often claim I saved Wyatt and Teo from the terrible life they might have had if they were with their father. But the truth is the opposite. From the moment Wyatt and Teo stormed into my life, they saved me.

Pondering over the people who played a significant role in my life, the image of a smug-looking Federick Archer presented itself in front of my eyes.

Continuing to undress, I couldn't figure out why Federick has been invading my mind for the past few days. Like a blood-sucking parasite, the thoughts of Federick were unwilling to let go for even a decent minute. Staring into the mirror in front of me, I knew damn well it was incredibly wrong of me to be thinking of the empty void inside Federick's cold grey eyes burning with the intense fire of passion.

Instead of seeing the reflection of me peeling off my clothes, the image of Federick slowly undressing me played in the reflective oval surface. Experiencing an outer-body moment, I was transported to a passion-filled world. Holding and caressing my naked body, Federick's murmurs into the soft curve of my neck invaded my thoughts. Planting sweet lingering kisses all over my back and front, Federick's hot breath made my skin feel alive.

His strong warm hands sliding up my tingling skin and slipping under my hair, Federick wrapped the back of my neck and dragged my mouth to his with raw passion and yearning. Standing there, between his arms, I wanted Federick to take care of the pool of warmth between my legs. To make me sore with an overpowering pleasure and to quench my thirst for him.

My body temperature rising to an insanely hot degree, I snapped back to reality. Coming face to face with my flushed self, I slowly breathed out the insanity imprisoning my thoughts.

But did my brain get the message? . . . Obviously not!

Eyeballing the redness covering the olive skin of my visage, the fervour of the lascivious visions intensified like a spreading fire in the middle of summer. Dangerous and hot.

Pushing me against his office wall with a roughness I ached, Federick held my hands up and kissed me with possessiveness. Moaning against each other, we were like two starved animals.

Gasping, I forced myself out of that sensuality-filled world and splashed cold water on my sweltering face.

Droplets rolling down my face, I gradually peered back up. But like a wicked curse, head-bent on eating me alive, Federick's cold grey eyes longing for me stamped itself inside my brain like a tattoo. A stranger in my own body, I found myself plunged back into the pool of salaciousness — craving Federick's touches.

My wild imagination taking the lead, I gaped as Federick roughly bent me over his expensive mahogany office table and slowly leaned in. His wide body closing around me. His firm muscles pressing against mine.

My chest tightening and my ears burning to crisp, Federick' smell and bodily warmth seeped into mine; melting my heart and confusing my already over-confused brain.

My lustfulness forbidden like an erotic movie to the innocent eyes, I fought to shake the consuming waves of lecherousness. But the more I resisted, the deeper I was thrust into this insanity.

Feeling more real than a ridiculous fantasy created by my bloody mind, my breathing grew heavier at the image of Federick spreading my legs apart and pulling my hair to bring my head up. His firm hand hot on my flesh, slowly running up and down my inner thighs, the wetness between my legs increasing, I was just as aroused in real life as I was in my imagination.

Visioning Federick's lips grazing upward, from my spine to my neck, a tingling sensation coursed through my bones, confirming I, Phoebe Smith, sexually desired *The Greatest Playboy'* of the century. The one person I should have never felt this way towards.

It was utterly wrong, particularly when we just became friends after years of disdain. I had no idea how or when I started looking at Federick in such a different light, but dear God, I needed to resist whatever was happening between us.

For now, though, a cold shower was due.

"Mom. Grandpa and grandma are here," Wyatt called out from the living room.

Hastening downstairs to meet Joseph and Alicia, I blocked all thought of their invasive, arrogant, peace-stealing playboy of a son. Trust me, Federick freaking Archer deserved much worse insult for his intrusive and non-stop thrusting inside my mind. If not for him, I would have long gotten out of that freezing shower!

"Hey, sweetheart. What's up?" Alicia greeted between hugs.

Given the mood I was in, I was immensely tempted to reply, *'Attempting to stop fantasising about your son's eight pack abs, strong arms, smirk, mesmerising eyes or anything sexual happening between him and me.'* But with great restraint, I managed to control myself and my sassy mouth. Because if they did find out — mainly Alicia — I will be in deep shit.

"Just a family dinner. I owed you guys this much after bailing out last time. Plus, as my assistant informed you, I have two major surprises for both of you." Bringing myself to the moment, I responded with a smile.

Curious as ever, Joseph tried to cajole details of the surprises out of me, but there was no way I was going to give in easily.

"After dinner, Mister. Be patient." I jocularly mused, loving his pouting look.

Joseph was such a father to me, and I loved him for that. I loved how he looked at me the same way my dad did when I would behave childishly or do anything stupid and crazy. I guess this was the main reason why I still acted like a teenager around them. It reminded me of what I lost way too soon in life.

CHAPTER 34
PREVENTION IS BETTER THAN CURE

PHOEBE

"Alicia. Mr Archer." Stepping into the living room, Maria respectfully and amicably greeted.

"Hello, Maria. How have you been?" Ready for a chit-chat with her friend, a smiling Alicia silvery saluted after Joseph greeted Maria.

"I'm doing very well, thank you. The vacation really helped."

"I'm glad to hear. We should catch up over some lunch. I want to hear everything about your vacation." Alicia proffered with childlike excitement.

"Absolutely." Sweetly smiling, Maria assented and led us to the dining room.

"I kept the file on top of your office table." Luke softly mumbled as he passed by me on his way to the dining table.

Swiftly and stealthily nodding in acknowledgement, I took my seat at the head; with the kids on my left and the Archers on my right.

"So, how about those surprises?" Finishing the delicious dinner Maria had prepared with so much love, Joseph once again questioned.

Regarding me with a knowing look, hidden behind their pretence of impatience and curiosity, it didn't take a genius to know they had gotten news of Damien's arrival from one of my two stubborn and pissed-off best friends. Yet, here they were — feigning ignorance. Which under another circumstance would have upset me, but after the day I had, I couldn't complain.

To be honest, I was amazed at Alicia and Joseph's restraint. I was expecting them to be already drowning me in sermons, warnings and advice. It was both stunning and suspicious how they weren't already talking ill of Damien — let alone, mentioning his name.

Choosing to welcome the anomaly of their behaviours, I eased into the heavy discussion that was bound to take place by revealing Luke's adoption into the family first. Exploding with excitement and joy, Alicia and Joseph decimated the lingering fear that my decision to adopt so quickly was rash — that the timing was wrong.

Halting in-between her incoherent celebration planning, "What's surprise number two?" Alicia prodded.

Right on cue, the doorbell rang.

Holding my heart. Praying it wasn't Federick deciding it would be nice to crash another one of my family dinners, especially after what happened earlier in the bathroom, I breathed out a sigh of relief when Maria stepped into the room and presented Damien. If it had been Federick, I don't know what I would have done. I fear I wouldn't be able to look that jerk directly into the eyes without turning crimson red.

"Damien is surprise number two." Hugging Damien and giving him an encouraging smile, "But from the looks of it, it appears either Talon or Logan have already brought you up to speed."

"Both of them did, actually. Right before you invited us over for dinner." Her smile completely wiped off her face, Alicia courtly enumerated.

"Good evening, Mr and Mrs Archer." Nervously rubbing the back of his neck, Damien tried his best to sound cordial and friendly.

Prepared for their outburst at any given moment, I was left astounded when Joseph and Alicia did the complete opposite of what was expected of them and reciprocated Damien's handshake without a grimace. Sure they were neither smiling nor warm. And the stern lours decorating their face promised a heated conversation. But at the very least they were being civil, which was more than could be said of Logan and Talon.

Putting their personal feelings aside, Alicia, Joseph, Luke, Teo and even Wyatt — the king of sarcasm — behaved courteously for the entirety of the night. At awe, despite the awkwardness and lingering tension, I was grateful to finally have a typical, drama-free family dinner.

Then again, everyone else seemed to have an entirely different stance than me.

Openly sighing in relief when I put an end to our *'Fun family night'* after Talon called for the scheduled conference meeting, all of them happily sent me off. Even Wyatt and Teo who usually submerge me in questions excitedly bid their goodnights and rushed upstairs to do their *'Homework'*.

Never before in my motherhood life have I had it so easy.

Marching into my office shortly after me, Luke barely gave me enough time to secure Blair's package inside my drawer' secret compartment. Aware my rule of thumb was; *'Prevention is better than cure'*, Luke waited, knowing there was no chance I would conduct an official D.S.I investigation outside the soundproof office hidden behind the library. Particularly when Wyatt and Teo were unsupervised. Clasping onto his file with a giddy glimmer, his excitement to lead his first detective case with the Elite Team had still not worn off.

Locking the secret room behind me and taking a seat behind my mahogany desk, "Hi team, found anything special for me?" I jocularly mused after Luke transferred them onto the monitor which covered at least half of the wall.

"It took me a lot of time and effort but —"

"Don't forget a major irritation explosion." Interrupting Talon, "Mister, here, was so vexed he couldn't get through the hacker's game that he nearly did some serious company damage." Xylan teased, earning himself a hateful glare from Talon.

"Phebes, you should thank God we were here to lend a helping hand. Otherwise, bye-bye tech room and hi, repair cost." Matt pinched in, earning himself a glare from Talon and a grin from the rest of us.

"Aren't we the best. . ." Leaning back on his couch in the comfort of his home, "What will you do without Matt and me?" Xylan joyfully exclaimed.

"We would all be saved from seeing your bare chest. Not to mention, have an amazingly peaceful and quiet life." The only one still at the agency, Talon retorted without humour.

Seriously, that man was in dire need of a life outside the agency. When we have pressing one-after-the-other missions, I understand the need to stay at the agency. But God damn, if not for the team and me pressuring him, Talon would spend every second of his life enclosed within the walls of the agency. Heck, I would be surprised if he still has a properly functioning apartment.

Sharing a knowing look with me; Luke returned his gaze to the scene of my top agents' bickering and acting like twelve years old. I pitied my poor head. My day started with bickering among male adults. Continued with bickering teenage boys in the evening. And is finishing with bickering male adults at night.

Perhaps there was an epidemic going around, affecting all the male specimens, no matter what age range. I wish someone would have had the decency of informing me, and I would have happily stayed home, in the comfort of my bed; probably overthinking my whole life.

"Excuse me!" Luke interjected in a high tone. "Might I suggest we get back to the main topic. Some people have school early in the morning, you know." With confidence, Luke demonstrated he understood the importance of our talk from last night.

"You're right. As I was saying before being rudely interrupted by those two morons, I bypassed and deciphered the bug implanted by the hacker to manipulate the museum's primary system. According to the information, I recuperated so far; the hacker wiped the existence of a few valuable artefacts from the inventory records — suggesting the thief also stole whatever was wiped from the database." Talon cleared some of my earlier questions. However, he also brought new queries to light.

"Why didn't the museum manager share that some of their other pieces were also missing?" Annoyed the manager hid crucial details from us, I abruptly voiced out.

If the manager had fully corporated as I asked of him, this whole *'Hacking the hacker'* could have been avoided. Saving my time and resources. I might be a billionaire, but that doesn't mean I love going about, unnecessarily wasting money.

"He probably wasn't aware the items were gone," Matt answered my question.

Infinitesimally tilting my head, my expression clearly read, *'As if! It was on his record. He knew.'*

"Since those artefacts were still in the inventory port, where they are identified, cleared, processed, then recorded into the main museum database, it's highly possible the erased items were recent arrivals and had yet to go through the entire identification process. With all the commotion at the museum, the lack of digital footprint and the many valuable pieces they receive each day, it's safe to presume the missing artefacts went unnoticed." Noticing my disbelief, Luke explained in more detail.

"Another school project." Just as astonished as me by Luke's knowledge of art, Xylan inquired.

"Nope. After reading the case file last night, I researched the museum and its movements." Luke proudly announced.

Proud of Luke and his engagement, there was no doubt in my mind that Luke would soon crack this case wide open.

"Has the museum been made aware of the situation?" Writing something on his notepad, Luke questioned.

"Yes, Matt and Xylan drove down to the museum this afternoon to inform them. They have now agreed to fully corporate with us. By tomorrow night, the manager will fax a preliminary report of what's missing from the inventory." Talon summarised.

"I take it, you handed him a copy of everything that was wiped from the system to see if they were all stolen, or if only a specific one were taken," I confirmed with all three; to which they responded with a nod.

"Selling the items from the list on the dark market before they are reported stolen would be hugely profitable for our thief and The Fox. And even if The Fox doesn't want to sell right away, he has the advantage of time. By the time the museum would have figured out all the stolen items, it would have been too late." Luke pointed out a strong motive.

"Great. We have a motive. Find the means and confirm the opportunity. Before *The Fox* knows it, he will be caught, and the case will be close." Doing the one thing I promised I wouldn't unless absolutely necessary, I took the reign and overshadowed Luke.

Part of me knew it was wrong of me to obliterate Luke's leadership after personally handing him this case. But, the other, more nasty part of me couldn't care less. That part was impatient and only cared about revenge — about the folder that was peacefully laying in my drawer' secret compartment.

As if reading my mind, and unfazed by my bossiness, Luke handed the team their tasks. Explaining how they all needed to broaden the scope of their investigation, Luke dismissed them with such a calm demeanour; I was more convinced he was ready.

A fake smile plastered on my face, my anxiety internally killing me, I bid Luke good night and locked the office door. Slumming down on my chair, I slowly exhaled. The long-awaited moment was here.

New information on Cole Vanderwill.

Soon, I would know more about Vanderwill's movement. Have concrete evidence of what he has been doing for the past ten years. Where he was. What he is presently into. And more importantly, how I can get a firm grip on him.

At this point, I didn't care about the Archers' attempt to keep me at bay, nor my promise to them to be patient. It was high time I stopped counting on Pierce to find all the information I required. That man was useless.

The question now was — how valuable and accurate Blair's new information was?

The answer was merely a drawer away.

***

THE END

Hey there, thanks for sticking to the end of this story. My hope is you loved it and are looking forward to the next instalment in the series. There are so many questions that still need to be answered and so many things that are to be discovered.

Before you leave here today, could you please review this novel on Amazon for me (or the place where you got this book)?

I would really appreciate it. Not only will your small action encourage me, but it would also help other readers to discover this novel. And who knows, it might make their day, and that would be all thanks to you.

Scan the QR code to be sent directly to the Amazon review page:

Here's the link if you would prefer just the review link: https://www.amazon.com/review/create-review?&asin=B08H4XMWW1

If you liked this series and my style of writing, or just want to know more about me, sign up for my monthly newsletter. I promise to keep you up to date and even give you teasers when it's available. Scan this QR code to sign up to my monthly newsletter:

https://plumitifpress.ck.page/7d0fad7c2c

READ MORE FROM LAVINIA DASANI

⚒ COMING NEXT ⚒

BOOK 3 OF TAME SERIES

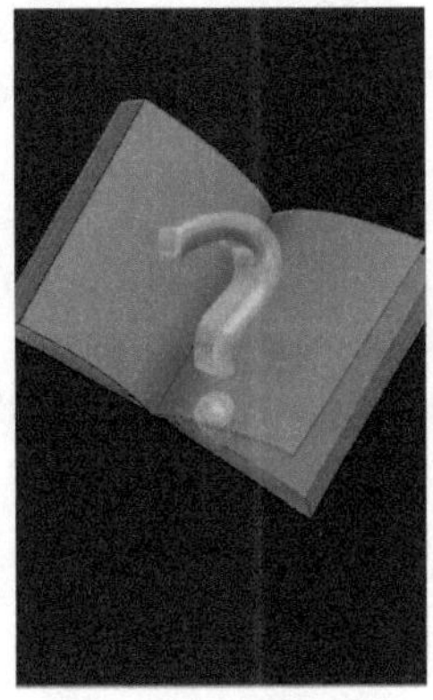

https://laviniadasani.com/

ABOUT AUTHOR

Lavinia Dasani is a Self-Published Author and Founder/CEO of Plumitif Press, LLC. Originially from the beautiful island of Mauritius, she migrated to the United States at 16. She enjoys travelling, reading, fashion, animals, the beach and connecting with people.

She started writing at 10 years old and published her first ever online novel on Wattpad in 2013, around the age 13. Her favourite genre is Romance.

When she is not busy writing or making good use of her Psychology degree, she enjoys connecting with her readers.

She goes by Lady Lavinia Dasani on all social platforms and have other books under that name. Connect with her on any social platforms now:

https://laviniadasani.com/contact/